High Praise for Shelly Thacker's
Timeless

"POWERFUL AND SENSUAL ... Part captive/captor, part 'Highlander,' *Timeless* is a magical novel that will more than satisfy readers of historical and new-age romance."
—*Romantic Times*

"This one sweetened my dreams. *Timeless* has a dreamlike quality with just enough mystery. The audience will bask in the sensual aura. A keeper!"
—*Rendezvous*

"THIS IS A STORY NOT TO BE MISSED!"
—*The Literary Times*

"ONE OF THE BEST BOOKS OF THE YEAR. Shelly Thacker's latest tale is a wonderful blending of a medieval and a paranormal romance into a *Timeless* novel that will elate fans from both sub-genres."
—Harriet Klausner

"YOU SIMPLY MUST READ *TIMELESS*. This poignant, bittersweet, and emotionally touching love story brought joy to my heart and tears to my eyes. It's Shelly Thacker's best book yet. Magical, mystical, and marvelous!"
—*Old Book Barn Gazette*

Dell Books by Shelly Thacker

Published by
Dell Publishing
a division of
Random House, Inc.
1540 Broadway
New York, New York 10036

ISBN: 0-440-22518-3

Printed in the United States of America

Published simultaneously in Canada

May 1999

10   9   8   7   6   5   4   3   2   1

OPM

SHELLY THACKER

Into the Sunset

A DELL BOOK

*To Uncle Dale and Aunt Mary
with love and congratulations
on more than 50 years together.
Here's the Western you've been
waiting for, Uncle Dale
(even though it's still got "all
that kissin' and mushy stuff").*

1

How *many men were hunting her by now?*

Antoinette Sutton pressed her cheek against the coach's musty upholstery, keeping her eyes shut as the Wells Fargo stage to Leadville rattled up the mountain trail. She struggled to breathe evenly, couldn't seem to get enough of the thin air into her lungs. Sweat trickled down her face and stained the dress she wore, a stylish French sateen in solid black. Widow's black.

Her stomach lurched with every nauseating sway of the coach. And her fever was getting worse. Annie sank her teeth into her lower lip to hold back a moan.

She felt sick enough to throw up on the nice, shiny kid boots of the lady squeezed in beside her. And not just because of the smothering crush of nine passengers. Or the stale smells of horse sweat and miners who didn't bathe often enough and the macassar oil the men used on their hair. Or the annoying buzz of conversation as her fellow travelers chatted oh-so-pleasantly about crop prices and how nice the August weather had been and the latest silver strike up in Central City.

Annie remained silent, tenderly, protectively resting one hand over the gentle swell of her belly, hidden by her full skirts. Questions circled and preyed on her mind like merciless vultures.

How many men were on her trail? A handful? A dozen? Or every sheriff and marshal in five states?

How long would they keep tracking her?

And how far?

Trying to swallow the cold lump of fear in her throat, she opened her eyes and lifted the flapping leather curtain on her left. Glaring sunlight blinded her for a second. She blinked, dizzy and half afraid she'd see a rider chasing the stage with badge flashing and gun drawn, like in the dime novels her brother used to love.

Instead she saw only air: empty, heaven-blue sky above *and* below. The stage had climbed high into the Rockies since leaving Trout Creek this afternoon. A ledge fell away sharply beneath the wheels, revealing the jagged green tops of pine trees trailing down the mountainside into a gulch so deep she couldn't glimpse the bottom.

Annie shuddered and let the curtain fall. After a week of jostling along old Indian trails and back roads day and night, she hated the West. Hated every hot, dirty, wild, godforsaken mile of it. Only once before had she been west of the Missouri River, on a visit to Abilene when she was six, with Mama, to look for Papa.

She knew she was the very picture of what folks out here called a "tenderfoot." But she needed to disappear—and this was the best place to do it. She had to keep going, changing stage lines, changing directions, covering her trail. Had to put plenty more miles between her and the law back in Missouri. She couldn't stop to rest, to wait until she felt better.

Or to grieve.

James. Annie shut her eyes again, curling up in her

corner of the darkened coach while the other passengers kept chatting and laughing.

James, oh God, I'm so sorry.

Even now, she longed for his company and his comfort. *Even now.* Droplets of sweat mixed with the trail dust on her cheeks, and felt like tears. But they weren't tears. They weren't. Her mama had raised her not to be any man's fool.

If only she had listened.

One of the wheels struck a rock and the stage bucked like a wild horse. Annie clung to the padded seat, trembling. The uncomfortable feeling in her stomach was getting worse—and it was different from the queasiness she had gotten used to the past weeks.

She tried to tell herself it was only this awful case of the ague. Or the meager food that had been available when they stopped for lunch in Trout Creek: fried cornbread with slices of fat pork and gritty coffee that had tasted like it was three days old.

But she was beginning to fear it was something else. Something far worse.

Annie's heart seized up like it would stop beating. Like it would break. She had never been the sort to pray much, but she began to pray now, silently, desperately.

For forgiveness.

For the precious new life growing inside her.

"You feelin' any better, Mrs. Smith?"

Annie lifted her lashes and regarded the young soldier seated across from her, his blue uniform so new it all but gleamed. He was on his way to Fort Collins, he had told them all proudly, had just turned twenty and been promoted to corporal.

Twenty. He seemed merely a boy. How could he be the same age as her?

"Yes, Corporal Easton." Annie shrugged, managing a smile and yet another lie. "I'm feeling a bit better, thanks."

She had told none of them about her delicate condition; her fellow passengers were only worried about her ague—mostly about catching it.

As she started to turn away and close her eyes again, the boy offered her his canteen and a smile. "You thirsty, ma'am?"

Annie hesitated, her natural wariness sharper than usual. She wasn't used to people showing her kindness. But then, these folks didn't know who she was.

Or what she had done.

With a grateful nod, she accepted the canteen and drank, spilling some when the coach rocked over a deep rut in the road.

A gentleman with gray sideburns down to his chin and a southern drawl offered her his handkerchief. "How far did you say you were going, Mrs. Smith?"

Annie tentatively took the offered square of snowy linen and lowered her gaze, dabbing at her ruffled bodice, worried by the way everyone's attention turned to her.

She hadn't said where she was going. Had barely spoken ten words to anyone. Dared hope the black dress and wedding ring would be enough to explain her silence and why she was traveling alone. She didn't want to make any kind of impression; she wanted to be as forgettable as the fake name she had chosen.

Besides, she was no good at polite conversation, hadn't spent much time with people like these.

Nice people. Respectable people.

"Montana Territory," she said at last. "I have family there." More lies. If any lawmen managed to track her this far and ask her destination, she wanted them galloping off in the wrong direction.

"I'm surprised they didn't come east to meet you," the whiskered man commented. "The northern territories are a might unsettled yet. There's still trouble with the Indians, sometimes even here in Colorado. A lady traveling alone must have a care."

"Indeed," the skinny matron next to Annie said with a disapproving cluck of her tongue, hooking her arm through her husband's. "Why, it's dangerous venturing into these mountains even with a well-armed escort. Colorado is fairly teeming with gamblers, claim-jumpers, speculators, and unsavory types of every ilk these days."

Annie barely listened as everyone launched into a discussion of the need for better law enforcement, now that the latest silver rush was attracting so many new arrivals to the Rockies. She splashed some water from the borrowed canteen onto the borrowed handkerchief and used it to cool her brow, feeling too light-headed and sick to pretend interest while they tried to persuade her that this was no place for a woman alone.

Don't you think I know that? she wanted to shout. She hadn't planned to come here. There hadn't been time to think, back in St. Charles, on that horrible afternoon when she had run through the rain.

Had run in a blind panic beneath thundering clouds and lightning that stabbed the red Missouri earth. She had stumbled into a clothing shop and pointed out the mourning dress and paid cash and left quickly—before the proprietor could wonder why she kept her blue silk cape clutched so tightly at her throat.

Then she rushed around the corner and changed in an alley out back, leaving the cape and her bloodstained clothes and her entire life behind in the mud.

Somehow she made it to the train depot—only to realize her mistake. James owned half the railroads in Missouri. The conductors and porters all knew her from the trips she'd taken with him—to New Orleans and Philadelphia and a luxurious suite at the Biltmore Hotel in New York City. She couldn't escape by train.

Soaked to the bone, sobbing, she'd hurried to one of the livery stables instead. And ten minutes later, had a six-dollar seat on the first stage out of town, headed west.

"And the *winters*," one of her traveling companions was saying with a shudder. "The territories really ain't a place for any lady who—"

"Thank you." Annie interrupted the chorus of advice being directed at her. She handed the soldier his canteen, keeping the wet handkerchief pressed to her hot skin. "Thank you, but I'm sure I'll find Montana to my liking."

The skinny matron next to her pursed her lips and raised a disapproving eyebrow. "I assure you, you would be much happier elsewhere, Mrs. Smith."

Shaking her head wearily, Annie closed her eyes and sank back against the upholstery. *Happy.* She would never be happy again. Had lost all right to be happy.

But she would give her child a good life, she vowed. A safe, healthy, good life. There was enough money in the leather satchel under her seat to make sure of that. They would live in San Francisco, or maybe Virginia City. In a real house, just like regular folks. And they would be decent and respectable. And they would be together, like a mama and her child should be.

That thought almost made her smile, in spite of everything. Just for a moment.

Then the image shattered in a burst of hot pain that knifed through her. She gasped and slumped forward, her jaw going slack.

"Oh, God." It twisted through her again and she doubled over. *"Oh, God, no."*

* * *

Annie didn't realize she had passed out until the coach jolted to a stop. She opened her eyes to a blur of pain and noise and shifting shadows. Wrenching spasms in her belly. Voices shouting. Distantly, echoing strangely.

". . . Over here . . ."

". . . Well, wake him up, damn it . . ."

She was too weak to move. Shivering with cold. Something soft was wrapped around her, beneath her, but she was so cold. Strong arms held her, lifting her.

". . . Poor thing kept callin' out for 'James.' Guess that were her husband . . ."

Suddenly there was a night sky overhead. Stars. So many stars. The whole world seemed made of stars and pain. Someone was carrying her. She felt wool against her cheek. Scratchy blue wool. Uniform. The boy. Heavy boots pounded on wood. Running. Oh, God, please, no. Stop. Every small movement tore through her.

". . . Too much blood . . ."

". . . Made a detour 'cause you're the closest doctor . . ."

A creak of hinges as a door opened. Flood of light. The smells of burning wood and smoky oil lamps and rubbing alcohol. The boy laid her down on something hard, smooth. Table. A single, choked word slipped past her lips. "Help . . ."

"We're going to help you, ma'am—"

"My baby . . ." She tried to shake her head. "Not me . . . save the baby . . ."

Efficient hands began removing her dress. Her widow's dress. "How far along are you, Mrs. Smith?" The man's voice was low, soothing.

"F-Four," she whispered. "Four months . . . I think."
James.

Another voice, a woman's. Soft and insistent. "Y'all can wait outside. Doc Holt don't need an audience."

"Mrs. Smith," someone called, "God be with you . . ."

". . . We'll be prayin' for you . . ."

The sound of jostling feet on a wood floor. The rattle of the door again. The clatter of metal. The woman appeared on the other side of the table, with a silver tray. The man took it from her.

Annie summoned all her strength, reached up and clutched the doctor's arm.

"Money," she whispered on parched lips. *Money could buy anything. James had always said so.* "I h-have money . . . pay you if . . . save my baby."

The man leaned over her. Tried to ease her back down on the table. "Ma'am, I'm sorry." His eyes were gray and gentle and sad. "It's too late. We have to do all we can to save you now." He turned to the woman. "Chloroform, Mrs. Owens. Quickly."

No. A soft cloth covered Annie's nose and mouth. She tried to push it away. A thick, sweet smell invaded her senses. *No, he didn't understand.* The baby was all she had. All that mattered. Her own life wasn't worth saving. Even if he could save her, it wouldn't be for long. She had only come a few hundred miles. Not far enough to be safe.

Not near far enough.

He would find her, by God.

That thought had burned in his gut and robbed him of sleep for days now. Five days. Or was it six? U.S. Marshal Lucas T. McKenna rubbed his eyes with the heel of his palm, his other hand resting near the Colt .45 Peacemaker holstered on his hip. The smells of smoke and hot iron choked the afternoon air, the train engine a few yards away belching great clouds of steam and ash toward the Missouri sky.

Time had unraveled into one long, shapeless blur since the telegram had reached him in Indian Territory, urgently summoning him home to St. Charles. He could remember only moments of the past week. Fragments, like shrapnel: the cold that had drenched him when he read the words on the small white piece of paper. The endless clacking of metal wheels over railroad tracks. Dozens of unfamiliar faces milling around rooms draped in mourning. The awkward reunion with his sisters. A gleaming coffin with brass fittings.

And the quiet sound of James's children, crying.

Lucas clenched his jaw and glared down at his worn boots, trying to push it all away. He had to treat this like any other assignment. Subdue the need for retribution that burned him hotter than the August sun high overhead.

Hunt down the coldhearted bitch who had murdered his brother.

The train's bell clanged as the whistle made its long, mournful call. A conductor shouted "All aboard!" and the last few passengers spilled out of the depot, clutching their baggage. The stationmaster hustled along with them, handing out the last few tickets as people hurried across the platform to catch the 1:15 to Jefferson City.

Lucas forced himself to wait patiently, as requested. He yanked at the open neck of his shirt, unknotted his kerchief, and mopped sweat from his face before stuffing the sodden piece of cloth into the pocket of his black trousers. He had almost forgotten how hot St. Charles could get in August—hot enough to make him feel like he was standing in the middle of a frypan.

Finally, the last passengers were on their way and the stationmaster rushed over to him. "Sorry for the delay, Marshal McKenna. But like I said, I'm not sure I can help you. I talked to the town constables last week—"

"I was hoping maybe you'd remembered something more since then," Lucas said, loud enough to be heard over the noise. "Anything that might be useful."

The man's spectacles reflected the sunlight as he looked up to meet Lucas's gaze. "Well, sir, like I told the constables, it was raining that day. Hard enough to drown a man. None of us could see much, what with everyone ducking their heads in that downpour. And the women were all decked out in traveling cloaks, carrying parasols and such—"

"And no one remembers seeing this woman?" Lucas dug the wanted poster out of his pocket. "Dark, curly hair she always wears long and loose. Brown eyes—"

"Oh, I know her, Marshal. Saw her many a time." The man shook his head as he handed the paper back. "Mr. McKenna always treated her real well—first-class Pullman compartment, champagne, caviar. We all called her Lady Antoinette," he admitted with an apologetic smile. "It's just, with the rain and all, I can't say if she was here that day, and I can't say if she wasn't. Wish I could help you. It's a damn shame what happened to your brother. He was a good man."

Lucas nodded curtly and folded the paper, wanting to crush it in his fist or tear it into pieces. *A damn shame* didn't begin to describe what had happened, and *good* didn't begin to describe his older brother. James hadn't deserved to die, cut down at the age of thirty-two. Shot by a woman to whom he had shown only generosity and compassion.

Too much compassion; if James had had one flaw, it was that. "If you hear anything," Lucas said, sick of repeating those four words, uttered so often the past days, "I'm staying up at the house for a while."

"I'll pass along any word, Marshal, I surely will. Something's bound to turn up. Everyone in town admired your brother. And the local constables are doing all they can."

Lucas shook the man's hand and left, keeping his opinion of local law enforcement to himself. In the week since the murder, they hadn't even been able to pin down how "Lady Antoinette" had left St. Charles, much less what direction she had taken. But at least they hadn't protested when he stepped in to help with the investigation.

His boot heels echoed on the wooden platform, then on the steps that led down to the street. After talking to the constables, he had personally questioned the witnesses to the crime: James's servants, who had never seen Antoinette at the house before that evening, when they overheard her arguing with their employer in the study.

James had been telling his mistress he never wanted to see her again. Then there had been a gunshot. Then Antoinette had been seen fleeing the grounds, covered in blood—with a sackful of money taken from James's safe.

Obviously the old saying was true: Hell hath no fury like a woman scorned.

And where was she now? Lucas wondered as he stalked back toward town. Living high on the hog in some fancy hotel back East? Spending the money she had stolen from James on ball gowns and jewelry down in Natchez? Decorating the arm of some rich *señor* in Mexico? Enjoying a sea voyage to Europe?

The possibilities made bile rise in his throat. One thing had become clear: "Lady Antoinette" might have the morals of an alley cat, but she was smart. Lucas had hunted down some of the most wily criminals ever to plague the territories; he hadn't expected this light-skirt to be much trouble. But she had apparently planned her escape as carefully as the crime, because she had managed to evade the law, so far.

But not for much longer.

Lucas stopped at a street corner, next to a three-story brick building that had the name JAMES MCKENNA, ESQ. lettered in gold on the door, half-covered by a sign that read CLOSED. He felt his throat tighten, remembering how proud he'd felt of his older brother the first time he'd seen this place—the offices that took up an entire block, the business James had established and managed with such skill. Soon it would be sold.

His head lowered, Lucas moved toward a lamppost and leaned against it, arms folded as he tried to think. From below the brim of his hat, he watched carts and carriages and townsfolk crisscross, kicking up red Missouri dust as they went about their lives on this sultry afternoon.

Every time he returned to St. Charles, it astonished him how much the town had changed since he was young; it had been little more than a scattering of cabins and cornfields in the woods back then—like the one where he and James had done the backbreaking work of plowing and planting beside their father . . . and challenged each other to races when they hauled feed and water for the animals . . . and snuck off to the swimming hole together on summer afternoons.

Until the war. Everything had changed after that, when marauders began stalking Missouri looking to drown their bitterness in blood and fire.

Lucas spat in the dirt, forcing the memories away, not wanting to feel the fresh grief and loss that knifed through him. He had to keep his mind on the hunt. Plot his next move.

He was supposed to meet up with his deputies back in Indian Territory as soon as possible—and the Territorial Governor wouldn't look kindly upon him taking an extended leave to pursue a personal vendetta. Not when he and his men were finally closing in on the Risco gang after two years of work.

When the telegram about James had arrived, Lucas had told his deputies to go on without him, but ordered them to stay together and stay coolheaded. To a marshal, emotion could be as dangerous as any bullet or bowie knife.

He lived by that adage, had lived by it for so many years he no longer had to think about it.

But he thought about it now, as he turned and headed down the street toward the telegraph office, to send a message to his men. He needed more time here in St. Charles, had more people to question, had to find some lead he could follow. He wouldn't be returning to the territories. Not yet.

Not until he saw Antoinette Sutton pay for what she had done.

It was almost eight by the time darkness fell over the town, bringing a summery hush disturbed only by droning cicadas and the chirp of a cricket now and then. Lucas felt grateful for the cool that descended as the moon rose, but the silence and peace didn't match his mood. Lamplighters had just begun their work as he made his way quickly back to the house, the mansion James had built on a hill above St. Charles.

He finally had a solid lead to follow, but even that didn't lessen the thick, hot feeling that choked him as he looked up at his brother's home—the place where James had died.

The moon's silvery glow haloed the east and west wings and illuminated the pillars that seemed to stretch halfway to the sky. In the back, the mansion's southern windows looked out over the woods where the McKenna homestead had once been; on this side, each commanded an impressive view of everything the McKennas' eldest son had helped build from nothing but ashes after the war.

Lucas shifted his gaze to the sidewalk as he hurried toward the front gate.

If only he had come here more often, accepted the invitations to Thanksgiving or Christmas. A couple of times, he'd said yes—but something always came up. His work. His duty. There was always another criminal that had to be hunted down. He'd always thought there would be time later to spend with his brother, his family. *Later.*

Now it was too late for anything but regret.

Olivia's floral arrangements and black wreaths, draped so carefully around the front gates, had gone limp in the heat. Lucas strode past them and up the walk and took the steps two at a time. He lifted his hand to knock, then hesitated, still not sure whether he was supposed to announce his arrival each time or walk right in, like a member of the family.

A servant solved the problem by opening the door before he could decide. An efficient bunch, they were; Lucas had given up trying to remember the titles of the various doormen and housekeepers and under-whatnots, never mind their names.

"Evening," he said with a nod as he stepped inside.

"Good evenin', Mr. Lucas, sir. The ladies just finished their supper," the gray-haired man told him in a deep baritone. "There's a plate warmin' for you in the kitchen, and the ladies are takin' their tea in the drawin' room. They asked if you would please join them directly when you returned." He motioned toward the ornate double doors at the far end of the hallway.

Lucas felt his gut clench. The stage would be leaving in an hour. He had hoped to talk to Olivia alone, then take his leave. Without facing his sisters again; all three were staying with Olivia to comfort her in her time of sorrow, even though she wasn't always the easiest person to get along with, under the best of circumstances.

"Thanks," he said reluctantly. "I'll do that."

The servant was still holding out one hand. It took Lucas a moment to remember he was supposed to surrender his hat. He took it off and handed it over, raking his fingers through his mashed-down hair before he headed for the drawing room.

A series of red Persian carpets muffled his steps on the marble floor as he walked past framed daguerreotypes, porcelain vases displayed on stands, and paintings illuminated by miniature crystal chandeliers. He caught a glimpse of his reflection in a gilded mirror and stopped, grimacing.

The man grimacing back at him had bleary eyes and a dark stubble of beard on his jaw, his skin darkened and clothes faded from too much time in the sun. A thorough coating of dust and sweat hardly improved matters. He looked as unfit for polite company as a rangy wolf that had just loped in from the woods.

He thought to make himself more presentable, and wasn't quite sure how to achieve that, when he heard the creak of a door nearby, followed by a quiet voice.

"Uncle Lucas?"

He glanced over his shoulder. "Peter?" His thirteen-year-old nephew hovered in the shadows of a doorway. "What is it?"

When the boy remained silent, looking from him to the polished floor and back again, Lucas tried to think of something more to say.

But the words seemed to clog up in his throat; every time he looked at Peter, he saw James, the boy favored him so much. "You all right?"

Stupid question. Of course he wasn't all right. Peter

had just lost his father, at an age when a boy needed one more than ever. Lucas knew how that felt, yet he didn't know what to say to ease his nephew's pain; he couldn't offer platitudes, assure him it would be all right.

Because it wouldn't be.

Lucas felt another fierce shot of anger at the woman who had taken his brother's life—and torn up so many others.

"Uncle Lucas, I . . ." The boy looked uneasily toward the drawing room, where the sound of feminine conversation could just be heard from the other side of the doors. "I want to . . ."

Before Peter could finish, one of those doors slid open. "Lucas? I thought I heard you. I'm so glad you've returned."

The voice was soft, polite, proper. Even in mourning, Olivia McKenna was still completely a lady, well suited to her place as James's wife.

Or rather, his widow.

She clasped her hands at her waist, her skin pallid against the black dress she wore, her blond hair pulled back in a neat chignon. "Did you have any luck today?" Only her blue eyes conveyed what she felt: hope that was almost desperation.

Conscious of the boy's presence, Lucas didn't want to go into details. "Yes."

Olivia closed her eyes and lifted a hand to her heart for a second before turning to her son. "Peter, would you be a dear and go up and see how Cordelia is feeling? She might like some more tea."

James's nine-year-old daughter hadn't been eating much, had barely left her room since the funeral.

Young Peter frowned at the request. "She's got her nurse and her nanny—"

"And a kind, considerate brother." Olivia walked over

and ran her hand through her son's sandy hair, then leaned down and whispered something to him. Peter nodded sullenly and moved toward the staircase, his gaze on the floor.

Lucas wanted to say something more to the boy, tell him they could talk tomorrow. But that wouldn't be possible; Lucas wouldn't be there tomorrow.

And he would only say the wrong thing anyway. He wasn't any good with children, wasn't cut out to be a family man.

He was not his brother.

As soon as Peter disappeared up the stairs, Olivia ushered Lucas into the drawing room, closing the doors behind them. Inside, his three sisters waited amid the mahogany and velvet furnishings and soft lamplight, looking warily of the man who had just stepped into their midst. They just didn't seem to know what to make of him, this brother who was almost a stranger, who wore a gun and a badge. And he didn't know how to fix that.

Lucas glanced away. He hardly knew them anymore, they were all so grown up and sophisticated: Callie, the eldest at twenty-three, home from her medical studies in Philadelphia; Eden, who was in her final year of college in New York and dreamed of being a writer; and Faith, so sweet and elegant, fresh from her Boston finishing school.

James had taken good care of them, always saw that they had the best of everything.

Now, as one, all three girls looked up at him. Silence reigned.

"He's got news," Olivia said, sinking down on the edge of an upholstered settee. "Tell us, Lucas. What have you found out?"

He looked at his sisters, trying to think of some nice, polite, proper way to explain. They had suffered enough in the past week: first James's death, then the revelation that he'd had a mistress for three years.

After clearing his throat, Lucas settled for just stating the facts plainly. "A stage driver who came in from Independence today thinks he remembers her. A woman on his coach that night matches Antoinette Sutton's description." He clenched his jaw. "And she was wearing widow's weeds."

Faith gasped at that particular, offensive detail. Callie, who had always been the strong one, put a comforting arm around her. "And where did she go?"

"She's not going to get *away*, is she?" Eden asked with a look of disbelief.

"No," Lucas vowed. "The driver said she was headed west. I just came back to collect my things and I'm catching the nine o'clock stage. I'm going to retrace her route." He glanced at Olivia. "I'll find her."

Olivia blinked up at him, a slight tremble visible in her hands, folded in her lap. "Thank you, Lucas. I know you'll keep us informed."

"Of course." Lucas couldn't think of anything more to say, his eloquence around children surpassed only by his grace and charm around women. "Well, I need to be going." He began a retreat toward the doors.

Until a tremulous voice stopped him. "You are coming back, aren't you?"

It was Eden. As he turned around, she stood up—all five feet two inches of her.

"I—I mean," she continued haltingly, "I know your work is important, out in the territories, but . . . you will come back to us, won't you?" She regarded him with tear-brightened eyes. "At least for a little while?"

Lucas felt a lump in his throat, and though he swallowed hard, he couldn't dislodge it. Suddenly, standing before him was not a sophisticated young woman, but the girl he used to carry on his shoulders around the farm, when he was almost Peter's age and she was only three.

A girl who had lost too many people she loved and depended on. Who had always looked at him as if he were her hero.

And he realized then that his sisters still needed someone to depend on. They might be financially secure, thanks to James's will, but that didn't mean they could fend for themselves. Hell, they were all of marrying age. There should be a man around to watch over them, guide them, keep their suitors in line.

He didn't know how he could be what they needed.

But he knew he couldn't fail them . . . like he had before, when they were all so much younger.

"Yes," he promised. "I'll come back." He repeated it as he left the drawing room. "I'll come back."

He heard slippered footsteps following him down the hallway. Olivia caught his arm. "Lucas, wait. I must speak with you in private before you go—"

"Olivia—"

"It won't take a moment. Quincy," she called to the servant who stood by the door, "would you please pack Marshal McKenna's things in his saddlebags and bring them down?" She was already tugging Lucas toward her private sitting room.

He gave in and followed, both annoyed and curious at her behavior. While she turned up one of the lamps, he flipped open his pocket watch, "I don't have a lot of time—"

"I know, I'm sorry. But I thought I should . . . thought you should know . . ." She closed the door and moved to a writing desk in one corner, opening the top drawer and withdrawing a sheet of paper.

When she handed it to him, Lucas almost dropped his watch. He forgot the presence of delicate feminine ears and cursed, vividly.

The word REWARD was printed boldly atop a long column of type—with a number at the bottom. "*Five thousand* dollars?"

"I know we discussed this, and you said it wasn't a good idea, but I—I placed that advertisement in the paper this morning. And they sent it on to a number of other papers. By tomorrow it will be—"

"Everywhere." He flung the paper aside. "God damn it, Olivia—"

"It's been a whole week, and nothing has turned up," she said defensively. "I had to do something. The advertisement will help—"

"A five-thousand-dollar reward will *not* help. A five-thousand-dollar reward will bring out every flea-bitten, trigger-happy bounty hunter in ten states. I'll be lucky if I don't get shot in the crossfire!" He paced away from her, fists clenched. "It would've been better to let her think she got away, Olivia. When she was confident she was safe, *that's* when she would've come out in the open. Now she'll go to ground like a scared rabbit."

"Keep your voice down, if you please," Olivia requested. "I have every confidence in you—"

"No, you don't." He spun to face her. "That's why you placed that ad. Because you thought I wouldn't see this through. Because you don't think I give a damn about my family."

Olivia turned away, and said nothing.

Lucas felt the sting of her condemnation as if she had slapped him. He shook his head, studying her while she studied a fern in front of the curtained window.

"And what the hell happened to 'let's handle this quietly'?" he demanded. "I thought you wanted to avoid a scandal—"

"There has already been a scandal. What I want is justice."

Whether it was something in her voice, or the way she stroked the fronds of the plant, Lucas finally understood. "You want her dead."

Olivia glanced over her shoulder, and for the first time he recognized the emotion in her eyes: a thoroughly improper, unladylike hunger for vengeance.

"Three years, Lucas. For three years I was understanding. When I first heard the whispers in town, I didn't believe it. Even after I discovered the whispers were true, I . . ." Her voice wavered. She took a breath before she continued. "I never said a word. Because after Cordelia was born, I was the one who asked that . . ." She paused again, lowering her gaze.

Lucas shifted his attention to the flocked wallpaper and almost told her to stop. She didn't need to explain. He had talked to James's friends, had already guessed why his brother had taken a mistress; it was a common enough practice among men of James's social class.

Olivia started pulling dead leaves off the fern. "I suppose it was naïve of me to think that he might love me so much, he wouldn't . . . go elsewhere. But to carry on with a woman like *that*," she said bitterly, tearing the leaves into bits until they stained her fingers. "The daughter of a *whore*. To take her on trips, parade her around like some rare prize . . ."

Lucas felt a muscle flex in his cheek. *That was just James.* Always taking care of the people around him, treating them to the best of everything.

Olivia let the shredded leaves fall to the rug, and her voice became soft. "I was always understanding. But no more. Lucas, if you find her first . . ." She turned to face him, flicking a glance at the .45 holstered on his hip. "I see no reason why she shouldn't receive your usual treatment."

Lucas knew what she meant. "You've read too many newspaper stories, Olivia."

"Are you saying your reputation is undeserved?"

He hesitated, shrugged one shoulder. "I'm saying reporters tend to exaggerate. I've faced a few nasty S.O.B.s who preferred to shoot their way past me rather than take their chances in front of a judge."

"I see." She was all pale politeness again—except for her blue eyes, which seemed to burn with intensity as she held his gaze. "But it's possible Antoinette Sutton may resist arrest as well, and the West is an uncivilized place . . . and I don't think any questions would be asked."

Lucas didn't need her to explain that fact to him, either.

"Don't worry, Olivia." He nodded before he moved to the door, his fingers fastening tight around the handle. "I intend to see that she gets what she deserves."

2

The tiny grave was in a corner of the cemetery, in the shade near a picket fence that might have been white some years ago. Annie knelt in the grass, barely aware of the autumn wind cutting through the calico dress and woolen shawl that Mrs. Owens had loaned her. She looked at the ground, not blinking, not moving, so still that a chirping sparrow hopped within a few inches of her.

The bird flew away in a burst of flapping wings when Annie lifted her hand. She reached toward the scant mound of earth, her fingers moving over it, back and forth, brushing away the leaves that had fallen since her last visit.

Beneath the leaves lay a few sprigs of columbine tied with ribbon, faded by the sun, dried by the mountain air. She picked them up and they crumbled, the petals blowing away on the wind. Annie stared down at the parched stems left behind, unable to remember when she had brought the flowers, or even if she had been the one who placed them there.

It might have been one of the townsfolk; they had all been so kind to her, so filled with sympathy for the "unfortunate young widow" who had been stranded among them two months ago, who had hovered near death for more than a week. Even the doctor hadn't expected her to survive. While she was still unconscious and fevered, the local preacher had held a ceremony here for her lost little one, gathering a few people for prayers and hymns. They had even provided a small pine cross.

BABY SMITH, someone had carved in the weathered wood.

Annie closed her eyes and hung her head. A low sound escaped her, full of pain that was still as fresh and deep in her heart as it had been eight weeks ago.

She had given her child nothing. *Nothing.* Not life, not the secure, loving future she had dreamed of . . . not even a real name.

Only a cross on a cold mountain hillside, in a cemetery filled with drunks shot in saloon brawls, miners killed in cave-ins, lawmen who had died trying to bring order to this remote, uncivilized corner of the West.

Hunched over the mound of dirt, Annie covered her face with her hands, and felt the dust of the columbines against her cheeks, and began to cry.

The afternoon sun cut long shadows across the grass by the time she stirred, lifting her head, realizing she must have drifted asleep. Since losing the baby, she hadn't been able to rest at night, would lie in bed staring into the darkness.

Annie wiped at her cheeks and sat up, shivering in the wind. Gray clouds had slid into view, threatening rain or maybe snow; it was hard to tell, hard to make sense of the weather or much else in this place, so high above the world it seemed to belong more to the sky than to the earth.

The crocheted shawl had fallen to the ground. After a moment, she picked it up and pushed herself to her feet, unsteadily.

Only the thought of getting another talking-to from Dr. Holt made her wrap the shawl around her. She walked toward the cemetery gate. He kept warning her that she wasn't fully recovered yet, that she was still weak and shouldn't exert herself. Annie didn't care.

Not when part of her soul lay buried in the cold earth.

She looked back at the small cross as she stepped through the gate and latched it behind her. The moment her fever had passed and she was able to get out of bed, she had started coming here each afternoon. And still she didn't understand.

She had taken James's life. Had failed to give her child life.

Why wasn't she *the one buried here in the middle of nowhere?*

She let go of the latch and turned away, head lowered. A carpet of meadow grass dotted with white flowers and fallen aspen leaves silenced her steps.

It didn't take long to reach the town sprawled on the rocky mountainside below. Annie might not understand why God had seen fit to spare her life, but she was beginning to suspect that He had deposited her here on purpose, that in some strange way she belonged in this place.

Because she felt like a ghost, just drifting through the days, and Eminence, Colorado was well on its way to becoming a ghost town.

Dirt gathered along the hem of her dress and petticoat as she walked down the main street, past clapboard buildings that needed paint and doorways cluttered by unswept leaves. From what everyone said, Eminence had once been worthy of its name, six years ago when silver had been discovered here—a rich vein that had made several men into millionaires. Thousands of prospectors had poured in and the town sprang up practically overnight, saloons and bawdy houses first, then the land office and livery stable, hotels and mercantiles, later a schoolhouse and a pretty stone chapel with a bell tower.

Then last year, the boom went bust: The silver played out and people started moving on. Now, many of the shops and once-grand hotels stood empty, the population dwindled to a hundred or so stubborn types—homesteaders, a few merchants, a couple of Lutheran missionaries, and some optimistic miners hoping to strike another vein.

And a woman by the name of Smith who wasn't at all what she claimed to be.

As she approached the livery stable, Annie noticed that the stage had arrived. It came through once a week, bringing mail and a handful of passengers, carrying away more residents who had decided to seek their fortunes elsewhere. The stage and an occasional mule train offered the only connection to the outside world; even the new Denver Pacific Railroad had snubbed Eminence, declining to build a link because narrow mountain passes made the town inaccessible in winter.

Mr. Ballard, the livery owner, smiled and waved to her as he unhitched the lathered horses from their traces. Annie lifted a hand to return his greeting, though she couldn't summon a smile. For these few weeks she had been safe, hidden in this forgotten scrap of a town. But people had been talking about her dramatic arrival—and though news traveled slowly in these parts, it did travel.

And she wasn't far enough from Missouri.

Strangely, that fact no longer filled her with terror; she had awakened from her fever with only a numb . . . emptiness in her heart. As if all her fear, all her feelings but sorrow had been burned away, her sense of urgency lost with her baby.

She couldn't bring herself to leave here. Couldn't bring herself to part from that little cross on the hill.

Even if she got captured. *What did it matter?*

She glanced back at the stage, noticing that it was already empty; the passengers must be quenching their thirst in the saloons or gobbling platefuls of roast chicken and baked beans over at Kearney's Boarding House. When she looked down the street toward the general store, she also noticed that the mail flag had already been hung out front.

"Damn," she whispered, hitching up the dragging hem of her skirts and hurrying on. Mrs. Greer would be needing her.

In her rush, she almost tripped on the uneven planks of the wooden boardwalk out front. Through the store's tall windows, she could see what looked like half the folks in town inside, all eager to collect their letters and newspapers. Annie opened the door and squeezed in.

"Excuse me." She coughed on smoke from the men's cigars, the tobacco smell overpowering the familiar scents of freshly ground coffee and the cured hams that hung from the ceiling. Someone had stoked up the pot-bellied woodstove in the center of the store and a few people gathered around it, warming their hands, while others perused shelves piled with tools and soaps and patent medicines, and barrels and kegs heaped with seeds and buckwheat flour and oranges fresh from California.

Most people, though, pressed toward the back counter where a fancy brass sign hanging from a chain read U.S. POST OFFICE. Everyone was talking at once. Annie tried edging through sideways. "Excuse me, please."

"Mrs. Smith! A pleasure to see you, ma'am." Cyrus Hazelgreen, the town's lone remaining banker, turned to her with a tip of his bowler hat and a gallant bow. "You're looking well today."

"Hello, Mrs. Smith," Mrs. Gottfried said brightly, try-ing to hold onto her two-year-old son, who was lunging toward a display of glass jars filled with peppermint and horehound candies. "How are you feeling?"

"Did you try that yarrow tea I sent over?" another lady asked, studying Annie in the light of the oil lamps suspended overhead. "Yes, I can see you surely did. Much better color in your cheeks today, dearie. It worked a wonder, if I do say so—"

"Yes, thanks, I—"

"Ann? There you are." Mrs. Owens, who worked as Dr. Holt's nurse, emerged from the throng at the counter, delightedly ripping paper and string from a package in her hands. "This is the China silk from San Francisco I was telling you about." The bolt of emerald-green fabric drew admiring *oohs* from other women who closed in for a better look. Mrs. Owens held it out toward Annie. "The color would look so pretty on you, and there's more here than I need—"

"No, I . . . thanks, but . . ." Conscious of the borrowed shawl wrapped around her shoulders, Annie looked down, her hands wringing the faded blue calico of her skirt. "The clothes you've loaned me are more than enough. You've already been so generous." She lifted her head, gazing at the women who had gathered around her. "All of you."

They responded with soft "not at all"s and gentle expressions and friendly smiles, and Annie felt something knot up inside her.

Never in her life had she known the sort of kindness these ladies had shown her the past few weeks. Back in St. Charles, no respectable woman would even *speak* to her; they crossed the street when they saw her coming or looked right through her like she was made of air. She had gotten used to it, growing up, telling herself she didn't care. Didn't care about being turned away from the school. Didn't care about having no playmates except her brother.

But here, everything was different.

Here, no one knew what her mother was, or what she was.

And so Mrs. Greer, who owned this store, had taken Annie in to share her living quarters upstairs. And each of these women had helped care for her—without asking anything in return, without knowing anything about her except that she had suffered a miscarriage and was all alone.

"I—I owe you all so much." Annie found it hard to speak past a tight, dry feeling in her throat. "I know I said it before, but . . . thank you."

One of the women placed an arm around her. " 'T'ain't nothin', Ann, what we done for you. It's how folks treat folks out here."

Annie tried not to flinch away, tried to relax and summon a smile. If she had learned one thing about life in the West, it was that women stuck by each other, with a fierce loyalty forged by loneliness, hardship—and the fact that they were outnumbered by men four to one in this rugged place.

And yet she kept waiting for these good, upstanding ladies to whisper and point, unable to believe they couldn't tell just by looking at her that she was a liar. A fraud. When she glanced down again, the gold ring on her left hand caught the light, mocking her.

She didn't deserve their friendship. Or their respect.

A stout blond girl emerged from the crowd at the back counter, a baby balanced on her hip. "There ain't no letter from Joe," she said softly, her eyes full of disappointment.

"Sakes alive," one of the women said in disgust.

"The dickens take that scalawag!" another commented.

Annie seized the opportunity to sidle away from the group. "Let me check the mail sacks again for you," she offered.

The other women turned to express their sympathies to the girl, many of them sharing her predicament—left behind in Eminence while their silver-hungry husbands were off chasing the next big strike. Annie overheard one wife mutter a few choice words about men and their "hell-fired habit of always ridin' off to somethin' more important than their loved ones."

As she threaded through the chattering crowd, Annie couldn't help remembering what her mama used to say: Sooner or later, a man always left you high and dry, usually right when you needed him most. So it was best not to depend on him in the first place. Not to get used to having him around.

Not to give him your heart. Not ever.

Annie swallowed hard. She would never forget that lesson again, not after learning it the hard way.

At last she managed to reach the back counter—but she didn't see anyone behind the envelopes and packages piled up between the tins of soda crackers and the crocks of honey and jam. "Mrs. Greer?" she shouted above the crowd's noise.

"Lord amighty, if everyone would just stop yelling— Ann, is that you?" Only the purple ostrich plume in Rebecca Greer's hat showed until she straightened, rising from the floor with an armful of envelopes that had apparently slid from the pile.

Her pink dress bore several inky fingerprints, her bustle was askew, and her dangling green earrings bobbed as she turned her head left and right before squinting in Annie's general direction.

"Ah! There you are. I'm managing just fine, dear. You go on upstairs and take a rest. Did you enjoy your walk today?" She released her armful of letters atop the others, then picked one up and held it close to her nose, babbling on before Annie could answer. "By the horn spoons, there's a peck of mail this week, and half of it ad-dressed to folks who don't even live here anymore—"

"It might be a help, ma'am, if you were to wear your spectacles." A lanky sixteen-year-old leaning on the counter looked up from the penny dreadful he was read-ing, its lurid cover showing a blazing shootout beneath the title TRUE TALES. He held a licorice stick clamped be-tween his teeth at a rakish angle. "I'm gonna be lucky to get home by suppertime—"

"You hush up, Travis Ballard." Mrs. Greer snatched the periodical from his hands and thwacked him on the shoulder with it. "And stop reading other folks' mail. And did you pay for this?" She plucked the licorice stick from his mouth. "I'm paying you a dollar a week to help out, you lazy rascal, not to eat up what scanty profits I got—"

The rest of the crowd groaned and complained loudly at yet another delay by their official U.S. postmistress, and Annie stepped around the counter without waiting to be asked. While Mrs. Greer took young Travis by the sleeve and hauled him toward the back room, Annie grabbed an apron from a nearby hook and slid onto her vacated stool.

A few minutes later, a steady stream of townsfolk were on their way out the door, gratefully clutching the latest issues of *Godey's Lady's Book* and *Wards' Illus-trated Catalogue*, week-old newspapers from Denver, and messages from family and friends "back in the States," which was how folks here still referred to the East, even though Colorado itself had been a state for two years now.

As she worked, Annie discovered one letter addressed to her—or rather, to *Mrs. Ann Smith*—from young Cor-poral Easton up at Fort Collins, the soldier who had car-ried her off the stage on that harrowing night when she arrived here.

He had written to her twice since then, inquiring after her health and asking if he might visit when he got leave. She hadn't replied yet. Just seeing his name brought a rush of painful memories, and Annie slipped the letter into her pocket and kept handing out mail.

As soon as she was well enough, she had insisted on helping out around the store in return for her bed and board. Mrs. Greer had admonished her for being "prideful and stubborn," but accepted, admitting that she had been struggling to keep this place open since her husband passed away last spring, and they'd had no children. With her eyesight so poor, the mail was the chore she dreaded the most, so it was the chore Annie had claimed first.

"Mrs. Smith?"

Annie looked up from sorting letters to see a prospector known as Big Horace standing in front of her. Dirt obscured his features, he had a length of rope slung over one shoulder, and the sour smell of whiskey and sweat came off his clothes—strong enough to make the other people at the counter give him a wide berth.

"Yes?" she asked politely. The mountain of a man with a scar on his face had given her quite a fright the first time she saw him, but Rebecca had explained that he was harmless; some of the miners only came in from their diggings now and again, and they got a bit rough around the edges.

"Ma'am, I think you're . . ." Big Horace took off his hat. "Why, you're huckleberry above a persimmon, ma'am, and I'd be right peart were you to join me tonight for some chicken fixin's over t' Kearney's, if you're not still feelin' poorly."

Annie blinked up at him, unable to make sense of what he'd just said.

Mrs. Greer appeared at her elbow. "Horace, what are

you doing staring at Mrs. Smith like that? She's a lady, not a gingerbread pudding on a Christmas platter." She gave him a playful poke in the belly before she turned to Annie. "I'll manage the rest, lamb. You're still looking a might pale, and it's too warm in here." Mrs. Greer scooped up one fat stack of letters. "Since Doc Holt ain't come in to pick up his mail yet, maybe you could take it to him."

Annie met the older woman's squinty gaze and thought of arguing. But she had yet to meet the person who could win an argument with Rebecca Greer. "All right."

"Good. Then you come straight back here and take a rest, like I said before."

Annie nodded, almost smiling, thinking that Mrs. Greer sounded very much like a mother.

Except that her own mama had never sounded like that.

The thought brought a sharp sting to her eyes. Annie quickly took off her apron, picked up Dr. Holt's mail, and stepped around the counter.

"Ann, before you go . . ."

Annie turned back. "Yes?"

Mrs. Greer had an uncertain, hopeful look in her eyes. "I've been meaning to ask . . . you said you had kin in Montana Territory, and I know Doc Holt said you'll be well enough to travel in another week or so . . ."

For the first time since Annie had met her, Mrs. Greer seemed at a loss for words, fidgeting with a charm on one of the bracelets she wore.

"By the horn spoons," she continued at last, "if you want to get there before spring, you'll have to go soon, before the snow flies. But if . . ." She hesitated again, and her voice became quiet. "Lord knows this town ain't got much to offer anymore, but if you could think of staying on, I'd surely appreciate it. Most everyone who needs work has left, and Travis ain't much help, and I . . . I just can't manage this place on my own. I could pay you a few dollars, to go with the room upstairs and meals."

Annie couldn't speak for a moment, her voice stolen by surprise. Not because the idea was outlandish.

But because it was tempting. People accepted her here, treated her like an equal. Maybe she *did* belong here, where so many folks were left over or left behind, like bits of gravel in a prospector's pan after all the gold had been sifted away.

A life in Eminence wouldn't be anything like the leisurely, indulged life she had known the past three years, filled with rich clothes, rich food, rich trappings. But it would be a life.

"I . . ." She reached toward Mrs. Greer, only to knock a glass jar of cinnamon sticks off the counter. It crashed to the floor.

Annie cursed, then realized how unladylike it sounded. "I'm sorry. Mrs. Greer, I'm so sorry." Annie started picking up shards of glass. "I . . . it wouldn't . . . you don't want someone like me around," she finished lamely. "Believe me, you don't."

"That's not true," the older woman argued. "I like you, Ann Smith. And I don't like many folks." She knelt beside Annie with a whisk broom. "You go on now. Go on and think about it. I'll clean this up."

"Thank you, Mrs. Greer—"

"Rebecca," the older woman corrected.

Annie met her gaze, feeling as broken as the glass on the floor. "Rebecca," she said quietly.

She scooped up Dr. Holt's mail from the counter and left. Her steps echoed on the wooden planks outside, beneath the fading afternoon sun, and she thought she finally understood why God had brought her here and spared her life.

To punish her. Surround her with everything she'd dreamed of in the most secret places in her heart since she was a little girl. Respect. Friends. A home. A *real* home.

Everything she could never have.

As she crossed the street, her gaze on the dust, something made her glance up. Maybe a shift in the wind. The sound of a door creaking as it swung open. A strand of her unruly hair blowing into her eyes. She wasn't sure.

But that was when she saw him. Watching her.

A stranger. He stood in front of one of the saloons, directly ahead of her, almost hidden by the darkness and shadows beneath its balcony. Silent and still. In the shifting afternoon light, she got only an impression of a tall, lean figure standing alone. But her heart started beating harder. She didn't know why, couldn't even tell what had drawn her attention to him, what made her so certain he was staring at her.

But some instinct lifted the fine hairs on the back of her neck. Even as she looked right at him, she could glimpse no more than an outline of broad shoulders. A western hat tilted low over his eyes. A pistol holstered on his hip.

And all at once, the fear that she had thought burned away by sorrow came rushing back in a flood. She almost stopped in her tracks, almost turned around, but forced herself to keep walking. Steadily, casually.

He didn't move. Didn't seem especially threatening. Wasn't nearly as big and frightening as Big Horace.

She tried to breathe evenly, calm herself. He was probably just another miner who'd come in from his claim after weeks away from civilization. Was probably staring at her because he hadn't seen a woman in a long time. Or maybe he was a traveler passing through, newly arrived on the stage and drunk from his visit to the saloon.

He stepped down from the saloon's porch and started across the street. Directly toward her.

And the way he moved wasn't drunken or casual, but slow and purposeful. And Annie knew that there was something different about this man.

Something dangerous.

Her heart thudded a hard stroke. A single panicked thought rioted through her mind.

She'd been found.

All the breath seemed to leave her lungs. She had thought she no longer cared about being captured—but she'd been wrong.

Oh God, oh God, oh God. She lowered her gaze and remembered the letters in her hand. Started leafing through them as she walked. Told herself she looked like any ordinary homesteader who'd just come from collecting the weekly mail. She tried to hum but couldn't remember a single tune.

She could hear his footsteps now as he came closer, the sound heavier than she would've thought for a man who seemed so lanky. *Muscle,* some part of her brain supplied. *Every lean inch of him must be pure muscle.*

An uneasy fluttering sensation filled her belly. Dear God, what should she do? *Think, damn it.*

Annie lifted her head and nodded politely and said a cheerful, "Good afternoon."

Without saying a word, he reached up to touch the brim of his hat. His fingers were long and tanned, his face as lean and spare as the rest of him, his jaw stubbled by a dark beard, his mouth bracketed by deep lines. He had black hair that curled below his collar.

And clear, green-gold eyes that fastened on her with an intensity that made her legs feel weak.

Cowboy, she thought desperately as they passed almost shoulder to shoulder. Maybe he was a cowboy. He was dressed like one, had the rough, hard look of a man who'd spent his life on the range. And cowboys were reputed to be men of long stares and few words.

But what would a cowhand be doing so far from the cattle trails?

It seemed to take her forever to reach Dr. Holt's house on the corner. Her hand trembled as she knocked on the front door, barely aware of the sound over the rising buzz that filled her head. There was no reply. A tingling feeling began between her shoulder blades.

Like she was about to be shot in the back.

Unable to stop herself, she nervously glanced behind her. The dark stranger stood in front of the general store.

Watching her.

She forced a smile.

He didn't return it.

Annie knocked on Dr. Holt's door again, her heart hammering now. *Open the door. Open it. Please, Dr. Holt, open the door!*

It couldn't be her.

That wan, demure little creature dressed in faded calico couldn't possibly be Antoinette Sutton. Lucas stood on the board sidewalk in front of the general store, staring at her, and told himself he'd gone without sleep for too long. He'd been on the hunt so many weeks—talking to stagecoach drivers and passengers, going in circles, losing her trail and picking it up again—that he was ready to pounce on an innocent homesteader.

From what Olivia had told him, he expected his brother's killer to be a brazen, lusty, bold figure of a female who would just as soon curse him and spit in his eye as look at him.

This elfin lady who'd emerged from the general store with a handful of mail looked so pale and slender, it seemed a good breeze could knock her down. She matched part of the physical description everyone in St. Charles had given him—dark-haired and brown-eyed and pretty enough to make any man look twice. But she seemed too . . . small.

When he passed her on the street, her manner had been polite, her voice soft, and she barely came up to his chin. He didn't even know why he was still staring at her.

The door she was knocking on finally opened, and a man greeted her warmly and ushered her inside the whitewashed, two-story house.

Obviously some friend or kin, Lucas thought sourly. Perfect. He had just wasted five minutes glaring at an innocent homesteader. Another pointless end to another useless day.

Even if Antoinette Sutton had been dropped off in this dusty nothing of a town suffering from "female trouble," as he'd been told, she was probably long gone. He doubted this was the kind of place she would loll about for very long.

And the sooner he put Eminence behind him, Lucas decided, the better. He usually got his best information in saloons, but the barkeeps here had proven annoyingly discreet, responding to his questions with shrugs and long, silent stares.

"Can I be a help to you, mister?"

Lucas turned to find a bright-eyed kid of about sixteen standing on the boardwalk beside him, chewing on a striped peppermint stick.

"Name's Travis. Travis Ballard." The boy extended his hand, palm up. "Saw you standing out here a spell and figured you might need directions. Or information. I know 'bout all there is to know 'bout this town. You want anything, I'm your man." He waggled his fingers encouragingly. "I can show you where to get a good shave and a bath. You need a room for the night, I'll take you to the best place. And we still got a couple of decent whores left in town."

Lucas arched one eyebrow and started fishing in his pocket for a coin. "I'm only interested in one woman."

The kid laughed. "Well that's good, 'cause I think they charge extra if you want 'em both at once—"

"A woman by the name of Smith." Lucas pressed a half-dollar into Travis's palm. "Mrs. Ann Smith."

The boy fell silent for a moment, pocketing the money. "You don't say."

A wariness had come into the kid's eyes and voice, a subtle shift that told Lucas a great deal.

By hell, maybe she was still here. He ruthlessly subdued the hope that surged through him. "I'm down from Montana Territory," he continued smoothly, tossing out a potentially useful detail he had gleaned from one Corporal Easton of Fort Collins.

Travis seemed to relax a bit, nodding. "You her kin, then?"

"Yeah." Lucas felt his stomach turn at the very idea— and felt his pulse pick up as he sensed he was closing in on his quarry at last. "Distant relation."

"That explains it, then."

"What?"

The boy glanced across the street, looking directly at the house where the pretty brown-eyed elf had disappeared, then pointed.

"Why she didn't seem to recognize you."

Lucas choked out a vicious curse. *Damn the little bitch, she had fooled him.* He was already running, drawing his pistol.

But before he was halfway across the street, he saw a dappled mare light out from behind the house and take off at a gallop—its rider's skirts and long hair streaming behind her on the wind.

3

The dappled mare's hooves pounded the earth, clods of dirt and grass flying. The rocky landscape whirled past in a dizzying blur of green and gray. Annie clung to the reins with one hand, the horse's mane with the other. Her pulse roared in her ears as she fled blindly into the sun's fading light. The wind tore at her hair, at her clothes. She barely felt its cold fingers.

Panic had already turned her to ice. After she had stepped into Dr. Holt's house, she had looked out the front window—and saw the black-haired stranger talking with Travis. Saw the boy point right at her. Knew that her first terrified guess had been correct.

She had been found. By a lawman, a bounty hunter— she didn't know which. Didn't want to find out. She had run for the back door, shouting to Dr. Holt that there was trouble and she needed his horse.

The little mare seemed to fly over the meadows, leaping over every rock and branch in her path. Annie's whole body felt bruised and jolted and she wished there had been time to saddle the animal. Wished she remembered better from childhood how to ride bareback. She clung desperately to the mare's neck and glanced behind her again.

Oh, God, he was getting closer! Minutes ago, she had dared hope that she'd lost him. That she'd had enough of a head start. But now he was gaining ground. She could see his black hair and the bay color of the horse he rode.

And the metallic flash of a pistol in his hand.

A terrified cry rose in her throat but Annie choked it back. Faced forward. Tried to make sense of the jouncing landscape in front of her. *There, to the north.* She tugged hard on the reins, turned the mare. Headed up the mountainside. Toward the pines and aspens blanketing the uneven slopes.

It was almost dusk. If she could reach that forest, maybe she could lose him in the darkness. It was her only chance. She loosened her grip on the reins. The mare stretched out her neck and galloped headlong for the woods.

They splashed across a creek. Barely lost speed as they raced up a hill and down the other side. Annie could already see the gold of the aspen leaves. Felt desperation and hope surge inside her. They raced up another steep rise. Reached the crest.

And suddenly the ground fell away sharply from beneath the horse's hooves.

The mare whinnied, pawing at empty air as they plunged forward.

And tumbled straight down.

Lucas swore as his quarry disappeared in the distance. Vanished as if she had dropped right off the mountain.

Where the hell did she go? Fury shot through him. *Not this time, damn it.* He dug his heels into the bay gelding's sides, kept his Peacemaker drawn and ready. He wouldn't let Antoinette Sutton slip through his fingers again. Wouldn't fall for another of her tricks.

All dressed up in calico and innocence. He felt sick at the way she'd duped him with her disguise. Made him think that such a sweet face and gentle smile and big brown eyes couldn't belong to a coldhearted killer. She'd played him for a fool.

He kept his gaze fastened on the place where she had vanished. Blocked out everything else. As the bay galloped toward the trees, Lucas felt a familiar, icy cool slide through his veins—a sensation that always overcame him when he neared the end of a long, grueling hunt. It made him all the more aware of the pistol in his hand, heavy and hot, powder and steel ready to ignite and explode.

In some remote part of his brain, he noticed the peacefulness of the meadows around him, thought it strange that this was where his search for his brother's murderer would end. And it *would* end. Today. Here. Now. She might be tricky, but the dappled horse she had stolen was no match for the bigger, faster gelding he had taken from the livery.

And she was no match for him.

It was almost too easy to follow the swath cut through the tall grass. He rode within yards of the spot where she had disappeared—and yanked the bay to a sudden, rearing halt.

He studied the crest of the steep rise, his eyes narrowing as an obvious explanation for Antoinette's disappearance hit him.

She might have one last bit of treachery up her calico sleeve. Maybe the direction of her headlong flight hadn't been random at all—maybe she had led him here on purpose.

This would make a perfect spot to bushwhack him from below as he came galloping over the top. She could very well be armed. Could've been carrying a pistol in her skirts all along.

Lucas dismounted, dropping quietly to the ground, holding his Colt ready. He hadn't survived eight years in the Federal Marshals' service by making careless mistakes. He slapped the bay on its lathered flank and sent it trotting back down the way they had come.

Then he crouched low and silently crept toward the top.

The clouds high overhead played with the vanishing sun, made its light shifting and deceptive, bright rays and black shadows dueling over the green landscape. The wind moving through the grass sounded unnaturally loud, his own breathing even louder.

His every muscle tensed. His boot crushed a dried leaf and he flinched. Paused. Kept moving.

The last few feet he covered on his belly, his eyes never leaving the fringe of grass that marked the crest of the hill. When he was just inches from it, he stopped and remained still, flattened against the ground. He waited. Listened. Heard nothing.

Only the peaceful twitter of meadow birds.

He waited a moment more.

Then he lunged to his feet and brought up the .45 and swept the hillside below in a swift arc.

But he didn't see her standing at the bottom, waiting to kill him.

He saw her lying at the bottom, on her back, a patch of crumpled, faded blue among all the green.

His heart thudded a strange, doubled beat. Her horse was nowhere in sight. It looked like she had come up on the sheer drop too fast and fallen—

No, it was a trick.

"Antoinette Sutton," he shouted, starting to walk down the hill toward her, aiming right at her.

He called her name a second time and she stirred, moaning. She lifted her head, pressed her hand against the ground as if struggling to raise herself up on one elbow.

He couldn't see her other hand. Kept waiting for her to whip out a gun. Instead she froze, staring up at him. He looked down into her lovely face.

And knew it had been the last thing his brother saw before he died.

Cold, blinding fury seized him. He thumbed back the hammer on his Colt. His finger tightened on the trigger.

Her eyes widened, locked on the barrel of the .45.

His breathing became harsh. He could feel the steel curve beneath his finger. So smooth, so hard. *So easy.*

One shot and it would all be over.

But still she didn't pull a weapon. Didn't beg for mercy or curse him or spit in defiance. She just gazed, transfixed, at the Peacemaker, with those brown eyes so like a doe's.

And a second later she lowered her lashes, her expression shifting to one that held no terror or even resignation but . . .

Acceptance.

Lucas felt a tremor go through him. He ignored it. Held his hand steady. Sweat trickled into his eyes. He blinked it away, remembering young Peter and Cordelia, crying. His sisters, looking to him for justice. Olivia, pleading with him. *The West is an uncivilized place . . .*

No questions would be asked.

Before he knew what he was doing, he was at the bottom of the hill, standing over her, the pistol still in his hand. Antoinette flattened herself against the ground with a cry that might have been fear or pain or both.

This close, he could see her cheek badly bruised, her lip bleeding. No gun in her hands. He eased the hammer forward.

And holstered his pistol.

She blinked up at him with a look that mirrored his own surprise at what he had just done.

And *now* she looked terrified. "W-what do you . . . what . . ."

He reached down for her but she shook her head and tried to scramble away—only to stop, gasping sharply.

He caught her arm, his fingers clamping around her wrist. *So soft.* Quickly, he searched her for weapons—sure that he would find a pistol, a knife—and found none. When he pulled her to her feet, her right leg gave way beneath her and she crumpled to the ground with an exclamation of pain.

He told himself he didn't care. Took a pair of handcuffs from the pocket of his trousers.

"Federal Marshal," he bit out, his voice heavy with disgust—for her and for himself. "Miss Antoinette Sutton, you are under arrest for the murder of James McKenna, your lover." He knelt in front of her, jerked her hands together, and locked the steel manacles around her wrists.

Then he pulled her close to him, glaring into her eyes as he revealed the rest. "My brother."

She uttered a choked, wordless sound. Her eyes filled with disbelief. Shock.

Panic.

He slid one hand behind her back and the other beneath her knees to lift her up. She fainted in his arms.

It took one hell of a long time to make his way back to town.

The sun dropped behind the white-capped peaks in the west, leaving the mountainside gray and soft and shadowy with dusk as Lucas rode across the meadows. He kept the gelding to a slow walk, his right arm around his unconscious prisoner, the reins in his other hand. The dappled horse limped a few paces behind.

He'd found the mare stumbling back toward town with a lame leg, and at first had considered just putting her out of her misery. God knew he wanted to put a bullet in *something*. But it wasn't his horse, so it wasn't his decision.

He only wished he had such a simple explanation, any explanation, for why he hadn't shot the woman now cradled in his lap.

He looked down at her, this wisp of a female, her weight almost nothing against his thighs and his shoulder, her slender throat arched back over his arm, her dark curls tumbling down the horse's side. Her face was so delicate, her features so flawless, she could pose as a model for an expensive china doll. He could see why James had found her attractive, he thought bitterly.

James would have wanted to protect her, take care of her.

Lucas felt fresh anger simmering in his gut. Anger at this innocent-looking lightskirt . . . and at his own weakness. It had come as an unpleasant surprise to discover that—despite his hunger for retribution, despite all the god-awful things he had seen and done in his life, despite the hatred he felt—he didn't have it in him to shoot Antoinette Sutton.

And he didn't understand why.

Because she was unarmed, he told himself. *Because she was hurt and vulnerable.*

He briefly thought it might be her beauty, but it had been a long time since Lucas was an inexperienced kid, hypnotized by every pretty female who came within ten feet of him.

He had no real answer. Only the fact that, so far, nothing about Antoinette Sutton was what he'd expected.

Her clothes and her thinness and the dark circles under her eyes told him she hadn't been living the carefree life of ease and luxury he'd imagined. Nor had she been waiting to ambush him out on that hill.

She had, in fact, simply fallen from her horse. And gotten badly hurt. The bruise on her cheek and cut on her lip were the least of it. He could tell she had broken a rib or two. And maybe her ankle. Hell, if the fall had been bad enough, she could be bleeding inside.

If he had any sense, he would just dump her here in the middle of nowhere and leave her to the slow, painful death she deserved.

Yet he kept riding. And tried to figure out what he intended to do next. Things would've been simple if he had taken vengeance, let his Colt dispense justice.

But he had allowed that moment to pass, like the storm clouds that had vanished from the sky overhead without releasing even one flash of lightning.

The bay gelding stumbled and Antoinette moaned, her lashes fluttering upward. When her gaze met Lucas's, she made a sound of distress and started struggling to break free.

He tightened his arm around her. "Don't even *think* about it, lady. You cause me any trouble, you give me just one reason to put a bullet in you, and I'll take it."

She went still, her breathing shallow and uneven, her body tense in his hold. Her dark eyes, glassy with pain, searched his face.

And somehow he sensed what she was thinking. "Yes," he said harshly, "James's brother, Lucas. I favor our father. James favors our mother—or rather, he *did*. Until you shot him dead."

She swallowed hard, looked away.

"Aren't you even going to try and deny it?" he demanded, his fingers digging into her arm. "Tell me I've got the wrong woman, *Mrs. Smith?* Insist there must be some mistake?"

He could feel her body trembling against his. She remained silent for a long moment. The horse's hooves clopped through the grass.

"There's . . ." Her voice was soft, and bleak. ". . . No mistake."

Surprised, Lucas couldn't respond for a moment. Then he whispered a curse. Hearing her admit her guilt brought him no satisfaction. It wasn't enough. Not nearly enough.

And perversely, he felt like a brute, like he was bullying the confession out of her when she was hurt. He relaxed his grip on her arm, just slightly. "I didn't think so."

She looked up at him, clearly struggling for words against the pain of her injuries. Her voice was scarcely a whisper. "I . . . didn't mean to . . . do it—"

"I wish I had a dime for every outlaw who ever told me that," he said caustically.

Her expression held both fear and confusion. "Why . . . didn't you . . . kill me?"

It was the same question that had been plaguing him—the one question he couldn't answer. For the second time, she rendered him mute.

Why did you close your eyes? he wanted to ask.

"Because I'm taking you back to Missouri to stand trial," he told her at last. "You're on your way to face a judge and jury, *Miss* Sutton. And then you'll spend the rest of your life in prison—if they don't sentence you to hang."

She flinched, whether from the pain in her ribs or the coldness of his words, he couldn't tell.

But again, she didn't argue with him. Simply closed her eyes, remained still in his embrace, and didn't say another word.

Damn the woman, couldn't she do what he expected just once? Why did she have to lie quietly in his arms looking so fragile and—

He ruthlessly cut off that thought. He was *not* going to be deceived into feeling sympathy for her. Regardless of how she looked, she was a cold-blooded killer who had murdered his brother. The last thing she deserved was his sympathy.

Lucas looked out across the sea of grass that stretched before them. As the moon rose and the first stars blinked into view, he began contemplating the long trip back to Missouri . . . wondering how he was going to stand it. If an hour's ride with her left him feeling this edgy and off-balance, he didn't want to think about what it was going to be like sharing close quarters with her for the next several days.

Night had fallen by the time they approached the town, visible only as a dark silhouette and a scattering of firelight ahead. Eminence apparently lacked street lamps, but he could make out lanterns and torches, carried by about twenty people gathered in the street. When they caught sight of him, shouts went up and they hurried in his direction.

The kid, Travis, raced ahead of the rest, holding a lantern aloft, the bouncing light illuminating his stricken expression when he caught sight of Antoinette, who had fallen unconscious again. "Tarnation! She ain't dead, is she?"

"If she were dead, I wouldn't have her in handcuffs." Lucas kept riding toward town. "She just needs to be patched up—"

"You said you was her kin." Travis jogged alongside, his voice accusing. "I told everybody I only pointed her out 'cause you said—"

Lucas cut him off with a dry look and didn't bother

explaining to the boy that he shouldn't trust strangers. "You got a doctor in this town?"

Before Travis could reply, the rest of the crowd surrounded them.

"Lord a'mighty!"

"Sakes alive, what happened?" A matronly woman with a purple ostrich plume in her hat touched Antoinette's cheek.

"Who the devil are you, mister?" one man challenged.

"Poor Mrs. Smith!"

"Her name isn't Smith and she's never been any man's Mrs." Lucas reined the bay to a halt, shifting Antoinette's weight to dig in his pocket for his badge. "I'm a federal marshal and this woman is wanted for murder—"

Shouts of dismay and disbelief drowned him out, even as he held up the silver star with the words U.S. MARSHAL on it.

"That can't be true!"

"You've got the wrong woman—"

"She already confessed." Lucas practically had to yell just to be heard. To his amazement, the crowd had quickly turned hostile—toward him.

He awkwardly swung his leg over the gelding's neck and slid to the ground, still holding her in his arms. She moaned softly as his boots hit the dirt.

"Her real name is *Miss* Antoinette Sutton," he continued, "and there's a warrant out for her in Missouri. Right now she needs a doctor. Do you have one in this town or not?"

The man who had challenged him a moment ago stepped forward. "I'm Dr. Holt. My office is over here." He reached out to take Antoinette from Lucas.

Lucas shook his head adamantly. "I've got her. Let's go."

The townsfolk raised their torches and lanterns to

light the way, swarming around him as he carried his injured prisoner across the street.

To his surprise, the doctor led him straight to the two-story, clapboard house on the corner that Antoinette had entered earlier. Lucas abruptly recognized him as the man who had greeted her so warmly when she knocked on the door.

The man whose dappled horse she had used to make her getaway.

As they stepped inside, Lucas assessed Holt in the brighter light. Early thirties, brown hair and gray eyes, a match for Lucas at about six feet tall. Something about his furrowed brow and rumpled clothes suggested a schoolmaster, but his tanned face and hardy build seemed more suited to a bullwhacker or a blacksmith than a doctor. Already Lucas didn't trust him.

A dozen people followed as Holt led him through a simply furnished parlor and into an adjoining room. After lighting a pair of oil lamps, he directed Lucas to lay Antoinette on an examining table.

One of the women came forward to help as the doctor bent over his patient, his expression concerned. "Take these cuffs off, Marshal—"

"Just patch her up and get her ready to travel."

Holt straightened and fixed him with a stare. "Look, lawman, you can't just flash a badge and start giving orders. I don't know who you are and I don't—"

"Lucas McKenna. The brother of the man she murdered."

A shocked chorus of gasps and exclamations came from the gathered townsfolk.

And Travis, who had lagged behind in the doorway, came hurrying into the room so fast he almost tripped over his own feet. "Did you say McKenna?" he asked, his voice rising. "*Lucas* McKenna? You're U.S. Marshal Lucas T. McKenna of Indian Territory?"

Lucas looked at him warily, braced for what he feared was coming next. "Yeah."

"Tarnation!" The kid took a step back. "Don't anybody else know who this is?" he asked incredulously, turning to his neighbors. "This is . . . tarnation, this is one of the best, most wrathy lawmen ever to ride the Red River! Tough enough to chew nails an' spit out tacks and so quick on the draw they say he's got rattler blood in him—"

"Kid—"

"He brung in Mad Jack Pickett single-handed, and him and his deputies shot up the Blevins gang and—" Travis looked at Lucas as if he were Wild Bill Hickok come back to life, then stuck out his hand. "Marshal McKenna, sir, I've been readin' about you for years. Why, you're a gen-u-ine hero—"

"Don't believe everything you read, kid." Lucas didn't shake his hand. "I'm nobody's hero."

"But the rattler part might be accurate." Holt looked up from gently examining Antoinette's side and gestured to her bruised face. "Did you take a bit of revenge for your brother's death, *Marshal*? Is that how Ann got hurt?"

"She fell from her horse." Lucas was rapidly losing his patience and his temper, especially since it didn't look like Holt or anyone else believed him—regardless of Travis's glowing biography. "Or rather, *your* horse, *Doctor*. You own that dappled mare she used to escape?"

"I let her borrow it—"

"Then I guess I won't have to add horse-thieving to the murder and robbery charges."

"Sorry to disappoint you." Holt started rolling up his

white sleeves. "Just take the cuffs off so I can examine her properly. She may be seriously hurt—"

"Yes." The woman with the ostrich-plume hat kept hovering over Antoinette and generally getting in the way, her eyes full of worry. "The poor lamb's barely recovered from losing her baby."

"What?" Lucas asked in astonishment. "What did you say?"

The woman rushed over to him. "Ann came here two months ago in the middle of the night, dropped off by a stagecoach makin' a detour on its way to Leadville 'cause she was having a miscarriage. She *can't* be the woman you're looking for—"

"Rebecca, would you and the marshal and everyone else get out of here?" Holt demanded. "Mrs. Owens is all the help I need. I have to examine this patient more thoroughly and I am *not* going to do it in front of half the town."

Lucas tore his gaze from Rebecca, with her pink dress and plumed hat and bobbing earrings, and looked down at Antoinette, so slender and pale in the faded blue calico. Nothing about this made sense. He felt like he had stepped into some bizarre dream. *Miscarriage.*

"Get her ready to travel," Lucas ordered, when he could find his voice. "Keep in mind I'll be right outside. And the cuffs stay on."

He moved through the parlor and out into the night with everyone else, his mind reeling.

Miscarriage. No wonder she looked so wan and fragile. The people he'd questioned had mentioned only "female trouble." He'd had no idea that Antoinette was pregnant—

All at once, he recognized the emotion he was feeling as pity, and shook it off.

Whatever she had been through, it didn't matter. And

it didn't come close to the pain she had inflicted on his family—on James and Olivia and their children and his sisters.

And it didn't change Lucas's mind about taking her back to Missouri to face every bit of suffering the law could inflict. He took a deep, steadying breath of the cold night air. There was no way to know, he told himself, if it had even been James's child.

Lucas doubted the daughter of a whore would be faithful to a lover.

Maybe *that* was what she and James had been arguing about that night.

He had walked several paces outside before he realized everyone was peppering him with questions again.

"I do *not* have the wrong woman," Lucas insisted, raising a hand to quiet them. He turned to Travis, who had followed close on his heels. "Go get my saddlebags, kid. I left them at the livery when I came in on the stage."

While Travis hurried down the street, Lucas glanced from one frowning, unfriendly face to another, some of them as weathered as the buildings in this forgotten town.

"The *lady* you're all *so* concerned about," he said tightly, "is no lady. She's not a respectable young widow who was on her way to Montana Territory. She's nothing but a low-born tramp." Anger made his voice sharp. "She was my brother's mistress for the last three years. He took her in off the streets, set her up in a fine place of her own, gave her the best of everything. And she showed her gratitude by stealing all the cash from his safe and shooting him through the heart."

One tall, skinny matron pursed her lips, turning to a friend. "I just *knew* something wasn't right. *I* knew all along there was something not right about that girl—"

"You hush up, Priscilla Kearney. You did not," the woman named Rebecca said, her earrings and the plume in her hat bobbing as she shook her head. "It's not true. He's made a mistake!"

Few people looked or sounded convinced of Antoinette's guilt. Travis came running up with Lucas's saddlebags and black drover's coat, and his hat, which had fallen to the dirt when he lit out on the bay gelding. Lucas put on the coat and hat and pulled a crumpled wanted poster from his bag. He smoothed it out, then took his hunting knife and stabbed it through the top of the paper, attaching it to the wooden clapboards of the doctor's house.

The townspeople gathered around it, lifting their lanterns to study the sketch and read the description of Miss Antoinette Sutton of St. Charles, Missouri.

"It *is* her," Rebecca whispered, echoing the stunned and distressed opinions of many others.

"But . . . but what kind of *evidence* do you have that she's guilty?" one lady asked plaintively.

"There's no question of her guilt." Lucas didn't understand why they were so damned reluctant to believe him. And he wasn't used to having to explain himself in situations like this. Normally when he rode into a town and arrested an outlaw, people were *glad*, grateful to have their streets made safer, eager to see justice done.

"You keep sayin' that." Another woman turned toward him. "But what kind of *proof* is there?"

Lucas gritted his teeth. He proceeded to describe the crime, trying to do it the way he had described dozens of crimes before to fellow lawmen or lawyers.

Coolly. Unemotionally. "My brother apparently wanted to end the relationship, and she disagreed. So she went to his *house*, where his wife and children live. The servants overheard Antoinette arguing with him, in the study. Then they heard a gunshot. She was *seen* running from the grounds, through the gardens. The murder weapon was never found—which means she must have brought it with her and then disposed of it later. Everything was planned and carried out perfectly. She got her revenge and she got away with fifteen thousand dollars."

"Fifteen thousand?" someone asked.

Travis whistled in disbelief.

"But she doesn't *have* any money," one man said. "She's poor as Job's turkey—"

"And if you could have *seen* the way she mourned her baby," Rebecca added, her voice quivering, "visiting the cemetery every day—"

"She's so tenderhearted—"

"How can you stand here and *defend* her?" Lucas stared at them in disbelief, feeling ready to explode. "After everything I've just told you, you *still* don't believe she's guilty?"

The crowd fell silent for a moment.

"We *know* her, mister," one of the women told him quietly, her eyes as stubborn as the tilt of her chin. "We don't know *you* a'tall."

A few of the townsfolk—the skinny matron by the name of Priscilla Kearney, and three or four other sensible types, who were apparently in favor of law and order—started to drift away from the crowd, whispering among themselves.

But most stayed right where they were.

Lucas shook his head in disgust. God Almighty, how many people in this town had Antoinette duped with her lies and her pretty smiles? "I don't know what kind of theatrical act she's put on for you people—but I'm telling you she is *not* a sweet, innocent widow. She's the daughter of a whore. She's a thief who doesn't care about anything but money. And she's got *blood* on her hands. My *brother's* blood."

Everyone continued talking and debating with him, but Lucas decided to stop wasting his breath. He turned to Travis. "Where's the telegraph office in this town?"

"We don't have a telegraph here, sir," the kid said, stepping forward and looking pleased to be asked even a simple question. "Too high in the mountains. Too hard to string the wire up these ridges and keep the poles standing, what with all the winds. But the mail express ain't left yet . . . uh, on account of you took one of the fresh horses they needed for the team." He gestured toward the end of the street, where the coach still sat outside the stables. "My pa owns the livery. Stage'll be leavin' in the morning, if you want to send a letter."

Lucas grimaced. What he wanted was to send word home, to give his family a little peace by telling them he'd caught James's killer—but he would arrive in St. Charles at the same time a letter would. "No, I don't want to send a letter. But tell your pa I'm going to want two tickets on the stage. One way." He headed back into the doctor's house.

Holt had closed the door to his examining room. Lucas opened it without knocking. The doctor turned on him with a glare.

The pungent scent of smelling salts filled the room. Supported by the doctor's female assistant, Antoinette was sitting up.

And wearing nothing but her petticoat and her camisole, lifted so it just covered her breasts while Holt was wrapping a white bandage around her ribs.

Lucas got an eyeful of porcelain skin and full, round breasts spilling over the scanty bit of cotton and lace and ribbon. Her dusky nipples showed through the thin fabric. He couldn't move, couldn't speak. Their eyes met and she tried to cover herself better.

But she couldn't quite manage it with the handcuffs.

Lucas felt like he'd just been kicked in the gut. "She fit to travel in the morning?" he demanded hoarsely.

"No." Holt left the rest of the bandaging to his assistant and stalked toward Lucas. "She needs rest—"

"A day? Two days?"

"Five or six weeks." Holt curtly gestured for him to leave and followed him out, shutting the door behind them.

"If that's supposed to be a joke, Doc," Lucas bit out, "it's not real funny."

"Do you see me laughing, Marshal? She was just starting to recover," Holt said as they faced each other in the parlor. "She was just getting back on her feet after everything she'd been through—and then you ran her right off the side of the mountain."

"That what she told you?" Lucas scoffed.

"What I'm telling *you* is you can't take her anywhere until her ribs heal. She'd never make it down the mountain in this condition. I've taped her up, but out on the trails, getting bounced around in a stagecoach . . ." He shook his head. "One of the broken bones could puncture a lung."

"Well, Doc, accidents happen."

Holt's gray eyes turned icy. "Are you listening to what I'm saying? She could die—"

"And I'm supposed to care?"

"Allow me to put this in language you understand, Marshal. If you're responsible for this woman's death, you'd better kiss that shiny badge of yours good-bye. You may be the biggest toad in the puddle down in Indian Territory, but this is Colorado. You don't legally have jurisdiction here. I'm willing to bet you can't even enforce your Missouri warrant here."

"It's been taken care of," Lucas replied slowly.

Sometimes, having a famous reputation *did* prove to be useful. He narrowed his eyes. "You seem to have more than a passing knowledge of the law, Doctor. Makes me wonder how you came by it."

"The hard way." Holt's voice dropped lower, his stare unflinching. "Let's just say I don't have a big soft spot in my heart for lawmen—especially lawmen who use their badge as an excuse to do whatever the hell they please. You take this girl out of here before she's fit to travel and *you'll* be the one facing a judge. Because I will shout about it all the way to Indian Territory and Missouri and Washington, D.C.—and your illustrious career as a hero to gullible kids will be finished."

Lucas told himself it wasn't worth the effort, or a bruised hand, to knock the good doctor on his self-righteous ass.

"What's in this for you, Holt?" he shot back. "You trying to rescue her? You want to protect her? I'd be careful. The last man who took Antoinette Sutton under his wing got paid back with a bullet in the chest."

For a moment, he almost thought the doctor was going to dare say *maybe he deserved it.*

Until Lucas let his right hand settle on the butt of his holstered Peacemaker.

The doctor's gaze settled on the gun. "All I'm trying to do, McKenna, is save a life. It's what I do for a living." He glanced up, returning Lucas's glare. "Trust me, she won't be leaving Eminence. She can't. You go on your way and come back in five weeks, she'll still be here."

Lucas choked out a derisive laugh. "I go on my way, and you and the other hornswoggled people in this town will be buying her a first-class ticket on the next train out of Denver." He turned on his heel. "I'll be back shortly—and by that I mean later tonight." He stopped at the door. "And she'd better still be here."

He yanked the door shut behind him, wondering how in the name of God and all the angels one smallish woman could cause such huge upheaval.

Outside, a few people lingered, studying the wanted poster and talking among themselves. Frustration and exasperation knotted together inside Lucas.

Now that he had spared Antoinette's life, it seemed her life had been made his responsibility. He wasn't sure whether Holt was telling the truth about her condition, whether she *might* be able to travel to the nearest train depot—but if he took the chance and things went wrong, it could cost him everything.

He glanced around. The idea of cooling his heels in this worthless scrap of a town for five weeks almost made him retch.

But he wouldn't be here that long. He had seen people in worse shape get out of bed and hit the trail in less time. Hell, he'd had broken ribs himself more than once, and never had he been lain up for an entire month.

Two weeks, he figured, maybe three, and she'd be ready to go.

Until then, he had no choice but to stay here. He sure as hell couldn't trust the townsfolk to keep her in custody. Not when Antoinette had so many of them hoodwinked into believing she was every bit as sweet and good as she appeared.

Travis stood a few feet away, standing watch over Lucas's saddlebags like some kind of loyal puppy.

Lucas sighed and walked over to him. "Where's the jail in this town, kid?"

"Uh, we don't have one, sir."

Lucas regarded him for a long moment. "There's no jail?"

"No, sir. It's the truth, sir. Jail burned down this summer and our town marshal left to take a job up north, and we ain't found anyone willin' to take his place since. Nearest law's the county sheriff down in Central City, and that's—"

"Seventy miles down the mountain." Lucas ran a hand over his unshaven face, tried to remember the last time he'd slept, and muttered a word that started with "f" that made Travis blink.

Yet the admiration in the kid's eyes only seemed to grow. "So . . . so what're you going to do with the prisoner, Marshal?"

"What am I going to do with her?" Lucas echoed, wondering the same thing as he looked at the shops and houses and stone chapel and abandoned buildings that made up Eminence. For a moment, all he could think about was a hot meal and a decent bed.

Then an idea occurred to him. He glanced sideways at Travis. "Post office is in the general store?"

"Yessir."

Lucas headed across the street.

"Marshal? Sir?" Travis followed at his heels. "What have you decided to do?"

4

A *nightmare. She had been swept up in a nightmare.*
The dose of laudanum Mrs. Owens had given Annie
helped dull the stabbing pain in her ribs and made
breathing easier—but it didn't relieve the sick feeling of
panic in her stomach.

And the haze of the drug seeping through her veins
only brought her memories of this room more vividly to
life. They whirled around her, like ghosts.

*The feel of the hard, smooth examining table beneath
her. The flickering lamplight. The odors of rubbing alcohol and smelling salts. The sound of distant voices.*

She closed her eyes. Tried to shut it all out. Couldn't
escape the echoes of her own words, pleading.

My baby . . . not me . . . save the baby . . .

Annie sobbed, the sound scratchy and thin. Her
throat had gone dry. She lifted her head, glanced into the
dark corners, frightened by a dizzying sense that the images were more than memories, that they were happening now. The walls seemed to move, tumbling toward her,
the ceiling closing in to crush her. "Mrs. Owens . . ."

But Mrs. Owens wasn't here. She had left after buttoning up Annie's dress and bandaging her sprained ankle.

Leaving Annie alone. Alone with the heavy steel manacles around her wrists. And the memories.

She sank back down on the table, whimpering softly as the sounds and smells and other fragments of time floated through the numbing fog of laudanum.

One image was of a dark silhouette standing above her on a hill, aiming a pistol at her in the fading light of day. She stared up the black barrel of that gun and held her last breath and waited for the end. The end of all the pain, all the horror she felt at what she had done.

Only it didn't end.

She kept waiting for the gunshot that never came. *He had changed his mind. Why had he changed his mind?*

She turned her head toward the door of the examining room, seeing in her mind's eye the lawman's expression when he had stormed in right after she'd been awakened by the smelling salts.

James's brother. The one who had left Missouri years ago. Lucas. He didn't look anything like James. Didn't talk or act anything like James. She had sat there feeling mortified and naked and defenseless, and Lucas McKenna had stared at her—not with the hatred and anger she had seen earlier in those gold-flecked green eyes, but with a feeling that unsettled her even more.

A feeling she had seen often when men glanced her way on the streets of St. Charles: a volatile mix of cool disdain . . . and heated desire.

And what did he have planned for her now?

The door opened and again Annie had the unnerving sensation that a moment torn from the past was happening in the present. She tried to sit up, wincing, bracing herself—but it wasn't the black-haired, glittery-eyed lawman this time.

Only Dr. Holt entered the room.

"How do you feel?" He returned to her side, speaking

in the same quiet, gentle way he always addressed her. "Is the laudanum helping?"

He looked down at her with concern as he checked her pulse, whispering a curse when the handcuffs got in the way.

Annie shook her head. "I . . . want to get . . . out of here."

"Mrs. Smi— I mean, Miss—"

"Annie." She couldn't meet his gaze. "It's . . . Annie."

"Annie," he said, no condemnation or reproach in his voice as he used her real name for the first time. "I wasn't lying about what I told the marshal out there." He inclined his head toward the door. "The laudanum may've eased your pain some, but those cracked ribs are serious. If you try to escape before they heal, you could—"

"I didn't mean out . . . of town." Her vision suddenly swam with tears. "Out of . . . this *room. Please.*"

Understanding finally dawned on his face. "Of course. I'm a fool. God Almighty, we shouldn't have left you in here all alone."

He slid one arm beneath her shoulders and the other beneath her knees and picked her up, gingerly, as if she might shatter in his arms. She bit her lower lip, every movement causing a fresh wave of pain. Without another word, he carried her out of the examining room.

In the darkened parlor, he settled her on a worn, velvet-upholstered couch. Then he tucked round pillows behind her shoulders and her head to prop her up and covered her with a counterpane. "Better?"

She nodded, grateful for his kindness, relieved to be away from that room where she had lost everything that mattered to her, lost the last dream she would ever dream.

Annie blinked tears from her eyes, giving in to the drowsiness of the laudanum, gazing down at the dying flames on the hearth. She couldn't bring herself to look at Dr. Holt again.

Couldn't bear that he now knew the truth about who she was. What she had been. What she had done.

He moved toward the fireplace and crouched in front of it, picking up a poker to stab at the charred logs. "Mrs. Owens and Mrs. Greer are upstairs preparing the guest room for you. The marshal . . . hell, I'm sure you overheard our shouting match out here. I don't know where he went off to." The doctor sounded disgusted.

The clock on the mantel chimed seven times and he glanced up at it. "I told Rebecca I think it'd be best if you stayed here tonight, where I can keep an eye on you." His voice gentled as he turned to face her. "Annie, you don't have to tell me, it's none of my business, but—"

"You want to know . . . if it's true," she whispered, not looking up from the flames, every shallow breath hurting. "If I . . . killed James McKenna."

He remained silent a moment. "Some men," he said, "need killing."

She lifted her eyes to his, surprised by the fierceness of his voice—and by what she saw in his expression.

He wanted to believe in her, wanted to think the best of her.

And she had to disillusion him.

"Some men, maybe . . . but not James," she whispered. "He had his faults. But he didn't deserve to die." She paused to take another shallow, aching breath. "He was good to me. And I cared about him." *And I thought he cared about me.* A pain that no drug could ease wrenched her heart, and she dropped her gaze, staring down at the patterned wool rug on the floor. "I never wanted . . . to hurt him. I wouldn't hurt anyone on purpose. It was an accident." Her voice almost gave out. "I swear it was an accident."

She lay still, unable to bear what she would see now in Dr. Holt's eyes: doubt, disapproval, shame. Perhaps anger that she had misled everyone in Eminence for so long. Maybe even pity that she had been foolish enough to care for the wealthy man who had bought and paid for her company.

The crackling of the fire made the only sound.

Finally she summoned her courage and looked up again.

The doctor was simply regarding her with those soft, dove-gray eyes, his expression of concern and compassion unchanged. Then he nodded.

Annie swallowed hard past a lump in her throat. She didn't understand how he could just accept that she was telling the truth—without judging her, with no proof other than her word.

Lucas McKenna would certainly never believe James's death was an accident.

Nor would the judge and jury back in St. Charles.

"Dr. Holt—"

"Annie, I've been telling you for the better part of two months now to call me Daniel," he chided softly.

She plucked at a loose thread on the counterpane, the steel manacles around her wrists jangling. "Daniel, I'm grateful for all you've done for me. And God knows I"— she inhaled a shaky, shallow breath—"don't want to go back to Missouri to face a trial, but I . . . don't think you should keep trying to help me. It'll only get you into trouble—"

"Trouble and I are old acquaintances. And I figure no one from Montana Territory is going to be riding down to help you," he said, adding gently, "There *is* no family in Montana Territory, is there?"

She shook her head, lowering her lashes, remembering the countless lies she had told to conceal her identity.

"I figured they would've come for you long before now. You're a woman who . . ." He cleared his throat. "You remind me of . . ."

When Annie glanced up, Daniel moved away from the hearth to stand before the front window, staring out into the night. "I had a sister," he continued haltingly. "Sweet and pretty. Had a real tender heart, like you. Just picked the wrong sort of man. She . . . died when she was about your age."

He fell silent, picking up a porcelain figurine of a cat that lay in the middle of a table before the window.

"Daniel, I'm sorry," Annie whispered with genuine feeling, understanding now why he had always shown her such special caring and concern. From the beginning, he had treated her like a little sister.

He set the figurine down and turned to face her again, running a hand through his disheveled hair. "Is there anyone who might be able to help you if—when you go back home to Missouri? Any family?"

Family. Home. Those two words pained Annie far more than her injuries. "I . . . have an older brother," she said, "but . . ."

She gazed past Daniel, through the window and into the darkness, remembering the night Raphael Sutton had left St. Charles four years ago. Rafe had galloped off with a smile and a boast. *I'm gonna make us rich, Annie. You'll see. Rich enough to buy this whole damn town.* He had written a few times after that—once to ask for money—and then disappeared. Just like Papa.

Just like men always do, Mama had said.

And yet, when Annie had first started handling the mail over at Mrs. Greer's general store, she had secretly placed a letter in the outgoing bag—a note addressed to Rafe's last known whereabouts and signed only *Half-*

pint, the name he used to call her when they were young and inseparable.

In her heart, she had known her long-lost big brother wouldn't come riding into Eminence to scoop her up and comfort her and carry her away to some place safe. She didn't even know if he was still alive.

And yet she kept hoping.

"No," she said finally. "No family back in Missouri, or anywhere else. Not anymore." She looked up at Daniel. "It's only . . . been two months, but you and the others have . . . have been more of a family to me than my real family was."

Footsteps sounded on the staircase as Mrs. Owens and Mrs. Greer came down from the upper floor.

Annie held her breath, her side burning, and waited for them to come around the corner into the parlor. She wished she could sink into the couch and disappear. They had done their duty as good Christian women, saw that her injuries were tended and that she had a room for the night—but now they would despise her for what she had done, spurn her like all the other respectable women she had ever met, and walk out the door without a backward glance.

Rebecca came bustling in several steps ahead of Mrs. Owens.

And with one look at Annie, she promptly sank to the floor beside the couch in a heap of pink silk and tears, the purple ostrich feather in her hat bobbing as she shook her head. "Oh, dearie! Oh, lamb! By the horn spoons, I can't believe what that huffed-up, mean-eyed critter of a lawman said! Tell me it isn't true! Please tell me it isn't—"

"Rebecca . . ." Annie felt a sharp pain in the center of her chest that had nothing to do with broken bones.

Everyone in Eminence had been so generous to her, but Rebecca most of all—and in return Annie had brought her only hurt. "I'm not going to lie to you anymore," she whispered. "What the marshal told you *is* true—"

"You mean . . . you planned to murder that man?" Mrs. Owens sank down in an armchair next to the couch.

"W-What?" Annie glanced from her to Daniel and back to Rebecca.

"That was what he told the folks outside!" Rebecca cried. "He's an awful, terrible critter!" She proceeded to recount at length the marshal's version of what had taken place back in Missouri.

And for the first time since her arrest, Annie felt an emotion other than guilt and fear.

Anger. "He thinks I *plotted* to kill James? For *revenge* and the *money*? Why would he . . ."

She didn't finish, already knowing the answer: Lucas McKenna was like everyone else back in St. Charles. Everyone who had always thought the worst of her, always believed she was her mama's daughter.

"Anyone who knows you would know better." Rebecca dabbed at her eyes with a lacy handkerchief. "You wouldn't hurt a flea, never mind plot a murder!"

"Tell us what happened," Mrs. Owens suggested gently.

"Yes, lamb, just tell us." Rebecca reached down to brush a damp strand of hair from Annie's forehead.

Annie closed her eyes, the motherly gesture wringing her heart. "Rebecca, some of it's true. I *am* the daughter of a prostitute," she whispered. "And I *was* James McKenna's mistress for three years. The child I was carrying"—her voice broke—"was his. I've never had a husband. And I *did* take James's life . . ."

She turned her face away, choked with guilt and remorse, tears sliding down her cheeks. "B-But I didn't go there that night to kill him. I didn't bring a gun. I went to tell him about the *baby*. And he . . . he threw fifty dollars at me and told me to get out and . . ." A sob tore from her. "I don't *know* anything about guns. There was one on the desk and . . . I didn't know it could go off like that. It all happened so *fast*." She was sobbing so hard, she couldn't continue.

After a moment, to her astonishment, she felt Rebecca's gentle touch again, smoothing her tangled hair in that comforting, motherly gesture. "Shh, lamb. It's all right."

"You're no murderer," Mrs. Owens added quietly. "Maybe not all the folks in town are going to believe you, but some of us . . ."

"Some of us believe in forgiveness. And second chances," Daniel said. "Unfortunately, the marshal is never going to believe the shooting was unintentional. He's ready to march Annie off to face a hanging judge at the first opportunity."

"Well, we're not just going to leave this poor dear at that critter's mercy," Rebecca declared.

Mrs. Owens nodded in agreement. "We'll do whatever we can—"

"Wait." Annie couldn't seem to catch her breath, glancing between the three of them. "Didn't you hear everything I just said? You shouldn't get involved with—"

"We're already involved," Mrs. Owens said simply. "We're your friends."

Annie's vision blurred again and she blinked to clear it. "But I took a man's life. I'm a wanted criminal. And I lied to all of you. I claimed to be a widow when I'm a . . ." She lowered her gaze. "A fallen woman. I shouldn't even . . . be in the same room with ladies like you."

"You really believe that?" Mrs. Owens asked gently.

When Annie looked up, she found both ladies regarding her with the same expression as Daniel: no condemnation, only compassion.

"You're not the only young woman who ever came West to leave a troubled past behind," Mrs. Owens continued slowly. "Or the only woman ever to run afoul of the law."

"What are you saying?"

"We're saying," Rebecca told her, "that nobody walkin' on this here Earth is spotless perfect—especially in these parts. Only saints you'll see around here is the ones painted in the stained-glass windows up at the church."

"And not everybody in Eminence," Daniel added quietly, "has chosen to stay here because they're hoping for another silver strike or can't afford to move on."

Annie stared up at them, unable to find enough breath to form words. She felt dizzy, like the whole room was turning upside down.

"And some folks aren't going to be too happy that a man with a badge has come to town." Mrs. Owens sat back in her chair, rubbing her hands up and down her arms as if she'd taken a chill. "Some folks here have secrets they'd prefer to keep."

"True." Daniel leaned one shoulder against the hearth, folding his arms. "But a lot can happen in five weeks. A whole lot." His voice became strangely calm. "Let me tell you what I have in mind."

"Hold the light higher, kid. I can't do this in the dark."

"Sorry, sir." Travis complied so fast, he almost whacked Lucas in the shoulder with the lantern. "This better, Marshal? How's it look, sir?"

Lucas frowned at the boy. For more than two hours now, Travis had been tagging along beside him, alternately chattering, helping, and getting in the way while Lucas set out to put his idea into action.

After stopping at the general store, he had tracked

down the stagecoach driver and personally handed him three letters—one addressed to Olivia and his sisters, one to the constables in St. Charles, the third to his deputies in Indian Territory—telling them he would be returning to Missouri with his prisoner in a couple of weeks.

Then he had followed Travis to the charred remains of the jail, and began a tour of the town's abandoned hotels.

At the moment, the kid was grinning at him in the lantern light, chewing a stick of horehound candy, looking as bright-eyed and eager as a chipmunk.

Lucas suppressed a sigh and pulled the canvas measuring tape across the window, while Travis held the heavy velvet curtains out of the way. It was at least the twelfth window they'd measured in the fifth hotel they'd visited so far tonight, though Lucas was starting to lose count. Somehow, the boy's excitement and energy made him feel all the more trail-worn, tired . . . and older than his twenty-eight years.

After double-checking the height and width, he motioned wearily for Travis to let the curtain fall shut. "This place'll do."

"Good. Glad to hear it, sir." Travis nodded as if in agreement, then perched on a nearby armchair, raising a cloud of dust. "So, uh . . . what'll it do *for*, Marshal? I still don't"—he sneezed so hard he almost put out his lantern—"reckon why you'd want to stay in one of these empty hotels, sir. Old man Dunlap never even finished this place. Just these here rooms he used for himself—"

"It'll do," Lucas repeated tiredly, wadding up the measuring tape and shoving it in a pocket of his drover's coat. He stepped back from the window and picked up his own lantern, raising it to study the suite he had chosen on the hotel's first floor—a large bedchamber of about fifteen by twenty feet, with a smaller sitting room attached.

The proprietor might not have finished the place, but he was obviously a wealthy sort with a taste for self-indulgence. The glow from Lucas's lantern fell across flocked paper in shades of garnet and gold, and a hearth bordered in fancy tiles that took up most of one wall, beside the door. Across from the hearth sat a massive bed of burled walnut with a carved headboard that had to be six feet tall.

It also seemed Dunlap treasured his privacy: The bedchamber had just two slender windows, to the left of the bed, both hung with crimson drapes. And the only way in or out was through the sitting room—which made it ideal for Lucas's purpose.

Scavengers had apparently helped themselves to the more portable, practical furnishings, but they had left behind the bed, the chair Travis was sitting on, a chest of drawers, and one overstuffed chaise longue.

And an extravagant item that hung on the wall opposite the windows: a mirror in a gold frame, so huge it almost reached floor to ceiling. It reflected Lucas's puzzled look back at him from the lamplit darkness. "Eccentric codger, is he?"

"Dunlap? Sorta, I guess. Made a fortune in the mines hereabouts. Married himself a beautiful gal from Denver and started building this place for her as a weddin' gift." Travis crunched on the candy stick, swinging his foot so that it thumped the chair. "Bragged it was gonna rival the Teller House down in Central City—eight-course banquets, fancy balls, a millionaire in every room. He did up this here suite first and moved in with his wife while the rest was bein' finished."

Lucas nodded, stifling a yawn as he headed into the sitting room. A bridal suite. That explained the desire for privacy. And the oversized bed.

And, he thought, glancing back and arching one eye-

brow, the oversized mirror. It reflected the full length of
the bed perfectly.

Randy devil, that Dunlap. "So why'd he never finish
it?" Lucas stopped in the doorway between the two
rooms, hunting in the pockets of his coat for a pad and
pencil.

" 'Cause he went broke when the mines went bust,
and his wife up and left him."

Lucas shook his head in pity. *Poor, misguided fool,
that Dunlap.* "What a loyal and loving female," he said
dryly. He had started to think these accommodations too
good for Antoinette Sutton—but maybe they suited her
after all. She apparently had a few traits in common with
the previous lady of the house.

"She sure broke old Dunlap's heart." Travis stood and
dusted off the seat of his pants. "When she packed her
bags, he didn't have it in him to finish the place, so he
just locked the door and left it like this. Been up for sale
for months."

The kid fell silent while Lucas leaned one shoulder
against the doorjamb, making a sketch and jotting down
the measurements he had taken. He also made a quick
list of items he would need to buy, borrow, or scavenge.

"Marshal McKenna, sir? Uh . . . do you think you
could show me that trick you used to get past the lock? I
surely would—"

"Never mind that now, kid." Lucas rubbed his bleary
eyes, then finished adding a column of figures. "Where
can I find this Dunlap?"

"Don't rightly know. Back east, south, wherever folks
go when they leave here." Travis scuffed one boot along
the floor. "Hell, sir, ever'body with a lick of sense left this
town months ago. I don't know why my pa's so danged
set on stayin' here and muckin' out stables the rest of *his*
life."

Lucas picked up his lantern and headed into the hotel's main room, the boy following at his heels.

"Marshal, I . . . I'd give my back teeth to get out of here. I always . . . Well, sir, it's sorta been a plan of mine to get work down in New Mexico Territory or Tombstone or . . . or maybe even the Red River, like you. I know I'm young, but ain't nobody in three counties a better shot than Travis Ballard. I think I'd make a mighty fine deputy marshal."

Lucas paused in the cavernous main room. The walls had been plastered, but not painted; his lantern revealed a long hotel desk of unfinished oak, a fireplace in the opposite wall, a scaffolding in one corner, a chandelier on the floor that had been delivered but never installed. "You partial to sunburns, dust storms, blisters, and saddle sores, boy?" He moved on to check the rest of the hotel.

Travis stuck to him like glue. "Sir?"

"It's not all showdowns and shoot-outs like they say in the papers, kid." Lucas could hear the fatigue in his own voice. "Federal marshal spends most of his time on the trail. No place to call your own but a room in a flophouse. Paid two dollars a day and six cents a mile, if you live long enough to collect it. And the only thing worse than the money is the food." He stopped, turning to meet the kid's gaze. "That sound real exciting to you?"

The boy blinked up at him, looking like he'd just had a brightly wrapped Christmas package snatched from his hands. "But . . . but if it's so . . . then why do *you* do it, sir?"

Lucas furrowed his brow, unable to answer, surprised that he couldn't. He hadn't asked himself that question in years.

All he could remember was one moment of time—bright and sharp as the point of a needle—that had filled him with a thirst for justice, a burning need to see right triumph over wrong. He'd been younger than Travis, that day when he'd learned that evil could wear a friendly face.

They said they had food to share, and Lucas had let them in. Even though he and Ma were alone. He'd let them in.

And then he'd heard his mother scream.

"Defend the weak and the fatherless, do justice to the afflicted and needy, deliver them from the hand of the wicked," he said softly.

Travis smiled, looking awestruck. "That from the marshals' code, like a book or something?"

Lucas shook his head, not realizing he'd said the words aloud. He turned away. "You never been to church, kid?" he asked, irritated at himself. "Psalm 82. Fancy way of saying somebody's got to protect the good folks of this world from the bad ones." He *must* be dead-on-his-feet tired; it wasn't like him to reveal anything about himself to someone he'd just met.

Lucas decided he could explore the rest of the hotel later. He strode back into the half-finished main room, changing the subject. "So if Dunlap's long gone, who holds the deed on this place?"

"That'd be the bank—last one in town. You'll have to talk to Cyrus Hazelgreen." Travis scrambled to keep up. "But, Marshal, you mean you're lookin' to *buy* this whole hotel, sir? There's lots of places to stay in town—"

"None that'd let me make a few improvements. And it's more like *commandeer*, not buy. Let's go see Hazelgreen."

"But it's after eight o'clock. Shouldn't you wait until tomor—"

"Kid, you wanted to know what it's like to be a marshal. Well, it usually ain't pretty and half the time you're doing it in the middle of the night. Here's your chance to learn firsthand." Lucas opened the door and gestured with his lantern for Travis to proceed. "Let's go see Hazelgreen. Then we're going to need some tools. And some cement."

Annie opened her eyes, moaning softly, not sure what had awakened her. Darkness surrounded the bed, and the last dose of laudanum still fogged her senses, dulling the pain that throbbed in her side. A clock somewhere chimed twelve. She remembered Rebecca helping her undress and wash up, and Mrs. Owens lighting a fire on the hearth in Dr. Holt's guest room, and a feeling of warmth that had nothing to do with the quilt covering her. A feeling so tentative and new she hardly dared name it *hope*.

But now she shivered, all too aware of the cold handcuffs around her wrists.

And the sound of two male voices downstairs, arguing.

"Can't you just leave her be for the night?"

That was Daniel. The other, deeper voice was less familiar, but Annie knew who it belonged to.

"You the only doctor in town?"

"Yes—"

"Then you'd best get out of my way. Because there won't be anyone to treat you if you end up bleeding and unconscious on the floor."

Annie's heart pounded, louder than the footsteps on the stairs. She sat up, feeling dizzy at even that small movement, as she heard a door across the hallway open and slam. Then the door to the guest room burst open.

"Well, Doc, this *is* a surprise." Lucas McKenna appeared out of the darkness, a shadowy figure in a black coat and low-slung hat, his broad shoulders all but filling the doorway. "Here I thought you'd have her cozied up in your own bed."

Daniel was a step behind him. "Damn you, McKenna, this woman is my patient—"

"And my prisoner." The marshal's arm shot out to block the doorway. "I'm taking her into custody, Holt. I've got a warrant. A *legal* warrant. You try to stop me again and you can have a cell next to hers."

Even in the dim light from the hearth, Annie could see fury brewing in the doctor's expression, and it frightened her. "Daniel, don't . . . please." The laudanum made her so drowsy, it was difficult to form words. "I don't want . . . anyone to get hurt."

The marshal chuckled, a low, mocking sound. "Yeah, Daniel, don't," he drawled, his gaze fastening on her. "The woman who murdered my brother doesn't want anyone to get *hurt*."

Annie clutched the quilt, holding it in front of her, her cheeks burning. The drug might have numbed her senses, but she remembered vividly that she was dressed only in her camisole and knee-length pantalettes. "I'll . . . I'll go with you, peacefully," she told him, trying to face him without flinching. "If you'd just give me a moment to—"

Before she could even finish the request, he crossed the room in two strides and scooped her up, quilt and all—though his hold on her was much more gentle than his voice. "Save the demure act for someone who buys it, lady."

"Take it easy, McKenna—"

"Sure, Doc." The marshal turned toward the door. "Kid gloves. I'll let you know when visiting hours are. You can come over for tea."

Daniel took a step forward, clenching his fists. Tension ricocheted through the air and Annie knew she had to try and stop it. Quickly. This close, she could see how tired and haggard the marshal looked—and guessed his fuse to be dangerously short. He wasn't going to back down.

And though she was keenly aware of the hard, muscled strength of his arms, he wasn't hurting her. "Daniel, *please.*"

For a moment longer, the two men remained in place, standing almost toe-to-toe, glaring at one another.

Then the doctor stepped aside, eyes narrowing as the lawman carried her past him. "You're a real son of a bitch, Marshal."

"Yeah, Doc, and believe it or not, you're not the first person to tell me that." The marshal held her securely against his chest as he started down the stairs. "But unlike some people around here, I have a real easy time telling the good folks apart from the bad."

"Where are you taking her?"

"Across the street. Don't worry," the marshal called back. "I mean to take care of her. The sooner she heals up, the sooner we're on our way to Missouri."

Annie shut her eyes at that threat, and by the time she dared open them again, Lucas McKenna had carried her outside, beyond the safety of Daniel's house, into the deserted, moonlit street.

"I have to hand it to you, Antoinette," he said, his tone silky as he looked down at her. "You're sharp. Already got him and half the town wrapped around your little finger, don't you?"

Annie didn't bother trying to argue, his eyes so cold they made her wonder if he had ice where his heart should be. "Where *are* you taking me?"

"Jail."

The word rang with finality.

All at once, the hope she had felt earlier evaporated. Safe in Daniel's parlor, surrounded by friends—the first real friends she'd ever known—it had been easy to believe in the simple plan they'd devised. All they needed was time, Daniel had said. Time and a little help from nature, and she would be well enough to escape and her friends would help her disappear. Nobody would get hurt. He had promised her that.

But now, alone with Lucas McKenna, five weeks suddenly seemed like a long time.

Five *minutes* suddenly seemed like a long time.

Maybe it was some strange effect of the laudanum, but even with the thick quilt wrapped around her, even through the fabric of his coat and shirt, she seemed able to feel every muscle of Lucas's arms. And the hard, lean shape of his shoulder and chest beneath her cheek. And his hands on her arm, her thigh, as if he were touching her bare skin.

An odd, prickly warmth flowed through her. For a man with such a cold voice and frosty eyes, his body seemed awfully . . . hot. A fluttery sensation began in her stomach—which couldn't be from the laudanum.

Because it was the same sensation she had experienced this afternoon, when she first saw him standing in front of the saloon, watching her.

She didn't understand, hadn't felt this way when Daniel had carried her in his arms. Or when any other man had looked at her. Even James.

"You cold?"

"No," Annie said quickly, caught off guard, unable to tear her gaze from his face.

"You're shivering."

"M-Maybe the laudanum is wearing off," she said.

"Maybe you're afraid." His voice seemed to soften, almost imperceptibly. "Because you realize that whatever scheme you cooked up with your doctor friend isn't going to be easy to pull off."

Annie shook her head. She wasn't afraid. For some ridiculous reason, she believed what Lucas had told Dr. Holt: that he intended to take care of her.

If he wanted to hurt her, he would've shot her out on that hillside. Or dumped her in the middle of nowhere and left her to die. Or ignored Dr. Holt and just set out for Missouri tonight regardless of her injuries. But he hadn't done any of those things.

And at the moment, despite his mocking words and icy glares and foul mood, he was walking slowly, and seemed to be taking care not to touch her injured ribs or jostle her much as he carried her.

Which only confused her all the more. Marshal Lucas McKenna wasn't an easy man to figure out.

And he wouldn't be easy to escape.

At the far end of the street, he stepped up onto the boardwalk, walking toward what looked like a hotel.

"I-I thought you said we were going to the jail—"

"This muddy excuse for a town doesn't have one right now. This'll have to do."

A curved sign above the entrance had THE DUNLAP HOUSE lettered on it in fancy gold script. Annie's heart gave a strange, doubled beat as Lucas pushed open the door and carried her over the threshold, into what might've once been a magnificent hotel.

A lamp had been left burning on the front desk, the light glimmering off a chandelier on the floor. The room was so big, she could hear the sound of Lucas's boots echoing back from distant, unseen corners. He carried her past the desk and straight toward a room at the back of the hotel—which turned out to be a suite.

He snagged a lantern that had been left on a table, moving quickly through a sitting room and into a bedroom that almost looked luxurious.

Except that it had bars on the two windows: three vertical, iron bars on each one.

He put the lantern on a table and set her carefully on the bed, then arranged a few pillows against the headboard to prop up her shoulders, as if he knew how much it would hurt her to lie flat.

Then he started unwrapping the quilt from around her. Annie gasped in alarm as he pulled it aside. She tried to cover herself, suddenly feeling vulnerable.

"Stop it," he said derisively. "Stop trying to convince me that you're some shy, sweet, proper lady. You might have managed to fool the yokels around here, but you're forgetting that I *know* what you really are."

She froze, staring up at him, aware of the tension in his body as he towered over her, aware of his hands, the harsh sound of his breathing.

But when he moved, he only reached into his pocket and withdrew a key. He used it to unlock the handcuffs from around her wrists.

"Get used to having bars on your windows, Antoinette. You'll be seeing a lot of that from now on."

Not taking her eyes from his, Annie gingerly reached for the quilt and drew it over herself. "If . . . if you would just listen." She could barely find enough breath to speak. "If you would let me tell you the truth about what hap—"

He cut her off with a movement so quick she didn't even see it.

One minute he was standing next to the bed, the next he was caging her with his arms, his fists planted in the pillow on either side of her head.

His face was only inches from hers. "Let me tell *you* the truth, lady. Every outlaw I've ever tracked down has had a thousand excuses. *I didn't mean to do it, Marshal. It was an accident. You just don't understand. I was in a tough spot. There was no way out.*"

Beneath the cold of his stare and the heat of his body, Annie couldn't speak. Some of what he'd just said *was* what she had meant to tell him. *Except in her case, it was true.* But he wouldn't believe it. And her attempts to explain only seemed to make him angrier.

"Everyone," he said, breathing hard, "*everyone* gets into a tough corner at some time or other. Most people don't try to solve their problems by blowing a hole in whoever happens to get in the way."

"That's not what happened."

"Right." He thrust himself away from her. "And every jail is full of innocent people and you and every other outlaw behind bars has a sad story to tell. Well, I'm not buying it and I'm not crying, lady. *You* made your bed. Lie in it." His gaze left her face, moving lower. "And while we're on the subject of the truth . . ."

He took her left hand.

And slid the gold wedding ring from her finger.

Somehow, she felt even more vulnerable without it. Stripped of the last of her disguise. Naked before him. "Why does that matter to you?" she asked.

"Because it's a lie, Antoinette. We both know what you are. My brother's whore." He flung the ring away with an angry snap of his arm. "My brother's killer."

He grabbed the lantern. "Pardon me for not leaving you a light," he said as he stalked out, "but I thought you might take a notion to try and burn the place down. With me in it."

Annie's eyes adjusted quickly to the moonlight that filtered through the barred windows. She watched him carry the lantern into the sitting room, expected him to keep going, walk out and leave her in complete darkness, without even a fire for warmth.

Instead, he set the light down on a table in the sitting room. Then he took off his hat, shrugged out of his coat, and started unbuttoning his shirt.

Her eyes widened in surprise. "What are you . . . doing?"

"Staying right here," he said curtly, stripping off the shirt. "I intend to keep an eye on my prisoner. Day and night." He kicked off his boots. "Tomorrow you'll get a nice cell door to match those windows."

He turned to look at her. "Until you're well enough to travel, Antoinette, you and I are going to be spending all our time together." He stood in the doorway, clad only in his tight-fitting black trousers and his gun belt. "Close as two quills on a porcupine."

5

At least an hour had passed since Lucas had turned down the lamp and flung himself onto his cot in the sitting room. Yet he still lay wide awake, staring at the wall, one arm behind his head. Long after his eyes had adjusted to the moonlight, he kept counting the leaves on the patterned wallpaper, down one row and up the next.

This hell-fired, jaw-cracker of a day had left him feeling like he'd been dragged behind wild horses, yet for some reason, he couldn't sleep.

He finally had Antoinette Sutton in custody, so why didn't he feel any peace? He had expected a sense of victory. Triumph. Or at least the usual satisfaction that came from the successful end of a long pursuit.

Instead, he felt nothing but a strange ache, right in the middle of his chest. And he didn't even know what it was.

Hope, maybe. Hope that what he had accomplished today might bring his family some measure of comfort. Might help his sisters and Olivia and the children begin to heal.

Might allow his brother's departed soul to rest.

I got her, James, he thought as he lay there, looking up into the darkness. *I got her.*

A muscle worked in his cheek. His throat felt dry and

tight as he tried to picture James's face; he could summon only a blurred image from memory, like a photograph taken while the subject moved. The last time he had seen James, they had both been moving, both so busy with their work. Four years ago. Or was it five?

He tried to remember what they had said, but couldn't recall a word.

And all at once, it hit him like a fist in the chest. The tearing sense of grief and anger and pointlessness. *This was all he had left.* Unfinished memories, blurred images, forgotten conversations. And it was all he would ever have.

Because he would never see James again.

He shut his eyes. Why had he believed that catching his brother's killer would lessen the pain of losing him? Until tonight, he'd had a goal, a mission, a chase to keep himself from thinking or feeling.

But now it was over.

And having Antoinette in custody only made everything worse.

Because even as he lay there, with that hollow ache burning a hole through him, he couldn't stop himself from listening to her . . . to every small sound she made.

Every squeak of the bed beneath her slight weight. Every movement. Every sigh.

And he couldn't keep his gaze from drifting to the mirror. That damned, decadent mirror that Dunlap had installed so he could cavort with his bride in carnal abandon.

Lucas had wanted to take it out, but the thing was so big, the bedroom must have been built around it. And since he'd been rational at the time, he had actually thought it might help him. Had even angled his cot in the sitting room so that he could keep an eye on his prisoner, watching her in the mirror without her knowing he was watching. She couldn't make one move without him see-ing it.

Trouble was, she couldn't make one move without him seeing it.

And he was no longer feeling the least bit rational.

Moonlight filtered through the bars on her windows, enough to illuminate the outline of her body, so slender beneath the quilt . . . and her hair, a dark, shimmering mass. As she shifted restlessly, he would catch a glimpse of a slim calf here, a bare thigh there, a shoulder, a wrist.

It was like some slow, hypnotic, erotic dance, and he couldn't look away. In the past hour, he had memorized most of her in the moonlight.

And imagined the rest.

With a stifled curse, he raised one arm to cover his eyes, wishing he had closed the drapes before stalking out of her cell. He couldn't very well stalk back in and close them now.

Damn it, how could he feel anything, *even lust, for the woman who had taken his brother's life?*

He angrily reminded himself that she was a born se-ductress, a prostitute's daughter, no doubt well-versed in the ways of stirring desire in a man. She was probably doing this to him on purpose.

He heard her moving again, restlessly, heard the sheets caressing her skin.

"Would you go to sleep?" he shouted into the darkness.

She went silent and still.

"Sorry," she said after a moment, "if I'm disturbing you."

Her voice was soft, but not the least bit seductive; in fact, it held a note of sarcasm.

Lucas tried to get his breathing under control. "Not at all," he bit out. "I imagine a guilty conscience makes it tough to get much rest."

"I haven't been sleeping well since . . ."

She didn't finish.

"Since what?" He wasn't sure why he was asking, why it should matter to him.

When she spoke again, her sarcasm had vanished.

"You don't care about the truth," she said, sounding as tired as he felt.

"*Your* version of the truth? No, I don't. You'd say anything if you thought it'd keep you out of jail. Maybe *do* anything, too." Lucas sat up on the edge of his cot, the air cool against the bare skin of his chest. "Is that how you got the good doctor feeling all mush-brained over you? I'll bet your mama taught you a lot of tricks—"

"I am *not* my mother. I was *never* a whore."

For the first time, he detected a hint of steel beneath that delicate, feminine surface.

"You shared a man's bed for money," he said coldly.

"Because it was better than . . ."

Again she didn't finish.

He watched her in the mirror, saw her bury her face in the pillow. "Better than what, Antoinette?"

She didn't answer. Didn't move.

After a long while, he thought she might've finally gone to sleep. Or decided to ignore him. He muttered a curse and lay back down. What did it matter whether she answered him or not?

"I haven't been sleeping well," she said quietly, "since I lost the baby."

He froze, startled by her words, by such an unexpected answer to the question he had asked before. *Of course.* How could he have forgotten about her miscarriage? That was why she hadn't been able to . . .

Annoyed, he chastised himself for being so easily drawn into her web. His gaze fastened on the mirror. "God Almighty, you want me to believe you care about

everything and every*one*, don't you? If your baby mattered to you so much, you wouldn't have risked taking
stagecoaches over the worst back roads in the West—"

"I didn't *know*—"

"Did you even know who the father was?"

"*James* was the father of my baby." Her voice rose
sharply. "And I wanted that child with all my heart."

Her heart? Lucas felt like he was going to be sick.
"Now I know you're lying, *lady*—because if the child you
were carrying was my brother's, he would've taken care
of you. Both of you. My brother *loved* children. You
should have seen the way his daughter and son cried at
his funeral—"

"Don't—"

"A nine-year-old girl and a thirteen-year-old boy." He
shot the words at her like bullets. "Sobbing for their
daddy—"

"Please, *don't*—"

"Two innocent children who'll have to grow up without a father because of you. And you want me to believe
you have a heart?"

"Stop it," she pleaded, "stop it!"

Lucas thought it must be a trick of the moonlight, or
some flaw in the mirror, because he swore he saw tears
in her eyes.

Bright, silvery tears that slid down her cheek and into
the dark tangle of her hair.

*Tears of remorse for what she had done? Of sorrow
for James's children?*

He would've called them crocodile tears, just part of
her act, meant to make him believe her story that it had
all been an accident.

Except that he was fairly sure she had no idea he was
watching her.

"I know what I did," she whispered brokenly, lifting

trembling hands to her face. "God forgive me, *I know what I did.*"

Lucas stared at her, unable to speak as he watched her cry—so quietly it seemed she was trying to keep him from hearing, so hard that her slender body shook beneath the quilt.

Then he turned his back.

He wasn't going to do this. Wasn't going to look at her anymore, or talk to her—not when the two of them were alone together in the night. It felt too . . . intimate.

He couldn't let Antoinette Sutton seduce him with her wiles, or wring pity from him with her tears.

"God will have to forgive you, lady," he said, his voice flat and cold. "Because I never will."

Sleep, Lucas thought, shutting his eyes against the sunlight streaming in his window, was a wonderful thing. Maybe the best thing God had ever invented. Better than a morning spent trout fishing in a Montana river. Better than a thick steak and a beer at the end of a long day's ride.

Or maybe it only seemed that way because he hadn't been able to *get* any sleep.

He had lain awake the entire night. Thinking. About her.

The stiffness in his muscles made him groan as he sat up. When his feet hit the plush carpet on the floor, he slouched over and rested his elbows on his knees, blinking the dry, parched feeling from his eyes. He glanced toward the mirror.

His prisoner was sleeping peacefully.

He scowled in her direction. No woman had ever robbed him of a night's rest before. And he had known his share of women over the years.

Beautiful women with kind hearts and tender hands,

the kind most men *would* lose sleep over. Women who had helped him forget, for a moment, all the sunburned miles he rode and the guns aimed in his direction. That was all he ever asked of women, all he ever wanted— moments. An hour or two of physical bliss now and then.

If there was one thing he had never done, would never do, it was let himself get all fool-headed over a female. That sort of thing never turned out well, for either the man or the woman. Just look at poor Dunlap, abandoned by his pretty young bride.

Or James and Olivia, who had seemed so perfectly suited when they married.

Lucas shook his head, running a hand through his disheveled hair. Since he was awake, he might as well get up. Travis had said he'd be back this morning. And Lucas had plans for the day.

He had to return to the burned-down jail and get the cell door he had picked out last night, then install it between Antoinette's room and the sitting room, since he couldn't watch her every minute of every day. After that, he meant to keep busy. Explore the rest of the hotel. Round up a more comfortable bed, if one could be found. Maybe even get himself a shave, he thought, rubbing at his bearded jaw. And a bath and some clean clothes.

But the first thing he wanted, he thought as he stood, his stomach growling, was to secure himself some food. And some coffee. And some wood for the potbellied stove in the corner of his room; the temperature had dropped so low, he could practically see his breath.

He grabbed his gun belt from the floor beside his cot and buckled it on over his trousers, then pulled his .45 from beneath his pillow and holstered it, stepping toward the open doorway that led into Antoinette's cell.

She lay huddled beneath the quilt, which was pulled

up to her nose. She must be freezing—especially since he'd left her in there all night with no fire on the hearth and no clothes but her underthings.

Guilt gnawed at him for a second, but he forced it away. If Antoinette was suffering, it was her own damn fault. She was the one who had broken the law, not him.

And she'd better get used to hardship; the Missouri prison cell that would be her future home would be a lot less cushy than this one. A lot less.

Grumbling under his breath, he turned and picked up the woolen blankets he had kicked off during the night. Then he moved into her cell with silent, barefoot steps and draped the blankets over her. Carefully, so as not to wake her.

Purely out of concern for her health, he told himself adamantly. If anything happened to her, Holt and the others would take pleasure in having him brought up on charges in front of a judge.

For a moment, he lingered there, looking down at her. His plans for the day had included asking Miss Sutton a few questions. Starting with where she had hidden the murder weapon and the fifteen thousand dollars she had stolen from James's safe. But his interrogation would have to wait. She was exhausted, and hurt, and she needed rest.

So that she could get well enough to travel, he thought as he turned on his heel and went out. That was his only concern.

He had no sooner picked up his shirt from where he had dropped it on the floor last night than he heard a commotion at the hotel's entrance. His hand on his Colt, he stepped to the door of the sitting room.

And found himself facing a gaggle of females—three of them, two full-grown and one younger, all carrying baskets and bundles. The aromas of fresh biscuits and fried apples and bacon wafted in with them, making Lucas's mouth water as the three swept toward him. Their leader was the woman who had been wearing a purple ostrich-feather hat yesterday.

Today she wore a peach-colored dress, a blue hat festooned with ribbons, and a mutinous expression. "We've come to see Annie," she declared.

"Well, come back later," he told her in a low voice. "She's sleeping." When he glanced toward the cell, he realized it was too late; his prisoner was already awake.

Antoinette's brow furrowed in puzzlement as she looked at the extra blankets that had materialized over her. With an expression of surprise, she lifted her gaze to his.

"Oh, poor dear!" The gaggle's ringleader hustled into the sitting room, setting down the basket she carried. "Are you all right, lamb?"

"Wait a minute." Lucas moved to block the open doorway of the cell before any of them could go any further. "I haven't said you could—"

"What sort of rig *is* this he's got fixed up here?" The blue-hatted woman frowned as she looked past him, squinting at the bars on the windows. She turned a glare on Lucas, looking like a mama snapping turtle protecting her nest. "He didn't hurt you, did he, Annie?"

"No, Rebecca, I'm all right."

Lucas belatedly started pulling on his shirt. "She's perfectly fine, as you can see for yourself." He shoved his arms into the sleeves, missing on the first try; he wasn't used to having a feminine audience when he got dressed in the morning. "As for visiting, Rebecca—"

"*You* can call me Mrs. Greer." She planted one hand on her prodigious hip and gestured at the other ladies in turn. "This is Mrs. Owens and Miss Lazarillo. We've brung Annie some food and necessities. Someone has to take care of her—"

"*I'll* be taking care of her." Lucas realized he had just buttoned his shirt in the wrong holes. "You intend to help her escape."

"Surely, Marshal, you don't think we could break through solid iron bars?" Mrs. Owens asked coolly.

"I never thought she'd be able to fool people into trusting her, either. But it seems I was wrong about that." He glowered at them as he finally got his shirt buttoned up respectably. "I worked damned hard— sorry," he amended with an apologetic glance at Miss Lazarillo, who only looked to be about sixteen. "I worked hard to find Antoinette Sutton, and I am *not* going to let her get away."

Mrs. Greer squinted up at him. "If anything happens to this girl, you ornery critter—"

"This *girl* is an outlaw. And while she's in my custody, she'll be treated the same as any other outlaw. Nothing will happen to her. She's my prisoner, my responsibility."

A soft sound came from Antoinette's cell. All of them turned.

"Annie?" Mrs. Owens asked worriedly. "Are you all right?"

Antoinette had closed her eyes again, one hand pressed to her ribs. "The . . . last of the . . . laudanum's worn off."

Lucas felt his gut knot up, seeing her in pain.

Stop it, he told himself. *Stop feeling pity or anything else for her.* It was probably another trick. The bunch of them had probably put their heads together last night and cooked up this whole thing. "I suppose you want the doctor?"

She shook her head on the pillow. "No, I . . . think I'd better keep . . . the two of you apart."

Lucas arched one brow in surprise. "Probably smart," he agreed. "Don't count on him or any of these ladies helping you escape, Antoinette. Even if you could—which you can't—I doubt you'd live long."

"There's no need to threaten her, Marshal," Mrs. Owens said with a look of disapproval.

"It's not a threat, ma'am. Just passing along some information you folks may have been unaware of, up here in the mountains. There's a five-thousand-dollar bounty on her head."

"*Five . . . thousand?*" Antoinette gasped.

"Offered by my brother's widow," he informed her. "And it's five thousand dead or alive. You might keep that in mind when you're thinking about how much you want to get out of here. Every bounty hunter in ten states is looking for you. And some of them aren't as nice as me."

"You're . . . telling me I'm . . . safer here, with you?"

Even in pain, Antoinette still had that hint of steel he had noticed last night. And a hint of sarcasm.

"Yeah," he bit out. "You're safer here, with me."

"Well, the poor lamb has to eat," Mrs. Greer insisted, picking up her basket.

"And I brought *mi madre*'s special ointment," young Miss Lazarillo added, holding up a clay jar. "For her hurts."

"*I* will take care of her," Lucas insisted.

"Does that mean you intend to change her bandages?" Mrs. Owens asked.

"And help her wash and get dressed each day, too?" Miss Lazarillo inquired, her mouth forming a round, shocked "O."

Lucas folded his arms, realizing they had a point. He

already felt like he'd become too intimate with Antoinette; it was hard enough just talking to her, looking at her. The less physical contact he had with his prisoner, the better.

"All right," he relented, "she can have visitors. But only one at a time—"

"But we all came to see her," Mrs. Greer complained.

"My jail, my rules," he said flatly. "If you can't abide by them, the front door's right there. One visitor at a time, no more than twice a day. And I'll need to search any packages you bring in." He took the basket from Mrs. Greer's hands, lifting the hinged top to look inside.

The sight and scents of a pie pan full of hot griddle cakes covered with melted butter, of bacon and biscuits and fried apples and a jar of honey almost made him feel light-headed with hunger. "No sharp objects," he said, hoping they couldn't hear his stomach growling. "Nothing that she might use as a weapon." He confiscated a knife and fork. And a biscuit.

"Annie wouldn't hurt a fly." Mrs. Greer frowned at him as he plundered her foodstuffs. "Or even a bigger, meaner sort of critter."

"So you've told me." He handed the basket over and bit into the biscuit. Which turned out to be a damned fine biscuit. And it didn't have any flies baked into it. He wolfed it down in two gulps, motioning for Mrs. Owens to give him the bundle of clothes she held.

He untied the fabric knotted around it and discovered that Antoinette's friends had brought her some new undergarments and, thank God, more substantial clothes to wear: woolen skirts and plain blouses, a shawl, a flannel nightgown.

After handing the clothes back to Mrs. Owens, he tipped open the lid of the earthenware pot in Miss

Lazarillo's hands, wrinkling his nose at the fragrant, clear oil inside. "So which one of you is going to be this morning's visitor?" he asked.

"Me," Mrs. Greer said.

"Fine. I . . . uh . . ." Lucas turned toward her, feeling sheepish all of a sudden, like he was eight years old and facing his schoolmarm. "I'm also going to have to search you, ma'am."

Mrs. Greer tilted her head to one side, looking like some fluttery, blue-headed bird. "But you just did."

"I mean search your *person*, ma'am. For all I know, you could be concealing a pistol that you're smuggling in for her."

"Why . . . why you catawamptious coyote!" The lady blinked as if the idea had never occurred to her. The others both started chattering at once.

"*Señora* Greer would not *do* such a thing," Miss Lazarillo said.

"How do I know that?" he asked.

"You are *the* most suspicious man I ever met." Mrs. Owens's voice was decidedly hostile.

"Goes with the job, ma'am."

Mrs. Greer squinted at him—it was her fierce squint; he was already learning to tell them apart—then gave her basket to Mrs. Owens and raised her hands, a dramatic gesture of surrender accompanied by an equally dramatic sigh. "Very well then, Marshal, do your job."

Lucas made it quick, checking her voluminous sleeves, and her hips, where any hidden pockets in her underskirts might be. After he patted her bustle, he decided to leave it at that. "Uh, you're fine to go in, ma'am."

She had turned red as a beet. "Well, of course I am!" she blustered, brushing at her gown as if to rid herself of his touch. "Land sakes, of all the . . . I have never . . ."

She turned toward the door that led out to the hotel's main room. "Travis Ballard! I *thought* I'd find you here!"

Travis had just entered the sitting room with a few sticks of firewood under his arm, which he dropped on the floor as he just about jumped out of his boots. "Mrs. Greer? What are you . . ."

The kid's gaze landed on Miss Lazarillo, and he seemed to forget whatever else he was going to say. He flushed a shade of red that rivaled Mrs. Greer's, and his Adam's apple bobbed up and down several times before he managed to utter another word. "H-Howdy, Valentina."

The Mexican girl lowered her lashes, smiling shyly. "*Buenos días,* Travis."

Lucas hadn't noticed before now, but the young lady was about the same age as his would-be deputy. And rather pretty.

Mrs. Greer stalked over and pointed an accusing finger at the boy. "Are you helpin' this here varmint on purpose?"

"Varmint?" Travis blinked as if he had forgotten anyone else was in the room. "Who? I . . . uh . . ." He looked helplessly at Lucas.

"He's working for me," Lucas said to rescue the kid.

"Hmph. I thought as much." Mrs. Greer promptly turned her back, giving Travis a cold shoulder. "Don't you be bothered comin' back to my store, boy. You're fired!"

"What? Why? What did I do?" Travis looked stricken—and embarrassed to be fired right in front of Miss Lazarillo.

Mrs. Greer didn't bother to explain; she hustled the other two ladies out with the efficiency of a field general directing troops, then gathered up all the items the women had brought. "So, Marshal McKenna, do you intend to let me in to see Annie or not?"

"I'll give you half an hour, ma'am." Lucas stepped out of the way to allow her into Antoincttc's cell. "And I'll he right outside. And I've got the hearing of a"—he searched for an appropriate comparison—"a big, mean sort of critter," he said dryly. "You might want to keep all that in mind."

Mrs. Greer squinted at him as she entered the cell—the squint of extreme dislike. "Hmph."

Lucas decided to grant the two women some privacy . . . since there might be some changing of bandages or clothes or whatnot taking place. He pulled on his boots and followed Travis, who had retreated into the hotel's main room.

The kid was at the front window, watching the other womenfolk depart, his nose practically pressed up against the glass. "You think Val—Miss Lazarillo will be comin' back? I don't never get to see her. Her pa don't like me much."

"Apparently they'll *all* be coming back." Lucas sank onto a stool behind the hotel's front desk. "Daily." He rested his head in his hands for a moment, his fingers plowed through his hair.

Two weeks, he told himself. Antoinette would be ready to move in two weeks. He could endure this for two weeks.

Travis came over to the desk. "Marshal, sir . . . did you mean what you said to Mrs. Greer? 'Bout me working for you?"

Lucas shrugged, looking up. "You said it yourself last night, kid. You're a little young to be a deputy."

"But we don't have to *call* it that, sir. I could be, say, a . . . an apprentice. You'll be needin' somebody to fetch firewood and get provisions and keep the place swept up an' all, won't you?"

Lucas considered the idea. It would be good to have

some help with the chores; he sure as hell wasn't much of a housekeeper.

And if he had to put up with that trio of females fluttering in and out, it might be good to have a little male company around, too. Especially company that didn't glare or squint at him. "Can your pa spare you?"

"Hell, sir, we don't get but one stage through here a week. And not many riders come to town anymore." Travis flicked a hand in the general direction of the stables. "Livery ain't real lively these days."

"Can't promise things'll be much more lively around here," Lucas warned him. "Being a lawman can be near as boring as mucking out stalls sometimes. And I couldn't pay you much. Maybe . . . two bits a day."

"That's plenty, Marshal McKenna, sir! Tarnation, sir, for a chance to work with you, I'd . . ." The kid looked as happy as a bear cub up a honey tree. "Why, I'd pay you, sir!"

Lucas felt a rare grin tug at one corner of his mouth. "Consider yourself hired, kid, at the rate of two bits a day. Your first job is to go rustle up some breakfast and coffee." He fished a silver dollar out of his pocket and tossed it in the air.

"Yes, sir!" Travis caught it with one hand, his smile rivaling the coin for brightness as he headed out.

While the door closed, Lucas remained sitting where he was, stomach growling. He glanced back toward the suite where his prisoner was no doubt enjoying a breakfast feast served up with tender loving care. God Almighty, he thought tiredly, if his deputies could see him now . . .

They'd be laughing until they couldn't stand up, enjoying every minute of this—the fearsome L. T. McKenna of Indian Territory being cussed out and chased away by a gray-haired little lady in a ridiculous blue hat.

He frowned ruefully, scratching his jaw, wondering

how his men were doing; where they were, how close
they had gotten to hunting down the Risco brothers—a
ruthless pair whose gang counted train robbery, kidnapping, and murder among their life's accomplishments.

Lucas had arrested one of the gang in a whorehouse
in Red River back in July. With a little pressure applied
to his gunshot leg, Hughes had sung like the proverbial
canary and named several hideouts in New Mexico Territory and Texas favored by Jasper and Willie Risco. After two years of work, Lucas and his deputies were so
damned close . . .

And as soon as he was done cooling his heels here,
and Antoinette was permanently behind bars in Missouri, he could finish the job.

The hotel's front door opened and Lucas glanced
up, surprised that his new apprentice was so quick and
efficient.

But it wasn't Travis who entered. "Marshal McKenna,
good day to you, sir!"

The cheerful voice belonged to the banker, Cyrus
Hazelgreen, who wore a wide grin, a bowler hat, and a
three-piece suit with an expensive gold watch dangling
from the vest. He was accompanied by two men: a red-
haired, slim fellow whom Lucas recognized as one of the
saloonkeepers he'd tried to question yesterday, and a
barrel-chested man he didn't know, dressed all in black.

The three walked over to the desk, Hazelgreen holding up a sheaf of documents. "I've had the papers drawn
up, sir, the ones we discussed last night, granting you the
deed on this place. Thought I'd bring them over first
thing and introduce you to our town council." He gestured to the two men. "Mr. Camden Fairfax, I believe
you've met."

The saloonkeeper extended his hand, his quiet voice

marked by a refined English accent. "I trust you will accept my apologies, Marshal, for my being rather less than hospitable yesterday. Had you identified yourself as a peace officer—"

"Forget it, Fairfax." Lucas shook his hand.

"And this," Hazelgreen said, gesturing to the man in black, "is Reverend Gottfried."

"A pleasure to meet you, Marshal." The preacher grasped Lucas's hand in both of his; for a man of the cloth, he had the crushing grip of a wrestler. "A true pleasure. I understand you are quite a lawman." His wide grin revealed dimples in his apple-red cheeks.

Lucas shrugged. "Sounds like Travis has been passing around his penny dreadfuls."

Hazelgreen laughed as he set the documents on the desk. "No need to be modest, sir. Your reputation is well known throughout the West. As soon as I spoke with my fellow councilmen here this morning, we unanimously decided we would like to make you an offer."

"An offer?" Lucas asked warily.

"Yes, indeed." Hazelgreen doffed his hat, clearly enjoying the opportunity to make a speech. "You see, some view this town as nothing more than a motley assortment of misfits, ne'er-do-wells, and dreamers. But I— that is, we—believe in Eminence. We want to save this place, make it what it once was. And we think we can do it in two words."

Lucas managed to stifle a yawn, and wished more than ever for coffee. It didn't even have to be good coffee. Lousy coffee would do. Just one measly cup.

"Narrow gauge," Hazelgreen announced grandly, spreading his arms like a magician who had just pulled off an impressive trick.

"Mr. Hazelgreen," Lucas said slowly, wondering if the

banker might be a few dimes short of a dollar, "I'm familiar with ten-gauge, twelve-gauge—"

"It's not a firearm, sir, it's a railroad."

"Railroad?"

"Narrow-gauge railroad. It's been quite a success down in Pueblo, Florence, other parts of these mountains—"

"It is a new type of railroad," Fairfax explained, "that allows trains to get through the high mountain passes."

Gottfried nodded enthusiastically. "If we could persuade the Denver & Rio Grande to invest in a narrow-gauge line to Eminence—"

"It would bring in new settlers and help restore this town to its former glory," Hazelgreen said confidently.

"Sir," Lucas said, trying to remain polite, "I'm not sure I see what all this has to do with me."

He also didn't see how anything could restore Eminence to its former glory. He'd seen towns like this all over the West—and most boomed one year and went bust the next. Smart folks cut their losses and got out while they could.

"Marshal, if we only had a few hundred more residents," Gottfried explained, "this area could be declared a county. And if we were declared a county, Eminence could be voted the county seat. Which would bring in new businesses and even more people—"

"And that is where you come in, my good man," Fairfax said.

"Huh?" Lucas still couldn't see what any of this had to do with him, though maybe his confusion came from lack of sleep, lack of food. Lack of coffee.

"If we're going to attract more settlers, decent folks," Hazelgreen told him, "we need law and order in this town. And . . . well, we've had something of a struggle in that area."

Lucas frowned. "And why would that be, exactly?"

"A few rowdy fellows come through now and then," Fairfax said, "especially around this time of year. Drifters. They come in for the winter, and sometimes they cause a bit of trouble—"

"You've already got yourself a fine place to stay, free of charge." Hazelgreen tapped a finger against the documents on the hotel desk. "And we'll pay you a salary of seventy-five dollars a week."

The amount of money they were dangling almost made Lucas's jaw drop. "To do what?"

"To become the town marshal, of course."

Lucas shook his head, practically shuddering at the idea. The last thing he wanted was to stay here permanently; he couldn't get out of Eminence fast enough. "I'm not planning to be here for long."

"I understood from Travis that you would be with us several weeks," Hazelgreen said. "Why not make something of your time while you're here?"

"It would be quite a feather in our cap," Fairfax said, "to have the renowned L. T. McKenna as our town marshal, even for a short while."

Gottfried nodded enthusiastically. "Put this town back on the map. Probably get us mentioned in all the papers—"

"No thanks," Lucas said flatly. He didn't need a job; his money could hold out for two weeks, or even three or four, if it came to that. And he wasn't going to be used as some kind of publicity stunt, in a misguided effort to lure settlers to a town that had seen its better days. "I'm not your man. I'm only interested in one prisoner—the one I've already got."

"But Marshal—"

"Sorry." Lucas shook his head adamantly. "Thanks, but the answer is no."

The three men exchanged crestfallen glances. Hazelgreen sighed and pushed the documents toward Lucas, producing a fountain pen and small jar of ink from inside his suit coat. "Very well, sir. But if you change your mind—"

"I won't." Lucas signed the papers and handed them back.

After Eminence's town council left him in peace, Lucas didn't have much to do but sit and wait for his breakfast. As he stared at the door, the next two weeks seemed to stretch out before him like an endless desert. He wasn't used to long periods of inactivity. Hell, he wasn't used to staying in one place more than a few days.

Two weeks, he told himself.

Much longer than that, he'd be lucky to leave Eminence with his sanity intact.

The prospector waited until after dark before he risked walking into town from his cabin on the outskirts. He kept his shoulders hunched and his head low, hoping he looked unworthy of notice with his scruffy beard and patched clothes. He ambled along at a slow, casual mosey—except when he passed old man Dunlap's hotel, to which he gave a wide berth.

He was nervous, and being nervous, he was careful.

Music reached his ears before he pushed open the swinging doors of Fairfax's Saloon and Gambling Emporium, squinting in the bright light. Some fool was doing his drunken best to pound "My Darling Clementine" out of the piano in the corner, though half the keys didn't work. The saloon was crowded—if a dozen people could be accounted a crowd. Which it could these days, in Eminence.

The prospector spotted his friend in his usual place at the bar, making short work of tall glasses of beer, like this was any other night.

He walked over and took the next stool, slouching forward casually, keeping his voice low. "Looks like we got us a lawman in town."

His friend studied the foamy rim of his glass, running a dirty finger along it. "Hyup," he replied softly, licking his finger.

The drunken piano player began caterwauling a solo. *"In a ca-vern, in a can-yon, ex-ca-vaaaa-ting for a mine . . ."*

"A federal marshal." The prospector's mouth went dry just saying the words. "Some famous, federal goddamned marshal. Looks to be stayin' a spell."

"Dwelt a min-er, for-ty nin-er, and his dauuugh-ter Clem-en-tine . . ."

His friend took another long swallow of beer, looking as unconcerned and contented as a fly in a currant pie. "Hyup."

"Oh my dar-lin', oh my dar-lin', oh my daaar-lin', Clem-en-tine . . ."

"Could be *trouble*," the prospector whispered, annoyed that he had to point out the obvious, "if he chances to take a good long look at us. Unless you fancy movin' on?"

"Nope."

". . . You are lost and gone for-e-ver . . ."

Slowly, the prospector began to smile. "You already got it planned, don't you—to do somethin', mebbe make it look like an accident?"

His friend finally looked up from his drink, with a familiar, dangerous glint in his eyes. "Hyup."

". . . Dread-ful sor-ry, Clem-en-tine."

6

Trio of desperadoes gunned down on the North
Platte

Marshal L. T. McKenna honored by mayor of
Guthrie

Hero of the Red River strikes again

Annie barely tasted the last few bites of the waffle she
was nibbling. She could hardly draw a breath—never
mind eat her breakfast—and not just because of the pain
throbbing across her ribs. As she skimmed one story after another, a queasy feeling began in the pit of her stomach, yet she couldn't stop leafing through the newspaper
clippings and penny dreadfuls strewn across her bed.

Yesterday, Travis had struck up a conversation with
her about his favorite subject—the marshal—but Annie
hadn't believed the boy's wild tales. So he'd brought over
a few items from his collection this morning to prove he
wasn't making it all up.

Each one described Lucas McKenna's daring, his re-
sourcefulness, his bravery under fire. She wasn't sure
which she felt more: fascinated or frightened.

"Annie, you have to eat more than that if you want to
get well," Mrs. Gottfried admonished gently.

Annie glanced up at the preacher's wife, who was setting out dishes of ham and sliced oranges and spoon
bread with pumpkin butter on a marble-topped table beside the bed. Rebecca was indisposed today and Mrs.
Owens was busy, so Mrs. Gottfried had been kind
enough to bring Annie's breakfast.

"I'm . . . not very hungry," Annie replied.

"Hungry or not, you need your strength." Mrs. Gottfried handed her a plate of orange slices. The young
woman's blue eyes were gentle, her voice soothing. "You
mustn't give up hope, you know, even though . . . well,
even though things look discouraging right now." She
frowned at the handcuff around Annie's right wrist, then
at the entrance to Annie's room.

Or rather, her cell.

As Annie set the plate aside, the chain that attached
the handcuff to the bed rattled. Lucas had spent several
hours yesterday installing two more security measures:
The wide doorway between the bedroom and sitting
room had been fitted with a jail-cell door, made of black
vertical iron bars, with a shiny new brass lock.

And as if that weren't enough, he also took the extra
precaution of handcuffing her to the bed whenever he
left the hotel for a while—as he had this morning. He'd
disappeared with no explanation, left Travis to keep an
eye on things.

The boy was currently out in the hotel's main room,
playing a harmonica.

As Mrs. Gottfried poured tea from a chipped pot into
a china cup, she glanced at the clippings strewn across
the bed. "I don't think those are going to help you get
well," she said with a rueful expression. "Are you feeling
any better today?"

"I'm . . . I'm all right." Annie gratefully accepted the
cup of tea and sank back against the pillows, wincing.

Every small movement still brought pain, but thanks to her friends' gentle care and hearty meals, and Miss Lazarillo's ointment for her injuries, she was feeling a little better.

Or rather, she *had* been feeling a little better. Even as she sipped at the tea, her eyes were drawn back to the *Trio of Desperadoes Gunned Down* story.

"I can't believe these are all true." Mrs. Gottfried set the teapot down and sat on the edge of the bed, picking up one of the newspaper clippings. " '. . . *And then Marshal McKenna fired. One shot. From a distance of fifty yards* . . .' Fifty yards?" she asked dubiously, glancing at Annie. "I don't think that's even possible."

Annie shook her head, not certain *what* was possible where Lucas McKenna was concerned. She wrapped her hands around the cup of tea, trying to draw warmth from it.

" '. . . *and his quarry perished forthwith, thus saving the good citizens of Guthrie the necessity of a trial* . . .' " Mrs. Gottfried's voice trailed off and she didn't finish. She started scooping up the clippings from the bed, putting them back into the cigar box Travis had brought them in. "Hokum. Fiddle-faddle. These journalists make him sound more like a gunslinger than a peace officer. What lawman worthy of being named a *hero* would purposely shoot a suspect?"

Annie gulped a mouthful of hot tea that burned her throat, remembering what had almost happened when Lucas found her. "I—I don't know. But I think he's . . . he's very . . ." She couldn't come up with words to describe him.

"Difficult," Mrs. Gottfried suggested with a frustrated sigh as she rose and carried the box away, sliding it sideways through the barred door into the sitting room. "Obstinate."

"Confusing," Annie added softly. She glanced at the floor beside her bed, where one stray clipping had fallen: the *Hero of the Red River* story. The accompanying illustration riveted her attention.

It showed a solitary, dark-haired lawman looking cool and confident despite being surrounded by armed opponents in a rocky ravine. Annie had to admit it was a good likeness: The artist had perfectly captured the lean, strong lines of Lucas's face, the frosty stare, the look of determination.

And the gun in his hand. She would never forget that particular Colt. Not after seeing it from a criminal's eye-view.

Hero . . . or heartless? she thought as she studied the picture. *Man of peace . . . or avenging angel?*

She *should* be thinking about getting well and trying to devise some kind of plan to escape. But the man who held her prisoner also seemed to hold her thoughts captive.

Last night was the first time she'd noticed it, when the day's light vanished and she had been left in the darkness, alone with him again. She hadn't been able to tear her gaze from him as he stood on the other side of the barred door, stripping off his shirt.

For a moment, before he turned down the lamp, she had glimpsed an expanse of corded, rippling muscles, all tanned and hard and powerful, like he was made from the same steel as the .45 holstered on his hip.

Annie blinked to chase the memory away, trying to reassure herself that Lucas McKenna *did* possess some tiny shred of gentleness. After all, he was allowing her friends to take care of her.

And he had slipped into her room that first morning and covered her with a blanket when she was cold.

But though his actions bespoke gentleness, the man

himself could be so cold, colder than any Rocky Mountain wind that might slip through her windows. And gruff and harsh and curt. He hadn't hesitated to torment her about what she had done, about James's children. With cutting words that had struck more deeply than any bullet.

Because they were true.

"Annie?"

"I'm sorry." Annie looked up from the sketch on the floor, embarrassed that she had lost track of the conversation. She wasn't even sure how much time had passed, noticed the tea in her hand had gone cold. "What were you saying?"

Mrs. Gottfried gave her a puzzled look, standing at the foot of her bed. "Is there anything you might like me to bring for you when I return this afternoon?"

Annie looked around and couldn't think of one more thing she might need; yesterday afternoon, when Rebecca had visited for the second time, she had cleaned Annie's room top to bottom and brought along some thoughtful touches to make the place feel more comfortable and less like a jail cell: clean sheets, warm blankets, extra pillows, a rug for the floor.

"No," Annie said quietly, glancing down into her tea. "You've already been too kind."

Mrs. Gottfried walked over to the hearth. "I thought perhaps some flowers, or a cheerful painting for you to look at."

Annie noticed that Mrs. Gottfried had started pacing, that she seemed fidgety, almost nervous. In fact, she hadn't sat down for more than two minutes since Lucas had locked the door.

Of course, the preacher's wife had probably never been locked in a cell with an outlaw before.

Annie lowered her gaze. Mrs. Gottfried was only a few years older than herself, but she was a genuine lady, with her gracious manners, her light brown hair always pinned up in an old-fashioned style, and her prim dresses like the one she wore today, of pale yellow that was softer than sunshine. She was the very picture of respectability, refinement . . . virtue.

There couldn't be a woman in Eminence who was more her opposite.

In fact, Mrs. Gottfried's arrival this morning had been a surprise; though she had always been friendly before, Annie had assumed the minister's wife would want nothing to do with her now.

"Mrs. Gottfried, you . . . you don't have to come back at all this afternoon," she offered, keeping her gaze lowered. "I mean . . . I know what some people think of me—"

"Oh, Annie, I hope you're not still smarting over what Widow Kearney said yesterday." Mrs. Gottfried returned to her side.

Annie couldn't look up, and couldn't change how she felt. Though Daniel and Rebecca and her other friends had been steadfast, several people had reacted just as she'd feared.

Mrs. Kearney, who owned the boardinghouse, had been the most vocal, blustering into the hotel yesterday while Rebecca was here to voice her opinion: that Lucas should remove "that despicable murderer and disgraceful little tramp" from the vicinity as soon as possible, because women like herself were working hard to make this a *decent* town for *decent* people.

Annie took a sip of cold tea. "Some folks might be offended by your helping to take care of me—"

"Some folks are easily offended."

"But, ma'am—"

"Other folks realize that things aren't always as simple as they appear." Mrs. Gottfried sat on the bed. "Don't let Widow Kearney bother you. She rarely has a nice word to say to anyone about anything. She's been bitter since the day she lost her husband, seems to think that because she was robbed of her happiness, nobody else deserves any, either."

Annie stared down into her tea, at the black leaves that had settled on the bottom of the cup. She knew what she herself deserved . . . and it wasn't happiness.

"Annie, nobody has the right to judge you," Mrs. Gottfried insisted. "Mrs. Kearney and those others would be shocked if they knew there were *already* quite a few less-than-decent people living right under their noses. In some rather unexpected places."

Annie looked up, startled. "What?" She hadn't suspected that the minister's wife might be aware of what Daniel had revealed last night. "Do you mean . . . you *know* . . . ?"

"I mean me." Mrs. Gottfried rose from the bed and walked toward the windows. "I'm no different from you. No different and no better."

"That's not true!" Annie replied instantly, thinking of all the times she'd seen Mrs. Gottfried in the general store—chatting with the women in town who all sought her approval, or cuddling her young son, or getting a hug from her gentle bear of a husband. "You're . . . you're respected and important and *good*. You're the finest, most upstanding lady in this town."

"If you judge by appearances." Mrs. Gottfried stood in front of the window and reached out to touch one of the iron rods, tentatively, her hand trembling. "I take it you'd be surprised, if I told you this isn't the first time I've been behind bars."

Annie gasped in shock, barely even aware of the pain

that wrenched her injured side. For a moment, the wail of Travis's harmonica was the only sound in the entire hotel.

"I don't tell everyone about my past." The young woman glanced over her shoulder, her expression as soft and gentle as the pale sunlight that streamed through the window. "But I think you should know the truth. There was a time in my life—a few years ago when I was about your age—that I got into some trouble. I thought stealing was the way out." Her eyes became sad and she shifted her gaze back toward the window, toward the sky outside. "But someone got hurt. And it was my fault. And I got caught and spent two years in prison, back East."

Annie could hardly believe what she was hearing. It wasn't possible. The minister's wife had once been a *thief*? Had spent time in *prison*? "Does . . ." She could hardly gather enough breath to speak. "Does your husband know?"

"Oh yes, Uli knows. He was . . ." Mrs. Gottfried smiled ruefully. "He visited the prison to minister to the inmates. That's how we met."

"And he . . . a man like him, he . . ."

"Knew what I had done." Mrs. Gottfried nodded. "And came to love me anyway." She paused and turned toward Annie, her eyes suddenly glistening with dampness, and shook her head, as if she still had trouble believing it herself. "My time in prison changed me, Annie. You can't imagine . . ." She seemed unable to continue for a moment, wrapping her arms around herself, shuddering visibly. "I don't know if I could've endured it, without Uli."

Annie set her tea on the table beside her bed. "Mrs. Gottfried—"

"Katherine is my Christian name, but I prefer Katja, the German version." She came back around the bed.

"It's about the only German I can pronounce, much to Uli's frustration." She smiled, pulling up a chair and taking a slice of orange from Annie's plate. "So, does knowing all of this change how you think of me?"

"No," Annie said without a second's hesitation. "What you were before doesn't change who you are now. You're kind and caring, you're still . . . you."

Katja held her gaze steadily. "And regardless of the mistakes *you've* made in the past," she pointed out softly, "you're gentle and good-hearted and someone I'm proud to call my friend." She ate the orange slice and put the rind aside.

Annie looked down. It wasn't the same at all. Katja hadn't been a man's mistress, paid to share his bed—and nobody had lost his life at her hands.

Her throat tightening, Annie lifted her gaze. "I just wish . . . I wish . . ."

"That you could go back and change everything. Undo what happened." Katja's eyes filled with understanding. "That's the one thing we can never do, Annie." She shook her head. "All we can do is go on with our lives, and try to put the pieces together somehow. I know how hard prison is, and I don't want you to suffer like that. Law and order are important . . . but so are mercy and forgiveness."

Annie lowered her lashes. *Forgiveness.* How could she ask anyone's forgiveness?

She couldn't forgive herself for what she had done.

Lucas entered the general store through the back, as silent as the dust particles that drifted down from the rafters in the chilly morning air. He closed the door behind him and stood still, wary, letting his eyes adjust to the abrupt change from bright sunlight to the darkness of the storeroom. He slipped off his leather gloves and stuffed them in the pockets of his drover's coat, listening.

He didn't hear a sound. No voices, no whispers.

No gaggle of females plotting Antoinette's escape.

Damn. He supposed it had been too much to hope that he might overhear a few choice details of their scheme. Either Rebecca Greer really *was* indisposed this morning and Mrs. Owens really *was* busy—or the women were just smart enough to do their plotting somewhere else.

In any case, he was free to proceed with plan B.

Quietly, he slipped off his boots and left them next to a barrel of sugar. If Mrs. Greer had been telling the truth, she might still be around. He had seen a hand-lettered CLOSED sign in the window, and the front door was locked.

The back had been locked as well.

He wove his way through barrels and baskets and crates in the darkness, hunted for the stairs, and made his way stealthily to the living quarters above.

In the first room at the top of the steps, he discovered Mrs. Greer resting in bed, with the curtains drawn and what looked like a damp cloth over her eyes. She appeared to be asleep.

Maybe she was suffering a headache, or a fit of the vapors or some such. Women were said to be prone to all kinds of mysterious ailments. Or so he'd been told.

Without disturbing her, or announcing his presence in any way, he left her door and moved silently down the hallway, somewhat surprised that she had been telling the truth. It didn't change his plans, however. This wouldn't take long.

In minutes, he had checked the other rooms—kitchen, small parlor, office—and found the one that interested him.

The spare bedroom. The one Antoinette had occupied for two months before he arrived in town.

Lucas stepped inside and pushed the door partly closed behind him, leaving it open just enough so he would hear if his unwitting hostess stirred. He assessed the room with a quick glance.

It was the kind of place a woman would no doubt call "cozy" and "charming," with sunlight pouring through gingham curtains at the window, a brass bed piled with lacy pillows, a patched velvet chair. The dresser and washstand overflowed with doilies and a clutter of knick-knacks and whatnots.

He started with the dresser, rifling quickly through the drawers, then moved on to search the bed, the pillows, the chair, even under the braided rug on the floor.

All he found were a few garments in the dresser and a worn cloth satchel under the bed, the kind with a flat leather bottom, one of its handles mended with string. He sat on the bed and opened the bag, sifting through the few belongings inside—some coins, a bottle of stomach bitters, a handkerchief, writing paper, a torn stagecoach ticket.

In other words, nothing.

He snapped the bag shut, muttering a curse under his breath. It was possible, even likely, that Antoinette had ditched the gun she used to murder James; unless she had wanted to keep it for protection, she had probably tossed it out the window of one of the stagecoaches that carried her west.

But she would *not* have parted with the fifteen thousand in cash she had stolen. That particular piece of evidence had to *be* here. Somewhere. Hazelgreen had told him Antoinette hadn't made any deposits in the bank.

So where could she have hidden it?

Lucas set the bag aside, taking off his hat and raking a hand through his disheveled hair. It might be easier to think if he had been able to sleep last night, instead of lying awake for hours. Again.

Listening to her breathing, her restlessness.

He had thought having a cell door between them might help, but instead last night had been even worse than the first: He had actually started to imagine what it might be like to take off the demure flannel nightgown she wore . . . starting at the high collar and slowly working lower . . . unfastening one tiny pearl button at a time.

Lucas stood and stalked over to the window, lifting the sash, hoping the cool breeze would chill the sudden heat from his blood. *What the hell was wrong with him?*

Maybe the air in this place was so thin it was affecting his brain. Maybe he was suffering from some strange Rocky Mountain madness. That had to be it. What other explanation could there be?

He had expected Antoinette to *try* and seduce him, tease him with her wiles until he couldn't think straight. Like she'd done to Holt. And his brother. And God knew how many other men who had fallen for her charms in the past.

He kept waiting for her to use her tricks. Any number of tricks. All she had to do was . . . maybe leave her blouse open a bit, allowing him a glimpse of her breasts . . . or run her tongue over her lips now and then, slowly . . . or look at him in a certain way, with coy invitation.

Or when she changed her clothes at night, she could do a slow, teasing strip in the moonlight, on the other side of the barred door, just out of his reach.

Lucas felt his heart thudding against his ribs. Yes, that would work. That would be very effective. Turn him into a dazed, crazed animal in about thirty seconds flat.

Shaken, he closed the window and turned away, rubbing his eyes to try and banish the image. So far, Antoinette hadn't made a single effort in that direction. Not a one. He almost wished she would, damn it.

Purely to confirm his low opinion of her.

But the fact was, every time he looked at her for more than a few seconds, she turned her back, covered up, glanced away. And blushed like an innocent.

Innocent? Lucas shook his head. *Bullfeathers.* Innocent was the one thing Miss Antoinette Sutton definitely was not. Her shy reactions were just part of her disguise, meant to keep him and everyone else in this town from suspecting her true nature.

With a frustrated grimace, he grabbed the satchel from the bed and tossed it back underneath. It landed on the rug with a heavy, rattling sound.

He froze, glancing toward the door, but there was no sign that he had awakened Mrs. Greer down the hall.

After a tense moment, he reached for the bag, frowning. The coins and the bottle of stomach bitters couldn't have made that noise. It sounded like there was something large and loose inside. How could he have missed something that big?

When he opened the satchel again, he found nothing but what he'd seen before.

Then he shook it carefully—and heard the odd, heavy rattle again.

Eyes narrowed, he pulled his hunting knife from his belt and sliced the lining open. *Of course.* He should've thought of this in the first place. A woman as smart and tricky as Antoinette Sutton wouldn't walk around carrying her stolen riches in an ordinary traveling case.

The bag had a false bottom. He pried it up.

Underneath, he found a wooden box. A simple box of carved walnut, about six by ten inches, with a tiny brass lock. The sort of box ladies used to carry vanity items like a fancy brush and a mirror and powder puffs and perfumes.

But if this one contained such innocent possessions, why take care to hide it?

Lucas felt a rush of vindication surge through him. The box was the perfect size to hold about fifteen thousand dollars' worth of banknotes. And maybe even the pistol she had used to murder his brother.

How like Antoinette to cloak her treachery in innocence.

A sound came from Mrs. Greer's room—a creak of bedsprings, a yawn. Lucas slid the box into his coat pocket, deciding he'd better go before he had any explaining to do. He put the satchel away and headed swiftly for the door, his mouth curved in a grim smile.

Finally he had what he'd been looking for. Proof of Antoinette's crime. Proof that she had been lying.

Proof that would put her behind bars for the rest of her life.

Annie knew he was back even before she heard his voice.

She looked up as she heard the hotel's front door open, heard his footsteps—unmistakably his. Already she was familiar with the sound of his boots, the purposeful way he walked. Her stomach tensed. She and Katja fell silent. He said something to Travis.

Then he entered the sitting room and stopped in front of the barred cell door, still wearing his black coat and his low-slung western hat.

And an expression she had never seen on his rugged face before. He almost looked . . . pleased.

Except that his eyes glittered like green ice.

Annie's fingers dug into the soft ball of red yarn in her lap. She didn't know where he had been, but the way he was looking at her almost made her drop the crochet hook in her other hand—the hand that was cuffed to the bed.

He unlocked the cell, his gaze never leaving her. "Mrs. Gottfried, it's time for you to go." His voice was cool, curt. And quiet. Somehow *too* quiet.

"Of course, Marshal." Katja, who had been sitting on the bed, gathered up her things. "You keep practicing that stitch, Annie." She touched Annie's arm and caught her attention, holding her gaze for a long moment, her blue eyes filled with reassurance. "Remember what I told you."

She clearly wasn't talking about needlework, but about all she had said and shared this morning. About *hope* and *mercy* and *forgiveness*.

Annie nodded. She would try.

Katja smiled, looking hopeful herself as she picked up the basket of breakfast dishes. "I'll see you again later. If that's acceptable, of course," she added politely as she walked past Lucas.

"Fine." He didn't give her a glance.

Annie felt very much alone as her friend left. Lucas didn't move, standing there, regarding her with that odd expression; she caught a hint of straight, white teeth. He looked almost . . . wolfish.

Her stomach did a little flip and she forgot about the ball of wool in her hand. It slipped from her fingers and tumbled off the bed—one end still attached to the hook in her hand—and unraveled as it rolled across the floor.

It hit the toe of Lucas's boot.

He bent down and picked it up. "And what is this?" he asked, his voice a slow, soft drawl.

"Katja—Mrs. Gottfried was teaching me how to crochet."

He studied the ball of yarn as if it were something foreign. Then he started winding up the loose end, moving closer to her inch by inch. "How nice."

Annie's pulse suddenly seemed very loud in her ears. "I doubt a crochet hook could be used as any kind of weapon." She held up the short wooden stick with a stubby curve on one end. "It isn't dangerous."

"Doesn't appear to be."

A strange thought flashed through her mind—that she knew how a fish felt as it was being reeled in.

"I have to pass the time somehow," she said nervously, not sure why she felt the need to fill the silence with words.

"Yes, I suppose you do." He kept moving closer as he wound the yarn, his gaze traveling over her—boldly, directly. The way he always looked at her.

Annie felt her breath catch and her ribs throbbed in protest. She thought she had gotten used to men staring at her back in St. Charles, and had always ignored it. But somehow when Lucas did it, it made her feel . . .

Flushed and warm all over. Her face. Her fingertips. *Everywhere.*

She lowered her gaze, pretending to study the uneven rows of crochet she had been working. He came closer until he stood right beside her. Close enough that his scent surrounded her—a musky, clean scent of leather and the outdoors and the mountain air.

He dropped the ball of yarn in her lap.

She kept waiting for him to say something. He didn't. Didn't speak. Didn't move away. When she glanced up, she saw him looking at her intently.

Or rather, at her clothes. She didn't understand why her pin-tucked blouse and plain brown skirt would hold such interest; they were the same garments she had been wearing when he left earlier. The only thing different about her was that Katja had braided her hair, which now hung down her back in a loose plait.

His eyes seemed to be focused on her high collar, on the buttons at her throat.

Then he leaned closer and grabbed the long chain that bound her right wrist to the bed, unlocking the handcuff. "They can dress you up like a proper lady, Antoinette." His voice was rough, his eyes stormy. "Make you look like a proper lady. Teach you how to do needlework like a proper lady. But that *doesn't* change what you are." He dropped the manacles on the floor and straightened. "What you are inside. Where it *counts*."

Annie rubbed at her wrist, thinking that was almost the same thing Katja had told her—though her friend hadn't meant it the same way at all.

For once, she resisted the urge to shrink from Lucas's glare. She didn't understand what had suddenly made him so angry. "And you think you know what I am."

She said it as a challenge.

And regretted it a second later.

Because he reached down and touched her. Tilted her chin up with one hand. Her heart seemed to stop. All at once she was aware that she no longer heard the sound of a harmonica in the outer room. Lucas must've sent Travis on some errand.

Which meant the two of them were alone.

"Yeah, I know exactly what you are." His voice was low and husky. He ran his fingers along her jawline, slowly. "And you're not proper, and you're no lady."

Annie couldn't reply, couldn't even *think*. Not with him stroking her that way. God help her, she *must* be what he thought: a woman without virtue. Fallen. Ruined. A respectable lady wouldn't melt this way at the merest brush of his fingertips. Wouldn't shiver when he looked at her like that.

Or stare at his mouth.

Or like the feel of him touching her.

He leaned down, and Annie knew then that no matter

how Katja tried to convince her otherwise, she would never be a lady.

Because she didn't protest. Didn't even try to pull away.

"How good are you, Antoinette?" he murmured, his mouth close to hers. "I'll bet you're damn good. Is that how you kept my brother wrapped around your finger for three years?"

For a moment, she thought he was going to kiss her.

She must be losing her mind. He was taunting her. Tormenting her. She jerked her head away, hoping he couldn't tell how she was trembling and breathless. Her body's wanton reactions to his touch only proved he was right to have such a low opinion of her.

How could she respond this way to a man who despised her? "You . . . you made up your mind about me before you even *met* me."

"Yeah." He straightened, looking cool and unaffected by what had just happened. He turned his back, reaching into his coat. "And it seems I was right."

He tossed something onto the bed.

Annie flinched, stared at the object, for a moment didn't even know what it was.

Then she gasped, dragging air into her lungs, ignoring the pain that shot through her body. The physical agony from her ribs couldn't match the far deeper hurt in her heart. "Where did you find that?"

"You know where I found it," he snapped, turning to pierce her with a hard stare. "Right where you hid it. With your devoted Mrs. Greer indisposed, I—"

"Invaded her home and pawed through my personal things?" She glared at him, incensed.

"Decided to search for evidence. Judges and juries are rather fond of evidence."

Annie's side ached and hurt as she stretched one hand

toward the box—then she hesitated and got off the bed, moving away from it. Then she reached for the box again. "You had no right—"

"I have every right."

He stopped her, his hand closing on her wrist.

Their gazes locked. He held her there for a second, his fingers so strong and hard and hot against her skin, Annie felt like she was being branded. Once more she had the unsettling sensation that he was going to pull her against him, seal his mouth over hers, and . . .

"Where's the key?" he grated out.

"I don't . . . have it." Her voice was halting, wavering.

"Where'd you hide it?" He released her arm.

"That box doesn't contain anything that would interest a jury—"

"If you want to do this the hard way, that's fine with me." He grabbed the box.

"No!" Though every movement wracked her, she tried to stop him. *"Don't—"*

It was too late. He stalked over to the door of her cell—and smashed the edge of the box against one of the iron bars.

The wood splintered, the hinges broke, and the contents fell across the rug.

Annie shut her eyes, covering her mouth with one hand to hold back a sob.

"What . . . ?" Lucas demanded in a tone of disbelief. "What the hell is this?"

Annie shook her head, lifting her lashes slowly, reluctantly, aching with a pain that filled her heart until she thought it would shatter like that precious little box. The contents lay strewn across the carpet, stark white against the deep red and green.

A bib, a tiny knit cap, an ivory rattle, and a lacy pair of booties.

"I told you," she whispered. "I told you there was nothing in that box that would interest a jury."

"I don't understand." He looked and sounded utterly bewildered.

"They're just some things I bought for the baby," she choked out, slowly walking over to them and sinking to her knees, not caring about the agony in her side. "For my baby. Just a few . . ." She couldn't speak anymore.

He dropped the jagged pieces of the box onto the rug. "Where's the goddamn gun, Antoinette? And the fifteen thousand you stole?"

"I don't know what happened to the gun." She ran one fingertip over the tiny knit cap, afraid to touch it, unable to resist. "I told you, it was an *accident*. I was terrified and the gun fell and I ran—"

"And the money? Are you going to tell me you took that by accident?"

"I only wanted the money for my baby. So I could raise my child somewhere safe and give him a good home, a good life . . ." Tears spilled over her lashes. "I spent some on a black dress, and a wedding ring and . . ." She gestured to the baby items. "I—I saw these in a shop window, next to the stage depot in Independence, in this pretty little box, and I . . . wanted them. But after . . ."

Tears streamed down her cheeks. "I didn't want to see them anymore." She picked up one of the booties. "But I couldn't bring myself to throw them away."

He stood there. Just stood there and didn't say another word. Like he didn't feel anything. Like he was as cold and remote as the mountain peaks outside her barred window.

"And what did you do with the rest of the money?" he demanded.

"You wouldn't believe me if I told you."

"Try me."

She lifted her head and looked him straight in the eye. "I gave it away."

He remained frozen for a moment. Then he blinked, once. Slowly. "Gave it away," he echoed, shaking his head. "*You* gave away almost fifteen thousand dollars."

"After I lost the baby I didn't *care* about the money anymore! I didn't care what happened to the money . . . or . . . or to me."

"And who do you *claim* has it now?" he asked sarcastically. "Mrs. Greer? Your precious Dr. Holt?"

Slowly, she stood up, facing him, still clutching the tiny bootie in her fingers. "I sent it to an orphanage in Denver that I read about in the paper. Anonymously. I wanted to . . ." She wiped furiously at her eyes. "It couldn't help my child, so I wanted it to help someone's child. A child who had nothing . . . and no one."

He folded his arms. "You really expect me to believe all this, don't you?"

"I don't care what you believe anymore!" She turned away, every part of her ablaze with pain. "It's *true* what they say about you in those articles." She gestured to the box of newspaper clippings on the floor of his room. "You are ruthless. Heartless!"

"I'm surprised you know how to read."

"So you thought I was stupid as well as a slut?"

"No, I think you're smart, Antoinette. I think you missed your calling. You should've been an actress. You would've been a big hit on the stage. Very convincing." His voice dropped to a low, dangerous tone. "Except that I know for a fact you're a mur—"

"*You're* the one who's a murderer. A cold-blooded killer, according to those newspapers. I suppose you think it makes a difference that you wear a badge—"

"You shouldn't believe everything you read."

"I'm *not* going by what I read. I'm judging by what I *saw*, with my own eyes."

Their gazes met and held. Those glittering green depths smoldered, darkening.

"You were going to kill me," she accused. "Out on that hillside when you found me. You were going to shoot me."

"And I didn't. So why do you believe a bunch of greedy half-wits who call themselves journalists?"

"You've judged *me* by reputation alone. By what people *told* you about me. People who didn't even know me at all, who would never speak two words to me. You've taken everything they said as gospel truth."

"Because they were good people," he shot back. "Not thieves and criminals—"

"Is that how you see the whole world? Good and bad?" She couldn't catch her breath, pressed a hand against her aching ribs. "And which category do *you* fall into, Marshal?"

He moved to her—suddenly, swiftly. Startled, she backed away. Came up against the wall. He closed in and she could see the gold flecks in his eyes, feel the heat radiating from him.

Feel his body against hers.

"You really don't want an answer to that," he growled.

With that he turned on his heel and stalked out, slamming her cell door and locking it. Annie couldn't move, couldn't breathe.

Because every inch of her was tingling, burning.

As if he'd just been branded on her soul.

7

A raw, biting wind tugged at Lucas's coat, making it flap noisily as he stood on the hillside beneath a tree, near a picket fence. Raindrops spattered his hat and his face, while tumbling leaves blew past him in a wet parade of shiny yellow and brown. It had been raining for most of the past week. Gray clouds lumbered across the late afternoon sky like a ghostly herd of buffalo.

But the damp weather wasn't the only reason for his discomfort as he stood there, one gloved hand resting on his holstered Colt, the other clenched at his side.

Stood there staring at the small pine cross. At the two words carved into it.

Baby Smith.

A muscle worked in his jaw. He wasn't sure what he was doing here, what he hoped to accomplish. He and Antoinette hadn't spoken much since their argument last week—but she had made one request, now that her ankle was healing up and she was able to walk more easily.

She had asked to come here, claiming that she had visited the grave every day, before he arrived in town.

He had refused, of course. It was obviously a trick. A scheme. A lie. The easier it was for her to walk, the easier it would be to try and escape. He wasn't about to let her out of her cell, not for any reason.

So he stood there, alone, not knowing why he had ventured outside in a cold rain, why he had climbed all the way up here.

He kept hoping he would find proof of her guilt. Evidence. *Something* he could hold in front of a judge and jury to show them she was a liar, a murderer.

Instead, he kept finding proof of something else.

Even here.

Rain dripped from the brim of his hat, splashing his boots as he gazed down at the tiny grave. He couldn't help noticing that the grass to one side was worn bare . . . as if someone had indeed spent a lot of time curled up on the damp ground, beside this small mound of earth. And a handful of wilted flowers was strewn nearby, scattered by the wind.

Even as he resisted, an image flashed into his head. The image that had haunted him for a week now: Antoinette crumpled on the floor of her cell, crying silent tears over a bib and a tiny hat and a rattle, a lacy bootie clutched tightly in her hand.

He crouched down, resting his elbows on his knees. *Baby Smith.* Her child.

And maybe, if she was telling the truth, James's child.

Which would make this poor, lost innocent Lucas's nephew or niece.

The thought made his heart feel strange. He took off one of his gloves and reached out to the mound of earth. It was cold. So cold and isolated, out here in the rain. He brushed away a few fallen leaves, not sure why he felt compelled to tend the little grave.

All he knew was that, despite his best efforts to deny it, he believed Antoinette on one point.

She had cared about her baby.

Miss Antoinette Sutton— daughter of a whore, mistress, thief, murderer—had truly wanted this child. Maybe even . . . loved this child.

He lifted his face to the leaden sky, wishing the rain could wash that certainty away. It confused the hell out of him. *She* confused the hell out of him. To think that she might actually have a heart, to hold even that one small, charitable thought about Antoinette was more than he wanted. More than he could stand.

Because it felt like a betrayal of his brother.

Lucas shut his eyes and shook his head in denial. He wiped stinging rain from his face. Yanked his glove back on. A few days ago, he'd spent an entire morning writing to every orphanage listed in the Denver paper, seeking to discredit Antoinette's ridiculous claim that she had donated the stolen money. Unfortunately, he wouldn't receive any replies for at least another week, mail delivery being what it was in the mountains.

He had probably wasted his time and postage. She had probably sent the money to a *bank* in Denver under an assumed name. Or maybe one of her friends was holding it for her. Or maybe . . .

Or maybe she was telling the truth.

Lucas stepped back from the little cross, then abruptly turned and walked toward the cemetery gate. None of this made any sense—and none of it made any difference.

Even if Antoinette *had* cared about her baby, even if she *was* telling the truth about the missing fifteen thousand, it didn't make her any less guilty of killing James.

She had taken the life of a gentle, kind, generous man. A husband. A father.

A brother.

Lucas latched the cemetery gate behind him and

headed down the hill, hunching his shoulders against the bitter wind that blew down from the north. It would be better, he decided, if he stopped looking for evidence he wouldn't find, stopped asking questions that had no answers. Stopped driving himself crazy.

Antoinette's fate wasn't for him to decide; a judge and jury would put her on trial and choose her punishment.

And since she was healing quickly, it wouldn't be long before she'd be well enough to travel. A few more days and they could leave for Missouri.

The sooner, the better.

The rain that had started out as a gentle patter earlier today had strengthened to a downpour that pounded on the hotel's roof and splashed noisily against Annie's windows.

The light of a candle was all that held the darkness at bay in her cell. A single candle in a tin cup. But Annie was grateful to have it, after spending ten nights surrounded by shadows and gloom. Disbelief battled a tiny spark of pleasure as she set the candleholder on the hearth, her movements slow and stiff.

The dull ache in her ribs didn't keep her from sighing as she watched steam curl upward from the metal tub at her feet, the warm white tendrils rising on the cool air.

Her jailer, she thought with a slow, confused shake of her head, was a man she would never figure out.

For the past week, he had been cold and distant, rarely letting her out of his sight but hardly speaking to her. He came into her cell only when it was necessary to put the handcuffs on her or remove them. When she had asked if he would take her to visit her baby's grave, he had refused in that sarcastic, mocking tone she had come to hate.

Then today, after he had gone out for a short while

and returned, she had made another request and he had granted it. Without arguing, without mocking her, without even saying a word.

He had simply sent Travis to fetch a tub and enough hot water to fill it. He even allowed her a candle so she could see what she was doing as darkness fell. Apparently he believed her when she promised she wouldn't try to burn a hole through the wall and escape using one stubby candle.

She was stunned that he would trust her even that much. After handing it to her, he had shrugged off her thanks, locked her cell and left her alone, granting her a rare moment of privacy.

And now she stood beside the tub, his unexpected kindness leaving her confused. And a bit nervous. She shivered, but told herself it was only because her room was so chilly.

The darkened hotel was silent, except for the sound of the rain; Travis had gone home for the night. Lucas was out in the main room, probably doing what he usually did to pass the time—reading the newspapers or pacing or writing letters.

Or cleaning his gun, which he did every day. As if he always had to be ready at a moment's notice to kill someone.

Annie shivered again. For tonight, she decided, for once, she would try not to think of Lucas McKenna and all the strange, conflicting feelings he aroused in her. Instead of puzzling over the reason behind his generosity, she'd better take advantage of it before he changed his mind.

And before the water got cold. She moved to the windows, as quickly as her injured side would allow, and closed the heavy velvet drapes. Then she picked up a cotton towel and a bar of herbal soap from her washstand—more gifts from Rebecca—and returned to the tub.

Her gaze on the steamy water, she set the soap and towel on a nearby armchair and started unbuttoning her blouse . . . until she happened to glance up and catch her reflection in the mirror that almost filled the wall on one side of the room.

She stopped, frowning. Whoever the original owner of this place had been, he must've been quite impressed with himself; most people didn't need anything bigger than a cheval glass to check their reflection.

Annie went to her bed, gingerly, and picked up a blanket, hanging it between the mantel and one of the bedposts, tying it securely in place with some yarn from her crocheting.

Lucas might come back into the sitting room, and she wasn't taking any chances. It was bad enough having him see her when she was fully dressed. Every time he regarded her in that bold, direct way of his, every time their eyes met and held, she felt strangely breathless, hot, tingly all over. The idea of him looking at her when she wasn't wearing any . . .

No, no, no. Upset by the fluttery sensation in her stomach, she stepped behind the blanket and finished unbuttoning her blouse. She had to get these unruly, unwanted thoughts under control.

Hadn't she learned her lesson? Learned that her mama had been right? *Men can't be trusted,* Mama had always said. *They're only interested in one thing.* And they weren't capable of caring or gentleness or loyalty or love. Not really, not for long.

Not when it counted.

Annie hadn't believed any of that when she was young, naïve, dreamy-eyed. And her foolishness had cost her everything she held dear.

But never again. She would never let herself be any man's fool again. Not ever.

Her fingers seemed to fumble with every button as she slipped out of her skirt and petticoat. She placed the garments on the chair, then gave one last, uneasy glance over her shoulder before she removed her camisole. After thinking a moment, she unfastened her bandage, too, and carefully unwrapped it; her ribs had been feeling much better, and she didn't want the bandage to become a soggy mess. She dropped it on the floor, slipped off her pantalettes.

Then at last she stepped into the tub. Slowly, she lowered herself down, sighing at the touch of the hot water against her bare skin, her bruised side. Even though there was only a foot of water in the dented tin bath, it felt almost luxurious after a week of making do with splashing herself at her washbasin.

The tub was just long enough that she could fit fairly comfortably, if she kept her knees up. She let herself go limp, resting her head against the edge, letting the heat soothe her body and her nerves.

After a few minutes, she hardly even noticed the throbbing ache in her ribs. They were healing well, Daniel had said a couple of days ago, when he came to examine her injuries; he had visited her twice this week, while making his rounds of patients. Fortunately, he and Lucas had been civil toward each other so far—but the air between them crackled with so much tension, she still feared they might come to blows.

Daniel had privately told her she might be ready to travel sooner than he'd expected—maybe in another two or three weeks, rather than four.

With that in mind, he had come up with an escape plan.

Apparently the lock on her cell was something called a fifteen-pin cylinder lock—which meant that to get past it, they would either need a master thief who had a great deal of time, or a skeleton key. Eventually, Eminence being the kind of place it was, Daniel had said, he might be able to come up with one or the other.

But there was still the problem of her being handcuffed to the bed whenever Lucas left the hotel. What they really needed, Daniel had decided, was a *copy* of the keys to the door and the handcuffs.

If one of them could get their hands on those keys for a minute, they could use some wax—a block of wax about the size of a thin bar of soap—to make impressions of each. Then they could have copies made.

And while Lucas was out one day, her friends could simply set Annie free.

Unfortunately, she had pointed out, there was one rather large problem: Lucas didn't keep the keys on a ring or hang them on a hook somewhere; he always kept them in a pocket of his trousers.

Those snug black trousers that molded so tightly to his lean body . . .

Annie opened her eyes and sat up, sloshing water over the side of the tub. *Why* did her thoughts keep wandering off in that direction? She was blushing furiously, felt all tingly and breathless.

She splashed her face. Maybe she had a fever. Or maybe being locked up was starting to play tricks on her mind. She had heard stories of people who went crazy from being imprisoned.

Somehow, she thought desperately, this escape plan had to work. And soon.

With a frustrated sigh, she leaned forward in the tub and reached toward the chair, carefully pressing one hand to her side, her teeth catching her lower lip at the discomfort. She scooped up the soap and dropped it in her bath, then rubbed it between her hands until it lathered.

The fresh, green scent of meadow herbs filled the darkened room. As Annie scrubbed at her skin and worked the soap through her hair, she vowed that somehow, she must find a way to repay her friends for all their kindness. And for taking risks to save her.

But then, she might never have that chance.

Because when she left this cell and left Eminence, it would be to spend the rest of her life as a fugitive—or in a Missouri prison. Either prospect that loomed before her looked bleak. Dangerous. Frightening.

And lonely.

She had never really felt that emotion, even though she had spent much of her life alone.

Maybe because she had never really had friends before.

Annie blinked, and it wasn't just soap that stung her eyes. She had been right before: God had only spared her life to punish her. For what she was, for what she had done.

One painful day at a time.

The bathwater had gone cold. Slowly, she tilted her head forward and finished rinsing the soap out of her hair, wringing the tangled mass of curls between her hands. But her enjoyment had evaporated with the steam.

She stood, shivering in the chilly air, water sluicing down her body and dripping on the rug. As she reached for her towel, a noise from outside startled her, made her glance up.

It didn't come from the sitting room—but from outside her windows.

She froze, her arm extended, her eyes widening. It had sounded like a footstep. A heavy footstep.

But who would be lurking out there at night? There wasn't anything in back of the hotel but an empty field.

She grabbed the towel and held it against her. The drapes were closed, the room lit only by one candle. No one could see in. And she couldn't see out. Maybe she *was* going crazy. It was probably just the wind. Or one of the town's stray dogs. Or—

She heard it again: definitely a footstep, so loud and startling, she jumped backward.

And tripped on the edge of the tub.

Her weight knocked it over and she fell, yelping in panic, water splashing all over. She landed on the rug, hard, crying out in pain.

All the air knocked from her, she lay on her back in the soapsuds. The world turned hazy for a moment. She heard booted steps pounding across the sitting room's wooden floor.

"What happened?" Lucas called from the door of her cell. "Are you all right?"

Annie couldn't speak, her ribs ablaze with pain. She managed only a groan.

The key turned in the lock.

"*No,*" she croaked, gasping for air. "Don't!"

As usual, he ignored her, yanking the door open. In a panic, she reached for her now-soaked towel and clutched it in front of her.

And just managed to conceal the bare essentials before Lucas came inside. He stepped around the blanket, carrying a lantern, his voice suspicious. "What the hell hap—"

He didn't finish, his jaw going slack.

"I . . . I tripped." Annie's entire body was aflame with embarrassment. The lantern in his hand offered enough light for him to see far too much. She had never felt so mortified, lying there at his feet in a puddle of water and suds, covered only with a wet towel.

But to her astonishment, he didn't mock her. Or pounce on her. He remained frozen where he stood. "Did you hurt yourself—"

"It hurts, but I . . ." She tried to sit up and stopped, inhaling sharply at the pain.

"Don't move, damn it. You could've punctured a lung."

"No."

She wasn't denying what he said but what he did: He set the lantern on a table, crouched down, and eased her back onto the rug, gently probing her bandaged side. "Can you breathe all right? Does this hurt?"

She flinched away. "Yes, it hurts." And she did feel breathless, but wasn't sure if that was from her injuries or from his touch, his nearness. "If . . . if I had punctured a lung, wouldn't I be dead by now?"

"Probably." He arched one brow. "And you definitely wouldn't be able to talk so much."

Annie almost forgot the pain for a second, gazing up at him in the candlelight. The flickering shadows emphasized the strong lines of his jaw and the deep, gold-flecked green of his eyes; with his tanned skin and his tangled black hair and his beard-stubbled cheeks, he looked so dark, almost fearsome, and yet somehow, so undeniably . . . appealing.

She really must be losing her mind.

When he touched her again, his hands closing on her shoulders, she tensed. "I'm fine," she protested tremulously, "really."

"Do you want to spend the rest of the night lying on a sopping wet rug?"

"N-no," she admitted, surprised by his gentleness as he helped her to a sitting position. She sucked in a breath between her teeth; every movement hurt, and she was shivering with cold. The wet towel she kept clutched against her wasn't doing much good. In any way.

He stood and yanked down the blanket she had hung between the mantel and the bedpost. Then he paused, glancing at the door of her cell, which he had left open.

"Yes," she said dryly. "My brilliant plan was to . . . whack you over the head with a bar of soap and . . . run for it." She gulped another breath. "Bend down and I'll give it a try."

She wasn't sure—couldn't believe it—but she thought she heard a chuckle come from deep in his throat. She had never heard him laugh before.

He did bend down, but only to wrap the blanket around her shoulders. Then he helped her up.

Her legs felt as wobbly as jelly, and for once, she was grateful for his strong grip. He eased her onto the chaise longue in front of the windows.

"I'm not trying to escape," she assured him, gathering the blanket around her as she sat on the edge of the plush chair. *At least not at the moment,* she amended privately. "Just . . . clumsy."

She flicked a glance at the window and decided not to mention the mysterious footsteps. Whoever it was had no doubt heard the commotion and was long gone. It could've been one of her friends, working on some new and better escape plan. Or just some drunken prospector wandering along in the dark.

Lucas righted the fallen tub and scooped her clothes off the chair. "Do you want the doctor?"

She noticed that the suspicion had returned to his voice. "No," she said, gingerly touching her throbbing side underneath the blanket. She didn't want to drag Daniel over here in the pouring rain; she would be fine until morning, when one of her friends came to take care of her. "I think I'm all right. Just . . . sore. And cold."

"That's probably because it's freezing in here." He dropped her clothes into her lap.

"It usually *is* at night," she said pointedly, looking up at him. "I doubt the stove in your room was meant to heat this one, too."

Without another word, he turned and walked out into the sitting room.

Annie watched him go, her brow furrowed. So much for helping her, she thought, not sure whether she was relieved or annoyed. She glanced at the clothes in her lap; she had intended to put on a nightgown after her bath. But for the moment, the clothes at hand were better than none at all.

Getting dressed wasn't easy, not with her aching ribs, especially since she tried to hold the blanket in place at the same time. She barely managed to wiggle into her pantalettes and camisole before Lucas reappeared, carrying an armful of wood.

"Now what are you doing?" she asked in surprise.

"As long as I'm in here with you," he said grudgingly, "you can have a fire."

Before Annie could decide whether to thank him or protest his continued presence in her room, he pulled the cell door shut behind him.

Then he took the key from his pocket and locked them in. Together.

Her heart made a nervous little skip. "I . . . I . . ."

"You're welcome."

"Thank you," she said belatedly.

He slid the key back into his pocket, walking across the squishy rug to put the logs in the fireplace. A few moments later, with the help of the candle, he had a fire started. "You're sure you don't need the doctor?"

"I'm sure." She mostly didn't want *Lucas* in here with her, but apparently she wasn't being given a choice about that.

"Good."

Annie wasn't sure how to interpret that soft, one-word comment. But she *was* grateful for the fire; it was the first time the room had held any warmth.

Lucas straightened and looked around. "So where do your lady friends keep your bandages?"

She blinked at him. "I can wait until one of them comes tomorrow morn—"

"You'll never be able to sleep. I've bandaged up my deputies before when they had busted ribs. It'll take two minutes."

Annie recognized that tone of voice, and knew better than to argue with him when he used it. The man was accustomed to giving orders and having them obeyed.

She gestured toward the dresser, surprised that her comfort mattered to him. Until today, he had never seemed all that concerned about her. "Top drawer."

He walked over and rummaged through the drawer's contents, while she watched him, wondering. *Hero or heartless?* It seemed whenever she believed he was cold and unfeeling, he would show some hint of gentleness, even thoughtfulness.

Enough to make her believe there might be a heart beneath that silver star, that this legendary lawman might have a side few people ever saw . . .

Annie cut that thought short, lowering her gaze, reminding herself that she didn't dare trust her *own* heart. Especially when it came to men by the name of McKenna.

She'd made mistakes in judgment before. Serious mistakes. Mistakes she wasn't going to repeat.

He returned to her side, carrying the roll of bandages. Annie held her breath and held the blanket tightly closed at her throat as he moved behind her. In one easy motion, he swung his leg over the chaise like it was a saddle and sat down.

There were only a few inches between them . . .

between his chest and her back. She remained very, very still. The scent of leather and the outdoors, his scent, surrounded her. The fire crackling on the hearth seemed to have gotten awfully loud. And hot.

"This isn't going to work if you're all wrapped up in that blanket," he said after a moment.

"I'm not . . . wearing much." She nodded toward her blouse and skirt, which were on the floor.

"I think I can handle it. You're not that irresistible, Antoinette."

He said it in that mocking tone. The one she hated. She gritted her teeth to hold back a tart reply, reminding herself that he *was* trying to help her, when he didn't have to.

She loosened her hold on the blanket, enough to let it slide down her shoulders, slowly, to her waist. She trembled at the touch of the air against her wet skin. She was still soaked, hadn't had the chance to towel herself dry. And her thin cotton camisole wasn't much in the way of clothing.

Everything would be all right, she told herself nervously; all he could see was her back.

On the other hand, she thought a second later, he was taller than her. Which meant he could probably see over her shoulder.

"Move your hair out of the way."

His voice had shifted again, gotten deeper. Softer.

She reached up with one hand and lifted the sopping mass of curls off her back, pulling her long hair around in front of her, glad that it offered a bit more coverage than her damp camisole.

"Now move this out of the way." He touched the bottom hem of the garment.

Take a breath, Annie ordered herself, the brush of his

fingertips against her spine sizzling through her like a lightning bolt. *Take a breath.* It took a moment for the command to travel from her brain to her lungs.

With trembling fingers, she tugged her camisole up, just far enough to expose her rib cage.

He swore, vividly.

Annie knew why: because he could see her bruise, the ugly black and purple and yellow mark that stretched halfway around her. "It only looks bad because it's healing," she told him. "At least, that's what Daniel says."

He didn't reply. She heard him unrolling the bandage.

And a second later, she couldn't form another rational thought.

Because he had leaned closer, reaching around her to start wrapping her ribs with the long strip of white fabric. She couldn't move a muscle, vividly aware of the rough feel of his wool shirt brushing against her back. And his hands. And every droplet of water sliding down the curves of her body. And his breath soft against the nape of her neck.

And his hands.

She had never experienced his touch this way before—strong and yet gentle, so careful of her, so . . . tender against her skin.

"You all right?"

"Yes," she lied, her voice a breathy whisper. She inhaled and exhaled in shallow, unsteady little gasps; and not just because it was always a bit painful having her injuries tended.

Annie shut her eyes, her heart thumping wildly as he continued working, smoothly and efficiently. She wished she had opened the curtains. The room felt so enclosed, so enveloped in heat and darkness and silence. Like they were the only two people in the world.

She blinked rapidly, trying to clear her vision, her thoughts. How was it that Lucas McKenna always rendered her so addle-brained?

How could he stir her blood as no man ever had?

"Never seen broken ribs heal up this quick," he commented, sounding perfectly calm, cool. Not the least bit addled. "Your *señorita* friend must put some magic ingredients in that potion of hers."

"Maybe." Desperate to fill the silence, Annie tried to think of something more to say. "Being a marshal must be dangerous work."

His only response was a noncommittal grunt, which she couldn't interpret. Did he mean it wasn't really all that dangerous?

Or he didn't care about the danger?

"The papers say you're one of the best." After a moment, she added, "Marshals."

"I do all right."

That sounded modest; odd, she thought, for a man she had considered arrogant.

"Where do you live?" she asked impulsively. "In Indian Territory?"

For a long moment, he didn't reply. The crackling of the fire on the hearth and the spattering of the rain against the windows made the only sound. She thought maybe he wouldn't tell her. Maybe it wasn't his habit to reveal personal information to anyone.

Especially not to an outlaw in his custody.

"I keep a few things in a rooming house thereabouts."

"Oh." That didn't sound like much of a home.

In fact, it sounded rather . . . lonely.

Annie batted that thought away, reminding herself she shouldn't—didn't—care about the man who held her prisoner. She looked around the room, trying to think of something else to talk about. Something neutral and safe.

Her attention settled on the mirror that filled the opposite wall.

She blinked, her eyes widening as she stared at their reflection, at the two of them in the firelight—sitting so close together, his hands so large and dark and strong against her pale skin, her body almost naked·except for the skimpy camisole and the blanket bunched around her hips.

A quiver went through her. He lifted his head.

And their gazes met in the mirror.

8

He'd made one hell of a mistake coming in here.

Lucas's heart thundered louder than a Comanche war drum as he stared at their reflection. Antoinette remained utterly still, her back as straight as one of the iron bars on her cell door, her eyes wide and dark.

A bead of sweat slid down his temple. Damn it, he never should have let himself help her. Or touch her. Should've left her lying on the floor. Should've left once he made sure she wasn't seriously hurt.

He should leave now.

But he didn't.

He didn't move a muscle, the roll of bandages gripped in his hand. Her breathing had become rapid, shallow. His whole body felt heavy and hard. God Almighty, he had been trying to do something considerate, something right.

Instead, everything had gone wrong.

Until this moment, she hadn't even seemed to understand the effect she had on him—sitting here within his reach, half-naked, all soft curves and wet skin.

And sweet, tantalizing scent. He longed to bury his face in her damp hair, kiss her throat, her shoulder.

Wanted to let his other hand slide beneath the blanket, to find out if those pantalettes were the kind with a slit in the center.

He wanted to pull her back against him and let his fingers seek her soft, feminine heat. Touch her breasts through the damp fabric of her camisole until her nipples beaded against his palm and her slender spine arched with the pleasure. Ease her down onto the chaise, shift her body beneath his . . .

Lucas shut his eyes and tore the bandage. Why the *hell* had he offered to wrap up her ribs in the first place? He should've gone for the doctor. Why hadn't he just gone and gotten the damned doctor?

But as he tucked in the frayed end securely against her side he knew why: because part of him was *glad* she hadn't wanted to see Holt. Not just because he suspected the two of them were cooking up an escape plan, but because he felt jealous every time he saw them together. He didn't want to think of her with any man.

Except himself.

Lucas glared at her back, resting his hands on his thighs, his fingers digging into the rigid muscles through the fabric of his trousers. The realization was stunning, unforgivable. Undeniable.

He wanted her, in a way he didn't understand. Wanted Antoinette all to himself. All of her. *All* . . .

"All done," he said, his voice low and sharp.

"Th-thank you." She stood up, wrapping the blanket around her like a cloak as she moved away from him, her steps wobbly.

He almost rose to help her but didn't trust himself to touch her again. If he dared move one muscle, he wouldn't be able to stop himself from making his fantasy come true.

You're not that irresistible, Antoinette.

A lie. Even when he'd said it, he'd known it was a lie. So he stayed right where he was, keeping himself absolutely still. She took a seat on the chair beside the fire, turning so her back was to him. And he sat there. Trembling with unsatisfied hunger.

Damn her, she actually made him *tremble*.

He couldn't take his eyes from her. The blanket now concealed her from neck to ankles, but it did nothing to lessen her attractiveness. If anything, she only looked more . . . vulnerable. Small and soft and vulnerable, with her hair all in tangles and her bare feet peeking out of the blanket. A fragile little brown-haired elf.

With a savage bruise on her side. He had felt like a mule kicked him in the gut when he saw that.

Lucas tore his gaze from her. *Why should her pain matter to him? He wanted her to suffer.*

Didn't he?

Yes, of course he did. She *deserved* to suffer for what she had done.

For God's sake, she had murdered his brother.

He glanced around desperately for something to take his attention from her. His gaze settled on a plate of fried chicken and peach pie that sat on a low table beside the chaise, left over from her supper. He grabbed a piece of chicken and bit into it.

"Are you . . . staying?" Antoinette asked warily, peeking at him over her shoulder.

"When I go," he said, trying to sound cold and remote, "the fire goes out, too."

She muttered something he couldn't quite catch. After a moment, she added, grudgingly, "Fine, then stay."

Lucas slouched back against the plush pillows on the chaise. He wasn't as worried about her setting the place on fire as he was about leaving her with a hearth full of firewood—since a log would make a mighty fine weapon if she ever took a notion to whack him over the head when his back was turned.

Yet he didn't want to deprive her of the fire's warmth.

Narrowing his eyes, he tossed the chicken bone back on the plate, not sure where this new habit of indulging her had come from.

He would only stay a little while. Everything would be fine, as long as he remained where he was and she remained over there. Antoinette picked up one corner of the blanket and used it to start drying her long, tangled curls.

Lucas picked up the pie.

"Rebecca didn't make that for you," she complained, not looking at him.

"I'm hungry," he growled.

Maybe she caught his true meaning; she didn't offer another peep of protest.

"And I don't have a regiment of women cooking daily feasts for me," he added, wolfing down the pie and reaching for another piece of chicken. "I've been making do with whatever old lady Kearney serves at the boardinghouse." He licked his fingers. "And Travis's coffee."

"Travis makes your coffee?"

"Almost the worst I've ever tasted."

She glanced at him over her shoulder. "You could make it yourself," she suggested dryly.

"My coffee *is* the worst I've ever tasted."

A hint of an amused smile curved her mouth before she turned back toward the hearth.

He had made her smile.

Lucas fought the small feeling of pleasure that curled through him. Forced his attention back to eating.

But he kept noticing the scent that clung to his hands. The scent of the herbal soap from the bathwater that had made her skin wet. It was fresh and sweet and tantalizing.

Thoroughly irritated with himself, he dropped the half-empty plate on the rug and rubbed his palms on the sides of the chaise, trying to get her off his hands, off his mind. Damn it, he wasn't going to do this anymore—let himself feel desire or concern or pity or *anything* for this woman. He would *not* betray his brother's memory.

Or make his brother's mistake.

James had been taken in by Antoinette's charms—and ended up with a bullet through his heart.

"I suppose none of this is new to you," he said bitterly.

She turned her head, looking at him over her shoulder again, her expression quizzical.

God, she was beautiful. He didn't think he had ever seen a woman quite that beautiful, with the firelight behind her making her hair shimmer and giving her cheeks a dusky glow . . .

"The food," he snapped. "You're probably used to daily feasts. And fancy accommodations." He flicked a hand at the various furnishings. "Velvet curtains, feather pillows, lots of leisure time. Spent on your back."

She lowered her gaze and didn't reply.

"You liked it, didn't you," he accused. "The clothes and the luxurious place to stay and the trips and the—"

"I like not being hungry."

That took him by surprise. Especially since her voice held no defensiveness—just that flash of steel he had noticed before.

"If you were hungry, Antoinette, there were other ways you could've made a living."

"Were there really?" Her head came up, those dark eyes flashing. "And who would hire the daughter of the town whore to work in their shop? Or to watch their children, or even clean the dirty floors of their house?"

He held her gaze, but couldn't think of an answer.

"And yes," she added, not flinching from his stare, "I liked the food, and the clothes, and having a place of my own. I never had anything like that before. Anything . . ." Her lashes lowered as she seemed to search for a word. "Nice."

Honesty was the last thing Lucas had expected from her. It surprised him even more than her grit. And stole the fire from his anger.

"James always took good care of me," she continued, more softly. "He protected me. Men in St. Charles used to stare at me and make comments, and some of them would . . . do more than make comments."

Lucas could easily imagine the type of men who would have come sniffing around her, making all sorts of lewd offers. Somehow it angered him.

"But after I became . . ." She turned, staring into the fire. "After it became known that I was McKenna's woman, they stopped. It was . . . at least a little respect. More than I had ever had before in St. Charles."

Respect?

Lucas looked away, raked a hand through his hair. That was what she had wanted? *Respect?* He had pictured Antoinette as a greedy, money-grabbing female strictly interested in her own profit.

But if he could believe what she was saying, that wasn't what she had sought from being his brother's mistress. McKenna's woman. *James* McKenna's woman.

A sudden image shot through Lucas's mind: James and Antoinette together. In bed. A fierce, unnerving emotion tore at him.

Jealousy.

Brutally, he forced himself to hang on to that image. To picture the two of them together. Burn it into his brain, so it would sear away all the thoughts and feelings

she stirred in him. "Tell me, Antoinette, what was it
like?" he bit out. "Did you see him every day, once a
week? How did it work?"

She regarded him with wide, shocked eyes.

"I want to know." He pierced her with a hard stare.
"Did you only entertain him at night? Did you slip into
his office during the day? Did you know about his family?
Did you care?"

"We . . . we didn't talk about our families. It was part
of our agreement."

"So you had an agreement. How cordial."

She turned toward the fire again, gathering the blanket more tightly around her. "I don't want to talk about
this."

"Well, I do. Tell me more. So you had an agreement—
but you *knew* he had a family, didn't you? You knew he
had children."

"I—I knew he had children, and three sisters. And a
brother who left home long before James and I . . . met."

"And how often were you with him? How much time
did you spend in my brother's bed?"

"I only saw him now and then, all right? Why does it
matter to you?"

Lucas folded his arms across his chest. Why *did* it
matter? This wasn't helping him at all. No matter how
he peppered her with harsh questions, no matter how he
tried to brand painful images on his mind, it didn't help.

Didn't change how much he wanted her in his own bed.

"Now and then," he echoed coldly. "Does that make
you any less a whore?"

That arrow-sharp barb found its mark, as he'd known
it would.

She turned to glare at him. "Apparently you've already made up your mind about that." Her dark eyes
glittered with anger. And hurt. "But maybe you'd explain

something to *me*, Marshal—how can you call me a whore and still hold your brother in such high regard? *James* knew he had a wife and family. James was the one who took vows and broke them."

Lucas looked away, regretting suddenly that he'd brought this subject up.

She persisted. "Why is it that a man can take a mistress and still be considered admirable, but the woman is considered dirt? By the very same people who admire him. Why is that?"

"It's a matter of right and wrong."

"And men are always right, no matter what they do, and women are wrong?"

"No—"

"That really is how you see the world, isn't it? Right and wrong. Saints and sinners. Well, James was no saint."

Lucas got to his feet. "I really don't want to hear any more of this."

"*He* was the one who came to me. I didn't go and knock on his door one day and say, 'Good morning, sir, I'd like to be your mistress.' He knew what he wanted—"

"Antoinette," he warned, "stop it—"

"And he didn't offer to put a roof over my head because he was starting some kind of charitable home. I was *seventeen* when he came to me. He was twenty-nine. Think about *that* while you're busy sorting people into neat rows of 'good' and 'bad'—"

A noise at the front of the hotel cut her off. The noise of the door banging open.

Lucas spun toward the sound, his hand on his Colt.

"Marshal?" It was Travis's voice, shouting. A second later, he came running into the sitting room. "Marshal McKenna, sir, we need your help!"

"*We* who?"

The kid grabbed the bars of the locked cell door. "There's a ruckus over at Fairfax's Saloon—"

"I didn't sign on to be the town marshal, kid." Lucas shook his head and let go of his gun. A lawman could get shot real easy breaking up a saloon brawl. "It's none of my business—"

"But it's *Valentina,* sir—Miss Lazarillo! There's drifters givin' her an awful time and her pa's down in Leadville and— Please, you've got to help!" The boy shook the cell door, his expression frantic. *"Please!"*

Women.

Difficult, feather-witted bundles of trouble. The world would probably be a saner place without them. His *life* would definitely be saner without them, Lucas thought with a grimace, standing in the darkness next to the front window of Fairfax's Saloon and Gambling Emporium.

His Colt drawn and cocked, he kept to the shadows as he edged closer to the window, his back pressed against the rough pine boards of the wall. It had finally stopped raining, but the clouds overhead blotted out the moon; he should be nearly invisible, especially in his dark clothes. The streets were deserted, the night air cold. He could see his breath as he peered through a corner of the glass to assess the situation.

By the light of oil lanterns hung from the saloon's ceiling, he counted three gunmen and nine townsfolk inside—with two others stretched out unconscious on the floor. Tables had been overturned, chairs were scattered. What the hell Miss Lazarillo was doing in there, he didn't know, but one swarthy-looking hombre had her cornered against the bar. She was struggling against his hold, crying.

Another man—a tall, heavily built half-breed with

waist-length black hair and a nasty sneer—was waving a twelve-gauge shotgun at Fairfax and the saloon's patrons, herding the prospectors and homesteaders to one side of the room with their hands raised. A third accomplice Lucas could only see from the back—but he appeared as big as the half-breed, and he had some poor idiot pinned to one of the tables, a pistol at his head.

"Oh, great," Lucas hissed under his breath as he recognized the poor idiot. It was Holt. "Just great."

There was a lot of shouting going on. It seemed like the drifters intended to relieve the locals of their valuables. Lucas had run into their kind before: two-bit thieves with more firepower than smarts, trying to steal from folks who barely had fifty dollars between them. Best thing would be to disarm the thugs, run them off, and make them some other lawman's headache—someone with a jail.

Lucas shifted his attention back to the girl. It looked like he'd better move fast. The swarthy drifter was heading for the rear exit, dragging her with him—and he clearly didn't have robbery on his mind.

Lucas turned and ducked around the corner of the saloon, slipping into the alley between buildings, running for the back.

He heard her scream. Blocked it out. Didn't allow anything to penetrate the icy cool descending over him, flooding through his veins. When he reached the corner of the building, he darted a look around it.

In the darkness, he could just make out the silhouettes of three horses that had been left behind the saloon.

And the fact that the scum now had Miss Lazarillo pressed up against the wall. She wasn't screaming anymore. Like her mouth had been covered.

There was no time to waste. Lucas holstered his pistol

and moved forward with quick, silent steps. The hombre was so intent on satisfying his lust, he never realized he was no longer alone.

"Excuse me, friend," Lucas said softly as he came up behind him.

The drifter whirled, eyes wide with surprise.

Lucas hit him with a quick left hook. His fist smashed into the man's jaw. The drifter staggered sideways and the girl broke free, sobbing, falling in the mud. Lucas struck again, with a kick to the groin that knocked the man off his feet. Even as he went down, groaning, Lucas grabbed his arm, forcing him onto his stomach and landing on top of him, one knee in the middle of his back.

"Kidnapping and rape is no way to treat a lady," Lucas snarled as he jammed the drifter's arm up behind him, twisting it at a sharp angle. A strangled sound came from the man's throat. His breath reeked of liquor. Lucas searched him quickly, confiscating a Smith & Wesson, which he slipped into the waistband of his own trousers.

And a bowie knife, which he unsheathed and pressed against the drifter's throat.

"Nice knife," Lucas said coolly, drawing a bead of blood with the point of the blade. "Now then, I'm willing to consider this a moment of drunken stupidity, but I'd advise you to change your ways. I'd also advise you to leave town. Lets you and I not meet up again. Nod if you agree."

The man nodded, very carefully.

"Good. In fact, I think it'd be best if you left the state. Tonight. I hear Utah's nice. Nod if you agree."

The man nodded again. Very carefully.

"Glad you see things my way. Now get out of here. Real quiet like."

As soon as Lucas released him, the drifter scrambled to his feet and limped over to his horse, grabbing the reins. When he glanced back over his shoulder, Lucas drew his Colt.

The hombre jumped into the saddle with an exclamation of pain and kicked his horse into a gallop. Lucas kept his pistol trained on him until he rode out of sight.

Then he turned to the girl. "You all right, Miss Lazarillo?"

"Oh, *s-señor* . . ." she sobbed brokenly, still crumpled in the mud, holding up her torn dress. "H-He was going to, he w-was going to—"

"It's all right now." Lucas walked over and helped her to her feet. "You go on home—"

"But . . . But my friend is still in there!" She looked toward the saloon's back door.

Lucas groaned inwardly. *Women.* "What were you and your— Never mind. You get out of here."

"But my friend, Lily—"

"Get out of here," Lucas ordered more sternly. "Go on over to the jail. Travis is there. I'll take care of Lily."

"Thank you, *señor*, thank you." She looked up at him, her eyes filled with gratitude, and with tears that glimmered in the darkness. "Y-you saved me. I will never forget this, *señor*. Never!"

She went running off in the direction of the jail. As soon as she was safely away, Lucas stalked over to the two remaining horses and confiscated every weapon he found on their saddles and in their saddlebags.

Then he headed back around toward the front of the saloon, his jaw clenched.

Sometimes a direct approach was best.

Concealed in the darkness, he walked to the line of horses at the hitching post out front. After setting the weapons at their feet, he grabbed a canvas rain slicker tied behind one of the saddles and pulled it on. Then he unloaded the various guns and left them in the mud— except for his own .45 and a short, double-barreled shotgun.

He concealed both beneath the slicker, the .45 against his belly and the shotgun down his back. Then he affected his best drunken swagger, started whistling off-key.

And stumbled right in through the saloon's swinging doors.

"Fairfax," he called in an inebriated yowl, "gimme a glass o' your finest tonsil varnish . . ." He staggered to a halt a few feet inside the doors, lifting his eyebrows as he glanced around. "Well, I'll be a poisoned pup, whatta we have here?"

Fairfax recognized him immediately, as did a few of the others, but Lucas tried to tell them with his eyes not to say anything as he looked around.

He didn't see another girl anywhere. The only person in any immediate danger was Holt, damn him; he was stilled pinned with a gun to his head.

"Come on in, cowpoke," the half-breed ordered, while the prospectors and homesteaders at the business end of his shotgun emptied their pockets. "But first get your hands up and hand over any guns and money you got."

Lucas pasted a terrified look on his face and raised his hands, still swaying drunkenly. "Ain't got no cash money. And ain't got no guns. Don't like violence. Hate violence." He staggered backward, away from the half-breed.

Toward the table where the other drifter—a tough-looking bastard with a scarred face and missing teeth— held the doctor hostage.

"Stop right there," the toothless one snarled.

"Ya mean right"—Lucas took one more stumbling,

backward step—"here?" He whirled, drawing both his weapons at once, aiming the shotgun at the half-breed and pressing the barrel of his Peacemaker under the other drifter's jaw, forcing his head up.

"Shit," the toothless one said.

"Exactly." Lucas thumbed back the hammer on his .45.

The drifter's eyes just about bugged out of his head. But he didn't remove his Remington from Holt's temple.

"Like I said, I hate violence," Lucas said lightly. "So let me explain this to you. I don't much care if you shoot this son of a bitch or not." He nodded to the prone doctor, who had a bruised face and a split lip. "But if you pull that trigger, then I'll have to pull this one. Just sort of on principle. And poor Fairfax here'll be cleaning brains off his floor for days."

Nobody moved a muscle.

"You," Lucas shouted, flicking a look at the half-breed. "You give a damn about your friend here, I'd put that shotgun down and start giving these folks back their valuables."

The half-breed hesitated, glancing from Lucas to the sack in his hands.

"Do it!" the toothless one shouted.

Swearing, the half-breed put his weapon on the nearest table.

"Fairfax, do me a favor," Lucas asked calmly, "and pick that up."

Fairfax obliged while the other men started digging coins and cash and watches and weapons out of the sack. Two of them pushed the half-breed up against the bar.

"Now then," Lucas said reasonably to Toothless, who still hadn't released his hostage. "I know Doc Holt here can make you feel madder than a rattlesnake on a hot skillet. Frankly, I can understand how you came to have him pinned like that. But the town's only got one doctor. And unfortunately, he's it. So put down the pistol and let him go." He forced the drifter's chin up another notch with the barrel of his gun. "I'm a Federal Marshal, by the way. Did I forget to mention that?"

The man's eyes widened and his Adam's apple bobbed up and down. "We was told there weren't no law in this town—"

"Looks like you were told wrong, doesn't it?"

"I ain't goin' to jail!"

"Well, that's just fine, because my jail doesn't have a vacancy at the moment."

Sweat trickled down the man's scarred face. "You kill me, I ain't dyin' alone!"

"I think we can find a more peaceable solution than that. I'm kind of fond of peaceable solutions at times like this." With the shotgun, Lucas gestured toward the saloon's rear exit. "I was thinking maybe you two could join your friend who went out back. He's on his way to Utah Territory. Should be nearing the border about now."

The drifter still hesitated, clearly having a hard time weighing the value of his miserable life against walking out of here empty-handed.

But finally, carefully, he put the gun on the table.

"Good. Now back away," Lucas said. "You gonna get up anytime soon, Doc?"

"Thanks," Holt bit out, rolling off the table with a curse.

Toothless backed up, his hands raised.

Then without warning the drifter darted sideways and lunged for his pistol. Lucas moved to block him and Toothless threw a hard left that hit him in the belly, grabbing the Colt. Lucas's pistol and shotgun both went off with a deafening roar, the shotgun blowing a hole in the wall, the Colt shattering one of the lanterns overhead. On the other side of the saloon, the half-breed tried to make a break for it.

Within seconds, the room became a free-for-all of flying fists, shouts, gunfire, and thrown glasses. Lucas and Holt pummeled Toothless to the floor, but the man was slippery as a snake. The heel of his boot struck Lucas in the jaw. Lucas grunted in pain, seeing stars for a second.

Holt managed to wrestle the .45 away from the man, who then grabbed a bottle and smashed it, swinging it at both of them. Holt rolled out of the way and the jagged edge sliced through Lucas's rain slicker and his shirt and shoulder. With a vicious curse, Lucas threw a punch that connected with someone—either the drifter or the doctor. Either would be satisfying at the moment.

When the dust finally settled, Toothless and the half-breed were bleeding and running for their lives, leaving their guns and even their hats behind as they fled through the rear exit.

Lucas stumbled to his feet, gingerly holding his bruised jaw as he scooped up his .45. "I only want to know one thing."

"And what is that?" Fairfax asked mournfully, standing in front of the bar and surveying the wreckage of his saloon.

"Where in the *hell* is a girl by the name of Lily?" Lucas took off the rain slicker and threw it on a chair.

Some of the men laughed, the sound breaking the tension. They started helping Fairfax clean up the mess, righting tables and chairs and picking up broken glass.

"Allow me the honor of introducing Miss Lily Breckenridge," an expensively dressed young man said in the smooth accent of the old Southern aristocracy. He walked over and knelt beside one of the two unconscious figures stretched out on the floor, while Holt tended to the other one.

The Southern gentleman grabbed a half-empty glass of bourbon off a nearby table and splashed the dusty face of what appeared to be a boy of about eighteen.

Lucas blinked in astonishment as the person in question sat up—looking dazed and groggy, spitting curses, and wiping at eyes that were fringed with long lashes. Clad in indigo trousers, boots, and a baggy wool shirt—all covered in dried mud—she didn't look like a Lily. She didn't even look like a *she*.

"I thought that was a prospector," Lucas said, shocked to find a young *girl* of about eighteen hidden beneath the layers of dirt and denim.

"I *am* a prospector," she declared, frowning in his direction, taking off her hat. Two long blond pigtails fell to her shoulders. "I just don't happen to be a man."

"Yes, our Miss Lily is a lady," the aristocrat kneeling beside her said with a broad grin, tugging at one of her pigtails. "No man in Eminence dares say any different—if he wants to avoid a black eye."

Miss Breckenridge gave him a dirty look. "I didn't see *you* rushing to Val's rescue, Morgan O'Donnell. You're a drunk and a coward and—" As she dabbed at the blood on her lip with slender fingers, the girl's gray eyes suddenly filled with alarm. "Where *is* Val? They didn't—"

"She's fine. In better shape than I am," Lucas assured her, walking over to accept a freshly poured whiskey that Fairfax held out toward him. He gingerly rested the cool glass against his jaw, wincing. "She's over at the jail, being consoled by Travis."

"Jail?" Miss Breckenridge regarded him blankly. "What jail?"

"Old man Dunlap's hotel," Holt explained as he stood up, helping his patient to his feet. "It's a long story."

The girl prospector didn't wait to hear it. She picked

up her hat and stood up, frowning as she looked around on the floor. "Did that bastard make off with my bowie knife?"

"I, uh, think you'll find your knife out front in the mud, miss," Lucas told her.

She hurried out, the spurs on her boots ringing with every step.

Lucas shook his head as he watched her go.

"Miss Lily grew up with a pickax in her hand." The Southern aristocrat stepped behind the bar and helped himself to a fresh bottle of bourbon, rubbing at a spot of blood on his brocade vest. "She just got in from her diggings tonight. Refuses to quit working her daddy's claim."

"Valentina came here to visit Lily," Holt explained as he walked over to accept a glass of whiskey from Fairfax, "and then the drifters showed up—"

"And you tried to save the womenfolk," Lucas asked dubiously, "without a gun?"

Holt glowered at him. "Anything broken on you?"

"No permanent damage." Lucas glanced down at the cut on his shoulder. It hurt like hell and it was bleeding, but it would heal. He looked at the Southerner on the other side of the bar; he had only one mark on him, and it was an old scar along his left cheek. "I notice you don't seem to have a scratch."

"I am blessed with excellent instincts for self-preservation. Morgan O'Donnell," the young man said in that elegant drawl, extending his hand. He had blond hair, a darker mustache, and a strong grip that belied the slight glassiness in his blue eyes. "I am the Gambling Emporium half of Fairfax's Saloon and Gambling Emporium. I'm the town's most skilled purveyor of poker and blackjack." He winked. "Helped by the fact that I am currently the town's *only* purveyor of poker and blackjack. And you would be a fellow Irishman, I believe—McKenna is Irish, isn't it, Marshal?"

"Yeah. Few generations back."

"Then here's to a braver man than I and a brother of the Auld Sod." O'Donnell lifted his glass in salute and drained it. "It seems Fairfax and I owe you our thanks." His grin flashed again, revealing dimples beside his mustache. "We've not had a decent fight in here in months."

"Glad I could oblige," Lucas said sourly.

Actually, it *had* felt good, he had to admit. Though his knuckles were bruised, his jaw ached, and his shoulder stung, he had needed *some* kind of physical release tonight. The brawl had filled the bill nicely. "Though if I'd known *you* were on the job," he said dryly, glancing sideways at Holt, "I might not have come. You ever think about carrying a gun in a town like this, Doc?"

"Haven't carried one since I was mustered out."

Lucas turned to face him, mildly surprised. "So you were in the war. Surgeon?" That couldn't be; he guessed Holt to be in his early thirties—which meant he couldn't have been more than twenty when the war ended.

The doctor held his gaze for a long moment before he replied. "Sharpshooter," he said evenly.

Lucas regarded him with disbelief. The sharpshooters had been the North's elite corps of marksmen. They had served as specially trained advance scouts—snipers who picked off Rebel officers from a distance. "And now you refuse to carry a gun?"

"Decided I'd rather be in the business of saving lives than taking them." Holt looked away and changed the subject. "Speaking of which, how's Annie today?"

"Your favorite patient is just fine," Lucas said coolly.

"Still healing up well?"

"Yeah." Lucas downed his whiskey in one gulp.

"Good to know. Wouldn't mind stopping by again tomorrow."

"Any time, Doc." Lucas's aching fingers curled into a fist. "Though Antoinette seems to think it's a good idea to keep us two apart as much as possible."

"Can't imagine why," Holt said, his gaze fastening on Lucas's.

"Can't imagine," Lucas retorted, putting his glass down on the bar a bit harder than necessary.

"Gentlemen." Fairfax came between them, perhaps fearing more damage to his saloon. He plunked down a bottle of expensive whiskey and a box of cigars in front of Lucas. "On the house, Marshal."

O'Donnell gave Fairfax a wounded look before shifting his attention to Lucas. "I *knew* this Brit partner of mine was hiding another bottle of O'Neil somewhere. What do you say, Marshal?" He whipped out a deck of cards from the pocket of his vest, fanning them out and folding them up in a nimble, one-handed maneuver. "How about we break open that bottle of lovely liquid gold, play poker 'til dawn, and sing a few Irish ballads? I know every verse to 'Oh, Danny Boy.' " He winked. "Including a few my da taught me that my ma never knew about, God rest their souls."

Lucas shook his head, one corner of his mouth curving upward. "No thanks." The scent of cigars was tempting, and he hadn't tasted five-dollars-a-glass whiskey in years. But he wasn't here to play games. Or make friends. He needed to get back to his prisoner. "Can't stick around."

"Marshal." Fairfax nudged the gifts toward him. "We are in desperate need of a man of your skills in Eminence, and the town council's offer of a job stands. After tonight, I'm certain I could persuade Hazelgreen and Gottfried to vote for a larger salary. You're worth ninety a week. A hundred—"

"Sorry, Fairfax. Not interested. This was a one-time-only exception. And there's no charge." Lucas handed back his empty glass, and waved away the bottle and the cigars. "Sorry about the hole in the wall," he said as he turned to leave. "Oh, and there's a few pieces of iron out by your hitching post you might want to gather up before morning. Might scare customers away." He headed toward the swinging doors. "Good night, gents."

"McKenna?"

It was Holt's voice. Lucas swung around, bracing himself to be grilled further about Antoinette. "Yeah?"

The doctor nodded toward the table where he had been pinned. "Thanks."

Holt said it with genuine gratitude . . . even though it looked like he was saying it through clenched teeth.

Lucas arched one eyebrow. This night had been full of surprises. "Forget it, Doc. Believe it or not," he said as he pushed open one of the swinging doors, "you're not the only one in the business of saving lives."

The fire still burned brightly on Annie's hearth when she heard the hotel's front door open. She sat up straighter on the bed, her bandaged ribs throbbing at the sudden movement, her heart skipping a beat.

Then she heard those familiar footsteps. And Lucas's voice.

And she released a breath she hadn't realized she'd been holding. As she sank back against the pillows, wincing at the pain, she frowned. The feeling rushing through her was *not* relief, she told herself adamantly.

Lucas McKenna was her jailer. A man who wanted her sent to prison for the rest of her life. A man who hated her. All the awful things he'd said to her tonight had made that abundantly clear. He considered her a whore and a heartless murderer, and he would never forgive her for either one.

She didn't *care* what he thought of her. Didn't care what happened to him.

Shouldn't care that she had heard gunfire coming from the direction of Fairfax's saloon.

But the sound had almost made her heart stop.

Her frown deepened. It was the *townsfolk* she'd been concerned about. And Daniel; Valentina had explained to Annie and Travis about the drifters, and how the doctor had tried to save her. Then Valentina's friend Lily Breckenridge had related a few more details when she arrived a while later—though the introductions had been awkward through the cell door, with Annie sitting there handcuffed to the bed, wrapped only in a blanket.

When Lucas had left in such a hurry, she hadn't had the chance to put on any clothes. He had just scooped her up blanket and all, put her on the bed, and handcuffed her before he rushed out, ordering Travis to stay behind with her.

At the moment, she could hear him talking to Travis, who sounded like he was falling all over himself thanking Lucas. Valentina and her friend had already left. After a few minutes, Lucas apparently managed to extricate himself from the boy and escort him out the hotel's front door. Which he closed firmly.

Annie heard a weary sigh as Lucas walked toward their suite. A moment later, he appeared in the sitting room, carrying a lantern.

She could make out blood on his shoulder, on his clothes. And a dark bruise on his jaw. "Are you all right?" she gasped, the question spilling out before she even finished the thought.

"Fit as a fiddle," he said sarcastically as he unlocked her door and came inside.

He didn't look fit; he looked terrible, bruised and bleeding, his shirt ripped, his trousers covered with dirt and splatters of mud. "I—I heard gunshots."

He set the lantern on a table. "Were you worried about me, Antoinette?" he asked dubiously, arching one black brow.

"No." She scowled at him. "I was . . . I was . . ." She couldn't figure out *what* she was feeling. "I was worried about Valentina."

"The gunshots came after Valentina was already over here, safe." He observed her with a curious expression. "And if I had gotten myself killed tonight, you'd be free right now. Don't tell me you didn't think of that."

Annie stared at him, blinking in surprise. Though he would never believe it, she *hadn't* thought of that. It hadn't crossed her mind for a second. She hadn't been thinking about herself, or escape.

The truth was, from the moment he ran out of this hotel with his gun drawn until the moment he came back just now, she'd had only one thought.

Him.

A fluttery, ticklish sensation filled her stomach as she admitted that to herself.

He walked toward her, digging the key to the handcuffs out of his pocket, and she lowered her gaze. "Valentina told me what you did," she said quietly, "how you saved her from that brute who was going to . . ." She looked up at him from beneath her lashes. "It was good of you to help when they needed you."

He shrugged his uninjured shoulder. "No more than any lawman would've done."

He was being modest again. As he leaned down to unfasten the manacles, she studied his bruised, rugged profile. Lucas had to be the most baffling man she'd ever met. He was famous in the West, practically a legend, yet he wasn't arrogant about his reputation or his skills.

He was a loner, yet he stood ready to help when someone needed him.

Even her. He had even helped her tonight when he didn't have to.

It didn't make sense. *He* didn't make sense.

But she realized that what the newspapers and penny dreadfuls reported about him was true, at least part of it: Marshal Lucas McKenna really *was* a hero, no question about it. He had risked his life tonight, to save people he barely knew.

As he dropped the manacles on the floor and straightened, their eyes met and held for a moment. Annie was startled by the feeling she saw swirling in his gaze. It wasn't anger, or hatred, but something she hadn't seen before, couldn't name.

And it lasted only an instant. "Dr. Holt sends his regards." His voice was cool, even.

Confused, Annie glanced at the jagged cut on his shoulder. "He didn't *do* that—"

"No." Lucas's mouth curved, as if in amusement. "He was a bystander. Mostly."

"Is he all right?"

He slid the key back into his pocket, turning away. "Your precious doctor is just fine."

"Why do you keep calling him that? Daniel is my friend. He's like a brother to me." When Lucas glanced back at her, she nodded toward the jagged cut. "How *did* that happen?"

"Broken bottle." He turned to leave, picking up the lantern. "It's nothing."

"It could be something if it gets infected. You should at least look after it. Take the bandages." Annie slid off the side of the bed nearest the chaise, realizing a bit be-latedly that she had to keep the blanket wrapped around her; she was still wearing only her camisole and pan-talettes underneath.

She grabbed the roll of bandages off the chaise and turned to toss it to him—only to find that he had come around the foot of the bed to meet her. She bumped right into him. The bandages tumbled from her hand, unravel-ing across the floor. He caught her elbow to steady her.

And both of them froze. The lantern swung in his other hand, making light and shadows dance around them. She could feel heat radiating from his body. Caught the faint scent of whiskey on his breath. Saw the gold-flecked, green depths of his eyes turn dark. The fluttery, ticklish sensation returned to her stomach.

And suddenly he drew her closer and lowered his head and kissed her.

Annie made a startled little sound in the back of her throat as his mouth covered hers. He let go of her elbow, his hand shifting to the nape of her neck. She grabbed his arms, her fingers closing around the taut, corded muscles beneath the rough wool of his shirt. And she wasn't sure if she meant to push him away or keep her-self from falling.

But she was already falling, tumbling into a bottom-less pool of heat and hunger as his lips moved over hers. He tasted of whiskey, fiery and intoxicating. Her heart was beating strangely. It was a startling kiss.

That became a deep, slow, bone-melting kiss.

He angled his head and molded his mouth to hers, his fingers tangling in her hair. The lantern hit the floor with a thump and she wasn't sure if he had set it down or dropped it. The sound in her throat became a soft moan. Her knees went weak. She no longer had the strength to stand, leaned into him, her breasts pillowed against the hard muscles of his chest. He groaned, deepening the kiss, his bearded jaw abrading her skin. She could feel his heart pounding against hers.

His other hand found her waist, drew her in tight against him.

And she felt exactly how much he wanted her.

A shudder went through her. A splinter of panic. *What was she doing?* "Lucas, *no.*"

He went still. She could feel his harsh breathing. Heard him curse. He pulled away from her, the flimsy cotton of her camisole clinging to his skin.

The blanket had fallen to her ankles and she had never even noticed. He stood staring at her for a second, his eyes almost black, a muscle working in his jaw. Then he let her go, turning away and grabbing the lantern as he stalked out.

He slammed the door to her cell and locked it. She heard him throw the key across his room. Heard it hit and shatter something made of glass. He turned his lantern down. All the way.

And vanished in the darkness.

9

"Why *is* that man in such an ornery mood?"

The sound of the disgruntled feminine voice made Annie look up from her chair beside the window, where she had been watching snowflakes float downward through the afternoon sunlight. After more than a week of clear, crisp autumn weather, a drizzle of rain that morning had turned into the first snowfall of the season.

"Rebecca!" Annie smiled with relief and rushed to the door of her cell as her friend entered the sitting room, carrying a wicker hamper. For most of the past week, Katja and Mrs. Owens had taken turns bringing her meals, since Rebecca had been indisposed. "I'm so glad to see you. Are you feeling better?"

"Yes, lamb. It was just another of my spells. I ain't the youngest filly in the herd anymore, you know." Rebecca set the basket down and brushed melting snowflakes from her woolen cape, which was a rich cardinal red, and untied the satin ribbons of her enormous purple bonnet. "Stage arrived this afternoon, so I thought I'd come over early and bring the marshal's mail. But did that man thank me for saving him the trouble of coming to the store? No, he did not. Stormed out of here without even lettin' me in your room."

As Rebecca turned to set her coat and hat on a chair, Annie's smile faded. She lowered her gaze to the scuffed toes of her patent-leather shoes.

Annie had no doubt that *she* was the source of Lucas's awful temper the past week, after the way she had surrendered to his kiss, his touch, the feel of his body against hers—and then rebuffed him a moment later. She had only confirmed exactly what he thought of her: that she was a temptress, a tease.

Her mother's daughter.

And it had made him hate her all the more.

"That cantankerous varmint." Rebecca glanced from the basket to the locked cell door, her cheeks pink from the frosty weather outside, her blue eyes full of sparks as she complained. "How am I supposed to serve you your supper?"

Annie shook her head. "You'll have to pass the food through the bars, I suppose."

"Hmph. I wonder what was in his mail." Rebecca bent down and lifted the basket's lid. "Wasn't but two letters, and he barely opened them 'afore he snapped at Travis and went out the door, looking riled up enough to eat the Devil with his horns on."

"Oh?" Annie asked mildly.

"But then, I heard tell he's been in an awful temper all week." Rebecca started handing items through the bars: a white tablecloth and a napkin and some silverware. "Here I'd been thinkin' maybe I had him wrong, after Daniel and Valentina told what he did over at Fairfax's last week—though I still ain't forgiven him for sneaking into my place and taking things from your room." She sighed dramatically. "One minute he's actin' like a thief and a scalawag, and the next he turns into a . . ."

"Hero," Annie suggested softly.

"Never did meet a lawman like him." Rebecca passed an empty china plate sideways through the bars. "It's near impossible to figure him out."

"Yes," Annie agreed, her voice so quiet it was almost lost beneath the crackling of the fire on her hearth.

Rebecca paused, still holding on to the plate; she squinted at Annie's hands, then looked up at her face. "By the horn spoons, I just realized you're runnin' around loose in there! He didn't handcuff you 'afore he left."

"No," Annie said lightly, not looking up as she took the plate.

Lucas hadn't entered her cell once all week. He hadn't handcuffed her when he went out, hadn't touched her.

Hadn't come near her.

"Ain't that a mite odd?"

"Um-hm." Annie turned away to carry the items to the table beside her bed.

But not before she caught Rebecca looking at her with wide, interested eyes.

"Annie Sutton," her friend said in a curious tone, "you know something you're not telling."

Annie shook her head, trying to look as if she had no idea what might account for the change in Lucas's behavior. She took a bit longer than necessary to set the table, smoothing out the tablecloth, arranging the napkin and plate and silverware . . . because she felt her cheeks warm, and feared the blush would give her away.

Reveal her shame.

She hadn't told any of her friends about Lucas's impulsive kiss. In fact, she had been trying very hard not to think about it or him or that night. She was too mortified by the way she had given in to the heated joining of their mouths.

On the morning after, she had counted herself lucky

that Valentina was the one who'd brought her breakfast; the sweet-natured girl hadn't noticed the reddened, irritated skin along Annie's jaw—or at least hadn't guessed what it meant. Fortunately, Valentina had been too busy thanking Lucas for saving her the night before.

If Annie's visitor that morning had been Rebecca, or Katja or Mrs. Owens, she wasn't sure how she would've explained the fact that she had obviously been the recipient of a passionate kiss.

"So?" Rebecca prompted impatiently. "Why do you think he didn't handcuff you? I can't believe he forgot, even if he *is* in a ripsnorter of a temper. He ain't gettin' careless, is he?" she asked hopefully. "He ain't goin' soft?"

"No." Annie fidgeted nervously with a corner of the napkin. *Soft* was the last word she would use to describe Lucas; the idea was almost enough to make her laugh.

Almost.

"Annie?" Rebecca sounded concerned now.

Annie forced a smile, turning and walking back over to her cell door. "He . . . um . . . he lost the key to the handcuffs, I think."

"Lost the key?"

"Well, he threw his keys across his room one night—"

"What? What made him jo-fired angry enough to do that?"

"—and he looked for them the next morning. He found the one to the door but I don't think he found the one to the handcuffs, so it must've fallen through a crack in the floorboards or something," Annie finished without taking a breath.

In truth, he had only thrown the key to her *door*, and found it again the next morning. But she had to make up some kind of explanation.

"You mean that key might be lying around here

somewheres?" Rebecca asked excitedly. She started pacing Lucas's room, peering at the floorboards.

"Rebecca . . ."

"Land sakes, even if the critter lost the key to the handcuffs, he still could've let me into your room before he went out," Rebecca muttered. "Somebody's got to tend to your ribs."

Annie lowered her lashes, feeling her blush deepen as she remembered, vividly, the night that Lucas tended her injuries. Telling Rebecca half-truths made her feel awful, but how could she tell her friend what had really happened?

The day Annie had left St. Charles behind, she had vowed that her life would be different. That *she* would be different. That never again would she allow herself to become a man's plaything—or a man's *anything*. She didn't trust men, didn't want one in her life.

Didn't want or need a man's touch, or his strength or his care or his kisses.

For one irrational moment last week, she had forgotten all that.

Lucas McKenna, who always seemed determined to remind her that she was nothing . . . had made her forget everything.

"Rebecca, I don't think you'll find it," she said at last. "And really, it's not necessary anymore, since he hasn't used the handcuffs. And my ribs are hardly bothering me at all today. In fact, I . . ." She glanced at the open door between the sitting room and the hotel's main room, where she could hear Travis's harmonica.

She lowered her voice. "I started thinking yesterday that I'm healed up enough to travel. Especially since the marshal has started making plans to leave for Missouri— buying supplies, checking the train schedules out of

Denver." She gestured to some torn newspaper pages tacked to his wall.

"Tarnation." Rebecca walked over to peer at them. "Ain't it just like that man to lose the key we *don't* need and keep the one we *do* need. Right when we need it."

"Are we still hoping to get copies of the keys?" Annie whispered.

"Lessin' you want me to take a sledgehammer to this here door." Rebecca frowned at the cell's sturdy lock.

"No, but I thought maybe . . ." She glanced at her windows, looking out through the iron bars at the softly falling snow. "Rebecca, I heard footsteps outside my window last week. And again two nights ago." She shivered with a sudden chill, despite the woolen dress she wore. The sound in the night had woken her up when she heard it this time—and scared her so badly, she had nearly called out to Lucas. "Katja and the others said they didn't know anything about it, but I thought maybe it was you, planning something?"

Rebecca shook her head. "I been laid up all week." She came back over to the cell door, her brow furrowed. "Did you mention this to the marshal?"

"No, but . . . but I guess I will."

Rebecca bent down and started taking Annie's supper out of the basket. "Well, if you're fit to travel and that varmint's lookin' at train schedules, we best do something about this here door, and right quick." She handed the foods through the bars—a pewter mugful of corn chowder, a sandwich of cold sliced turkey, and a dish of lemon cookies. "You eat up. I'll go to Daniel's place and see if he's back from birthin' Mrs. Hall's baby. Maybe he's found us a skeleton key or a good thief, and we can get you out of here."

Rebecca turned and grabbed her cloak and bonnet,

then hurried out, leaving the basket. With a sigh, Annie carried the foods over to the table, though she wasn't very hungry. She hadn't had much of an appetite the last two days, she had been so busy worrying about Lucas's plans to leave for Missouri, and wondering about the midnight prowler.

And trying not to think about that kiss.

She was setting the foods down when she heard the hotel's front door open again.

Annie turned with a puzzled frown. Had Rebecca come back?

From the sound of the heavy footsteps, it clearly wasn't her friend. And it wasn't Lucas. She heard Travis's harmonica cut out in the middle of a note. Heard him say something.

But whoever it was didn't reply. There was only silence.

Then the sound of something heavy hitting the floor.

"Travis?" Annie rushed to the door of her cell, grabbing the bars, a cold tingle going down her back.

The footsteps came toward the sitting room. A man appeared in the open doorway.

Annie froze, her eyes widening. "Who are you?"

Lucas had left the town behind before he even realized it, had stalked past the end of the board sidewalk and kept going, blindly, his blood hot with fury, his hand clenched into a fist around the two letters.

He'd passed townspeople bustling along the street, standing in front of the general store, collecting their mail and visiting shops. Some of them had greeted him but he hadn't even looked at them. Snowflakes swirled around him but he barely felt the cold, though he had left without his coat or hat or gloves.

He just kept walking, unable to think, unable to feel anything but rage. Gut-churning, helpless rage.

Thompson and Reynolds were dead.

The road narrowed to a steep trail winding down the mountainside before Lucas finally stopped. Realized he was going nowhere and couldn't do anything and stopped. His fingers tightened around the letters, crushing the pages. He wanted to smash his fist into the nearest rock. Wanted to shout his fury into the wind. Knew the mountain's echoes would only throw it back in his face, over and over.

Seth Thompson, the best of his deputies for more than three years, levelheaded and experienced and cool under fire. He had a wife and two boys.

And Henry Reynolds, the youngest, such a skilled rider that they always kidded he should go work for one of the new wild west shows and make some real money.

Dead. Both dead. Shot up by the Risco gang down in Las Cruces.

The letter from his men reported that they had captured one of the gang and killed two more during the gunfight—but Jasper and Willie Risco had escaped and were still on the run, racing for the Rio Grande and safety in Mexico.

Lucas stared up through the falling snow, into the dim afternoon sun, and realized only now that he had been walking south, without even thinking. His every instinct urged him to go after them.

But he couldn't go. He had to stay here.

With *her*.

He dropped his gaze, glaring at the other letter crumpled in his fist, the first one he'd opened—from an orphanage in Denver.

Yes indeed, the headmaster wrote, they had received

a large, anonymous donation two months ago: almost fifteen thousand dollars. If Lucas knew the donor's name, the children would like to thank their kind benefactor . . .

Lucas crushed the letter into a ball and flung it away. Like he wanted to push her away. From him, from his life. *She* was the one locked in a jail cell and *he* felt trapped. He wanted to get out of here. Get back to his duty. His work. While he still had some shred of sanity left.

Because that seemed to be slipping through his fingers more and more with each day he spent in her company.

With a curse, he tore the other letter in half, then in half again, and let the pieces fall to the ground. *Why had he kissed her?* He'd had no business kissing her. Didn't know why the hell he had given in to the impulsive desire to pull her to him and thread his fingers through her hair and feel the warmth of her mouth beneath his.

He was *not* impulsive. Hadn't done anything rash in years—hell, since he'd been a kid.

No, not true. He'd even been steady and sensible as a kid. He hadn't done anything rash in his whole *life*.

Lucas paced, raking a hand through his snow-dampened hair. He had kept his distance from her, kept his hands off her, but that wasn't helping. Even making plans for their return to Missouri wasn't helping. Not enough. It didn't stop him from wanting.

And thinking.

Thinking he might've been wrong about her.

He glared at the crumpled letter from Denver that lay in the snow a few yards away. *How much more evidence did he need?* She wasn't some greedy female who only cared about money. She hadn't given a damn about the money. Had given it to orphans. Orphans, for God's sake.

And in some part of his brain, he was beginning to suspect that maybe, just maybe, what had held his brother's interest for three years hadn't been Antoinette's beauty or any bedroom tricks she'd learned from her mama . . . but a tender heart, like her friends kept insisting she had.

His stomach clenched as he considered that possibility even for a moment. If Antoinette was capable of tenderness and caring, if she had told the truth about her baby, and about the money . . .

What else might she be telling the truth about?

I didn't mean to do it, Marshal. It was an accident . . .

Lucas stopped pacing, ground the heels of both palms into his eyes. *No.* God, no. It was wrong. To believe for a second that she could be innocent was wrong. He'd heard those same words from a hundred other criminals, every one of them guilty as sin. He was letting his desire for her distract him, blind him to his duty.

Being cooped up in that damned jail was making him crazy. He had to get out of here. Should be in Texas, on the Rio Grande, hunting the Risco brothers, pumping the bastards full of bullets. His men were risking their lives—*losing* their lives—and what was he doing?

Sitting on his ass in Colorado. Feeling this overpowering attraction toward an *outlaw*.

The woman who had killed his brother.

Lucas glared up into the sky, welcoming the sharp, biting sting of the snow against his face. There was only one explanation, one reason Antoinette had him so . . . beguiled. He'd been without a woman for months now. Too long.

That was why he couldn't stop thinking about the sweet taste of her lips, or the silky texture of her dark hair beneath his fingers. Or the way her brown eyes looked so soft in the firelight when she was sleepy. Or how he had felt when he made her smile . . .

With a vivid curse, he turned on his heel and stalked back toward Eminence, his steps echoing like gunshots when he reached the board sidewalk. He knew he needed to go write two letters, the kind he hated to write—one to Seth Thompson's widow and one to Henry Reynolds's parents, expressing his condolences.

But first he needed to douse this feeling that burned in his gut for Antoinette Sutton.

And he could think of two damn fine ways to do it.

The dissonant noise of someone playing "Nelly Bly" on the piano set his teeth on edge as he shoved open the swinging doors to Fairfax's saloon. There were only a few people inside: a scruffy prospector at the bar, another at the piano, and three more seated at a table with O'Donnell and Holt, playing poker.

O'Donnell—who had a curvaceous, scantily dressed redhead in his lap—grinned and raised a hand in greeting. "Marshal."

Lucas stalked over to the bar. "Beer."

Fairfax looked delighted. "Coming right up, Marshal McKenna, sir. Finest ale in the state of Colorado. And let me say what a pleasure it is to see you again."

Lucas didn't reply. He had said beer, not conversation.

Fairfax filled a glass until foam bubbled over the top and slid it down the bar. Lucas caught the glass, drained a quarter of it in one long swallow, and wiped his mouth with the back of his hand. The strong, dark brew burned pleasantly down his throat.

"And what brings you here this afternoon, Marshal?" Holt asked, sounding curious.

Lucas flicked a look over his shoulder. "You spend all your spare time in the saloon, Doc?"

Holt frowned at him. "First spare time I've had in a while. Spent three days riding the mountain to call on sick homesteaders, dug a load of buckshot out of a miner's backside at four this morning, and delivered a baby about an hour ago. And how's your week been so far?"

Lucas tossed a coin on the bar, scowling at him. "Just perfect." He shifted his attention to two of the other card-players: a pair of bearded, middle-aged prospectors who were staring at him. "And what are you two looking at?"

"Nothing, Marshal, sir." One stood up and grabbed his money off the table, dropping some. "We was, uh, we was just on our way out, wasn't we?" He headed for the door, without picking up the fallen coins.

His friend grabbed his own winnings and followed. "Hyup."

Lucas shook his head, recognizing a hasty retreat when he saw one. At the moment, he didn't especially care why the two were hightailing it out of his vicinity.

O'Donnell looked up in dismay, watching as half his players walked out in the middle of the game. He slanted Lucas a dry look. "Have you noticed, Marshal, that you seem to have a certain effect on people?"

The redhead on the gambler's lap giggled.

Before Lucas could reply, Fairfax came over to him, wiping his hands on his white apron. "Beer's on the house." He slid the coin back across the bar. "Anything else I can get you, Marshal?"

Lucas turned toward him. "You got any whores left in this town?"

Though his voice was low, the prospector seated at the bar overheard. "Whores?" he exclaimed, chuckling. "You lookin' to clean up our streets now, Marshal? Fill up yer jail with pretty ladies?"

Lucas gave him a quelling glare.

But the others in the room had heard the man; O'Donnell, Holt, and the third remaining card player now seemed more interested in what was being said at the bar than in their game.

Lucas took another long drink and told himself he didn't give a damn.

"Well sir," Fairfax said smoothly, ever the efficient host, "we used to have quite an array, but these days we've got but two ladies of the evening still with us. One of them would be Miss Ivy there." He gestured to the redhead seated in O'Donnell's lap. "And Miss Indigo can usually be found here when she's not with a customer, but I haven't seen her yet today."

Lucas turned and considered the redhead. She was young and attractive, her plentiful assets almost spilling over the top of her tight-fitting green dress. And she smiled prettily at him.

O'Donnell frowned, looping a possessive arm around the girl's waist. "Ivy, honey, why don't you go fetch Indigo," he suggested.

She sighed, linking her arms around his neck. "Aw, Morgan, you know I been trying to *avoid* her all day. She's been dogging my heels like a . . . oh, hell."

"Ivy!" A tall brunette appeared at the saloon's entrance, shouting. "What are you doin' lollin' around in there still? The stage will be leavin' in an hour."

"I'm not going," Ivy said sullenly.

"What did you say?" the brunette cried, pushing open the doors.

"I said I'm staying here!"

This, Lucas guessed, arching one brow, would have to be Indigo. He silently observed the new arrival as she came sauntering in, dressed in a gown of blue satin and black lace and a matching cape that was thrown back over her shoulders.

"The hell you are." The brunette marched over to the card players' table. "Ivy, we done decided already. We can't make enough money in this town. There's nothing

left here but a bunch of . . . a bunch of . . . well, just look
at them!" She gestured to the various men in the room.
"Any man worth more than two bits cleared out last . . ."
Her gaze settled on Lucas and she paused.

And her voice suddenly shifted. "My, my." She looked
him up and down, then took a black lace fan from a
pocket in her skirt and opened it. "You that famous lawman everyone's been talkin' about?" Her red lips curved
upward as she fanned herself slowly. "Just look at you."

Lucas returned her regard. She had dark hair, dark
eyes, a good body.

"Indigo, I'm staying," Ivy said.

The brunette's smile faded. "Be with you in a minute,
cowboy," she said to Lucas before she rounded on Ivy.
"Staying for what? For him?" She stabbed a finger
toward O'Donnell. "I bet you been givin' him free ones
again, ain't you?"

The gambler looked sheepish.

Ivy stood up, planting her hands on her hips. "He
doesn't have much money right now, but he's got plans—"

"Oh, sure, he's got plans. Big plans. That's *all* he's
got. That's all *any* man in this town has got. The ones
with money and sense all cleared out a long time ago!"

"And I'm going to be moving on soon as well," O'Donnell said, reaching for the bottle in front of him and re-
filling his glass.

"Horsefeathers! You been sayin' that for a year and
you're still sittin' here with a glass of bourbon in your
hand and five dollars to your name." Indigo looked from
him to the redhead. "How many times I *told* you, Ivy?"
She stamped her foot. "Don't fall in love with the customers. Y'ain't much of a whore if you give it away for
free. You think he's gonna marry you? You think he *loves*
you?"

Lucas took a long drink from his beer, feeling sorry for the naïve little redhead.

Ivy remained standing next to O'Donnell, clearly waiting for him to say something. "M-Morgan?" she asked tremulously.

The gambler didn't look at her as he spoke in that genteel, Southern drawl. "You go on home and pack, honey. Like Indigo says." He studied his cards. "I'm no good for you."

The girl blinked at him, covering her mouth with one hand. A stifled sob escaped her as she turned and ran out the swinging doors. They flapped in the chilly air behind her.

Indigo sighed as if in relief, giving O'Donnell one last, withering look before she walked over to the bar.

As she joined Lucas, her smile returned. "Now then," she said, fanning herself, "where were we, lawman?"

Lucas caught the scent of her perfume. Roses and musk. Her hair was brown. And so were her eyes. And she was voluptuous. And willing. What more could he ask? What more could any man ask?

She placed a hand on his arm. "Stage'll be leaving soon," she said, in a low, purring voice, "but I got about an hour left in this town. Wasn't planning on any more customers . . ." She smiled up at him, stroking the muscles of his arm through his shirt. "But I might change my mind. My, oh my, I surely might."

Lucas couldn't summon a smile in return. In fact, as he looked at her, he couldn't seem to summon much enthusiasm, either. His gaze traveled down her body and back up again, from her curvaceous hips to her artfully displayed bosom to her ruby-painted mouth. And he felt . . .

Indifferent. Unmoved.

He stared at her in silence, astonished that she didn't arouse his interest, when so many like her had in the past.

Indigo wet her lips with her tongue. "You sure look like you could make an hour memorable for a lady." She slid her hand up to his shoulder. "And something's got you all knotted up like a bale of barbed wire. I could soothe those kinks out of you. Real slow and easy like."

His fingers seemed to go numb around the glass of beer in his hand. Why was he even hesitating? This was exactly what he'd wanted, what he'd come here hoping to find. A woman to relieve his hunger. No complications. No questions. Just an hour with a willing, beautiful, available female. The type who had always satisfied him in the past.

This one was eager and no doubt highly skilled. But somehow, he found himself wanting something . . . different, something . . .

More.

Something he couldn't even name. This had never happened in his life. It was stunning—unnerving—to discover that she wasn't what he really wanted.

That the longer he looked at her, the more he thought of another woman.

A petite, vulnerable elf with soft brown eyes and lips that tasted impossibly sweet.

"What do you say, hmm?" Indigo ran a finger down his chest. "Come on back to my place and help me celebrate leaving this town for good."

"No thanks." He couldn't believe he was saying it, even as he heard the words coming out of his mouth.

Indigo arched one shapely brow, looking surprised. "My mistake," she said lightly, withdrawing her hand and taking his rejection with a shrug. "But something's sure got you all knotted up." She turned away from the bar, a sly, knowing look in her eyes. "What's her name, lawman?"

Without waiting for an answer, she sashayed toward the door.

One of the three remaining card players stood up and followed her. "*I'll* give ya a last go, Indy."

"You got money?" She kept walking, not even looking back at the prospector. "Cash money?"

"Just won twenty dollars." He waved the bills in the air.

She looked over her shoulder at him, sighing. "Come on, then."

Silence fell as the pair left. Lucas stood there, burning with a mix of unsatisfied hunger and befuddled confusion at what he had just done.

Made worse by the fact that the other men in the room seemed equally curious about his actions.

Holt in particular was looking at him with a furrowed brow and questioning eyes.

Lucas responded with a glower and turned his back, glaring down into his beer.

"Things sure have changed around this place," O'Donnell said morosely. "Remember the old days, Cam? Two hundred men a day coming through those doors, their pockets heavy from the silver mines, every one of them eager for a bottle, a woman, a game of cards . . ." The gambler sighed fondly. "And we all made so much money, we could hardly carry it to the bank."

Fairfax polished the bar with his apron. "That we did, Morgan, that we did."

"These days, all we've got left are a bunch of hard-working pioneers too damned careful with their dollars," O'Donnell said with distaste. "Half of them hoping for another strike they're never going to find—"

"Oh, Hell, Morgan, don't sink into one of your melancholy moods," Holt said. "You can't blame everything on the silver going bust. You know damn well Indigo was right. You should've done right by Ivy or left her alone."

"Don't *you* start in on me, Danny boy. I never told Miss Ivy any lies and I never made her any promises."

Lucas choked out a derisive breath. "Much as I hate to agree with the doc," he said, turning to face them, "any man worth a bucket of warm spit does right by a woman. If she's a proper lady, you marry her—and if she's a whore, you pay her. You don't just help yourself to a girl's favors and then toss her aside."

O'Donnell shoved his chair back and stood up, a bit unsteadily. "Now I'm not worth a bucket of warm spit? Would you care to take a boxing lesson out back, Marshal?"

Lucas stepped away from the bar. Punching something would feel damned good about now. "Anytime, O'Donnell."

"Do we have to have a fight in here every week?" Holt gathered up the cards on the table and calmly started shuffling them. "This keeps up, I'm going to stay home and play solitaire."

Fairfax chuckled. The prospector at the bar started laughing.

After a moment, O'Donnell shook his head, looking chastened. "Yeah, and with your luck at cards, you'd still lose." He sat back down and pushed away the bottle of bourbon that sat in front of him. "I didn't mean anything by it, Marshal."

"Forget it." Lucas finished his beer and tried to decide whether to have another. Since he had turned down Miss Indigo for some idiotic reason, and it didn't seem like another saloon brawl was going to present itself, getting good and drunk seemed about the only distraction he was likely to get at the moment.

"How about you boys smoke a peace pipe." Fairfax grabbed an open box of cigars from behind the bar, tossing one to Lucas and one to each man at the table. "Another beer, Marshal?" He refilled the glass before Lucas had a chance to reply.

Then the saloonkeeper lit a cigar for himself, took off his apron, and walked over to take a seat next to Holt.

"Since you scared off half the players, Marshal," O'Donnell said, clipping the end off his cigar, "the polite thing would be to sit in for a hand or two."

Lucas regarded the three of them warily, turning the fragrant Cuban cigar in his fingertips. This was another of Fairfax's recruiting efforts, and he wasn't going to be drawn in by it. He didn't want to get mixed up in the lives and problems and big plans of this town. He was *not* staying here. He was leaving. Soon.

But since he was leaving soon, he thought, a hand or two of poker probably wouldn't do much harm.

He picked up his beer and walked over to the table. "Deal me in."

The snow was falling more thickly through the dim light of afternoon as Lucas walked back to the jail, past the stage that was just pulling out of town. He felt a little better, another cigar clamped between his teeth, his pockets heavier by forty dollars, much of which used to belong to the good doctor.

Travis was no doubt starving—the kid was always starving—and eager to get home for his supper. And Lucas had two letters to write.

Which should be enough to keep his mind off Antoinette, he thought with a grimace. At least for the evening.

The night was another matter.

He opened the hotel's front door. And stopped dead in his tracks.

Travis was sprawled on the floor, facedown.

Lucas cursed, closing the distance in two strides and bending over him. He found a pulse at his throat, but the back of the kid's head was wet with blood. There were broken pieces of a heavy china plate scattered on the floor around him.

Lucas's heart hammered as he ran to Antoinette's cell.

He cursed, vividly. Furiously. The door was hanging open.

She had escaped.

10

The layers of blackness gave way slowly, one by one, until Annie could feel again. Could feel icy dampness pelting her cheek. And hard ground beneath her. And snow, bitterly cold through the fabric of her dress and undergarments. Pain throbbed at the back of her head. Where the stranger had hit her.

"You still alive, miss?"

The voice was soft, oddly polite. A booted toe nudged her in the back and Annie moaned. Everything hurt. The pounding ache in her head. Her ribs. And the muscles in her arms. Her hands were tied behind her. Her ankles were bound. She was lying in the snow, on her side. She opened her eyes and the cloudy sky and the white ground spun dizzily for a moment.

Then her vision steadied and she could see pine trees scattered around her. Mountain peaks everywhere. And the evergreens' limbs glittering with ice. A buckskin horse grazed a few feet away, pawing at the snow, its reins trailing on the ground.

The stranger stood over her in the faint light of . . . evening? Early morning? She couldn't tell. Didn't know how much time had passed.

Her mouth went dry with fear as he crouched beside her.

"I'm so glad you're still with me." His smile was warm, almost friendly. He wore a gray suit with velvet lapels, a striped satin vest, a string tie in his starched white collar. The falling snow stained his fashionable, wide-brimmed felt hat. He couldn't be more than twenty-five, almost looked like some prosperous young shopkeeper or lawyer.

Except for the spots of blood on his fine clothes and shiny black boots.

"Sometimes I don't know my own strength," he said, reaching down to brush a strand of her hair out of her eyes with his gloved fingers. "But I'm relieved I didn't kill you, Miss Sutton. A live body's so much more pleasant to transport than a dead one. Learned that the hard way. Dead body gives off such a disagreeable odor after a few hours—and then there's rigor mortis. You have no idea what a headache that can be." He tilted his head to one side. "You're really much prettier than on your wanted poster."

A bounty hunter. Annie stared up at him, numb with cold, with shock. *He was a bounty hunter.*

Terror seized her—just as it had when he'd stalked toward her cell and drawn a gun, threatening that if she made a sound, he would kill her, and Travis as well. Annie had watched helplessly as he'd unlocked the door with some kind of key. She'd had no weapons, no way to protect herself when he came inside, when he had grabbed her and struck her so hard, and the world had gone black.

He sighed, brushing his gloved hand along her cheek. "Didn't expect you to be this pretty." With a smile, he lifted a strand of her long hair to his lips. "And you smell so good. Think I'd like to keep you that way. At least for a while. I so rarely get the pleasure of bringing in a woman."

He looked up into the falling snow. "Unfortunately, we don't have time for this now, and good old Buck here has had enough rest. Better get back on the trail. People will be coming after us." He straightened and walked over to the buckskin. "Or rather, coming after *you*, the escaped outlaw."

Annie rolled onto her side, gasping at the pain, and managed to struggle to her knees. "What are you talking about?" She tried to keep her voice from wavering. "What did you do to Travis?" Quickly, she looked around for anything she might use as a weapon or to cut through the ropes. A broken stick. A sharp rock. Anything.

"The kid? I told you I wouldn't harm him as long as you cooperated," the bounty hunter said mildly. "I don't break promises, at least not to women. Always had a soft spot in my heart for the ladies." He bent down to tighten up the loosened cinch on the horse's saddle. "All I did was hit him good and hard. By the time he wakes up, I'll have collected my five thousand and be long gone."

Annie hoped that he was telling the truth, that Travis was all right. "And what makes you think you'll be *paid* the bounty?" she asked in disbelief, leaning to one side, biting her lip at the pain. Her numb fingers closed around a small, broken piece of rock. "I was already in jail. You *stole* a prisoner from a lawman's custody."

"No, no, you *escaped*," he corrected lightly. "This isn't the first time I've done this, you know. I prefer to let someone else take care of the tracking and capturing, then I just bide my time, wait for an opportunity." He led the horse over to her. "Even your lady friend fit nicely into my plan. It'll look like she helped you get free, then you ran off. I left my skeleton key behind on the floor, next to the basket. Nice touch, don't you think?"

Annie felt sick. "I suppose hurting Travis was a *nice touch*, too."

"Yes, in fact, it was. I made it look like a woman had done it. Took one of your dinner plates and busted it over his head. Something larger might've been nice, but I was in a hurry."

Annie shook her head, choking back a sob. It sounded like he had enjoyed every step—planning it, doing it. "Nobody will believe I would hurt Travis."

"Really?" He reached into one of his saddlebags and withdrew a creased, tattered piece of paper: the reward poster with her picture on it. "You're a wanted murderer, Miss Sutton."

Annie stared at the paper in his hand, shivering with cold. With shock. She had never seen the actual handbill that showed a sketch of her face beneath the words WANTED: DEAD OR ALIVE. The picture made her look cold, hard. Like an outlaw.

She shut her eyes, hanging her head, sinking forward. She *was* an outlaw. And Travis had been hurt because of her. Because she was worth five thousand dollars to any man who wanted to collect it.

The bounty hunter walked over and grabbed her bound arms, yanking her upright, ignoring her cry of pain at the sudden movement. "I'll be celebrated as a hero when I bring you in—an escaped lady outlaw wanted for murder, who also attacked a most unfortunate, gullible boy."

Annie wrenched her arm free, blinking hard. "It'll be my word against yours."

"No, you see, it *would* be your word against mine." He recaptured her easily, his grip tightening like a vise as he hauled her to her feet. "But when you tried to escape from me, I was forced to shoot you."

Annie froze, staring at him in horror. He had planned *every* detail.

This isn't the first time I've done this.

"Don't worry," he said, dragging her over to his horse, "it's a long way to Central City. You have several whole *days* left on this earth. And we'll have time to get to know each other much better, you and I."

He stepped up into the saddle and pulled her after him, slinging her across his lap, facedown. Annie inhaled sharply in pain. Her ribs felt like they were on fire and the saddle horn dug into her belly. But when she struggled, he held her still easily, linking one strong arm through her bound hands, pressing his elbow into her spine.

"What's this?" He found the rock she had clutched in her fingers, taking it from her. "A weapon?" He threw it away, laughing.

As he dug his heels into his horse's flanks and set off at a gallop, he was still laughing.

One horse, two riders.

Didn't add up.

Lucas knelt in the snow, staring at the hoofprints. As the last light of day began to fade into violet shadows, he turned up the lantern he had brought, studying the marks more clearly.

His first reaction when he had found Antoinette missing had been fury—that she had escaped, that he had been tricked. After he had carried the injured kid over to Holt's place, he had given the doctor a blistering earful.

But both Holt and Mrs. Greer, who had been at his house, had reacted with shock to the news that Antoinette was missing. As Holt went to work on the unconscious Travis, he insisted he knew nothing about any plan to help Antoinette escape tonight. And Mrs. Greer had been frantic, crying that she wanted to launch a search, telling some wild story about Antoinette hearing a prowler outside her windows at night.

Lucas had refused to believe any of it, refused their help, and set out alone to hunt down his escaped prisoner. He didn't want any more civilians getting hurt, and he didn't know who he could trust, who might be trying to help Antoinette.

The snow had made her path easier to follow down the twisting, treacherous mountain trails. But it kept coming down, thick and fast; for the first snow of the season, it had quickly become one hell of a storm—and the hoofprints began to disappear too quickly. Lucas had galloped down the mountainside at reckless speed, trying to catch up before nightfall, before the snow covered Antoinette's trail completely.

But now, as he knelt and studied the tracks more closely, he realized they'd been left by one horse carrying two people. And he felt a growing sense of unease.

From the beginning, some nagging, stubborn part of Lucas's brain hadn't been able to believe that Antoinette would hurt Travis.

And if someone was helping her escape, why would that person think the best chance to get away would be to share a horse?

Lucas stood, lifting the lantern and looking down the trail, through the snowfall and the deepening shadows. His instincts told him something was wrong—but he wasn't sure he could trust his instincts where Antoinette was concerned.

His eyes on the hoofprints, he walked over and

mounted the iron-gray gelding he had taken from the
livery stable and set off again. It was getting dark, the
icy white snowflakes kept falling, and the wind had become so cold it sliced through his drover's coat and
chilled him to the bone. But he didn't want to stop for
the night. Not yet.

Within an hour, the tracks led him to a copse of pine
trees, where he found a crushed place in the snow. Like
the two riders had stopped here to rest.

But when he dismounted for a closer look, he saw only
one set of footprints.

Made by a man's large, booted feet.

Lucas went still. It looked like the man had taken
some burden from his horse and laid it under the trees.
Maybe a bundle of supplies.

Or maybe a person.

A person who was tied up. Or dead.

Lucas felt like a lead weight had just dropped through
the pit of his stomach. He didn't see Antoinette's footprints anywhere.

Maybe Holt and Mrs. Greer *hadn't* been acting. He
remembered how the gray-haired woman had burst into
tears, the look of panic on her face. And her story about
a prowler outside Antoinette's windows.

Bounty hunter.

Lucas swore. He should have guessed. Didn't know
why he hadn't thought of it earlier.

But then he knew why: because he was always willing
to think the worst of Antoinette.

He returned to his horse and grabbed the reins and
vaulted into the saddle, three words ringing through his
head, over and over.

Dead or alive.

The reward Olivia had offered was for Antoinette
dead or alive. Five thousand dollars. There were plenty

of ruthless bastards in the West who would do anything for that kind of money. Anything.

Lucas spurred the gelding down the steep mountain trail, into the night. It was too dark to keep going, the moon and stars almost blotted out by the clouds and falling snow. He didn't stop to question why he was risking his neck.

Especially when he knew the son of a bitch could've killed Antoinette already.

Duty, he told himself, unable to explain his racing heartbeat. She was his prisoner—and if some goddamn bounty hunter had taken her from his custody, it was Lucas's duty to get her back.

If she was still alive.

Every muscle in his body had bunched up tight. He forced himself to relax. Managed to stay levelheaded, his hand easy on the reins.

Until a half-hour later, when he rode into a valley and lost the trail. He couldn't make out the hoofprints in the snow anymore. Or even the trail itself, not in the darkness. The storm had obliterated everything. And there were three different passes that led out of the valley.

He should stop, he thought logically, reining the gelding in ever-widening circles, looking for some sign of which direction they had taken. Should stop and wait until morning. Getting through the passes would be one hell of a lot safer in daylight. If the bounty hunter was smart, he had already stopped somewhere.

The thought of what he might do to Annie before dawn—what he might already be doing—brought a sound from Lucas's throat, a wordless growl of frustration and anger.

He tried to calm down. Think rationally. Find the usual detached, icy cool he had always relied on in situations like this.

But for the first time, he couldn't find it. Couldn't feel logical or steady or rational anymore. His pulse was pounding in his ears and he was soaked through and practically frozen solid and he just kept riding in circles through the hopeless mess of snow and sleet and darkness, refusing to give up.

And then he saw the shoes.

Annie's shoes, small patches of black against all the white.

They had either fallen off—or she had kicked them off. As a signal. A trail marker. To show which pass they had taken.

Smart girl. Lucas smiled grimly and hoped the latter was true. Because it would mean she was still alive. He dug his heels into the gelding's flanks and reined the horse forward.

"Get up, damn it. You son of a bitch, I said get up!"

Annie's heart thudded with fear as she sat pressed against the ice-slick rock of the mountainside, watching the bounty hunter curse at his horse by the light of a small lantern he held. His mood had changed abruptly when the buckskin had lost its footing on the steep trail, sending them both tumbling to the ground.

It looked like the poor creature had broken a leg.

"Worthless goddamn nag."

Annie flinched as the bounty hunter wrenched cruelly on the reins. "M-Maybe we should stop for the night and let him rest—"

"Oh, you'd like that, wouldn't you?" He turned on Annie, his eyes blazing in the light of the lantern. "I had different accommodations in mind, Miss Sutton—nice little place I found on the way up here. Got some supplies and a fresh mount waiting." He turned and kicked the injured horse. "Guess we'll just have to walk the rest of the way."

Annie shook her head, her teeth chattering as she tried to keep her bound, bare feet under her, hidden in the wet snow. With her long skirts, he hadn't noticed. Yet. "You're . . . you're not just going to leave the horse suffering like that, are you?"

"You want me to put him out of his misery? With a nice loud gunshot to signal anyone who might be tracking us? No chance." He bent to unfasten his saddlebags and weapons.

Annie glanced back up the trail behind them. She didn't know how anyone would be *able* to track them through this storm, which had turned into a blizzard as darkness fell and the temperature dropped. No *sane* man would risk traveling the steep mountain trails in this weather.

And the one man who had the most reason to follow her was definitely sane. Clearheaded. Logical. And he probably believed she had hurt Travis. After all, he believed she had murdered his brother in cold blood.

She doubted Lucas McKenna would risk his life simply to reclaim her as his prisoner.

But she prayed he was on her trail.

Because the one man who hated her more than any other was now her one hope of survival.

The bounty hunter slung his saddlebags across his shoulder and walked over to her, bending down with a knife to reach for the ropes around her ankles. "What happened to your shoes?" he demanded.

"I—I guess they came loose and fell off."

His eyes met hers and his expression turned ugly. "You smart little bitch."

Annie flinched as he raised his fist.

But he didn't hit her. After a moment, he relaxed and

smiled again. "A rather creative idea, Miss Sutton, but it won't work. No one would risk following us through this pass at night. Not in this storm."

He crouched down in front of her and sliced through the bindings on her ankles. Then he opened one of his saddlebags and pulled out a pair of soft, beaded deerskin boots, like moccasins but high enough to reach the middle of the leg. He shoved them on her feet. "Got these off a Cheyenne medicine man years ago. Snow'll probably ruin them but for five thousand dollars, I'll get a new pair." He stood up. "Now let's go."

"I—I can't walk very far in these—"

"Of course you can. Indians do it all the time." He drew his gun and aimed it at her head. "And the only reason you're not dead already is because a live body moves a whole lot easier than a dead one." He thumbed back the hammer on the pistol. "If I have to carry you, you might as well be dead right now. It's so cold out, you'd probably keep awhile, smell real nice all the way to Central City."

Annie stood up, shuddering. "All right."

"All right. Guess you should have thought of this before you went kicking off your shoes—to leave trail markers for someone who isn't even following us." He motioned her forward with the gun. "Ladies first."

Annie headed down the trail, the bounty hunter right at her back. His lantern offered just enough light for her to see in front of her. The moccasins had thick soles and fur lining, but after a while, her feet began to tingle from the wet snow. Every breath of the cold air seemed to burn her lungs. Her ribs ached from so many hours of being slung over his horse.

By the time dawn began to lighten the sky a couple of hours later, her limbs felt numb. Her whole body hurt.

She tripped on a branch, stumbling to her knees with a sob.

"Get up."

"I can't go any further."

He pressed the barrel of his gun to the back of her head. "You better hope that's not true."

She was breathing hard, so wracked with pain and so numbed by the freezing weather, she couldn't even feel fear anymore. "How . . . much further?"

"Another hour maybe. Get up."

"Let me rest. Please."

"I have several virtues, but kindness isn't one of them. Get up." He cocked the gun.

Annie staggered to her feet and turned to look up at him, her fatigue and frustration brimming over into defiance.

And that was when she saw him.

The rider. A black silhouette against the brightness of the dawn sky. Galloping toward them down the steep mountainside on a dark horse.

She couldn't catch her breath, for a second thought it was only a trick of the shifting light. But then she knew— knew the outline of those broad shoulders and the flash of silver in his hand and the hat tilted low against the sun. Knew who it was with every fiber of her being.

The bounty hunter turned, his arm still outstretched, his pistol glinting in the first rays of the morning. "Shit."

He aimed at Lucas and started to pull the trigger.

"No." Annie threw herself forward, slamming into his back just as the gun went off.

The shot went low.

And struck the horse.

The animal whinnied shrilly in pain and went down.

Annie screamed as she saw Lucas fall into the snow.

He was too far away for her to tell if he was hurt. The bounty hunter grabbed her by the arm and shoved her toward a jumble of rocks and boulders, taking cover behind them.

Annie strained against his hold on her, trying to see over the top of one of the boulders. *Dear God, what if he was dead?*

The bounty hunter fastened an arm around her throat and dragged her back against him, cursing under his breath. He shoved his saddlebags to one side and pulled out another gun. "Who the hell is that?" he hissed. "Who the hell would follow us through those passes? At night. In a *snowstorm*."

Annie didn't reply.

A moment later, a voice rang out from a few yards up the trail.

"Federal Marshal!"

Annie almost cried with relief as she heard that familiar bellow. He sounded unhurt. And just as ornery as always. *Thank God. Oh, thank you, God.*

The bounty hunter cursed and fired another shot in Lucas's direction. "I haven't come this far to lose my five thousand now!" he shouted up the hill.

There was silence for a while. The bounty hunter looked around wildly as if seeking some way to escape. But the pass was too narrow at this point; if they left the shelter of the rocks, he would be vulnerable to Lucas's gun.

"That woman was in my custody," Lucas snarled, closer this time. "I suggest you give her back while you still can."

The bounty hunter fired again, several shots this time.

Annie braced herself against the roaring of the gun so close to her. After it died down, she didn't hear anything more except the echoes of the gunshots off the icy walls of the pass. And the ringing in her ears.

And the pounding of her heartbeat.

There was nothing else. Nothing.

The bounty hunter emptied the spent cartridges onto the ground and reloaded his gun. And waited. For several long minutes. Still the pass remained eerily quiet. He chanced a look over the top of the boulders.

Then he stood up, dragging her with him, apparently satisfied with what he had seen. He kept his arm tight around Annie's neck, a pistol in each hand.

Annie cried out, glimpsing a crumpled form several yards up the trail, facedown in the snow—that familiar black coat, the hat, one black boot twisted out at an awkward angle. *"No."*

"Looks like I got him," the bounty hunter said with pleasure.

"Look again," a familiar voice snapped from behind them.

The bounty hunter whirled, losing his hold on Annie as he brought up his pistols. She lunged away from him, falling to the ground.

And everything seemed to explode around her. A deafening roar echoed off the walls of the narrow pass as Lucas and the bounty hunter exchanged fire. Shouts and a curse and the acrid smell of smoke and hot steel filled the morning air.

It was over within seconds. As the echoes died down, Annie lay very still, too frightened even to breathe.

Then she saw the bounty hunter stretched out on his back, his eyes unseeing, a single crimson stain spreading across his starched white shirt and satin vest.

She looked toward Lucas. He was still standing, smoke curling from the barrel of his Colt.

But it wasn't until she struggled to her feet, rushing toward him, filled with relief that he was alive, that she noticed the blood.

Blood on his face, on his shirt.

The pistol dropped from his fingers as he sank to his knees and fell forward.

"Lucas!"

11

Sleet pelted down from the gray skies as Annie huddled over Lucas, but the fear that drenched her was much sharper than the prickles of ice on her skin. The outcropping of rock a few inches above their heads offered precious little protection from the storm. The thin blanket wrapped around her shoulders, taken from the bounty hunter's saddlebags, wasn't much help either.

Her skin burned with cold, her legs and arms still felt numb—and she was ready to tear her hair out by the roots if the mess of wet curls didn't stop getting in her eyes as she worked.

"You have to wake up," she pleaded, cutting another strip of cloth from her petticoat with Lucas's hunting knife. "Lucas, you have to wake up and tell me what to do. I don't . . . I can't . . ." Annie realized she was babbling. Tried to swallow the panic bubbling up in her throat.

Two hours had passed since he'd been shot, maybe more. At first, she had thought his injury might not be so bad: A single bullet had struck him, cutting a deep furrow along his temple.

But it wouldn't stop bleeding. The snow all around him was stained dark red.

And she had no way to get him to safety or help; the first shot the bounty hunter had fired had killed Lucas's horse. When the snow had turned to sleet, slashing down out of the morning sky, she had dragged Lucas to a sheltered corner of the pass, but that had taken almost half an hour, and the last of her strength. He was too big, all muscle, too heavy for her to tug more than a few yards.

"I don't know how to help you," she cried, her shallow, unsteady breaths forming clouds on the frigid air. "I don't even know if I *can* help you. Or if you'll ever wake up again."

That possibility caused a hard tug on her heart that she couldn't explain. She tied the makeshift bandage in place around his head. Wasn't sure what else she should do. What else she *could* do. He was so pale, so still.

She didn't know anything about gunshot wounds. Didn't know how serious it might be. His pulse seemed steady, his breathing even, but he hadn't moved, or made a sound. Or opened his eyes.

All she could think was that she should try to stop the bleeding and try to keep him warm. But she seemed to be failing at both.

She tucked his coat and blanket closer to him, but they had started out damp—because he had left them in the snow up the trail, along with his hat and boots. He had arranged the bedroll beneath his coat to make a decoy. A clever trick that had allowed him to sneak over the rocks to surprise the bounty hunter.

And save her.

Gratitude, she told herself. This strange feeling in her heart was simply gratitude; she owed him her life. Owed him whatever help she could offer.

Exhausted, shivering, she hunched over him, trying to protect him as best she could from the shards of ice and snow that slanted in at them like arrows from some unseen enemy.

For one desperate moment, she considered leaving him to go for help. But as she looked down the trail, she didn't know where she might *find* help. Or how long it might take, how long she would last on foot. Or where in God's name she was . . .

And only then did it occur to her. Only then.

She was free. Outside. In the open. No cell, no iron bars, no handcuffs, no one pointing a gun at her. *Free.* For the first time in weeks.

Her heart pounded faster. The bounty hunter had said there was a shelter of some kind, further down the trail. A horse. Supplies.

A chance to escape. The first chance she'd had. Maybe the only one she'd get.

But when she looked at Lucas again, her heart thudded. If she saved herself, it would mean abandoning him. Leaving him here—alone, unconscious. He could freeze to death. If he didn't bleed to death first.

Annie shut her eyes, trying to think. To be logical and rational. Like he would. Even if she *did* stay, she wasn't sure she could save him. She would probably freeze to death with him. Already, her skin was turning red, and her muscles felt strange and shaky, her body wracked by more and more frequent shudders that left her trembling so badly she could hardly tie the bandages.

But when she opened her eyes, gazing down at him, she felt only confusion. Because there was no question in her mind.

Regardless of logic, regardless of all common sense, she couldn't leave him. She just couldn't.

She bent her head, tears of frustration in her eyes. They were both going to die out here, and there was no way she could stop it. All she could think of to do was pray, and she couldn't even manage that.

Annie hadn't prayed in a long time . . . not since she had begged God to save her baby's life.

And God hadn't listened then.

She wiped the tears and drops of melting ice from her face. She wasn't even sure He *would* listen to someone like her—a criminal, a mistress, someone who had taken a life, had been the cause of so much hurt for so many people.

God didn't owe her any favors.

But as she knelt there in the snow, she huddled closer to Lucas and began to pray, silently.

For the life of this man who hated her, and held her prisoner, and wanted to see her spend the rest of her days in a Missouri jail.

His head felt like he'd been hit by a cannon instead of a .44.

The pain jostling and bouncing around inside his skull made Lucas groan, made him wish he could sink back down into the soothing darkness that had cushioned everything. But a different kind of discomfort made that impossible.

It was hard to breathe. Felt like there was a weight on his chest. Like maybe he'd taken another bullet, near his heart.

He opened his eyes and immediately shut them again, blinded by a world bright with ice and sunlight and pain. Only after he remained still for a few moments and steeled himself did he slowly, reluctantly open his eyelids again, bit by bit.

He was lying on his back in the snow, under some sort of rocky overhang. Was covered with his coat, and a blanket. One of his saddlebags cushioned his head. When he reached up with one unsteady hand, he felt a frilly piece of cloth wrapped around his temples.

And there *was* a weight on his chest.

Annie lay curled up beside him, half on top of him, using him for a pillow.

He let his eyes close again, relief flowing through him. She was alive. Safe. For a moment, for reasons he didn't want to examine too closely, that was all that mattered.

As he lay there in the snow and ice and what he figured was an awful lot of his own blood, all he felt was gratitude.

When he looked up again, he shifted his gaze, moving only his eyes, until he saw the bounty hunter a few yards away—stretched out, dead. Lucas felt a shot of satisfaction, fierce and hot enough to warm every drop of blood in his veins.

There was no remorse. No regret. Not because the interloper had drawn first, or even because he'd shot Lucas's horse out from under him.

But because of the way Lucas had felt when he first spotted them, when he saw Annie fall to her knees, saw the bounty hunter draw his gun and aim it at her head.

Everything—the mountain, the snow, the gun, the whole world—had faded into a white-hot haze. A single, driving impulse. He had to get to her, had to get between her and that bullet.

His fury at the bounty hunter hadn't faded until the son of a bitch was dead.

Lucas opened his eyes again, feeling dizzy, like he'd lost his balance. And not just because of the .44 that had knocked him flat.

He had killed men before, but never like today. Never in a blind rage.

And never over a woman.

God almighty, the way he had charged down on them

like some kind of avenging demon. Then climbed a sheer rock face in the middle of an ice storm. And come up suddenly on his opponent at close range.

Too close, he thought, closing his eyes and swearing at the pain that kept ricocheting through his head. Stupid, stupid moves, every one of them.

Even more stupid than that, he didn't regret any of them.

Because he had done what he wanted—needed—to do: protected her. Saved her. Taken her back from the man who had taken her from him.

One corner of Lucas's mouth curved downward. He reached up to gingerly probe the wound alongside his head, clenching his teeth. Maybe the bullet *had* done more than just crease his skull. His brain didn't seem to be working right.

Annie stirred, lifting her head with a sound of discomfort, blinking sleepily.

Annie. Lucas stared at her, almost choking on his own breath. *When the hell had he started thinking of her as Annie?*

Their eyes met, and he couldn't speak, and she remained just as silent. The sleet that pelted them and the rocks and everything in the mountain pass made the only noise.

Her face looked pale, too pale, her eyes huge and dark beneath her wet, straggly curls. She was trembling as she brushed a strand of hair out of her eyes.

And then she smiled.

That was when it struck him—truly struck him, like a bolt from the blue: She hadn't left him.

She *could've* left him. Escaped. Done more than that. His gaze shifted to his Colt—which was still lying in the snow a few yards away, where he had dropped it.

She could've picked up the weapon, finished the job

the bounty hunter had started, taken the saddlebags, and walked out of there. To safety. To freedom.

Why hadn't she?

Maybe she couldn't. Maybe she was hurt. He looked up at her through narrowed eyes and tried to speak, his voice a dry croak. "You all right?"

"Me?" She looked like she was going to cry, though she was still smiling. She picked up his canteen from beside her and opened it. "I'm half-frozen. But I thought you were going to bleed to death."

"Why . . ."

She shook her head, looking puzzled at his unfinished question. "Because a bullet hit you in the head. And you were bleeding. A lot." She gently held the canteen to his lips.

That wasn't what he'd meant. But as he drank greedily, he decided he wasn't going to ask. Didn't want to know the answer.

Didn't want to think about it anymore.

He handed the canteen back. "Scalp wounds bleed a lot, Antoinette."

His voice was curt, derisive. Just as he'd meant it to be.

She flinched away from him, her smile fading. "Well, I didn't know that. I don't happen to know as much about guns and bullets as you do."

He pushed himself up onto one elbow, wincing, his empty stomach threatening to reject the water he had just gulped. "How long was I out?" He pressed one hand to his head.

"Most of the day." She nodded to the west, where the sun was disappearing behind the mountains, beneath clouds that threatened more snow.

He started to sit up.

"Lucas, are you sure you should—"

"We'd better find shelter before nightfall." He shut

his eyes against the pain that every small movement brought. Hunched over, he rested one hand on the ground, cursing as he waited for his surroundings to stop spinning.

His bandage slipped down to droop over one eye. Like some kind of lacy pirate patch.

Antoinette set the canteen down. "I can fix that for you," she said softly.

He pushed her hand away and adjusted it himself. Then he grabbed his coat in one hand and stood up. Unsteadily.

"Lucas—"

"Stop calling me that."

She looked stung, lowered her gaze. "Sorry, Marshal," she said tartly. "Go right ahead and walk around. I forgot, the newspapers said you're tough enough to chew nails and spit tacks." She took the blanket he'd left on the ground, wrapping it around the one she already wore. "Do what you want. Fall right off a cliff for all I care. And by the way," she added more quietly, "you're welcome."

Lucas turned away without thanking her. He couldn't find the words, couldn't even think straight. He felt dazed—and wasn't sure if it was from the way she was looking at him, the pain rattling around inside his skull, or both. He shrugged into his bloodstained black coat and walked toward his pistol, his steps wobbling like he was slightly drunk.

"In case you're interested," she called after him, "the bounty hunter said there's a shelter of some kind down the trail. He said he left another horse there. And some supplies."

Shelter? Lucas turned toward her, too fast, and almost lost his balance. Almost fell over. *A shelter and a horse?*

Why the *hell* hadn't she left him and tried to escape? "How far?"

"About an hour. At least, that's what he said."

He picked up his Colt, his head pounding with agony as he bent down, his stomach lurching again. He wiped the ice off the weapon as he walked back toward her, one careful step at a time. "We'll just have to"—as she stood, he abruptly noticed that her feet were clad only in a pair of fancy-looking moccasins—"walk. What in God's name are you doing sitting out here with nothing but those on your feet?"

"My shoes weren't in your saddlebags," she said defensively. "I thought you might find them, but I guess you didn't. I kicked them off to show which—"

"I found them."

"And you didn't bring them with you?"

"I wasn't thinking of your feet at the time." He flipped open the cylinder on his Colt, ejected the spent cartridge, loaded a new one, and snapped it shut. That familiar action, at least, seemed easy enough to manage.

"Well, these are better than nothing," she said, indicating her moccasins. "They're lined with fur—"

"Why didn't you take his boots?" He gestured toward the bounty hunter before he holstered his gun.

Antoinette's eyes widened, as if the thought had never crossed her mind. She looked like she might be ill. "Take bloodstained boots off a *corpse* and wear them?"

Lucas sighed. "No, of course you wouldn't." He started to shake his head, then stopped himself, wincing. "You are so damned . . ."

He didn't finish.

"What?" she asked archly.

Sensitive. Delicate. Tenderhearted. "Impractical." Frustrated by the pain and dizziness that kept threatening to knock him off his feet, he forced himself to ignore the feelings and stalked over to the dead bounty hunter.

Lucas pried both pistols from his hands, then rifled through the man's nearby saddlebags for anything that might be useful.

When he turned, he found Antoinette watching his actions with that same wide-eyed, faintly ill look. A visible shudder went through her. "Are . . . are we just going to leave him there?" she asked. "Shouldn't we at least bury the body?"

"Take too long. We spend an hour burying him, next person who comes along will have to bury us." Slowly, a bit more steadily, Lucas returned to the rocky overhang, stowed the bounty hunter's belongings in his own saddlebags, then picked them up along with his canteen.

Then he turned to Antoinette. She looked frightened, and he regretted his comment about someone burying the two of them.

She had never seemed quite so fragile before, her body wracked by shudders beneath the two blankets, her hair wet, her skin ruddy with cold. It was a miracle she hadn't died of exposure already. He doubted that she had enough strength left to walk more than a few yards, never mind a few miles.

Her lower lip quivered as she glanced from his bandaged head to the western sky, which had already darkened to shades of violet and purple. "Well, Marshal," she said lightly, as if she were trying to sound brave, "what are we going to do?"

He wished he could pick her up and carry her, hated that he felt too weak to even try it. "Get to the shelter before nightfall." He removed the blankets from her shoulders, then took off his coat and wrapped it around her.

"You can't give me your coat," she protested as he buttoned it. The garment swamped her, the bottom dragging on the ground, the sleeves hanging several inches below her hips. "You need it, or *you'll* freeze."

"The exercise will keep me warm." He tucked both blankets around her.

She immediately slid them off and handed them back. "At least take the blankets."

"I'll be all—"

"You're wounded, you've been bleeding all day, and you need some protection from the wind." She held them out toward him.

Reluctantly, he accepted them and put them on over his shirt. Before he could turn to start leading the way down the trail, she moved to his side and slid one arm around him.

"Put your arm around my shoulders," she said firmly.

He started to pull away. "You're barely strong enough to walk—"

"And you won't make it a quarter mile unless you let me help you." She hung on to him, looking up to meet his gaze. "And we have to get to that shelter before dark, or we'll both freeze to death."

He frowned at her. Stubborn, fragile, determined little elf.

Unfortunately, she had a point. Lucas fought off the waves of dizziness, ignored the pain throbbing between his temples, and allowed himself to lean on her.

As they set off, she muttered some comment he didn't quite catch about his head being harder than any bullet.

Tough enough to chew nails and spit tacks. The newspapers hadn't exaggerated, Annie thought, after they had been walking almost an hour, leaning on each other—Lucas helping her as much as she helped him.

It was snowing again, thick flakes that turned the darkness white around them. But despite all her fears, and the chills that raked her, and the danger they were in, somehow having him beside her made her feel . . . safe.

A short distance ahead, across an expanse of moonlit snow sprinkled with pines, their branches heavy with ice, the shelter finally came into view—an odd little cabin, built right up against the side of the mountain.

"We did it," she said in astonishment, her voice a raspy croak.

"Looks like a dugout." Lucas sounded exhausted. A few yards away from the cabin, they stopped in the trees. He slipped his arm from around her shoulders and settled her against a pine, handing her the blankets. "Wait here."

"Why—"

Before she could even finish the question, he vanished into the darkness, looking shaky on his feet as the night swallowed him up.

A few minutes later, she saw him circling around toward the front of the cabin, with his gun drawn, and she understood. The place might not be as empty as it looked. The bounty hunter might've had a partner.

She held her breath as she watched Lucas nudge open the door and disappear inside. He was in no condition to face any kind of enemy.

But a few minutes later, he came out, his pistol back in its holster.

"Deserted," he said as he returned to her side. "It's not much, but right about now, it looks damn good."

Annie sighed, too tired, too grateful even to speak. He put his arm around her again, they crossed the last few yards, and trudged through the open door.

A dank, musty smell filled the place, which appeared to be a single room with no windows. Annie couldn't see much else in the darkness, other than her breath on the cold air. Lucas settled her on a hard, wooden seat and lit a lantern that hung on the wall with a tin of matches next to it.

By the flickering glow, she saw that the dugout matched its name: half-cave, half-cabin, carved right out of the mountainside—no doubt for protection from the snow and wind. It looked like it might be an old trapper's place from fur-trading days.

Lucas had been right. It wasn't much, but at the moment, it *did* look damn good. A suite at the fanciest Denver hotel couldn't have looked better.

The back and part of each side wall were rough-hewn rock, the rest of it logs and mortar, and it had a dirt floor. Lucas set the lantern on a potbellied stove in the middle of the room, taking a few pieces of wood from a metal bucket nearby.

Annie started untangling herself from the blankets and his coat while she looked around. When she was very young, she had lived in a place much like this.

Before Papa ran off.

Other than the stove, the dugout had few furnishings: a couple of plain chairs and a table in one corner, some animal pelts and antlers on display. An old trunk sat against the rocky back wall, beside a bed of chipped white iron, with a striped ticking mattress rolled up at the foot.

She also noticed a black frying pan and some cooking implements hanging from hooks above the table, and dared hope there might be food somewhere as well. With a violent shiver, she set the blankets and Lucas's coat aside, and started rubbing her arms, trying to get some feeling back into her muscles. Her dress and undergarments clung to her body, damp and cold, and her feet felt numb, despite the moccasins.

Lucas arranged the logs inside the stove and lit the fire. Black smoke leaked from the wide metal pipe that led up to the roof—which also made an odd chirping noise. He coughed and whacked the stovepipe a couple of times with his fist.

There was the sound of something skittering up the pipe.

"Squirrels," Lucas said. The smoke stopped pouring into the room and flowed out through the metal chimney. Lucas took the rest of the wood from the metal bucket and set it on the floor. "You all right by yourself for a minute?"

Annie nodded, mute, still staring at the spot where she had heard claws skittering on metal. It had been a long time since she had lived in a place like this. A very long time.

Lucas picked up the empty bucket and went outside; as usual, without telling her where he was going or why.

Annie frowned as the door closed behind him. Lucas McKenna was definitely a man of action, not words. That was something else the newspapers hadn't exaggerated about.

She supposed a marshal had to be decisive and independent, that he had gotten used to just making decisions and carrying them out. Without asking what anyone else might think.

Or feel.

She looked down at the dirt floor. There was a lot between them that needed to be said. A whole lot. And neither one of them seemed to be saying it.

She wanted to ask why he had risked his life, gotten shot, to save her. But she was almost afraid to ask. Was it purely because he wanted to take her back to Missouri to stand trial? Was he so bent on seeing her punished? Did he still believe she was capable of cold-blooded murder?

Annie sighed, closing her eyes, shuddering with cold. If she knew one thing, it was that Lucas was not the most understanding, forgiving man. And she wasn't up to an argument. They were both exhausted, hungry, hurt.

Tomorrow, she thought wearily. Tomorrow would be soon enough to bring up everything that had happened, and what might happen in the future. Tonight they had more immediate problems to worry about.

She stood up and tried to scoot her chair closer to the stove, but quickly sat back down. Her feet and legs had started tingling painfully, like she was being jabbed with a thousand needles all at once.

A gust of cold wind and snowflakes blew through the door as Lucas returned. "No sign of any horse," he said, carrying the bucket, now heaped with snow, over to the stove. "Or supplies."

Annie whispered a curse, partly because of the pain in her legs, partly out of anger at the bounty hunter. "He lied," she said in disgust.

"Maybe. Or the horse might've got spooked by the ice storm and ran off," Lucas said, his voice low and tired. "Or some traveler happened along and helped himself when he saw nobody was around. Storm wiped clean any tracks that might've been out there."

He left the bucket of melting snow on the stove and carried the lantern over to the steamer trunk in the corner, crouching down to examine it.

"I don't suppose there might be food in there," she said hopefully.

"Let's find out." He straightened, drawing his pistol and aiming at the lock.

"Wait—" Annie winced, covering her ears as the roar of his Colt echoed off the stone walls. "Was that really necessary?" she asked in irritation.

"It was practical." He lifted the trunk's lid and started hunting through the contents, taking out an old quilt, a woven coverlet, a few tools of some kind, and a couple of small burlap sacks, one of which seemed to be empty. "Looks like there was some food."

"Was?"

"Something got to it first. Mice or some such." He dug a handful of grain out of one sack. "There's a hole in the bottom of this trunk."

Mice . . . or some such? Annie lifted her feet off the floor, drawing her knees in and wrapping her arms around them as she peered at the dirt in the dim light of the lantern. She didn't want to think about what *some such* might include, out here in the mountain wilderness.

Lucas closed the lid of the trunk, setting the quilt and coverlet on top and opening the other burlap sack.

"No horse," Annie said tremulously, beginning to understand the seriousness of their situation. "No food—"

"Coffee." Lucas held up the sack with an expression of pleasant surprise.

"I'm so happy the mice left the coffee for you," she said dryly.

He set it on the trunk, glancing toward the stovepipe. "Roast squirrel's not too bad."

Annie blinked, trying to tell if he was serious. "Is this what it's usually like on the frontier—living in a cave, competing with mice for food, roasting squirrels?"

"Colorado doesn't count as the frontier anymore. It's an official state. Frontier's a ways west of here."

She frowned at him. "Thanks for the geography lesson." She took off her moccasins and started to rub her feet, then stopped, inhaling a sharp breath as feeling started to return to them swiftly and painfully.

"Keep at it. You'd better get the blood flowing." Lucas walked over to her.

"It hurts."

"Good. That means maybe you don't have frostbite. And maybe you won't have to have them amputated."

She glared up at him. "Must you always be so—"

"Truthful?"

"Blunt." She started rubbing the soles of her feet again, cautiously, gingerly.

Lucas knelt in front of her and brushed her hands out of the way. "Not like that."

He took one of her feet in both his hands and started massaging.

"Ouch . . . ooh . . . ow . . . that . . . *hurts*," she protested.

But he didn't release her, no matter how she tried to wriggle out of his grasp.

And after a few moments, it didn't hurt so much. In fact, the powerful strokes of his fingers along her cramped muscles started to feel rather . . . pleasant.

Warm and tingly and . . . oh, yes, right there. The cold and pain faded, rapidly replaced by a flush of heat as Lucas's callused hands moved over her arch, and sole, and heel, and rubbed every toe, and stroked the surprisingly sensitive curve of her ankle bone.

She bit her lip by the time he shifted to her other foot, and not because of the pain in her muscles.

When he finally finished and released her, she drew her legs under her, feeling a bit breathless. For the first time all day, she was warm. "Th-thank you." After a moment she added, "Marshal."

"Next time you find yourself in a snowstorm," he admonished, looking up at her with a weary sigh, "keep your shoes on." He straightened and crossed to his saddlebags.

"Next time you find my shoes lying in the snow," she muttered, trying to gather her scattered senses, "pick them up and bring them with you."

He dug a tin cup and some other items out of his saddlebags, then returned to the stove, where the bucket of snow had become water. After unwrapping the bandage from his head, he started tending to his own injury.

Annie stood up, experimentally taking a few steps, relieved to discover that her feet and legs felt much better. The dirt floor, however, was cold, almost frozen. The pot-bellied stove might be good for melting snow—and maybe for roasting squirrels—but it didn't provide enough heat to make this place very comfortable. She could still see her breath.

"So we don't have a horse," she said again, "and we don't have much food—"

"We've got water. And the supplies in my saddlebags. And firewood. We'll get some rest, try to find the horse in the morning."

A plan. He had a plan. Annie felt a bit relieved. "And what if we can't find the horse?"

He didn't answer.

She turned toward him. Saw a muscle flexing in his lean, beard-darkened jaw.

And felt like she'd swallowed a chunk of ice, felt it settle in the pit of her stomach. She understood what he was trying not to tell her.

Without a horse, they were trapped here. Stranded in the middle of nowhere. And if the snows kept up like they had . . .

They wouldn't last long on coffee and squirrels.

"I—I may not know anything about survival in the wilderness," she said, her voice wavering, "but it sounds like . . . like we could . . ."

He didn't say anything for a moment.

His voice was quiet. "We're not going to die out here."

"You hesitated."

He looked over at her, his gaze meeting and holding hers. "We are not going to die out here," he said firmly. "If we can't find the horse, we'll wait for the weather to clear and walk out."

That plan was not as reassuring as his first plan. Not nearly. Annie shivered, realizing that for once, Lucas didn't seem quite as self-assured and fearless as he always did.

And for the first time, she missed that maddening, confident quality he always had.

She sank down onto one of the chairs in the corner. He finished cleaning the bullet wound in his temple, dabbing at it with his bandanna.

"You're bleeding again," she whispered.

He just nodded. And folded the bandanna into a pad and tied it in place with the strip of cloth from her petticoat. Then he went over to the bed, pulling it across the dirt floor, closer to the stove. He picked up his coat and their icy blankets, and hung them on the foot of the iron bedstead to dry.

Then he started unbuttoning his shirt. "You probably should get out of those damp clothes."

He said it casually, as if it were a simple and sensible idea, not shocking at all. And suddenly Annie realized what else being stranded here meant.

It meant spending the night alone with him. Several nights.

With no bars between them.

He hung up his shirt on the bed. Annie remained right where she was. In the corner. Fully clothed in her freezing, clinging dress and undergarments. And she watched him.

The muscles of his back and arms flexed in the lamplight as he unrolled the mattress, spreading the coverlet out across it. Along with the quilt. There weren't any pillows. He sat on the bed and took off his boots. Then he lay down and stretched out on his back with a muffled groan.

"What are you doing?" She still hadn't moved.

"Going to sleep," he said as if it should be obvious, sliding beneath the quilt and rolling on his side.

Annie frowned. So he intended to take the bed *and* all the covers? But then, she thought grudgingly, he needed them more than she did, since he was the one who'd been shot.

She started looking around, trying to think of where she was going to sleep. The moth-eaten animal pelts hanging on the walls didn't hold much appeal as blankets. And the freezing cold floor wasn't much of a choice. Especially since there were mice—or some such—running around in here.

"Are you coming to bed or not?"

Her stomach flipped at his grumbled question. She turned her head and stared at him blankly, her heart beating too hard. "You mean I . . . we . . . we're both going to . . ." Heat flooded her cheeks. "I—I don't think that's a good idea, Marshal."

"Antoinette," he said with exaggerated patience and a bleary-eyed stare, "I started out my morning getting shot. I spent all last night riding. I spent the better part of an hour hiking down this mountain on foot. And I haven't eaten much of anything since breakfast yesterday. Now, it's real flattering that you think I might be capable of something more than sleep right now." The hard line of his mouth curved downward. "But I'm not."

Annie lowered her lashes, realizing he was right. Of course he was. A bit too brusque and pointed, but right. Lucas might be tough enough to chew nails and spit tacks, but even he had his limits.

The man might be a hero, but he was also human.

"All I want is sleep," he continued, "and I'd just as soon not freeze to death while I'm doing it. This is no time to get all shy and squeamish. If we're not going to die out here together, then we have to survive, together."

Practical, logical. As always. And it was true: The question of whether or not they should share a bed was somewhat less important than other questions at the moment. Like whether they could stave off the cold and stay alive.

"Would you . . ." she said haltingly. "Would you . . ."

"What?" he snapped.

"Turn down the lantern."

He muttered a curse, but complied with her request, leaning over the side of the bed to turn the lantern down, all the way.

As darkness enveloped the small, dank, drafty cabin, Annie stood up and unbuttoned her dress, shivering as she let it fall to her ankles, followed by her ruined, tattered petticoat. But she decided to leave on her camisole and pantalettes. They were chilly and damp. But essential.

Grateful for the darkness, she walked over to the bed, reminding herself that she and Lucas had trusted each other with their lives today. She would just have to trust him to keep his hands to himself tonight.

The mattress was stuffed with cotton, and it felt lumpy, and the woven coverlet was stiff and scratchy against her skin, and the bed creaked. But the quilt felt soft and warm as Lucas held it open and covered her with it.

She curled up on her side, with her back to him. The bed wasn't very wide, wasn't really meant for two people. She thought he might make some effort to keep distance between them.

But he didn't. In fact, he looped an arm around her waist and drew her close to him. She tensed. "Marshal—"

"Need to conserve heat." He settled in beside her, his hard, muscled body going slack. "Go to sleep, Antoinette. You're perfectly . . . safe . . . promise . . ."

He seemed to barely have enough strength left to finish mumbling those few words. His arm around her relaxed.

But Annie didn't sleep. Couldn't. She just lay there, staring into the darkness. Listening to the wind battering the small cabin, howling through the stovepipe. And for some ridiculous reason, tears began sliding down her cheeks.

After all she had been through yesterday and today, why she should cry now, she couldn't figure out. She shut her eyes, tried to keep quiet. Didn't want to bother Lucas. Especially when he needed rest so badly.

But he must've heard her.

Because after a minute, she felt his fingertips on her cheek, his thumb brushing her tears away.

"Don't," he said quietly.

Annie buried her face in the coverlet. Why did men always say that when a woman cried? *Don't*. Like it would solve anything. Like she could just turn her emotions on and off. She was afraid. He might not understand or care, but she was afraid.

"Shhh, we'll be all right," he said. "I'll keep you safe."

Annie opened her eyes. He did understand. Without her having to say a word, he understood.

And he did care.

I'll keep you safe. Nobody had ever said that to her, not in her whole life.

And even though he didn't say any more, her tears stopped. His arm settled around her waist again, and he drew her close, and somehow she felt . . . protected.

Maybe because Lucas was the kind of man who really could keep a woman safe, who would always chase the dark things of the world away. Strong and unyielding, full of courage and fire and determination. And moments of unexpected gentleness.

The kind of man most girls grew up dreaming about. Dreaming that he would ride up on his horse someday and carry them off into the sunset.

But Annie knew better than to believe in dreams. Life had taught her too many times that they didn't come true. Not for women like her.

So as she closed her eyes, and tried to rest, she also tried very hard to remember that she didn't need a man's comfort or caring, or his strong arms around her. Didn't need this at all, she thought as she began to drift to sleep.

Didn't . . . need . . . Lucas.

12

Lucas remained still as he opened his eyes just a bit, his head hurting as if some persistent railroad worker was pounding a spike into him. He lay on his back beneath the quilt, blinking in the lamplight, realizing two things at once. First, he was alone in the bed.

Second, he could smell hot bean soup. And frybread . . . and coffee. His stomach growled at the warm, mingling aromas. When he recovered from his surprise enough to lift his head—cautiously, wincing—and look around, he discovered that Antoinette had been up for some time.

Apparently she had been busy while he was still asleep: She had not only brought in more wood for the fire, which was crackling in the stove, and made a meal, she had straightened the place up a bit, cleaned away some of the dust, arranged all the chairs neatly around the table in the corner, made everything tidy.

At the moment, she sat at the table with her back to him, wearing her plain brown dress, the food spread out around her: iron frypan, a metal coffeepot, the tin cup and plate from his saddlebag. Across from her sat another cup and plate she must have found somewhere in the dugout.

She had set two places. Had made him breakfast.

Lucas rested his head back against the mattress, regarding her in silent surprise for a moment. He never would have guessed that Antoinette might know how to cook—never mind be able to make something out of the few ingredients they had on hand. It only drove home what he'd been brooding about—or rather, trying *not* to brood about—since he'd opened that letter from the Denver orphanage.

Though he'd spent weeks hunting this woman down and almost a month in her company, the truth was he knew damn little about her.

Lucas sat up, groaning softly at the pain in his temple, and she turned toward him.

"Good morning," she said, a bit hesitantly. "How are you feeling?"

He considered that question for a moment, gingerly probing his bandaged temple. His head still ached, and his throat was parched with thirst, but the dizziness was gone. "Better." A good night's sleep had been exactly what he'd needed. "What time is it?"

"Almost midday, I think."

Lucas rubbed his eyes. A good night *and* half a day's sleep. He moved to sit on the edge of the bed and looked up.

Their gazes met and held for a moment, until she lowered her lashes and glanced away, a hint of dusky color in her cheeks.

He grabbed his shirt from the bedpost, studying her by the lantern's glow. She had tamed her curls into a long, thick braid that hung down the back of her chair, the end tied with a strip of cloth from her petticoat—a match for the one still knotted around his head. She almost looked like a schoolgirl at her desk, vulnerable and sweet, sitting there so quietly, her head bent.

Lucas pulled his shirt on and started buttoning it.

He'd kept his promise last night. She had been completely safe beside him. Unharmed.

Untouched.

He'd been left with nothing but vague, dreamlike memories of her soft, rounded shape curled against him beneath the quilt. And her body shifting during the night, snuggling closer to his warmth. And her leg resting against his, her skin warm even through the heavy denim of his trousers.

Last night, he'd meant what he'd said—he hadn't been capable of anything more than sleep.

But apparently he was feeling better.

Because just the hazy memory of her lying beside him, almost naked, was enough to heat his blood and stir a taut feeling low in his belly.

He grabbed his boots, tugged them on, and stood up.

"I was going to wait," she said, gesturing to the food on the table, her empty plate, "but I was starving, and I didn't want to wake you—"

"Don't worry about it." He went outside to heed the call of nature, and to take a few deep breaths of the frigid air, trying to chill the fire from his veins before he allowed himself near her.

Then he came back inside, a blast of snow and wind and sun blowing in with him as he shut the door.

"It hasn't stopped snowing." She sounded worried.

"No." He walked to the bucket of water that sat on the stove, poured some into a dented basin, and carried it to the corner, where there was a fragment of mirror nailed to the wall. He grimaced at his bearded, blood-stained face. When he unwrapped the bandage from around his forehead, he saw that at least the crease in his temple had stopped bleeding.

After tending the wound and washing up, he walked

over to the table, took a seat across from her, and dug into the food hungrily.

"Good," he said when he paused long enough between mouthfuls to speak. He tried the coffee and nodded appreciatively. "Damned good."

"Thanks." She sat watching him, her voice quiet. "Luc—Marshal . . . about the bounty hunter, I wondered . . ." She hesitated, shifted on her chair. "I never asked about Travis," she said finally. "Is he all right?"

"When I left town," Lucas said around a mouthful of frybread, "Holt seemed to think he would be fine."

"I'm glad." She was silent for a moment. "You thought I had escaped, didn't you? You thought I was the one who'd hurt him."

He lifted the cup of coffee and took a long swallow before he replied. "All the evidence pointed to that at the time," he admitted.

"All the evidence," she echoed softly. "Why did you risk your life to save me?"

She looked up at him from beneath her lashes.

He studied the rim of his cup. "It's my duty to look after anyone who's in my custody. You're my—"

"Prisoner," she finished for him, nodding. She picked up her empty dishes and stood, carrying them over to the bucket of water on the stove. "I understand."

Lucas set the coffee down and stared at the tabletop. She didn't understand a thing. She couldn't *begin* to understand why he had done what he'd done.

Damn it, *he* didn't understand any of this: why she stirred his blood like no other female he'd ever set eyes on. Why she had possessed his every thought for weeks.

How could he feel this way about *any* woman? Let alone *her*?

She had been his brother's mistress.

Had taken James's life.

And Lucas was so obsessed with her, he had almost died for her, had killed for her without remorse.

It was like being torn in half—part of him resisting and resenting her, part of him wanting so badly to take her in his arms.

To kiss her, learn the taste of her, feel her body soften and open and respond to his. He wanted that with an urgency unlike any he'd known before. *Need* was the only word he could call it.

He needed her. More than he needed shelter from the wind and the storm. More than he needed food or even air. For reasons he couldn't understand.

And she stood there with her back to him, silent, taking longer than necessary to wash one cup and one plate. And she thought she understood him.

With a frustrated curse, he pushed back from the table and paced over to the door, to the bed, to the stone wall at the back of the dugout. He found himself eye-to-eye with a wolf trophy on display, its pelt stretched out and nailed up by the paws.

Lucas frowned, feeling a certain kinship with the fallen predator—except that the poor son of a bitch was out of his misery.

And the wolf had probably died from a nice, quick rifle shot . . . not from having his guts all torn up by what he felt for a female.

He turned and settled in next to the wolf, resting his shoulders against the rock, crossing his arms over his chest. He expelled a harsh breath.

"Tell me how it happened, Antoinette."

"How what happened?" she asked.

"How you shot James. Tell me what happened that day."

With a startled gasp, she looked over at him.

He held her gaze across the lamplit darkness between them. There was no taking it back now, no more ignoring the question that had been gnawing at him for so long. He wanted her answer. Needed to know.

But she shook her head. "You decided a long time ago what you were willing to believe. I *tried* to tell you the truth the day you arrested me, and you wouldn't let me. You never even gave me a chance—"

"I'm giving you a chance now."

"Why? All this time you've only cared about *your* version of what happened. And now you want the truth? Why does it suddenly matter to you?"

Lucas looked away. *Because I can't believe you're a killer. Because you're so damned sensitive and gentle and softhearted. Because you are not capable of cold blooded murder.*

Because you're not what I thought you were.

When he hesitated, she turned away. "You're just like everybody else back in St. Charles," she said bitterly. "Not one of them ever gave me a chance. *Me.* Annie Sutton. Never mind what my mother was—"

"I know you're not your mother."

For a moment, she seemed unable to speak.

Then she pinned him with a glare. "Really?" she asked sarcastically. "I've lost count of the number of times you've called me a whore—like you thought I was born and raised in a cathouse while my mama was between customers."

He gritted his teeth. "I don't know where you were born and raised. You never told me."

"You never asked!"

"I'm asking now."

"In a backwater cabin that wasn't much bigger than

this place." She choked out the words. "In a patch of Missouri woods that couldn't be called a town. I started out with a big brother and a papa who was a farmer and a mama who was the prettiest lady around. And all I remember is Papa grumbling about bad weather and bad crops, and we were all hungry a lot, and it was the happiest time of my life."

She turned her back, her shoulders rising and falling rapidly as if she were struggling for breath.

Lucas didn't know what stunned him more: that her childhood had been similar to his own boyhood days on his family's farm—or that she'd grown up with a father and an older brother.

Men who should've taken care of her, watched over her. Protected her. "What happened to them—your father and your brother?"

"Papa left when the war started," she said bitterly. "The militia came looking for recruits and he ran off. We tried to find him—Mama and me and my brother Rafe—but we never did. That was when Mama moved to St. Charles. And *that* was when everything changed."

Antoinette reached down and picked up the empty tin cup she had washed, turning it around in her hands as she continued.

"We took rooms in a boardinghouse, an awful place down on the river, and Mama started getting lots of visits from what she called her 'gentlemen friends.' Yankees, Confederates, it didn't seem to matter to her. Nothing seemed to matter to her after Papa ran off. Nothing and . . . nobody."

Lucas felt sick, imagining what it must have been like: Antoinette couldn't have been more than five or six, watching an endless stream of soldiers and river rats and other men "visit" her mother. She would've been too young to understand why the people of St. Charles scorned her. People she didn't even know, who didn't know her.

Not one of them ever gave me a chance.

People like him.

"As soon as Rafe was old enough, he left." Her voice had become hollow. "Went off to make his fortune in the West so he could rescue us all. But he never came back either. He disappeared. Just like Papa." She set the tin cup down. "After that, it was just Mama and me."

Lucas studied her, understanding for the first time the flashes of strength he had always noticed beneath her fragility. And her spark of stubbornness. Even her cooking ability.

She had spent years making something out of nothing, fending for herself, with no one to take care of her and a mother who didn't give a damn about her. "Why didn't *you* leave when you were old enough?" he asked, shaking his head.

Her eyes widened in surprise. "I couldn't leave Mama. I couldn't abandon her like everyone else."

Lucas stared at her, astonished that she would be so loyal to her mother in spite of everything. It was beyond his comprehension that anyone could care *that* much for someone, flaws and all.

But she had stayed. Had sacrificed any hope of a normal life, of friends or a place in the community or a husband and children of her own.

Had chosen a far different life. "And how did you meet James?" Lucas asked tightly.

She hesitated, walking over to the table, reaching out to grip the back of one of the chairs. "It was my seventeenth birthday," she replied, looking down. "Mama gave me a pretty dress to wear—the first new dress I ever had. And she took me to one of the fancy new hotels in town for dinner. But everyone was looking at us, and whispering." She shrugged as if it didn't matter, as if she were used to it. "And they turned us away. But I didn't really care. The dress was enough of a gift."

A smile touched her lips—brief, fleeting—as if it were a favorite memory.

After a moment she looked up, staring into the darkness, into nothing. "The next morning, a gentleman in an expensive suit and a paisley ascot came to see us. He said he represented Mr. James McKenna, and he said Mr. McKenna had an offer for me. 'A mighty fine offer,' he called it." A look of pain crossed her features. "I remember exactly the way he looked at me when he said it."

Her eyes met Lucas's briefly before she shifted her gaze back to her hands, gripping the chair. "James had seen me from the window of his office," she told him softly. "And after Mama and the man in the ascot went and talked, she came back and said . . . said . . ."

Antoinette's voice choked out for a moment.

"She said I would have a fancy suite in that very same hotel that had turned us away, with a feather bed, and a maid, and a big coal stove to keep warm in the winter." She blinked rapidly, her dark eyes glistening in the lamplight. "And all I had to do in return was nothing, really. Almost nothing."

Lucas felt the muscles in his jaw harden. Maybe it hadn't occurred to Antoinette—maybe she was too innocent or naïve to see it this way, or too blind where her mother was concerned—but he would bet his last dollar that her mother had had a reason for dressing her up and parading her down St. Charles's main street. And it hadn't been a birthday celebration.

She had been advertising beautiful merchandise for sale.

"Did James offer to take care of your mother, too?" Lucas asked tightly, already certain of the answer.

She nodded. "He gave her some money every month. I never saw her so happy. She was getting older, and—"

"And her beauty was fading and she wanted to make sure she was taken care of. Even if it meant making you pay the price."

Antoinette's head came up, her eyes narrowing. "That's not true. She wanted *me* taken care of. She wanted me to have a better life than what she had, and she knew James would see to that."

Lucas didn't say any more, deciding to keep his opinion to himself. Any woman who would trade her own daughter for money wasn't worthy of being called a mother—though he could think of a few other choice words for her.

"I could've said no," Antoinette insisted, lifting her chin, clearly unwilling to spare herself any of the blame. "I knew it was wrong. But he was kind to me, from the first time we met. He was the first respectable gentleman who was ever *kind*. And Mama . . . she . . ."

Antoinette let go of the chair and turned away from him, wrapping her arms around her waist. "She said all I had to do was be . . . be careful not to make any . . . mistakes." Her voice became hoarse. "You always said that my mama probably taught me a lot of tricks, but she only taught me one." She hung her head. "How to be careful," she whispered. "How to avoid having a baby. *That* was the only trick she ever taught me, the only advice she ever offered me."

Lucas shut his eyes, wishing he could take back the brutal words he had flung at her so many times.

"So you see, it *was* my fault," she continued unsteadily. "It was my fault that it all went wrong. After three years, I . . . I must not have been careful enough, because this summer I realized I was . . . carrying James's baby."

She pronounced *baby* as if the idea, the very word itself, held all the magic and mystery and joy in the world.

"I denied it for weeks." She took a deep, shuddering breath. "I made up all sorts of excuses not to see him because I didn't know what would happen. Then I went to Mama—and she was furious. She told me I should just get rid of it, go to a woman she knew who would 'help' me. But I pushed her away when she grabbed my arm." Antoinette rubbed her bicep as if it were still bruised. "I couldn't do that to my baby, to James's baby. So I left. And I went to the only other person I could turn to."

"James." Lucas steeled himself, half dreading this, half needing to hear the rest of it. All of it.

"It was raining that day." She closed her eyes. "I was soaked through and covered in mud by the time I reached his house. I'd never been there before, but I was just so scared. I just kept thinking that it was happening all over again—that my child was going to grow up exactly like I did, poor and hungry and afraid all the time, with no father. No future."

She was breathing hard, started talking more quickly. "I didn't want to make trouble or cause a scene with his family. I slipped into his study, through the garden doors. He'd just gotten home from his office and he was putting something in the safe. He barely said two words before I just blurted it out. I told him I was pregnant."

A shudder went through her. "He didn't say anything for a moment. Then he . . . then he told me it was over. He said he'd had time to think while we were apart, and his children were getting older, and the last thing he wanted"—tears shone in her eyes and she looked up at the ceiling—"was to have any bastards running around the streets of St. Charles. He tossed his pocket money on the desk. Fifty dollars and a few coins. He told me that should be enough to get me a ticket out of town."

No. By God, that wasn't possible. Lucas felt every muscle in his body clench tight. He couldn't believe it, wouldn't believe his brother could be that cold. Not to anyone—especially not to a woman who had shared his bed for three years. A woman who was carrying his child.

"I—I could *see* sacks of cash in his safe," she whispered, tears sliding down her cheeks, "and all he gave me was his pocket change. That was all I meant to him, all I was worth."

"And when did you decide to pick up a gun?"

His sharp tone brought her gaze back to his. "There was a gun on the desk, next to his briefcase and the other things he'd brought home from the office. It was sitting right next to the fifty dollars. I—I was in a daze, and I was reaching for the money. I was going to just take it and leave. And then my hand was on the gun instead—"

"Why? Because you decided you wanted one of those bags of cash from the safe, too?"

"No," she retorted hotly. "I wasn't *thinking*. I wasn't thinking of anything except the pictures in my head—pictures of my child going through everything *I* went through growing up, and me ending up just like Mama . . . and for a second, as I was reaching for that money, it just seemed like it might be better if . . . if . . ."

"If you picked up the gun and demanded more than fifty dollars?"

"If I ended it all," she said in an emotionless voice.

Lucas stared at her, his jaw going slack with shock.

She had been thinking of shooting *herself*?

"But when I picked it up . . ." A sob tore from her and she covered her eyes with one hand. "James reached across the desk and tried to grab it from me. And it went off. It just went off."

Lucas turned away, bracing one arm against the wall, the stone rough and cold beneath his palm. Part of him still couldn't believe it. Didn't want to believe any of it.

"It all happened so fast," she said brokenly. "There was a sound like an explosion, and he fell backward. The servants came running. They were pounding on the door. I *tried* to help him, but it was too late. He was already . . . he was already gone."

Her voice dissolved in tears for a moment. "I was kneeling over him, covered in his blood. And they were pounding on the door and I *knew* what it would look like. Nobody in St. Charles would believe that it was an accident. I was his mistress. The girl from the boarding-house down by the river. The whore's daughter—"

"So you ran."

She nodded. "I looked up and saw those sacks of money in the open safe—and all I could think about was my baby, giving my child what I never had. A home, a future. So I took one. I took it and ran. I didn't even know how much was in it until later."

She seemed spent.

Lucas couldn't stand to watch her cry, but he couldn't make himself turn away from her again.

"I didn't mean to kill him." Her voice was less than a whisper. "He was the only person in my whole life who was ever kind to me." She sank forward, her head in her hands. "I didn't know anything about having a baby," she sobbed. "Mama only told me how *not* to have them. I didn't know what I was risking when I got on that stage-coach. I didn't want to lose my child," she choked out, "like I lost everyone else."

She buried her face in her palms and sobbed.

Lucas walked over before he was even aware of it, reached out to her before he could stop himself. Touched her arm.

She turned with a start, looking up into his face.

And he saw no deception in her eyes, only pain and loss.

"I didn't mean to do it," she said, her voice edged with desperation. "I only went to him that day because I was just so scared and . . . and alone . . . I wanted . . . I needed . . ."

He drew her into his arms.

She stiffened immediately.

"Shh," he whispered, his voice strained as he tried to convey that he wasn't coming to her out of vengeance, or anger. "Shh."

He just held her, somehow knowing instinctively what she had wanted from James that rainy afternoon and never got.

Strength and comfort and reassurance. She began to cry into his shirt.

And he felt burned by each salty tear.

13

Annie couldn't stop crying as he held her in his arms, enfolded so securely against his broad chest. Her cheek rested against the rough fabric of his shirt and she cried out all the pain that had been tearing at her heart, surrendering all of it to the warmth of his embrace, to his gentleness, to him.

And as the anguish poured out of her, a new emotion slowly filled her heart like a ray of light breaking through the darkness. Of all the ways Lucas could've reacted to what she'd told him, this was the last she had expected. But he understood. *He understood.* Never had she believed he might be capable of such tenderness and caring—for *her* of all people.

But he was a man like no other she had ever known. Fierce and strong, protective and gentle. A rescuer. A hero.

When she finally managed to get her tears under control and pull away from him, he let her go as carefully as he had taken her into his arms. As if she might shatter.

And a long, awkward silence fell between them.

They just stood there, staring at each other as if they'd never met before.

His eyes were dark, his expression strained. Unable to find words, she reached up, her fingertips brushing his stubbled cheek. And he cupped her face in one broad, callused hand, his thumb whisking away her tears—just like he had last night. So gently, so careful of her.

Neither of them said a word. He just drew her close, and she leaned into him, trembling with emotion as his mouth covered hers.

Annie's lashes lowered and she met his kiss with a sigh of longing. His lips molded to hers and she moved closer, needing his comfort, his strength. Needing *him*. His arms came around her, his hands tangling in her hair. She breathed in and he filled her senses with heat, and hunger, and the spicy, masculine taste of him.

His tongue parted her lips, his kiss so filled with passion that it sparked an answering ache deep inside her. A wave of unsettling heat poured through her. Her body melted against his.

Never had she been kissed this way—with such power and possessiveness. As if he were binding their souls together. As if there were no more yesterdays and no tomorrows . . . no one but the two of them in all the world. Her hands settled on his shoulders, slid around his back to draw him in tight, her fingers grasping his shirt.

When he finally lifted his head, her lips felt swollen, bruised—and her whole body felt burned. The sound of their breathing made harsh noise in the darkness.

He buried his face in her hair. "Annie."

The sound of her name on his lips brought fresh tears to her eyes. She didn't let him go. "Lucas." Her voice came out as a husky whisper.

Suddenly, his hands were fumbling with the buttons on her dress and her fingers were tugging at his shirt.

Warm, soft kisses brushed along her throat, her bared shoulder. She tangled her fingers in the hair at the nape of his neck. He was all lean muscle and molten gold in the lantern light, his arms rippling and sinewy, his flat chest covered with a mat of crisp, black hair that narrowed over his ribs and disappeared into the waistband of his trousers.

With a low groan, he bent and swept her into his arms, picking her up and carrying her toward the bed.

Her thoughts had scattered like snowflakes blown by the wind outside their shelter. But there were no questions, no hesitation in her heart. This was what she wanted. *He was what she wanted.*

The quilt was soft beneath her as he slid her dress off and dusted kisses over her every curve, Annie moaning at the touch of the cabin's chilly air against the dampness on her skin. His mouth sought and captured her breast through the thin fabric of her camisole, drawing her into velvety, liquid heat. He tore impatiently at the cotton fabric, bared her to his kisses.

His reckless hunger for her stirred a fierce response low in her belly, a desire beyond any she had ever known. Her body arched beneath him. His lips and tongue closed on her nipple, tugging, suckling.

A cry of pleasure dragged from her throat. A sensual fog descended around her as they shed the last of their clothes. He pressed his hips against her and she gasped at the hardness of his arousal, and then his mouth sealed hers in another deep, hot mating of lips and tongues and breath.

He shifted, covering her with his lean, muscled body, one arm sliding beneath her shoulders. His other hand slipped between her thighs. The bold intimacy of his touch stole her very breath, her cry of ecstasy lost beneath his groan of discovery and pleasure as he stroked her warmth, her wetness. A wordless sound tore from him as if he could bear no more.

He pressed one knee between her thighs. The blunt hardness of his arousal replaced his fingers at her feminine core.

Her eyes opened wide, her head tipping back at the feel of him entering her, her body parting and clasping his rigid length. Their voices mingled in a low sound of pleasure as he joined their bodies with a single thrust, deep inside her. She was stretched and filled by the size and heat and hardness embedded within her, her every muscle strung tight. He shuddered, kissing her cheek, her shoulder.

"*Lucas.*" It was a breathless sigh, a whisper of welcome and longing and passionate need.

And then she was beyond speaking, beyond hearing. All she could do was *feel* as he withdrew and thrust forward, deeper than before, filling her completely. She shut her eyes, giving herself to him, to the pounding emotions in her heart, to the wave of sensations that built as he moved inside her, again and again.

She gripped his shoulders, his hair, grasped handfuls of the covers beneath her as his rhythm became more powerful. The bed creaked with every deep, hard thrust.

And as suddenly as it had all begun, it was over. She felt his body tense, heard a hoarse shout tear from him, felt the rush of liquid heat as he spilled himself inside her. He collapsed, cursing, his weight pressing her back into the mattress, his body still sheathed inside her.

He was trembling. Actually trembling. Annie gave in to the impulse to wrap her arms around him and hold him. The sound of their harsh breathing made the only noise in the stillness, and the heat of their bodies seemed like the only warmth. After a long moment, he withdrew and settled beside her, his face buried in her hair.

And neither of them said a word.

Lucas opened his eyes in the darkness, blinking in the chilly air, realizing he had fallen asleep. He wasn't sure how many hours had passed. No light penetrated the dugout, only a bitter wind that rattled the stovepipe and howled past the door.

The lantern had burned out, and so had the embers of the fire, the stove a few feet away no longer giving off the least flicker of heat.

Annie lay curled up against him like a kitten. So soft, so delicate.

So trusting.

He opened his eyes wider. Though he couldn't see her in the darkness, he could feel every sweet, tantalizing inch of her. From the tendrils of her curly hair tickling his jaw, to her breath on his bare chest . . . to one slim, naked leg resting against his. Her hands were folded in front of her and the curve of her shoulder was tucked beneath his arm, as if he had drawn he close, even in sleep.

For a moment, he just lay there, breathing hard, fully awake now.

What the hell had he done?

Remorse and regret sliced through him like a double-edged blade. She had been vulnerable and in need of comfort—and he had taken advantage of her. Taken her to *bed*. He couldn't blame it on the effects of the bullet that had creased his skull; he might not have been at his physical best—but his mind hadn't been muddled. He had known what he wanted. Needed.

And it seemed not even a bullet from a .44 had been enough to stop him.

Annie shifted restlessly, one of her hands brushing his ribs, one breast now pillowed against the muscles of his chest. He inhaled a breath between his gritted teeth, his whole body suddenly taut, sexual heat flooding his nerve endings. The speed and intensity of his reaction to her dragged a groan from his throat.

He ordered himself to release her, forced himself to let her go. Slowly, he withdrew his arm from around her and she shifted again, away from him, onto her back with a little sigh. He levered himself up on one elbow. Now he could go. Could leave the bed without waking her.

Or he could lower his head and kiss her, find her with his mouth in the darkness. Make it better this time, make it right for her. Start at the slender curve of her throat and kiss every lush inch of her body . . .

Lucas shoved himself away and got out of bed, grabbed his trousers from the floor, pulled them on. The only thing to do was get out of here. Leave. Go outside into the frigid weather. Pray to God that the snow would be enough to freeze the fire and hunger from his blood.

But in some part of his brain, he knew that even a blizzard wouldn't help, that all the ice and sleet the Rocky Mountains could throw at him wouldn't help. From the start, *nothing* had been able to end this overpowering . . . attraction he had to Annie Sutton. He had tried distance, logic, seeking out another woman. But for the first time in his life, it wasn't just any woman he wanted.

It was one woman. One specific woman.

This woman.

He grabbed his shirt from where it had fallen, hunted for his boots. His gun belt made metallic noise as he buckled it on. For one moment—one stupid, heedless moment—he had forgotten everything. And he didn't *want* to forget.

Didn't want any of the soft, unfamiliar emotions that
had stolen through him when she responded to his kiss,
whispered his name. Gave herself to him.

All he was willing to feel for her was desire, raw
and physical and simple. That was all he wanted between them.

But if there were nothing but lust between them, he
wouldn't feel like hell now.

He headed for the door, grabbing his coat as he
yanked it open. Outside, he pulled it shut behind him and
went still for a moment, wincing, one hand braced
against the rough wood—and not just because of the
sudden, shocking brightness of the afternoon sun, or the
bite of the snow against his face, or the pain stabbing
through his temples.

What the hell had he *done*?

He thought of his sisters, and James's widow Olivia,
and young Peter and Cordelia. How would they feel, if
they knew that Lucas had developed this attraction to
James's mistress? That he had taken her to bed.

He pictured all of them staring at him, their eyes
filled with shock and betrayal.

Lucas straightened and moved away from the dugout,
walking blindly into the falling snow, his coat flapping
behind him in the wind. Instead of satisfying his desire
for Annie, making love to her only left him feeling worse
than before.

Hadn't he stood in Fairfax's saloon in Eminence not
two days ago, telling Morgan O'Donnell that any man
who just helped himself to a girl's favors and then tossed
her aside wasn't worth a bucket of warm spit?

So what did that make him worth this afternoon?

Lucas kept walking, not liking the answer. His mouth
hardened into a scowl. He had never had much charm or

tact around women—but he had sunk to a new low these past couple of weeks. Whenever he was with Annie, he acted like someone he didn't even know: hotheaded, irrational, impulsive.

Stupid. That was the word for it. Stupid.

And he seemed to conveniently keep forgetting that she was his prisoner. That she was in his custody. That it didn't *matter* what he felt.

It was his duty to take her back to Missouri and hand her over for trial.

Even if he believed she was telling the truth.

He almost wished he didn't. For the simple reason that he didn't want to believe that his brother had acted like a heartless bastard toward a woman carrying his child. Didn't want to accept that James wasn't the good, kind, generous man Lucas had always thought him to be.

There was also the question of what had happened to the gun. The constables had never found it. So if she hadn't taken it when she ran, where was it?

And yet, the story she'd told him was the only one that made sense.

The facts were just too plain. She had told the truth about wanting the baby. And giving away the money. He'd seen with his own eyes that she wasn't coldblooded. Wasn't *capable* of murder.

All the evidence added up: It had been an accident.

A tragic, goddamned accident had taken James's life—and cost the life of the child Annie had been carrying, and left two children without a father. And torn Lucas in half.

But did he believe her because of the facts?

Or because he wanted to believe her?

He lowered his head and hunched his shoulders as he walked toward the pines. Maybe he would find some sign of the missing damned horse. Maybe, in the light of day and the cold air, everything would get clearer. Including his senses and his thinking.

Or maybe, he thought sourly, he'd slip on a patch of ice and fall off a cliff and not have to think at all anymore.

14

Impossible. That was the only word. The man was impossible to understand.

The first night in the cabin, Annie had slept only fitfully, but after making love to Lucas yesterday afternoon, she had slept all through the night. Had felt so safe and sheltered beside him that she had enjoyed the first peaceful sleep she'd known in a long time.

But then she'd awakened early this morning—to find herself alone in the bed.

To find him stretched out on the dirt floor beside the stove, asleep.

At some point, he had apparently gotten up and decided not to come back: He had taken the wolf pelt and a few of the other furs down from the walls, piled them on the floor, and propped up his saddlebags at one end as a pillow. And he was fully clothed.

When she first opened her eyes, Annie had tried to tell herself that maybe it was some kind gesture of gallantry.

But that hope hadn't even lasted as long as it took her to pick up her dress and underclothes and put them on.

Now, as she washed up at the basin in the corner, she began to feel more and more uneasy. Looking at her reflection in the fragment of mirror hung over the washbasin, she noticed her lips, swollen from his kisses, and her hair, tangled by his fingers. The delicate flesh between her thighs still felt sensitive from where he had joined their bodies together so fiercely, so powerfully.

What they had shared yesterday had been quick and hungry and needy, but at the time, she hadn't regretted a moment of it, had given herself to him freely, with her heart.

But there had been only whispers of pleasure and sighs of passion between them . . . no words.

As she braided her hair, she frowned, telling herself she was asking the impossible; Lucas wasn't the sort of man who *ever* revealed his feelings with words.

His tender embrace and what had followed had *shown* her how he felt. She thought—assumed—that he understood her now, that he believed the painful truth about her past that she had revealed yesterday. That he cared.

On the other hand, he hadn't *said* so. Hadn't said any of that.

All at once, her heart fluttered with uncertainty. She knew better than to assume what any man was feeling. Or rather, she *should* know better.

As she turned away from the mirror, she remained standing in the corner, watching him while he slept. Tendrils of regret began to twine through her. For weeks, she had been trying to convince Lucas she wasn't a tramp—and now what had she done? Given herself to him. With no words of love or even caring between them.

Lord, she could hardly blame him if he thought the worst of her.

Annie started to pace. She had told him *everything* yesterday, spilled out every painful fact about her life, but did she really expect him to believe her—when the only proof she had to offer was her word? Lucas was a lawman; he made decisions based on facts and evidence.

Even if he *did* believe that James's death had been an accident, she wasn't sure he could ever forgive her. She was still the woman who had taken his brother's life. It was her fault.

Every time Lucas looked at her, he must think that. And he always would.

She heard him stir. With a little gasp, she spun toward him, feeling breathless and flushed, as if she'd been running.

He sat up, raking his fingers through his disheveled hair.

"Why are you on the floor?" she blurted.

He blinked at her drowsily, looked startled to find her standing there. "I, uh . . ." He stood up, running a hand over his beard-stubbled face. "Went to look for the horse yesterday. Couldn't find it."

He looked away as he continued. "When I got back, you were still asleep, and there was a lot that needed to be done. I went through my saddlebags and divided our supplies into daily rations. Chopped more firewood. Then did some hunting. Came back last night with a brace of grouse and a rabbit." He jerked a thumb toward the table.

For a man of few words, he was talking a lot.

And he still hadn't answered her question.

"I see," she said, clasping her hands in front of her, looking down at her interlaced fingers. "And why did you sleep on the floor?"

He fell silent for a moment.

And it wasn't the cool, remote silence she'd gotten used to back in Eminence. This was more like a tense . . . brooding.

"I thought it would be best if . . ." Again he paused.

She wished he would just tell her something simple, like he hadn't wanted to disturb her sleep.

Or say the words she longed for.

I understand now. I believe you.

I forgive you.

I care about you.

"What happened yesterday was a mistake."

Annie's head came up and all the breath seemed to leave her lungs. His words pierced her heart, no less painful for being what she had expected.

He turned away, his back stiff, his voice unyielding. "It was a mistake," he repeated, as if he wanted to make it absolutely clear. "It was a . . . moment of weakness. And it can't happen again. It *won't* happen again."

He walked away from her as if there were no more to be said.

Annie just stood there, unable to move, trying to blink away the burning feeling in her eyes.

She had thought Lucas *cared* about her, that he *felt* something for her—but she'd been wrong. What they had shared hadn't meant anything to him.

She didn't mean anything to him.

He was so upset with himself for giving in to a moment of *weakness* that he had left their bed. Didn't even want to come near her again. Could hardly even look at her.

"Antoinette," he said, his voice harsh, "I'm a federal marshal. You're my—"

"Prisoner," she choked out.

Annie, she wanted to say. *Yesterday you called me Annie.*

Her tears threatened to spill over. God help her, why hadn't she learned? Men only thought about *themselves.*

She had wanted Lucas's caring, his tenderness.

He had wanted sex. Any warm female body would have satisfied his needs; she had merely been conveniently close at hand.

And because Marshal Lucas McKenna viewed the whole world in terms of good and evil, saints and sinners, he had seen nothing wrong with taking what he wanted—because in his mind, she was permanently branded a sinner.

She stalked over to the stove and grabbed the empty water pail.

"Antoinette—"

"No, you're right. It was a mistake." Her voice wavered dangerously. She had to get out of here, didn't want to cry in front of him. "And we'll *both* make sure it never happens again."

She walked to the door and went out, pulling it shut behind her, her vision blinded by tears. A muffled sob escaped her as she slumped back against the rough wood, dropping the bucket in the snow. She covered her eyes with both hands.

She was the biggest fool who had ever lived. A few kisses, one embrace, a caress on her cheek, and she had stupidly heard tender words that he'd never spoken, and assumed he was feeling emotions that he'd never felt.

Dreams. Stupid, foolish dreams. When would she learn?

And she might, right now, be carrying his child.

Annie took a deep, steadying breath, trying to assure herself that she couldn't be pregnant. It had only been one time.

But once was enough, if she wasn't protected. Mama had made sure she understood that, had made her study Dr. Charles Knowlton's pamphlet *The Fruits of Philosophy* until she understood clearly how to be "safe," as Mama put it. Annie had always made sure she used one of Dr. Knowlton's methods of protection before James's visits.

And even that hadn't kept her "safe."

Yesterday, with Lucas, she had been swept away by his passion, so caught up in the newfound feelings in her heart, that she hadn't given a thought to the consequences.

But she couldn't be pregnant. God wouldn't do that to her, not like this. Not with a man who didn't care about her. Not after what she had suffered before.

Would He?

Annie shook her head in denial, shivering. But in spite of everything, the idea of a baby sent a tingle through her that was only partly fear.

When she lowered her hands, she saw that white flakes still swirled down from gray skies heavy with clouds. But it wasn't the sky that captured Annie's attention—it was the ground.

"Dear God." Her eyes widened. There had to be two feet of snow on the ground. Maybe more.

For a moment, she just stood there, her breath white against the bitterly cold wind. It looked as if Lucas had shoveled a clear place around the door yesterday, so they could get in and out more easily, but even that was half-full of fresh, white crystals that glinted in the morning sun. And the snow was still coming down, so thickly that she could hardly see more than a few yards in front of her.

A choked sound of distress slipped from her throat. She had never been afraid of snow before—but she had never seen snow like this.

She was used to Missouri snowstorms, like the ones that used to send her and her brother Rafe running out of their family's cabin on crisp winter mornings when they were little, to taste the icy flakes, and pelt each other with snowballs, and spell their names in huge letters with their footprints before it all melted.

Annie swallowed hard at the sweet memory. She wiped her eyes and picked up the empty water pail, forcing all her fears to the back of her mind.

There was no point in worrying about what had happened between her and Lucas, or what might happen in the future—not when the two of them might not survive beyond the next few days.

She moved a few feet beyond the door, starting to scoop snow into the pail. As soon as it was full, she turned to go back inside—but stopped halfway.

For a moment, she had thought she saw . . . No, it couldn't be. She shaded her eyes with her hand, peering through the falling cascades of snow, in the direction of the pines.

Yes, yes it was! A rider in the trees—a lone figure on a brown horse, trailing a pack mule behind.

Annie's heart started hammering. "Over here!" she shouted, dropping the bucket, waving her arms. "Help us! Over here!"

A second later she stopped, realizing two things: first, it wasn't necessary to signal him, since he was already heading straight toward the cabin; and second, not everyone traveling these mountains was necessarily friendly. It might even be the fur trapper who owned this place—and Annie doubted he would take kindly to strangers invading his dugout.

Then the rider stood up in the stirrups and waved one arm. *"Annie!"*

Annie blinked in surprise as she heard her name shouted across the distance—especially since it wasn't a man voice; it was a woman's.

In that same instant, the cabin door opened behind her and Lucas came rushing out, barefoot, his pistol in hand. "What the hell is going— God Almighty."

The rider had urged her mount into a gallop, racing

toward them, plumes of snow flying from beneath the horse's hooves, the mule braying in protest as it was tugged along behind.

"It's Lily!" As the rider drew near, Annie recognized Valentina's friend Lily Breckenridge beneath a wide-brimmed hat and heavy winter coat. Annie couldn't have been more surprised—or happier—to see a detachment of cavalry come riding up out of nowhere.

"Annie, Marshal!" Lily reined in when she reached them, smiling and breathless. Dressed in trousers and chaps and a wool shirt beneath her coat, she dismounted in an agile leap, her cheeks reddened from the cold, her voice filled with relief. "Sure am glad to finally find you! We've been searching for two days now—"

"We?" Lucas had been standing there looking stunned despite his bare feet, but he finally ducked back inside the open door.

"Folks from town," Lily explained. " 'Bout a dozen of us split up and went different directions." She took off her hat and knocked the snow from it, her blond pigtails falling to her shoulders as she shifted her attention to Annie. "Are you all right? Rebecca said some varmint ran off with you. None of us knew what in tarnation happened—"

"A bounty hunter kidnapped me. But Lucas—the marshal," she corrected herself quickly, "found me in time. He rescued me." Annie felt her cheeks redden and hoped Lily would blame it on the icy wind; she didn't want to supply too many details. "We're both fine."

Lily didn't ask what had happened to the bounty hunter—but maybe she didn't have to as Lucas reappeared, his boots on and his pistol in its holster.

"You rode all this way alone?" he asked Lily, disbelief and reproach mingling in his tone as he finished buckling on his gunbelt. "A woman traveling by herself in this weather—"

"I've been riding these passes since Sugarfoot here was knee-high to a June bug." Lily gestured to the mule, her chin rising indignantly. "And I can take care of myself just fine. I figured I owed you one, Marshal, seeing as you rescued Val and me from those drifters in the saloon."

"Thank you, Lily," Annie said warmly, smiling at her before giving Lucas a frown; he should be offering gratitude to their rescuer, not disapproving just because she happened to be a woman. Lily had risked her life to help them. "We're both grateful. I don't know what would've happened if you hadn't found us."

" 'T'ain't nothing. Folks in Eminence stick together." Lily walked over to the mule. "Lucky you two made it to old Peavy's dugout here. Nobody's seen weather like this since sixty-seven. I brought provisions and blankets and such." Lily started untying the canvas-wrapped bundles from the mule's back. "But you better eat and change right quick so we can skedaddle back to town before it gets any worse."

"Wouldn't it be better to wait out the storm?" Annie asked, walking over to help.

"Wait it out?" Lily shook her head, laughing. "Blamenation, Annie, we're about as high up in the Rockies as anyone can be, 'less they're a mountain goat. Snows only get worse from here on. We don't want to get stuck out here 'til spring." She handed over a small bundle. "Hard enough that we'll be stuck in Eminence 'til spring."

"What?" Annie blinked at her in surprise.

"What?" Lucas echoed sharply, walking over to them. "*What* did you say?"

"Storms started early this year." Lily shrugged.

"Passes usually don't close up for another couple of weeks, but seems they'll be closing right quick. Nobody gets in or out after that." She handed him a bundle. "Not even the mule trains will try to make it through now."

"We're *stuck*?" Lucas repeated. "In *Eminence*?" His expression turned as stormy as the clouds overhead. *"All winter?"*

Annie stared at Lily, shock and disbelief tumbling through her, then exchanged a glance with Lucas.

"Only if we get a move on and get back through that pass while we still can," Lily explained impatiently. "Otherwise, we'll be stuck *here*. Old Sugarfoot's an ornery cuss and he don't cotton to strangers, so I'll ride him." She untied another pack and handed it to Lucas. "You and Annie can share the horse."

Lucas had made himself a promise yesterday evening, while he was out hunting: He had resolved that he would start acting more like himself—steady, clearheaded, unemotional. Sane.

But just looking at Annie was enough to turn his thoughts to a muddle. Touching her was pure torment. And if she didn't quit wriggling in his lap, he was going to give in to his desire.

To deposit her in the nearest snowdrift.

"Would you stop that?" he growled.

"Sorry." She went still, settling back against him, her head tucked beneath his chin. "You were the one who insisted on riding this way."

Lucas grumbled a curse. He knew she was only trying to gain a little space between them, but it wasn't possible; before they left the dugout, he had decided it would be safest if she rode in front of him rather than behind, so he could hang on to her while the horse picked its way over the icy trails.

As they followed Lily along a snowy ledge with a sheer drop on their left, he kept one arm locked around Annie's waist, holding her securely against his chest.

Which was the problem. Even though Lily had given her a pair of trousers, two shirts, and a twill slicker to wear; even though Lucas had wrapped her in two blankets before scooping her up onto the horse, none of it helped.

No doubt it helped *her* keep warm, but it wasn't helping *him* at all.

He was still aware of the shape of her body beneath all those layers, the softness of the curves pressed against him.

She turned her head, looking at the sheer wall of rock that stretched above them on the right, her cheek resting against his throat.

Lucas, realizing he was holding his breath, forced himself to exhale. A few more hours of this and he'd be ready to dive into a snowdrift himself. Or check into an asylum. It was difficult to keep his attention on the trail and on Lily a few yards ahead of them.

Though Lily's mule seemed to have an innate, almost uncanny knack for choosing secure footing, the drifts had gotten so deep, they had actually debated turning back at one point.

Annie faced front again. "I didn't know," she said quietly, for the third time since they'd left the dugout.

"Right," Lucas finally responded. "It was just convenient that your ribs needed five or six weeks to heal," he said sourly.

"I don't control the weather—"

"No, but I'm sure Holt was thinking of this from the start. He knew if I waited around long enough we wouldn't be able to get off this godforsaken mountain—"

"How could Daniel have planned this? And it *did* take me almost five weeks to heal," she pointed out. "I only got here a few weeks before you. How was I supposed to know anything about snowstorms in the Rocky Mountains and passes closing?"

Lucas didn't reply. He knew he couldn't blame her for the weather. But the possibility that they might be stranded in Eminence for the next few months put him in a rotten mood.

"You're upset because you're still planning to take me back to Missouri." Annie's voice was soft, hurt. "You still don't believe I'm telling the truth."

A muscle worked in his jaw. "It doesn't matter what I believe," he told her honestly. "I'm a federal marshal. If I let you go, I'd be breaking the law."

"And you're nothing if not devoted to law and order," she said quietly, an edge of pain in her tone. "Good and bad, right and wrong—"

"If I don't take you in, someone else will. Another lawman, another bounty hunter—"

"And you'd rather it be you."

Lucas grimaced and looked away, out over the cliff. "I am not a judge and jury."

"No, of course not." Her voice held sadness, and resignation. "I understand."

Lucas's hand clenched around the reins. *I'm sorry.*

The words seemed to get stuck in his throat.

I'm sorry.

His whole life, he had rarely apologized to anyone about anything. For the first time, he wished he'd had more practice.

But he didn't want her forgiveness. Didn't want anything to add to this attachment growing between them. At first, he had been able to explain it away as simple, perfectly understandable desire. But it had changed and shifted somehow, into a different feeling.

One he couldn't recognize. Didn't trust.

All he knew was that this woman had turned his entire life upside down.

Lucas clenched his jaw. Before Lily had made her announcement this morning, he had been thinking it would be best to return to Missouri with Annie as quickly as possible. Explain everything to the courts and let them make sense of it. Put all this chaos behind him. Meet up with his deputies on the Rio Grande and get back to his work. Back to *himself.*

But now he had a different decision to make: If they really were stuck here, what was he supposed to do—keep her in a prison cell all winter?

As a marshal, his duty was clear: There was a warrant out for her arrest, he had taken her into custody, and he had to keep her in custody until they reached Missouri.

As a man, nothing was clear in his mind when it came to Annie Sutton.

And he didn't trust his motives for wanting to keep her with him.

He scowled into the falling snow, feeling unsure of himself. Unable to reach a decision.

And he hated the feeling.

It wasn't until sundown the next day that they finally approached Eminence, after spending an uncomfortable, sleepless night in a sheltered area of the pass. All three of them were worn out and half-frozen, and the animals were finished, stumbling the last few miles, ice crystals clinging to their muzzles and manes.

Lucas had never thought he could actually be *glad* to set eyes on Eminence, but when they came over a rise and spotted the town, he practically wanted to shout a hallelujah. As they rode, they came upon a few of the other searchers—a prospector, a miner, even a shopkeeper, each one sending up a whoop and a holler at seeing the objects of their search alive and well.

Lucas could hardly believe that these townsfolk—strangers, really—had willingly risked so much to save two people, or that they could feel so happy to find them safe. One man rode ahead to tell those who were waiting for news that "Annie and the marshal" were both all right.

Darkness had fallen by the time they rode into Eminence's main street, the town transformed by snow and moonlight into something that looked like a picture out of a kid's storybook, drifts sculpted into fanciful shapes against the buildings, everything glittering with ice, the roof and spire of the stone chapel at one end of the street blanketed in white.

But the deep snow and frigid temperatures didn't keep a noisy, happy-looking group from turning out to greet them—mostly Annie's friends, some carrying lanterns or torches.

Rebecca Greer came bustling ahead of the pack, her crimson cloak fluttering behind her. "Annie!"

Lucas barely had time to rein in and lift Annie gently to the ground before Mrs. Greer smothered her in a hug.

"Oh, you poor, dear lamb!"

"Rebecca." Annie fell into her friend's arms and held her just as fiercely. "I'm so glad to see you."

"Are you hurt?" The older woman set her back at arm's length, looking her up and down and squinting at her worriedly before shifting her attention to Lucas. "What in the blazes happened?"

"Bounty hunter." Lucas stepped down from the saddle, biting back a groan as every frozen muscle in his body clenched up in protest.

"By the horn spoons! I *told* you she was in danger." Mrs. Greer blustered at him. "I told you somethin' terrible must've happ—"

"Rebecca, I'm all right," Annie interrupted, gently

deflecting her friend's anger. "The bounty hunter was going to turn me in for the reward, but the marshal rode all night to find me and . . ."

While she started filling them in on everything that had happened—or rather, *almost* everything—Lucas took his saddlebags from the back of Lily's horse.

"You all right, McKenna?" Holt turned toward him after checking on Annie and Lily. He lifted his lantern and frowned at the bullet wound along Lucas's temple. "Better let me take a look at that."

"What's the rush, Doc?" Lucas gave him a dry look. "Sounds like we might be around another three or four months—not that that's news to you."

Holt furrowed his brow as if he didn't understand. "And how's that my fault? Snows came early this year."

"Yeah, I noticed." Lucas glanced at the dozen or so people gathered in the street, noting one conspicuous absence. "Where's Travis? He all right?"

"Resting at home. Told him to stay off his feet for a while, but he'll be fine."

"First good news I've had all day." Lucas flung his saddlebags over his shoulder.

"Can we go inside, please?" Rebecca wrapped her crimson cloak around Annie's shoulders, interrupting Annie's glowing description of Lily's heroic rescue. "Both these girls have near caught their death already, out in this weather. Poor lambs!"

Lucas noticed that Mrs. Greer didn't seem to give a fig if *he'd* caught his death.

Holt gestured for them to follow him. "Think I'd better take a closer look at all three of you."

"I'm fine," Lily said tiredly, still receiving hugs and hearty congratulations from everyone around her. "I'll be heading for the livery, Dr. Holt. I owe Sugarfoot and Wrangler here two nice big bags of oats."

Lucas led her brown gelding over. "Miss Breckenridge." He gave her the reins, then extended his hand.
"Thanks. Not sure we would've made it back here without you and that mule of yours. Next time I need a guide
through these mountains, I know who to ask."

She looked surprised, blushing and ducking her head
as if she wasn't used to receiving such praise. "I'd say
we're even, Marshal." She returned his smile as she
shook his hand. "Just glad I could help."

Lily headed off toward the livery and the crowd
started to disperse, a few following her to help her with
the animals, others heading home, all chattering at once
about the latest bit of excitement to hit their half-empty
town. Annie and Mrs. Greer trailed the doctor, who was
leading the way toward his place.

Lucas followed them.

Once they were all inside, the women settled on a
couch near the fireplace.

"Look, McKenna," Holt said as he closed the front
door. "I don't know what you think I had to do with winter storms hitting us early—"

"Five or six weeks," Lucas drawled. "Timing just
seems a little convenient to me."

"It wasn't a lie." Holt gave him an annoyed look as he
walked through the parlor toward his adjoining office.
"Broken ribs take a month or more to heal, but everyone's different."

"Land sakes, this critter thinks we were plotting to
keep you two here?" Mrs. Greer asked Annie as she
helped untangle her from the blankets she was wearing.
She squinted up at Lucas. "We were not hatchin' any
kind of snow plot—"

"I already explained that to him," Annie told her,
sounding tired and frustrated.

"Well, he is *the* most suspicious, ornery—"

"Rebecca, he did save her life," Holt said as he returned to the parlor with his medical bag. "And if that bullet had hit him a half-inch to the left, he wouldn't be here right now."

"And neither would I," Annie added softly.

Lucas arched one brow, surprised to hear them defending him. "I was only looking after the welfare of my prisoner," he said quickly, not sure who he was trying to convince. "And now that she's all nice and healed up, what are our chances of getting home to Missouri before next year?"

"There's no way out of here until spring." Holt set his bag on the chair and opened it, taking out vials and some nasty-looking instruments. "February maybe, March at the latest—"

"And I'm just supposed to take your word for that?"

"You don't believe me, give it a try," Holt retorted. "Passes around here are littered with the bones of idiots who got trapped by winter storms. First they eat their pack animals, then the leather straps on their packs, then their shoes. Then they die. Some were experienced mountain men. *That's* how dangerous it is trying to get through these passes in the winter."

Lucas felt his gut knot up. He had spent most of his adult life in the flatlands—Indian Territory, the Red River—had only passed through the Rockies a couple of times; he didn't know enough about this part of the mountains to know if they were telling him the truth.

But he remembered how grateful he'd been to set eyes on Eminence tonight—after just two days of getting to know these passes firsthand. Even with a skilled guide, they'd been lucky to make it through alive. He wouldn't want to count on that kind of luck a second time.

Still, he wasn't about to just accept that he and Annie were stuck here until spring. "This stuff could melt in a few days or a week, and we could get out of here."

"February or March," Mrs. Greer told him with an irritated sigh. "Ask anyone who's spent a few winters at this here altitude."

Lucas looked at her. "If all this is true, I suppose it means no mail until then, either?"

She shook her head. "Might be one last mule train that'll try and make it through, but probably not."

"So I can't even send a letter to my men, or a letter home to explain." He clenched his jaw. "My family and my deputies won't know what the hell happened to me."

His gaze settled on Annie.

"I'm sorry," she said, her eyes large and dark as she looked up at him.

"It's not your fault." His voice was sharper than he'd intended.

Holt came to stand between them. "McKenna, you want to join me in my office and let me stitch up that dent the bullet left in your head?" he asked with an annoyed expression. "I doubt a nasty infection will make you any more pleasant to be around."

Lucas eyed the instruments in the doctor's hands. "It's just a scratch, Doc. Not sure I want you coming at me with any sharp objects." He motioned to Annie. "Let's go."

"Hold on, McKenna. At least let me make sure she's all right before you lock her up again," Holt said. "She's been through a hell of a lot."

Lucas hesitated.

"Marshal." Annie clenched her hands tightly in her lap. "I may still be your prisoner, but you don't need to watch me every minute. I can't get out of Eminence at the moment."

Lucas glanced from her to her friends, and realized that much was true; at least for now, the passes were closed. She couldn't go anywhere tonight.

And maybe not for the next three months.

"Fine." Lucas headed for the front door. "When you're done, you know where you'll find me."

An hour later, when Lucas stepped into the darkened front room of Dunlap's hotel, he noticed two things.

First, a light was burning in the suite at the back.

And second, the place felt different. Maybe it was the cold weather, the ice on the windows, the moon shining through and casting everything in a silvery glow.

Or maybe it was that *he* felt different. Every time he'd walked into his makeshift jail before, he'd been filled with a sense of purpose. Driven by the need to see swift, sure justice done to his brother's murderer.

And now it was gone.

The fury, the determination, the need for retribution. Gone.

He walked toward the suite and entered the sitting room, dropping his saddlebags on a chair.

Annie stood at the open door of her cell, her face pale and her eyes wide. "God Almighty, you scared me," she said, releasing a wavering breath. "I didn't know who was walking in here."

"Didn't realize I needed to announce myself."

She frowned at him. "Your footsteps didn't sound . . ." She cut herself off, turned back into her room. "It brought back a memory of the bounty hunter, that's all. I wasn't sure where you had gone off to."

"Went to see Travis." He followed her into the cell, which was illuminated by a lantern sitting on the table beside her bed. She still wore the men's clothes Lily Breckenridge had given her: two shirts and trousers that were too big on her, rolled up at the cuffs, cinched at her waist with a belt.

The pants hung loosely on her, but they also revealed more of her legs than any skirt. For a moment, Lucas couldn't tear his gaze from her, finding every step she took somehow provocative.

Desire hit him so hard and fast, his heart and stomach did an odd somersault. He couldn't catch his breath.

God help him, how could just looking at her make him *ache*, make so many conflicting feelings crowd together inside him?

He glanced away, forcing himself to remember what was important: his duty, his family. He couldn't allow himself to forget that. Not again.

When he blinked to steady himself, he finally noticed what she was doing: She had an open satchel sitting on a chair next to the chest of drawers.

"Is Travis all right?" she asked, stuffing clothes from one of the drawers into the bag.

"Just fine. What, exactly, are you doing?"

"Leaving."

His eyebrows rose. "Excuse me?"

"I just came to get my things—"

"To go where?"

"Rebecca's. I'm going to stay at Rebecca's and help out in the store like I used to. Since I'm going to be here all winter, I have to earn my own way somehow. I can't keep living off my friends' charity."

Lucas frowned, though he couldn't help admiring her stubborn pride. And her willingness to work hard; some women would be perfectly happy to sit back and let others cater to them.

But Annie wasn't like some women. She wasn't like any woman he'd ever met.

Ever.

"And did you think of maybe clearing this with me?" he asked sharply.

She turned toward him with an irritated look. "Don't tell me you were planning to keep me locked up all winter?"

His eyes burned into hers, and he didn't reply. At the moment, all he could think of was that he wanted to kiss her. To ease that furrow from her brow . . .

No. It didn't matter what he wanted.

Or what he felt.

"Antoinette, nothing has changed," he said, trying to sound cold even as his gaze traced over her features, noticing every small detail: her skin like satin in the lamplight, the tendrils of hair that framed her face, her lashes thick as the black silk fringe on a surrey.

And the hurt in her dark eyes.

He turned his back. "And I'm not sure yet that we're going to *be* here all winter."

"And when do you think you'll be sure? Another week? A month?"

"When I know, I'll let you know."

"Am I supposed to stay in this cell until then?"

"Am I supposed to just let you walk out of here?"

"It doesn't make sense, Marshal! I can't leave town. You might not believe what everyone keeps saying, but I do." She resumed her packing. "You can't keep me here all winter."

"Legally, I can." *I have to.*

She slammed the drawer shut and gave him an exasperated look. "Why doesn't it surprise me that you would be difficult about this?"

"You're still in my custody—"

"And you're still taking me back to Missouri. So I can

stand trial. And probably spend the rest of my life in prison. If they don't hang me first."

He gestured angrily to the snow beyond her barred windows. "That just might be a moot question until next spring."

He didn't say the rest.

That part of him hoped the damned passes stayed closed, was grateful for the snow.

"If it's a moot question until next spring," she said, "there's no reason to keep me in a cell all winter."

Lucas stared at the rug, heard her close the last drawer and snap the satchel shut.

A muscle flexed in his jaw. "I haven't said you could go, Antoinette."

"Marshal," she said, her voice brittle, like it might shatter. Like she might shatter. "For once, *I* am making a decision."

She started to walk out.

"There's still the matter of a five-thousand-dollar bounty on your head," he said tightly. "Or have you already forgotten that nice gentleman who took you out of here a few days ago? You want to risk bringing someone like him—or worse—into Mrs. Greer's place?"

That stopped her. As he had known it would.

She turned in the doorway. He could see her thinking it over, knew she wouldn't do anything that might put her friend at risk.

"If nobody can get *out* of Eminence through those passes," she said, "I doubt anybody could get in, either."

"There's a lot of nasty SOBs in the West who'd risk more than frostbite for the chance at five thousand dollars," Lucas pointed out. "And there might already *be* another bounty hunter or two in town. How long do you think that first one was prowling around before he made his move?" He nodded toward the sitting room. "And five minutes ago, you thought *I* was someone dangerous coming in here."

Annie glanced from the barred windows to the door, and shivered.

Lucas moved to stand beside her. "You're staying here," he told her, "where I can keep an eye on you."

As he took the satchel out of her hands, she regarded him with a look of frustration and annoyance. And tears shone in her eyes.

Lucas felt like he'd just taken a double load of buckshot in the gut. All day, he had been trying to convince himself that he could subdue these unfamiliar, unwanted feelings she stirred in him.

But seeing her this way, seeing her almost in tears because of what he was doing, tore that idea to shreds. Because it tore him to shreds.

"Consider it protective custody," he said gruffly. "Anyone else tries to kidnap you or hurt you, they're going to have to go through me first."

He had to keep her safe.

And he had to keep in mind that she was his prisoner— because that was the only way he was going to make it through the winter days ahead.

And the winter nights.

The prospector slipped into the dark alley behind the abandoned mercantile, his boots crunching in the snow. Despite the frigid air, sweat soaked through his shirt and the patched woolen coat he wore. Twice, he paused to glance back over his shoulder.

Just when it seemed like a feller could get a break, everything had to go and take a turn for the worse. He'd been nervous as a long-tailed cat in a room full of rockers all night.

It wasn't twelve-thirty yet, but his friend was already

waiting, a cigarette in his teeth, the tip glowing red in the darkness.

"You heard yet?" the prospector whispered as he sidled up next to him. "He's *staying*."

"Hyup."

"All winter."

"Hyup."

The prospector glared at him in the moonlight. "*You* were going to take care of him," he hissed. "What happened to your ripsnortin' plan?"

"Couldn't get at 'im before." His friend blew a smoke ring that hung suspended in the air for a second. "Has to look like an accident, 'member?"

The prospector grumbled a curse, but knew it was true. From the day the damned marshal first showed up in town, he hardly ever left his jail for long—and with womenfolk going in and out, and that Ballard kid there all the time, things had been dicey. They couldn't just walk in and shoot him.

"Well, Jumpin' Jehosaphat, we got to do something. Can't even go to Fairfax's no more—I just about pissed myself when he came in like he done, in the middle of the day."

"Yeah, and you made sure to make a nice fast getaway. So now he'll think you had a reason. Sees us again, he's likely to take a good *long* look."

"Then we just have to do like we planned—somethin' that can't be pinned on us. Somethin' where there ain't no witnesses." The prospector started thinking. "Avalanche maybe. Or a cave-in, if we could get him out to one of them empty old mine shafts—"

"Be best if *we* wasn't around when it happened," his friend drawled. "That's sorta important for the 'can't be pinned on us' part."

The prospector scratched at his beard. "Give my last good tooth for a rattler or a gila monster long 'bout now."

"How many rattlers or gila monsters you ever seen in these parts? In the *winter*?"

"Well, I don't hear *you* coming up with nothing." The prospector hit his friend in the arm. "So far you been about as useless as a wart on a pretty gal's bottom. What ideas you got?"

"None yet. But I'll think of somethin'." He ground out the cigarette beneath his boot. "That lawman ain't gonna live long enough to see springtime."

15

A half-dozen townsfolk lounged around the potbellied stove in the middle of the general store, all chatting and laughing while some of their children played jacks on the sawdust-covered floor. With December snows holding the mountains captive, nobody had much to do in Eminence; most of the prospectors wintered in town, some with their wives, all staying at the various boarding-houses while they waited for the first touch of spring to work their claims again. Folks mainly spent their time visiting with friends and neighbors rarely seen in busier seasons.

Annie leaned on the counter, a frown curving her mouth as she sketched out an idea for a Christmas window display. She tried to find pleasure in the familiar smells of spices, tobacco, and coffee that filled the air around her, and in the genial buzz of conversation from the gathered homesteaders and miners.

But none of it lifted her spirits. Not even the tiny measure of freedom she'd been granted the past few days.

During the first two weeks after she and Lucas had returned to Eminence, he had kept her in her cell, like before. Then he had grudgingly accepted the fact that they were, indeed, stuck here for the winter—after talking to people in town, and several prospectors who'd lived in the area most of their lives, and even riding out to study the passes himself.

Finally, after much grumbling, he had relented a week ago and unlocked her door—though he'd made it clear he was only letting her out of the *cell*, not out of *jail*. She was allowed to work at Rebecca's during the day, but he had insisted on locking her in again each night.

Until a few nights ago when he stopped, with no explanation.

Maybe he had gotten tired of arguing with her. Or maybe he simply wanted his privacy. Whatever the reason, he had moved into a room down the hall and let her have the suite to herself; however, she was still expected to return to the jail every evening by dusk.

The two of them mostly kept their distance—and barely managed to be civil to each other. Like they were strangers.

But they weren't strangers.

Not since that day in the dugout, when she had told him everything, and he had held her so tenderly and kissed her, and . . .

Her frown deepening, Annie paused in her sketching and set the pen aside. She was *not* going to do this to herself. She had promised herself that she wouldn't let her thoughts and her heart get all addled again.

Lucas had made it clear that his duty and the law mattered more to him than anything. That he didn't care about her. He had risked his life to save hers—but only because he was seeing to the welfare of his prisoner.

A prisoner he intended to return to Missouri at the first opportunity, and hand over to the authorities. Regardless of what her fate might be in their hands.

His cold words still echoed through her memory.

Nothing has changed.

The sound of someone clearing her throat made Annie glance up and straighten.

Mrs. Kearney stood on the other side of the counter. She drew herself up to her full, imposing height, looking rather like a beady-eyed crow in her black dress, black bonnet, and black cape, a purse trimmed in jet beads clutched in front of her. "Where is Rebecca?"

"I'm sorry, ma'am," Annie said, putting her sketch pad away, "but Rebecca's busy this morning."

"I see. And when do you expect her to return?" As she spoke, Mrs. Kearney allowed her spectacles to slide down her long nose, looking at Annie with an expression of distaste as if she were a half-clad dancing girl who belonged in a cheap burlesque show.

Annie lowered her gaze, her hands wringing the white apron she wore over her dress of checked green gingham. All at once, she felt like sinking down behind the counter.

It had taken her only a few days to settle back into the life of the town—but it wasn't quite like it had been before. This time, everyone knew the truth about who she was and what she had done before she arrived in Eminence. During the past week, she'd been surprised by the way many townsfolk had accepted her presence among them.

And she hadn't been surprised that others—like Mrs. Kearney—had made it clear they would no longer shop in Rebecca's store when Annie was there. They didn't want to be waited on by someone like her: a wanted criminal, the daughter of a whore.

A woman who had spent three years as a rich man's mistress.

Annie kept her eyes downcast. "Rebecca will be busy in the storeroom most of the day."

Since it was Saturday, she and Rebecca had both ar-

rived at six in the morning, to greet the homesteaders
who came in once a week to trade their surplus eggs and
butter, or a cured ham from their smokehouse, or some
fresh-plucked chickens for goods they needed; folks had
harvested their gardens and butchered their animals in
the fall, so everyone's fruit cellars were filled with cured
meats and preserved fruits and vegetables.

The last mule train of the season hadn't been able to
get through, but the people of Eminence had more than
enough provisions to last the winter.

Rising so early had brought on one of Rebecca's
headaches, and she had decided to work in the darkened
back room, logging in and organizing the foodstuffs,
rather than in the lamplit brightness of the store.

Mrs. Kearney pulled on her black knitted gloves.
"Perhaps I'll come back another day," she said in a voice
that was even frostier than the temperature outside.

"I'd be happy to help you," Annie offered.

"You?" The woman sounded offended by the very
idea. "I hardly want someone like *you* touching food that
I'll be serving my guests."

Her tone made Annie flinch, flooding her with memories of St. Charles. All her life, people like this had made
her feel worthless. Annie had long ago gotten in the
habit of stepping aside when she saw them coming,
keeping her gaze lowered, getting out of their way to
avoid the whispers and name-calling.

Slowly, she forced herself to lift her head and meet
Mrs. Kearney's disapproving stare. "Whatever it is you
need, ma'am," Annie said politely, "I can help you with it.
Tomorrow's Sunday, so we'll be closed, but if you'd
rather wait until Monday . . ."

Mrs. Kearney pursed her lips—which, judging from
the deep lines around her mouth, she did often. "Indeed,
I believe I will." With a sniff, she turned and stalked away.

Before she could reach the door, it opened to admit Lucas and Travis, along with a blast of wintry wind.

"Marshal." Mrs. Kearney planted herself in his path, gesturing toward Annie with her black purse. "Isn't our town council paying you to keep our streets *safe* from people like this . . . *woman*? She's a known criminal. I really don't think she should be walking around free. And she certainly shouldn't be near these children—"

"She's hardly a danger to them, ma'am," Lucas said with a touch of impatience as he took off his hat and gloves.

"But she is hardly the sort of person who . . . who . . ."

"Ma'am, she's been working here for a week, and so far she hasn't committed one single crime." His gaze shifted to Annie. From his expression and his tone, he seemed to be in another of his thorny moods. "Now, she starts shooting up the town, or robs the bank, or disturbs the peace in any way, you be sure and let me know."

"Well, I . . . hmph!" With a swirl of her black cloak, Mrs. Kearney left.

Travis flattened himself against the counter as she swept past him and out the door. Then he chuckled, shaking his head. "That old bat Kearney always looks like she just swallowed a gulp of hair tonic."

Annie regarded Lucas in mute surprise as he walked toward her. "Thank you," she said when she could find her voice, "for defending me."

"Just doing my duty to keep things peaceful around here," he said curtly, tossing his hat on the counter. He headed for the stove in the center of the store, pouring himself a cup of coffee from the pot she kept brewing for customers.

Earlier this week, Lucas had visited Mr. Hazelgreen and accepted the town council's offer of a job, since his money wouldn't hold out all winter. Each day—morning, afternoon, and evening—he and Travis had been making the rounds of the various shops and buildings in town.

The rest of his time, Lucas spent here, keeping an eye on her and keeping watch over her; though so far, no more bounty hunters had appeared.

Travis walked toward her, pilfering a brown-and-white-striped horehound stick from a candy jar on the way. "We had a real exciting patrol this morning." He leaned his elbows on the counter, grinning broadly. "Chased a stray dog that got loose from a homesteader. Then a lady complained that her neighbor ain't cleaned the fall leaves off his chimney yet—we got a town ordinance against blocked chimneys. Fire hazard. Had to explain it to the feller—"

"And then Cyrus Hazelgreen asked us to chip the icicles off the eaves of his bank," Lucas said as he joined them, "because he considered them a threat to the safety of the citizenry." He took a drink from his coffee.

Annie noticed Lucas's frown; he seemed bored to distraction by the very events Travis considered exciting.

Then again, the boy seemed to find *everything* exciting, now that he wore a badge. The star bearing the words EMINENCE, COLO. above the words DEPUTY MARSHAL had him walking around like he was ten feet tall—even though it had been cut from the bottom of a coffee tin and the lettering was just painted on.

Lucas had given him the badge the day he himself became town marshal, officially swearing Travis in as a deputy; he'd wanted to honor the boy for being injured in the line of duty.

But true to his taciturn nature, Lucas hadn't mentioned it to her. Travis had been the one who related the story proudly, the first day he appeared in the store at Lucas's side.

"Travis," Annie said, wiping her hands on her apron, "Rebecca asked if I would send you back to the storeroom when you get a chance. She's got some heavy barrels that need to be moved. If you could help."

"Aw, Miss Sutton." Travis polished his badge with a corner of his shirt. "I'm a lawman now—"

"He'll be glad to." Lucas shrugged when the boy frowned at him. "Like I said, kid, it ain't all showdowns and shoot-outs. You signed on to serve the people of this town. Go on back."

Travis sighed in protest, but followed his boss's orders and ambled off toward the storeroom.

Lucas leaned on the counter toward Annie and set his coffee cup down, the steam from the dark brew rising between them.

She tensed. For three weeks, they'd barely touched, had come no closer to each other than the distance of this countertop. But every time he was near, her heart beat a little faster and an unsettling warmth went through her.

Annie lowered her lashes, irritated that she had so little control over her response to the man. She couldn't even help noticing how handsome he looked today, wearing a simple white shirt and a black vest that strained over his broad chest. The colors set off his tanned skin and dark hair, and the silver of the badge he always wore lately.

"Didn't hear you leave this morning," he said finally, his tone one of annoyance. "You were already gone when I woke up."

"It's Saturday, so I had to be here at six." She tried to ignore the uncomfortable, fluttery sensation in her stomach. "I didn't see a reason to bother you at the crack of dawn. Besides, I thought you decided to leave the cell unlocked so I could come and go—"

"I said you could help out at the store. I didn't say you could just come and go without a word to me."

Annie bit back a frustrated sigh. They stood there for a moment, staring into each other's eyes, the hum of conversation and children's laughter filling the store around them.

The man was truly impossible. Curt and unyielding and unreasonable and . . .

She was *not* going to let him upset her. Annie turned away to open a display case full of spice tins that needed rearranging.

"And speaking of coming and going," he continued, "on my way out this morning, I tripped on a woolen runner by the front desk. Never noticed it before—just like the table and chair that appeared in the front room yesterday. And the food and pots in the kitchen—"

"I want to start making my own meals," she said defensively, setting the tins on the counter. "There's no reason for others to keep cooking for me when I'm perfectly capable of cooking for myself. And there wasn't a table to eat at, so Rebecca found one in one of the abandoned buildings—"

"Along with the rug in front of the fireplace, and the settee with the embroidered pillow on it, and the curtains?" He scowled at her. "It's like some magical troop of elves has been visiting every day, decorating my jail."

"I didn't do it to annoy you," she said in exasperation. "The room was so empty, with nothing but a scaffolding in it. I thought it might be nice to make it a little more comfortable—"

"A jail isn't supposed to be comfortable. And a jail is no place for embroidered pillows." A glint of suspicion came into his eyes. "And what, exactly, does a settee have to do with cooking or eating meals?"

"I . . . well . . ." Annie hesitated, toying with a small tin of cloves in her hand, then decided it was time to confess. In a fit of pique a couple of days ago, she had planned a small act of rebellion. "Tomorrow's Sunday, so I don't have to work . . . and Katja Gottfried stopped by the store to invite me to a card party at her house—"

"No."

"I knew you would say that. I told her I wasn't allowed to leave the jail, so Katja suggested . . . she thought maybe . . ." Annie hurried to explain. "It would just be for a couple of hours, and we won't bother you. You'll probably be out patrolling with Travis. She's going to bring tea and cakes, and a few of her friends are coming over—"

"No." He shook his head. "They're not."

"But it would just be—"

"Antoinette, the answer is no."

Annie shut the door of the display case a bit too sharply. "Of course. You're right. What was I thinking? You never know where an afternoon tea might lead— a knitting bee. A box supper. All sorts of dangerous activities."

He frowned at her sarcasm. "No card parties. No bees. And no more decorating the jail." He picked up his coffee cup and started to turn away.

"Part of me actually thought you might understand," she said, anger and hurt making her voice shake. "How much I've always wanted to have friends, to be invited to things like card parties."

Their gazes met, his expression unreadable.

Annie looked down at her hands, clenched in her apron. "But it probably just seems silly to you," she finished softly.

He didn't reply for a moment.

"Antoinette," he said a bit more gently, "I'm not doing this to hurt you."

"Then why?" she asked in frustration.

"I have . . . obligations." He seemed to struggle to say the word. "I can't just forget them because I have . . ."

He stopped, as if unwilling—or unable—to explain further. An awkward silence fell between them. Then Lucas muttered an oath and turned away.

One of the prospectors waved him over to the potbellied stove. "Marshal, you want to get beat at checkers again?"

Lucas took off his coat, looking grateful for the distraction. "Depends, Ritter. We playing for pinto beans or real money today?"

One of the farmers surrendered a seat next to the cracker barrel, where the men had their own territory staked out, with comfortable chairs borrowed from one of the town's abandoned buildings, a spittoon nearby, and a large tin of chewing tobacco to share.

Annie shook her head, not even sure why she kept arguing with her jailer.

His reasons for his actions were always the same: his duty and the law. Right and wrong.

Nothing's changed.

He seemed determined to drive that point home at every opportunity—as if she needed reminders that she was still in custody. As if a day went by that she didn't dread what was going to happen when he dragged her back to Missouri to face a judge, a life behind bars.

Or a life cut short by a hangman's noose.

Her spirits even lower than before, Annie returned to her work. She was helping Rebecca organize the store into departments—grocery items on one side, dry goods in another, chewing tobacco and cigarettes in their own section, toys on a low shelf where they would appeal to children.

Rebecca knew where every last thing was in the shop,

down to the smallest tea leaf and sewing needle, but with her eyesight so poor, she sometimes had to struggle and search among the disorderly jumble to find a particular item for a customer. Annie wanted to make things easier for everyone.

Especially since she wouldn't always be here to help.

Only until spring.

Steam fogged the front windows of the darkened hotel as Lucas prowled the main room in the middle of the night, barefoot, dressed only in his black trousers. Annie was asleep in her suite.

He knew because her light had gone out an hour ago. He knew that because he kept glancing at the closed door of the sitting room now and then as he walked past, back and forth.

Like he had been doing almost every night.

God Almighty, he had hoped that moving to a separate room down the hall would help. He had hoped that staying out of her suite, not even locking her cell door would help.

But he still found himself lying in bed after dark, listening to the pounding of his own heartbeat.

She was still his last thought every night and his first thought every morning.

He glanced at her door again. Since their argument in the general store two days ago, she had taken to shutting herself in her suite after dusk. The sitting room door might even be locked . . . though he hadn't checked to *see* if it was.

The urge to walk over and try the knob was so strong it made his hand shake.

He forced himself to turn around. During the day, he managed to find enough distractions to keep his mind occupied and keep her at arm's length.

But at night, when the two of them were alone here together . . .

Lucas stalked over to the empty fireplace, and sat on the camelback settee in front of it. The braided rug felt scratchy beneath his feet. He slumped back and picked up the lacy needlepoint pillow from one corner of the couch.

He lifted the pillow toward him, could still catch the summery scent of meadow herbs, from the soap she used to wash her hair.

Yesterday, Sunday, he'd returned from his afternoon patrol with Travis to find that she'd fallen asleep here, curled up in front of the fire, a book in her hand.

And he'd sat down and just looked at her for the longest time, feeling like he did now. All tangled up inside.

Feeling like hell because she seemed so alone, and he'd denied her permission for a card party.

Lucas dropped the pillow as if it burned his fingers. If he felt like hell about ruining Annie's afternoon tea, how was he going to feel when he handed her over to the constables in St. Charles?

He stood up and started pacing again.

Women were trouble. No question about it. Trouble. Something Lucas usually tried to avoid. A federal marshal had enough of it in his life without going out and finding himself more. Like by getting all mixed up with a woman.

Especially a woman who was in his custody. A woman he *never* should have allowed himself to hold in his arms, or kiss.

Or take to bed.

Every drop of his blood heated at the memory that had made his nights restless for three weeks now: the two of them together. The feel of her naked skin against his, the soft perfection of her in his arms.

The sweet pressure of her body holding him so tight, deep inside her.

His throat went dry.

She was his prisoner.

But she wasn't guilty of the crime she was charged with.

She had been his brother's mistress for three years.

Even those words no longer held the firepower they once had.

Lucas walked to the front windows, looked out through the curtains at the snowy street. He flattened his palm against the cold window and refocused his eyes, looking at his own reflection in the glass.

He thought of his family, waiting back in St. Charles. Waiting for him to deliver them justice. Peace.

But for the first time in his life, he found himself wondering about the meaning of the word *justice*.

Annie wasn't a murderer. Was it right to turn her over to a court that would sentence her to life in prison—or hanging? Was that justice?

He closed his eyes, his fingers curling into a fist. More and more, it was becoming important to him to keep *Annie* safe. To protect her.

Her whole life, people had been turning their backs on her when she needed them—her father, her brother, even her own mother.

And James.

Lucas swallowed hard, opening his eyes. It was perhaps the sharpest irony of all that he'd started to see in Annie the goodness and generosity and warmth he'd always attributed to James.

And come to believe that James had committed the sort of callous, cold, selfish act that Lucas had once believed Annie capable of.

He still wasn't able to understand how James could

have treated her so badly, a woman as soft and vulnerable as Annie. And their unborn child.

She deserved better.

Just as she deserved better than what a judge and jury would do to her back in Missouri.

Staring into the night sky, Lucas turned the question over and over in his mind, the one he had never had to ask in all his years as a federal marshal.

What was the right thing to do?

16

"There comes a gal I used to know, swing her once and let her go! Swing your partner 'afore you trade, grab 'em back and promenade!"

Townsfolk wearing denim and homespun, work boots and sturdy leather shoes whooped and hollered as they danced to the raucous music of a fiddle, a banjo, and a squeeze-box accordion. Their feet thumped the floor planking hard enough to knock dust off the rafters and make bits of straw drift down from the hayloft overhead.

The grange hall had been decorated with evergreen boughs, garlands of cranberries, strings of popcorn. Angels and stars cut from pieces of tin glimmered in the light of oil lanterns hooked on every beam and crossbrace. A huge wreath hung on the front door, which kept opening to admit blasts of snow and icy wind, and yet another family that had braved the drifts to arrive by sleigh or on horseback.

The town's annual Christmas dance, held on the third Saturday in December, was apparently the social event of the season. Lucas stood in an out-of-the-way corner, leaning back against the wall with his boots crossed at the ankle, his arms over his chest. He hadn't been paying much attention to the festivities, staring blankly out at the crowd.

"Sir?" Travis was standing next to him. "What do you think I should do?"

"About what?" Lucas asked absently.

"About Valentina," the kid said with a hint of frustration. "Sir, ain't you heard a word I been saying? I thought her pa might be willin' to let me keep company with her, now that I'm a lawman and all, but he still don't like me much. And now Val says he's been talkin' about arrangin' a *marriage* for her next summer, to some high-falutin feller out in California who don't even *know* her." Travis's voice became bleak. "*I* known her since we was both tadpoles."

Lucas rubbed his eyes with the heels of his palms. He was the last man in Colorado who should be offering advice on how to deal with women problems; he still hadn't found any answers to his own.

He kept thinking of his sisters, Callie and Eden and Faith. And Olivia. Her children. All depending on him. How could he betray their trust in him?

Yet how could he abandon Annie, like everyone else in her life had done when she was in a desperate situation? She needed help.

She needed him.

Lucas clenched his jaw. The past few days, he'd been doing his damndest to just go on like before. To avoid thinking about what was going to happen weeks from now when the passes cleared. What *had* to happen. Because it wasn't in his power to change it.

Once they reached St. Charles, maybe he would be able to talk to the judge, make him understand the facts. Maybe his word offered on Annie's behalf would be enough to protect her. Maybe . . .

He raked a hand through his hair. He didn't know what he was going to do. All he knew was that he had to keep Annie in custody until they returned to Missouri.

But no law said he had to make her miserable all winter. Maybe the note he had left her at the jail tonight would, in some small way, begin to make things a little easier for her.

"Marshal?"

Lucas glanced at his young deputy. "Sorry, kid." He tried to think of something helpful to say; offering fatherly wisdom wasn't exactly his strong suit. "Shouldn't you, uh, talk to your pa about this?"

"Already did," Travis said with a forlorn expression. "Pa says I should just stop tormentin' myself over her, 'cause she's gonna be leavin' and there ain't nothin' I can do about it."

Lucas grimaced. "Sounds like good advice, Travis." He shifted his attention back to the crowd.

It looked like the town's entire population had turned out tonight—more than a hundred people, which meant there wasn't even enough room for all of them to dance at the same time.

Everyone took turns on the floor, visiting with friends and neighbors in between, or carting their sleepy children off to doze in the hayloft overhead, where they were watched by giggling girls who weren't quite old enough yet for dancing.

Men outnumbered women about four to one in Eminence, which made for some odd pairings of miners and farmers on the dance floor. A trio of grizzled prospectors played the music, while four others served up food and drink from laden tables at the back of the hall. The wizened old coot serving as the caller looked to be about seventy, but seemed to have been blessed with amazingly strong lungs.

"How will you swap, and how'll you trade, this pretty gal for that old maid! Chase the possum, chase the coon, chase that pretty gal 'round the room!"

"But, Marshal, how am I s'posed to just forget Valentina?" Travis sighed. "When she's around, I can't hardly *see* straight. Just lookin' at her makes me feel all funny inside. And when she ain't around, she's all I think about. Can't even sleep. Been pacin' so much, my ma kicked me out of the house the other night."

Lucas blinked, realizing that Travis had just described every one of the symptoms he himself had been suffering. "Maybe you should, uh, talk to Doc Holt. Might be some kind of . . . some kind of influenza or something going around town."

"I ain't sick, Marshal. I *love* her—"

"Evening to you, Marshal." Morgan O'Donnell approached them, a friendly smile on his face, his genteel Southern drawl just loud enough to be heard over the music. "Haven't seen you on the floor yet."

Lucas greeted him with a nod, glad for an excuse to change the subject. "I'm here on duty. Making sure everything stays peaceful."

"Ah, I do seem to recall this event ending in a drunken brawl one year, when some cad spiked the punch." O'Donnell winked, looking as dapper and glassy-eyed as ever. "And what about you, young Travis?"

"Not much for dancing," Travis said sullenly.

"On that, we are agreed." O'Donnell settled against the wall beside Lucas. "My talents most definitely lie elsewhere." He tipped his hat to a passing young woman, his smile widening. "I'm only here to see if I might get the chance to prove as much tonight."

Lucas slanted him a look. All the single men in town complained that Eminence suffered from two problems: a lack of unmarried ladies, and Morgan O'Donnell.

Apparently, the gambler set his sights on just about every pretty, available female in town, and managed to charm many of them into forgetting that other men existed in Eminence.

And with Indigo and Ivy long gone, the town's last bawdy house stood empty—and male tempers were getting noticeably shorter as winter wore on. Lucas had had to break up three fistfights in as many days this week. He was surprised guns hadn't been drawn. Yet.

No question about it, women were trouble, he thought morosely as he studied the toe of his boot. It was amazing the suffering that the female of the species could inflict, purely by walking around existing.

O'Donnell had his full attention on the crowd, or rather, the ladies in the crowd. "Married. Married. Too old. Spoken for. Hates me. Too . . . hmmm, yes, too young. Pity."

"You three critters just gonna hold up the walls all night?"

Lucas glanced up as Rebecca Greer approached them on her way to the food tables, carrying a platter taken from some folks who had just arrived. "Start eatin' at least," she admonished as she breezed on past toward the back of the hall. "We got Injun pudding. We got sweet-potato casserole. We got raspberry punch." She smiled at Lucas.

Lucas gave her a puzzled look as she bustled on by. For some reason, Rebecca Greer had grown more friendly toward him over the past couple of weeks, and he wasn't sure what accounted for the change.

He also wasn't sure which he preferred: her previous hostility or this new, almost motherly mood.

As O'Donnell continued studying the crowd, he released a melancholy sigh. "I do wish Miss Ivy had stayed in town. Never thought I'd be glad for such a damned cold winter."

Lucas had to agree with that; he'd taken up a new habit of long walks outside at night.

He was surprised he hadn't run into Travis.

The three of them stood there in silence for a moment, watching the noisy festivities.

Then O'Donnell surreptitiously produced a flask from inside his green silk vest. His mustache curving upward with a mischievous grin, he cast a sidelong look at the punch bowl.

"Try it," Lucas drawled, "and I'll have to arrest you."

"You are no fun at all, Marshal."

"So I've been told."

They glanced toward the door as it opened again and another group came dashing in, mostly hidden beneath bonnets and woolen shawls and capes. When Lucas recognized Annie among them, he felt his heart give an odd, doubled beat.

He remained where he was, watching as she handed her coat and gloves to someone who came forward to take them, and shook the snow from her long hair. She quickly looked around, talking with the ladies who accompanied her.

And then she saw him. Their eyes met across the crowded room.

Even from here, he could see the gratitude shining in her expression. In her smile.

He nodded in acknowledgment and looked away, trying to resist the warm, unfamiliar sensation tingling through his chest.

She had found the note he'd tacked to her door, telling her that if she wanted to join her friends at the Christmas dance, she had his permission.

He supposed he could've told her in person, but he hadn't wanted to make it into a big discussion. It was just one evening. A few hours with her friends. Didn't have to mean anything.

Lucas just couldn't see a reason to deny her something so simple that would make her happy for a while. Especially when everything else he did caused her so much hurt.

"Ain't that . . ." Travis glanced at Lucas in surprise. "Why, that's Miss Sutton."

"Yes, it is," Lucas said curtly. "Didn't see the harm in it. You and I are here to keep an eye on everything—"

"Sir, you don't have to explain to me. She's been workin' so hard at the store, I think it's right kindly of you to let her out for a bit. It *is* Christmastime." Travis studied him with a puzzled look before returning his gaze to the womenfolk. "That's Val over there with her." He released a besotted sigh. "And I don't see Mr. Lazarillo nowheres, so do you think it would be all right if I—"

"Go."

The kid didn't ask twice; he made a beeline across the room.

"Ah, women," O'Donnell said in an appreciative tone. "God love 'em." With a grin playing around the corners of his mouth, he gave Lucas a curious glance. "Should you ever wish to unburden your conscience, Marshal, about anything at all . . ."

"What's that supposed to mean, O'Donnell?"

"Nothing, Marshal. Not a thing." The younger man shrugged. "Please excuse me." He tucked his flask into his vest, his attention on a voluptuous blonde who had just walked in.

Lucas watched him go, his own gaze drawn back to Annie. She was chatting with Katja Gottfried, Valentina, and a few other ladies. They must have loaned her the outfit she wore: a chambray skirt that matched the dark color of the evergreen boughs, with a pair of western-style boots, and a white blouse that had long sleeves and ruffles at the high neck. Her hair had been swept back from her face in a simple style, woven with red and green ribbons that tangled through her long curls.

Lucas forced himself to blink, feeling it again—that strange tingling in his chest that kept hitting him every time he looked at her.

He also realized that he wasn't the only man in the room who had noticed her. Several fellows had glanced her way—including a few who had been spending, in his opinion, too much time in the general store.

All at once, he felt a compelling urge to go over there and stand at her side, but he fought it. He might have decided to let her enjoy a few hours with her friends, but he wasn't about to share the evening with her himself. He didn't intend to go near her. Lucas forced his gaze elsewhere.

The music changed as the dance-caller and squeeze-box player took a rest, both moseying off to the back of the hall to wet their whistles. The fiddler and banjo player slowed things down a bit, striking up an old-fashioned waltz that had been popular during the war.

As the fiddler began playing the sentimental tune, most of the men in the crowd headed off toward the food tables.

Lucas watched Travis escorting Valentina onto the dance floor, and saw O'Donnell walk up to the blonde he had spotted and bow gallantly.

But the girl shook her head, said something that made the gambler straighten with a jerk. A moment later, another fellow offered his hand, and she accepted.

Lucas almost winced for poor O'Donnell. Shot down clean, like a bottle off the back fence.

But before he had the chance to feel much sympathy for O'Donnell, he noticed three men converging on Annie—two of them glancing Lucas's way somewhat nervously.

He glowered at them. One stopped, apparently reconsidered, and changed direction.

But the other two didn't.

The idea of either of them touching her, holding her in his arms, drawing her close . . .

Before he knew what he was doing, Lucas straightened and stepped away from the wall.

She was already flanked by them, talking with them, when he approached and cut the conversation short. "Evening, gentlemen."

The two would-be dance partners fell silent. One man actually went a little pale.

Lucas realized that his greeting had come out as sharp and cold as a bullet from the .45 holstered on his hip.

"Good evening, Marshal," Annie said a bit hesitantly, her dark eyes uncertain, as if she were afraid that her jailer had changed his mind and decided to drag her back to her cell.

Lucas glanced down at her. How did he always manage to say or do the wrong thing around Annie? He hadn't meant to worry her. Hadn't had a plan at all when he walked over here.

But he heard a question coming out of his mouth.

"Would you care to dance?"

"I . . ." She blinked up at him, looking startled. "I—I was just explaining to these two nice gentlemen that I only planned to spend some time with my . . ."

Before she could finish, he took her hand and led her onto the dance floor, away from the two nice gentlemen.

He could feel Annie tense, felt her fingers trembling in his when he drew her toward him and settled his other hand at her waist.

As their bodies touched for the first time in weeks, his pulse was suddenly too loud in his ears. It was a pounding accompaniment to the slow, sweet music of the fiddle and banjo that filled the air around them. He eased her into the steps of the waltz.

She seemed a bit breathless, her voice wavering when she spoke. "Thank you for letting me come here tonight."

Lucas couldn't summon a reply. He was too aware of her hand resting on his shoulder, the warmth of her palm through his shirt.

"Didn't see the harm in it," he managed to say at last, his voice strained even to his own ears.

God help him, for so long he hadn't let himself touch her. Not like this. Not in a way that reminded him of how silky and warm her skin was. How perfectly she fit against him. How delicate and soft she felt in his arms.

Her lashes dusted her cheeks. "Still, it was kind of you," she said softly.

The notes of the music, full of the longing and loss of sweethearts parted by war, floated around them.

"Has anyone ever told you that . . ." She hesitated, as if reconsidering, then continued. "That despite being impossible most of the time, and tough enough to chew nails and spit tacks, you sometimes have a . . . rather appealing gentle streak."

"No," he replied gruffly.

When she looked up at him again, he could see her eyes sparkle in the glow of the lanterns, in the light reflected from the glittering tin stars and angels. "Well, you do."

That odd, warm feeling returned, right in the center of his chest.

"What?" Annie asked curiously as he stared at her in silence, his gaze moving over her face, her hair.

"Nothing. It's . . . you look . . . nice."

A blush colored her cheeks. "Thank you." For the second time tonight, she smiled at him. Then she shook her head, as if struggling to understand him. "You are full of surprises tonight, Marshal."

Lucas continued moving her gently around the dance floor in time with the music, not even trying to explain to her what he couldn't explain to himself. With the slightest pressure of his fingertips at her back, he drew her nearer.

Why shouldn't he tell her she looked nice? Annie always looked beautiful, whether she was wearing ribbons in her hair or a plain woolen dress . . .

Or nothing at all.

Suddenly the memories flooded him, the images playing havoc with his heartbeat: the taste of her mouth, their mutual whispers of urgent need, the feel of her slender body arched beneath him, the husky sounds of her pleasure when he thrust deep inside her.

His desire must have shown in his face, because he felt her tremble. They looked into each other's eyes as the fiddler played a long, tender solo. Her breathing had become shallow, unsteady, the color in her cheeks deepening—and her response to him only intensified the hunger already burning low in his belly.

But when the solo ended, the song ended. Everyone began leaving the dance floor. Lucas remained still for a moment as people milled around them, talking and laughing, seemingly part of some other world.

He *did* want to take Annie out of here right now and carry her back to the jail.

But not to lock her in her cell.

He clenched his jaw and forced himself to let her go, escorting her over to her friends with his hand at her elbow.

"Th-Thank you, Marshal," Annie said as he released her.

Lucas couldn't summon a single word, only gave her a curt nod and turned his back, blindly walking away into the crowd.

What was happening to him? What the *hell* was happening to him—to his logic, his reason? His last shred of common sense. He had no business leaving notes on her door. Asking her to dance. Wanting her by his side. Wanting her close. Wanting to . . .

Damn it, he was doing it again. Acting impulsive. Stupid. He only ended up tormenting himself. And he wasn't doing Annie any favors by granting her a few hours of freedom and happiness, making her think he was gentle and kind. It would only hurt her worse when he took her back to Missouri.

He stalked toward the refreshment table, needing a drink. A scruffy prospector held out a glass of punch and Lucas gulped it down, noticing that it had a stronger kick than he would've expected from raspberry punch.

He wondered if O'Donnell had spiked it, almost hoped he had, but he didn't see the gambler around anywhere.

Lucas was about to head outside for a long, cold walk through the snow when Mrs. Kearney bustled in his direction. She blocked his path.

"Ma'am," he said warily, draining his glass and setting it aside.

"Marshal." She sniffed. "Perhaps you could tell me exactly *what* is going on in this town of ours."

"And by that you mean . . . ?"

She flicked a hand toward Annie. "Is that *woman* a prisoner or is she not? Some folks might not mind the way you've been letting her flit around town, but *decent* people—"

"Ma'am." Lucas gritted his teeth. The last thing he

needed right now was Widow Kearney pointing out his
duty. He actually started to feel sick to his stomach.
"There *is* something in the Constitution about cruel and
unusual punishment—and I think keeping her locked in
a cell all winter would qualify."

"Would it indeed? One wonders if you treat *all* prison-
ers in your custody with such care and concern. *I* for one
do not like the idea of that . . . that . . ."

"Mrs. Kearney," he said tightly, "I'd suggest you
choose your words carefully."

"This is a small town, Marshal." She pursed her lips.
"People have been talking. Some have noticed that you
spend most of your time in your *prisoner's* company.
Tonight it seems rather obvious that you *enjoy* her company. And with the two of you staying together over at
the hotel—"

"It's not a hotel, it's a jail," Lucas said impatiently.
"Complete with bars on the windows, in case nobody
noticed—"

"But perhaps you can understand how people have
become confused, since you kept her *in* the jail before,
and now you simply let her come and go at will—"

"Mrs. Kearney," he said with all the patience he could
muster, "allow me to put your mind at ease. After
tonight, my *prisoner* will be living under lock and key
for the rest of the winter."

Without waiting for a reply, he moved past her and
stalked through the crowd, muttering a curse.

He had to do it—exactly what he had just said.
Clearly he couldn't trust himself around Annie anymore.
No other woman had ever made him *feel* like this. Like
he'd been hit by a runaway train.

It was the only way. He would lock her back in her cell
and keep her there. All winter. Put Travis in charge of

her. Move out of the damned jail and find somewhere else to stay until spring. Somewhere as far away from her as he could get.

He headed for the door, hoping a breath of the cold air would clear his head. She was going to hate him, but that didn't matter. Couldn't matter. He had to stop caring about—

Caring.

No, that was the wrong word. He didn't care for her. What he felt for Annie was desire. And a need to protect her. It mattered to him what happened to her. And he hated how he felt when he made her cry. But he didn't . . .

He couldn't . . .

As he stepped outside into the cold night, Lucas suddenly felt like he was viewing the whole world in one of those wavy mirrors at the circus. Like he had nothing solid to hold on to.

The sick feeling in his stomach started getting worse.

He almost ran right into Holt, who had just ridden up. "McKenna." The doctor knotted his horse's reins around the hitching rail out front. "Calling it a night a little early? Without your coat?"

"Just catching a breath of air." Lucas grabbed on to the railing to steady himself. "Where you been?"

"Treating a patient."

A noise from one of the sleighs a few yards down made them both glance that way.

There was a feminine squeal followed by a male voice saying "Shhh," and then O'Donnell's tousled blond head appeared over the edge of the seat. "Evenin', Daniel— aw, hell."

A woman popped up behind him, despite his apparent efforts to keep her hidden. Her hair was in disarray, her blouse unbuttoned. As soon as she saw their audience, she covered herself up with a nervous gasp and scrambled out the other side of the sleigh, hurrying away into the darkness.

"For God's sake, Morgan," Holt said with a frown, gesturing toward the hall. "There are families with children not ten feet away."

O'Donnell stumbled out of the sleigh and came toward them, a half-empty bottle of liquor in one hand. "I am a drunk and a scoundrel," he said with a bow. "Ask anyone." He looked in the direction the girl had departed, his voice turning angry. "Why the hell did you two have to go and scare her off like that?"

"God Almighty," Lucas said in disgust, "do you possess *one* shred of decency?"

"Listen to you." O'Donnell turned on him. "Saints preserve us, you're a fine one to be giving out lessons on decency, Marshal."

Lucas came away from the hitching rail. "What do you mean by that?"

"I mean, Mr. Holier-Than-Thou, that you once said any man worth a bucket of warm spit does right by a woman, so maybe you'd like to tell me what you're giving Miss Sutton in exchange for her—"

"You finish that sentence"—Lucas's hand closed on the butt of his Colt—"you better have more than a flask hidden in that vest of yours."

The gambler moved toward him. "I have never backed down from a duel, sir." He drew a .22 from inside his coat.

"You call that a gun?" Lucas said derisively.

Holt stepped between them. "Listen, you two—"

"Stay out of this, Daniel," O'Donnell snapped. "I'm tired of everyone in town acting like *I'm* a mangy cur for sharing the pleasure of a lady's company—when it's pretty damn clear *something's* going on at that 'jail' of his between him and Miss Sutton."

Lucas drew his gun with a curse. He was breathing hard, the sick feeling in his stomach turning painful.

"Stop it," Holt said angrily, turning from Lucas to O'Donnell with a look of disbelief. "Morgan, you have no idea how ridiculous that is. And do you have *any* idea what a .45 cartridge does to the human body? Even if McKenna's feeling generous and just nicks you, it could take your arm off. Try to imagine how hard it would be to earn your living one-handed."

"Good advice," Lucas snarled.

"Yeah?" Holt shifted an annoyed glare to him. "Well, I once treated a man who got shot with a .22. Bullet hit him in the side and ended up in his neck—after it turned his guts to mush."

"Stay out of this, Doc."

"Just offering some free medical advice." Holt remained between them, glaring from one to the other. "I'm also thinking about *me*. I have better things to do than spend the rest of the night digging lead out of either one of you!"

Lucas was still breathing hard. A dizzying buzz filled his head.

And the night suddenly turned a strange silvery-gray. He bent forward, doubled over by the pain in his stomach.

Holt spun toward him. His voice seemed to come from a distance. "McKenna? You all right?"

Lucas barely managed to choke out a one-word reply. "No."

17

As dawn broke through the windows, Annie kept pacing the front room of the jail, still wearing the green skirt, white blouse, and boots she'd been wearing at the dance. She straightened a pillow on the settee. Carried more empty cups and saucers to the kitchen. She felt like she was going crazy, had to *do* something.

Daniel had told her to try and get some rest, but she hadn't been able to sit still for five minutes, much less sleep. When she glanced down the darkened hall again, she saw the light still glowing under Lucas's door.

Daniel had stayed by his side all night, promising to come and tell her the minute there was any change.

If there was any change.

She picked up another teacup, but then sank down at the table, covering her face with one hand. The red and green ribbons in her hair tangled around her fingers. She couldn't stop shaking, fought a tear threatening to slide down her cheek.

It felt as if the whole world had spun to a halt in that moment when Mr. O'Donnell came running into the grange hall to tell her something had happened to Marshal McKenna.

Stunned, she had rushed outside and found Lucas lying in the snow, Daniel working over him frantically. At first she thought he'd been shot, but Daniel said that he'd taken sick all of a sudden, that he was unconscious.

When they couldn't revive him, they had brought Lucas back here, followed by her friends and Travis and at least a dozen townsfolk, who had stayed for hours, milling around and waiting for news. Finally, she had sent them all home with a promise to send word in the morning.

She closed her eyes. Lucas probably didn't even know how much the townsfolk liked him, how they had gotten used to his strong, steady presence among them. Everyone had come to admire his firmness and fairness, whether dealing with rowdy miners disturbing the peace or young boys getting into mischief.

Lucas McKenna had proven himself the sort of man people could depend on in any kind of trouble.

But it would probably come as a surprise to him that folks in Eminence cared what happened to him.

That she ...

Annie wiped at her eyes, unwilling to finish that thought. She had vowed to guard her heart. Stop dreaming. Stop imagining that Lucas McKenna was anything but unreasonable, unfeeling.

Then tonight, he had left her that note. That terse, wonderful note tacked to her door. He had tried to act as if it didn't really mean anything, but she knew better.

She knew how devoted he was to his duty, how difficult it was for him to budge even an inch. His small gesture meant a great deal to her—because it reminded her that he *was* capable of being kind, showed that perhaps her feelings *did* matter to him after all.

And when he had asked her to dance, his touch had ignited a storm of other memories: his hands strong and yet gentle as he touched her, the look in his eyes soft and yet full of fire.

Annie buried her face in the crook of her arm. She didn't want to remember, didn't want to let herself believe that she might matter to him. Didn't want to risk being hurt again.

Yet even as she tried to convince herself that she shouldn't care, she felt afraid for his life. Kept offering silent prayers and promises to God that if He would just—

"Annie?" It was Daniel's voice, tired and strained, coming from the end of the hall.

Startled, Annie knocked the teacup aside with a clatter as she straightened. "Is he . . . oh, Daniel, is he . . ."

"He's awake now." Daniel looked exhausted, his gray eyes bleary, his hair rumpled as if he'd been raking his fingers through it. "I think he's going to be fine."

"Thank God." Annie closed her eyes for a second, offering silent words of gratitude before she rose and hurried toward Daniel, into Lucas's room.

Inside, Lucas lay in the middle of his brass bed, under a pile of covers, his eyes barely opened to slits. His skin was pale, even a bit green. "Where . . . am I?" His voice was little more than a raspy whisper.

"Your room at the jail," Daniel told him. "Do you remember what happened tonight?"

"Hurt like hell." Lucas closed his eyes again.

Annie sat on a chair beside the bed, unable to fight the relief that flooded through her. She was trembling. "What was it, Daniel? What was wrong with him?"

Daniel picked up his open medical bag from the floor and set it on the foot of the bed. "Did you eat or drink anything at that dance, McKenna?"

"Punch," Lucas croaked, making a face.

Daniel nodded. "That must've been how they did it. Would've been fairly easy, actually."

"Did what?" Annie asked worriedly.

After taking out his stethoscope, Daniel leaned over his patient. "You have pain in your throat, McKenna? Feels like it's burning? And probably tingling in your hands and feet?"

Lucas nodded, his brow furrowed.

Daniel remained silent a moment, looking thoughtful as he listened to Lucas's heartbeat, then checked his pulse. "Severe gastric distress, dizziness, clammy skin, numbness in the extremities. And burning esophageal pain . . ." He paused, taking off his stethoscope as he straighted. "Arsenic."

Annie gasped. "Someone tried to *poison* him?"

Lucas choked out a curse.

"I wasn't sure at first," Daniel said. "Thought it could've been something you ate, McKenna, but no one else at the dance took sick. My next guess was a bad appendix, but you would've had a fever. The way you went down so fast, then lost consciousness, and your pulse kept dropping . . ." He put his stethoscope away in his bag. "Made me guess poison. Just wasn't sure what kind."

"But now you're sure?" Lucas asked, looking like he barely had the strength to keep his eyes open.

Daniel nodded. "Arsenic causes progressive circulatory failure, though it's usually a slow killer. If it had been done right, you would've died in your sleep last night and we might never have known why. Would've been hard to prove what had happened to you."

Annie shuddered at that thought. "But why did it affect him so quickly?"

"Whoever spiked his drink must have given him too much," Daniel replied. "Probably thought it would take a lot to kill a tough hombre like our famous Marshal McKenna here."

"Lucky for me," Lucas whispered, closing his eyes again, "you were so quick on the draw with that damned . . . stick."

"Tongue-depressor," Daniel corrected lightly. "Sorry about that." He shifted his attention to Annie. "Soon as I suspected poison," he explained, "I knew I had to get him to empty his stomach and quick."

Annie winced. That sounded awful. But apparently Daniel's fast thinking had saved Lucas's life.

"For once, Doc," Lucas said grudgingly, "I'm glad you were around."

"Happy to oblige." Daniel chuckled as he shut his medical bag and rolled down his sleeves, buttoning them at the cuffs. "Question in my mind is *who* did this." He arched one brow. "I hope you're not thinking of your *usual* suspect, Marshal."

Lucas frowned up at him. "If you had wanted to do me in, Holt," he muttered, "you've had plenty of chances before this."

"And I wouldn't have come to your rescue," Daniel pointed out dryly. "But someone in this town wanted you dead—and I'd say they put quite a bit of thought and planning into it."

Annie looked up at her friend. "But everyone in town seems to admire him so much—"

"Maybe not everyone. My guess is somebody got a little nervous having a lawman around." Daniel met and held her gaze. "Maybe somebody with a secret they'd rather keep."

She nodded in understanding, remembering what he had revealed to her weeks ago about some of the townsfolk.

Lucas blinked up at them, his eyes glassy and unfocused. "I'm not following."

"Well, see . . . it's like this," Daniel said hesitantly. "Some folks who've decided to stick around Eminence aren't here because they're hoping to find silver. They're . . . let's just say, they're here for reasons of their own."

Lucas looked drowsy and confused. "Huh?"

With a wry expression, Daniel picked up his medical bag. "I think you'd better get some rest, Marshal. Maybe we'll explain it to you later. Chances are, whoever did this vamoosed and decided to lay low as soon as he saw his plan went wrong. But just in case, I'll have a few friends keep an eye on your place here while you're recovering." Daniel picked up his wool coat from the back of a chair. "Be sure to give me a yell next time you need someone to break up a duel."

"Duel?" Annie asked. "What duel?"

Lucas grimaced. "Never mind."

"Why would Daniel need to . . . *you* were going to duel with someone?" She stared at Lucas in surprise. "I thought you were supposed to be *keeping* the peace around here, Marshal, not breaking it."

Daniel pulled on his coat, a grin curving his mouth. "Go easy on him, Annie," he admonished lightly. "The menfolk in town have been having a tough winter."

She glanced from one of them to the other with a frown. Daniel and Lucas exchanged a silent look of understanding that puzzled her.

"I'll leave you in Annie's care, for now," Daniel told him, his voice shifting, becoming more serious. "But I'll check back tomorrow." As he glanced toward the morning sun spilling through the room's only window, he winced, rubbing at his bearded face. "Or rather, later *today*." With a tired sigh, he turned to go.

"Holt?"

Daniel paused in the doorway, glanced back toward his patient. "Yeah?"

"Thanks."

The doctor nodded. "Consider us even, McKenna. You're not the only one in the business of saving lives, remember?"

Annie rose and followed Daniel down the hotel corridor. "Daniel, wait. Do you have any instructions for me? Is there anything I need to do to help him get well?"

"I think you'll do just fine, Annie." Daniel turned toward her. "Just make sure he stays put and keeps warm. And give him plenty to drink—tea, water. Oh, and milk. Some of the farmers keep cows through the winter to have milk for their little ones. I'll have some sent over to you. He may not like it much, but it'll help."

"So he'll be all right, then?"

"A week or so of rest and he'll be ornery as ever." He paused, looking at her curiously. "You going to be all right, Annie?"

"I'm fine. I'm not the one who's hurt—"

"I know. You just seem . . ." Daniel's voice became quiet. "We haven't talked about it lately, Annie, but I assume our plan is still in place." His gaze shifted from her to Lucas's room at the far end of the corridor and back again. "Unless maybe . . . something's changed?"

Annie glanced down, hoping he couldn't see the high color in her cheeks in the darkened hallway. Apparently it had become obvious that her feelings for the marshal weren't quite the same as they had once been.

She hadn't thought about the escape plan in a long time—not since her experience with the bounty hunter. Not after getting a taste of what it would be like to live on the run, hunted by men who would kill her without a second thought. Always looking over her shoulder, hiding, lying to everyone she met. Feeling afraid.

And alone.

She shook her head wearily. "Daniel, I'm so tired, I—I can't even think right now."

"You get some rest." Daniel laid a gentle hand on her shoulder. "There's a long time yet until spring. When you want to talk, I'll be here." He turned to go. "Always."

"Thank you." Annie watched him leave, grateful for his loyalty and understanding. Never in her whole life had she expected to have such good friends; she certainly never would've expected to find them here, in a half-deserted mining town in a remote corner of the Rocky Mountains.

But soon she would have to leave Eminence, and these good people. Whether it was to spend her life on the run . . . or return to Missouri.

Annie pushed the thought away, walking back to Lucas's room, wanting to reassure herself that he was all right.

He was still there, still quite alive.

And he still had that baffled look on his face. "What did Holt mean, 'they're here for reasons of their own'?"

"You're supposed to be sleeping," she admonished, looking around. She hadn't even set foot in here before today. Lucas's room was spartan, almost empty: just a bed, a chair, a sheet tacked up at the window for a curtain. No rug on the unfinished wood floor. No dresser for his belongings.

Just his saddlebags in one corner, which probably contained all his worldly possessions. She noticed he kept them near the door. Maybe out of habit. As if he always wanted to be ready to move on at a moment's notice.

"How'm I supposed to sleep?" he grumbled. "Tell me what he meant."

Annie sighed, recognizing one of his stubborn moods when she heard it, yet not sure how much she should reveal.

She walked to the window, pulling the makeshift curtain aside to look out at the sun and snow.

"What he meant . . ." she said slowly, "is that some people in Eminence aren't here because they're hoping to find silver. They're here because they're hoping nobody will find *them.*" She glanced over her shoulder. "Because they have . . . somewhat shady pasts. A few of them are in hiding."

"Are you telling me this town is full of *outlaws*?" His eyes widened.

"Not outlaws, exactly. And I wouldn't say *full.* But there *are* a few people with, um, less-than-spotless backgrounds."

He blinked. "Those nice farm folks at the dance . . ."

"Not all of them." The look on his face was almost enough to make her laugh. "Just some."

He narrowed his eyes. "Who?"

Annie glanced away. Revealing names could have consequences for those involved. Like Mrs. Owens. And Katja. And Cameron Fairfax. Their secrets weren't hers to share.

"I'd rather not say." Annie paused. "Some had trouble with the law when they were younger, and they've paid their debt to society and they're here to get a second chance, to start fresh. Others . . . well . . . let's just say that wanted posters never get *posted* around here. Seeing as there's no jail."

He frowned, saying nothing.

"What are you thinking?" she asked hesitantly.

"That it was no accident the jail burned down," he muttered. "Why was the town council so bent on hiring a new marshal?"

"Because they need someone to protect people and keep the peace. It's not an official policy of the town: 'If you're an outlaw, come and hide here.' Eminence is just a remote, isolated place, and apparently it sort of . . . happened over the years." She shook her head. "And not everybody knows about it. Lots of folks have no idea that some of their neighbors aren't quite as upstanding as they look."

"And nobody was going to tell me this?"

Now he sounded a little angry.

She glanced down, her fingers toying with the frayed edge of the curtain. "You're a lawman."

"And you didn't trust me."

"I'm trusting you now," she pointed out. "Lucas, these people are trying to make a new life for themselves here. You won't . . . I mean, you wouldn't . . ."

"Start hauling all the nice townsfolk off to prison?"

She looked at him from beneath her lashes.

"I can't make any promises," he said.

"No, I understand." It was almost painfully ironic, but she *did* understand. She actually admired how honorable and strong and protective he was, how he always wanted to do what was right.

Even as those very qualities sealed her own fate.

"Let me get you some tea," she said softly, heading for the door. "It might help you sleep."

"Wait," he said gruffly. "You don't have to do that. I was going to . . . I have to . . . ask Travis . . ."

She frowned, wondering if he was becoming delirious. He was rambling. "It's no trouble, Marshal. You're not in any condition to take care of yourself." Annie studied him. "I think we can declare a brief truce, while you're recovering. Christmas is supposed to be a time of peace, after all."

He held her gaze, his eyes dark with some emotion she couldn't name. "You are always so damned . . ."

She waited for him to say *stubborn.*

Troublesome.

Impractical.

"'Tenderhearted,'" he finished quietly.

Annie glanced down at the toes of her boots, resisting the warmth that unfurled inside her. She found herself remembering something Katja had told her about the people of Eminence, how so many of them had had their lives broken into pieces by hard times.

Sometimes, Katja had said, broken lives made for tender hearts.

"I just don't want to spend the whole winter at war," she whispered, glancing up. "Do you want me to go and get Travis for something? It's early, but I'm sure he'd come right over."

Lucas didn't reply, just kept looking at her, his expression strained. A muscle flexed in his beard-stubbled cheek.

Then that gentle look came into his gaze, the one that had taken her breath away last night.

"No," he murmured, closing his eyes. "Changed my mind."

"All right." Annie turned to go. "I'll make some tea."

She went to the kitchen and made a fresh pot, hoping a cup or two would also help soothe her jangled nerves.

But by the time she carried the tea back to his room, it looked like he was already asleep.

"Lucas?" She set the tray on the chair, since there wasn't anyplace else to put it. She perched on the edge of the bed, worried for a moment. But he was just sleeping.

He looked so vulnerable, she couldn't stop herself from reaching out to brush a dark tangle of hair off his forehead.

Annie sighed wearily, puzzled by her own feelings. Despite the time they'd spent together, the newspaper stories she'd read about him, the arguments they'd had, the rare tender moments they'd shared . . . he was still very much a mystery to her, this lawman. He was as hard-hewn and sometimes as fierce as the West itself. He could be as harsh as the winter storms that battered these mountains.

And at other times, he could be as gentle as a spring rain.

But what surprised her most was how different he was from his brother. Lucas wasn't anything like James.

James had been the picture of city-smooth refinement, civility, and charm, perfectly at home in a first-class Pullman car on one of the trains he owned, surrounded by champagne and caviar, speeding toward a business appointment in Chicago or New York or Boston. He had been generous to a fault, but he also enjoyed treating himself to the best of everything.

And there was one other, important difference between the two.

She had never felt this way about James.

Her throat tightened. She had felt gratitude for James's kindness, had admired his good heart, had even cared about him, but she had never felt . . . *this*.

Annie stood up and turned toward the door, quietly picking up the tray, telling herself she was confused, exhausted. She couldn't even think, much less make sense of the jumble of emotions in her heart.

She left Lucas to sleep, deciding she had better get some rest herself.

Now that they had declared a truce between them, she wasn't sure what the coming days might bring.

"Shame you went to all this trouble for nothing."

The sound of Lucas's voice calling from the jail's front room made Annie frown as she took a loaf of warm bread from the oven in the kitchen. On the one hand, she was glad he finally felt well enough to come prowling out of his lair; for the past three days, he had rarely set foot outside his room.

On the other hand, being ill only seemed to make him moodier than usual. She didn't know what to expect from him, from one moment to the next.

"It *would* be a shame," she called back, placing the bread in a basket and covering it with a cotton cloth, "if we wasted all this food. So we may as well go ahead and eat."

Lucas had granted permission for her to plan a small Christmas dinner for her closest friends. But Daniel had sent word an hour ago that he was treating a critically ill patient and couldn't get away, and Rebecca and Mrs. Owens had decided to take dinner to his house, to surprise him when he returned.

So Annie's Christmas dinner for five had unexpectedly turned into dinner for two.

But that was no reason to cancel the entire meal, she thought stubbornly as she headed down the corridor.

Out in the front room, Lucas stood beside the table she had arranged in front of the fireplace, shaking his head as he looked down at all the bowls and platters. "There's no way we could eat all of"—he glanced up and his voice shifted, deepened—"this."

Annie stopped, waiting for him to make another grumpy, irritable comment about how she was overdoing everything. "Now what's wrong?" She sighed. "It's the dress, isn't it? Or my hair? Or is it *all* wrong?"

Katja had loaned her the outfit yesterday: a wine-colored silk dress in an old-fashioned style, with a square neckline and long sleeves and a full skirt. Katja has also loaned her a pretty cameo to wear on a black ribbon around her throat. To show it off, Annie had pinned her hair up earlier, the mass of curls piled atop her head with a few trailing down her cheeks.

Lucas glanced away without comment, irritable or otherwise.

He still looked a bit pale, she thought. Or maybe it was just more noticeable, now that he had shaved the three-day growth of beard that had darkened his jaw. He wore black trousers and a white shirt, the rolled-up sleeves revealing his muscular forearms, a thatch of black hair just visible at the open neck.

She walked over and set the bread down between the plates. "I've never served as the hostess for a dinner party before," she said, feeling uncertain as she looked at the carefully decorated table. "I just wanted everything to be nice."

Valentina's mother had loaned Annie the white damask cloth. The Gottfrieds had offered the place settings of their English china and German crystal.

"You did just fine," Lucas said gruffly. "But I told you that you could go over to Holt's place with Rebecca and Mrs. Owens."

"Yes, but Daniel says you shouldn't be gallivanting around outside just yet. And I couldn't just leave you alone to spend Christmas by yourself."

He lifted his gaze to hers. "I've been spending Christmas alone for years."

Annie felt a tug at her heart. "Well, not this one."

Outside, beyond the windows, the night was silvered by moonlight and softly falling snow; inside, the candles in the center of the table and the fire on the hearth provided the only light.

Which made the room feel awfully . . . intimate, with just the two of them alone together to enjoy the Christmas meal she had prepared: a glazed ham, potatoes with dried herbs, mincemeat, fresh-baked bread, and a plum cake with currants.

Lucas walked around the table and held out her chair for her.

"Thank you." Annie sat down, smiling at his unexpected display of gallantry.

He returned to his side of the table and took his seat. There was an awkward pause.

"I suppose we should say grace, right?" he asked.

"Do you know any?" Annie could count on one hand the number of times she had eaten a meal where the saying of grace had been included.

"Yeah."

Annie bowed her head and waited.

"May the blessings of God, His peace and love, rest upon our table and all gathered here."

"Amen," Annie whispered. It was a lovely blessing.

She wondered where he had learned it. But she wasn't sure he would tell her if she asked.

For a while, there was only the quiet clatter of silverware on dishes as they passed foods back and forth. Lucas carved the meat and put a slice on her plate. She spooned potatoes onto his. He poured her a glass of wine.

When he lifted the bottle toward his own glass, she shook her head. "Probably not a good idea just yet." She pointed with her fork toward the milk she'd placed in a crystal decanter for him.

He frowned and set the wine bottle down. "I drink any more milk, I'm going to moo."

She grinned. "Daniel says it'll help you get better."

"I *am* better. Holt is just taking diabolical pleasure out of turning me into a cow."

"Still . . ."

Lucas grumbled something under his breath, but gave in and poured himself a glass of milk.

Every now and then a dark silhouette would pass by the front windows, since various townspeople were still taking turns watching over them; however, according to Travis, who had been investigating the attempt on Lucas's life with all the zeal of a bloodhound hot on a trail, two prime suspects had already vacated the vicinity.

The young deputy had questioned everyone who attended the dance, and discovered that of the four men who had been serving at the refreshment tables, two had disappeared: a pair of prospectors who had been in Eminence less than a year. Witnesses had seen one of the two giving Lucas the glass of tainted punch—and nobody had seen the pair since.

Some suggested they had decided to take their chances in the snowbound passes rather than face Lucas's wrath.

Annie shivered and turned her mind to more pleasant thoughts.

She noticed with approval that Lucas's appetite had returned in full. He made a sound of appreciation with each new dish he sampled.

"Who taught you to cook like this?" he asked, looking up at her.

She couldn't subdue a giggle.

He arched one brow. "What?"

"You have a milk mustache."

He frowned at her, which only made the white mustache look even funnier and made her laugh harder.

Still frowning, he reached for his napkin. "Moo," he said sardonically. After wiping his mouth, he picked up the half-empty glass of milk and set it aside.

That, Annie realized, still giggling, was clearly the end of that.

"Is there going to be coffee at the end of this meal?" he asked with a hopeful look in his eyes.

"Yes."

"Good." He took another piece of bread. "So who taught you to cook like this?"

She studied the edge of her wineglass. "I learned to cook when I was little, in St. Charles," she said, her smile fading. "Since I wasn't welcome in school, I had a lot of time to myself. And I . . . didn't like to spend it in the rooms that my brother and I shared with Mama."

She knew she didn't have to explain why.

"I spent a lot of time in out-of-the-way corners of the boardinghouse," Annie continued. "One day, the woman who ran the kitchens found me hiding in a pantry. She was French, from New Orleans. And she said I couldn't stay in her kitchen if I wasn't going to help. So I helped. Over the years, she taught me how to cook."

When she looked up and their gazes met through the candlelight, his eyes seemed thoughtful.

"What?" she asked softly.

"Just wondered if we ever met, when we were both younger," he said haltingly, "back in St. Charles. If maybe we met and neither of us even knew it . . ."

Her fingers traced the etched crystal of her glass. "I didn't spend much time in the part of town where you lived. And I doubt if your folks would have let you spend much time down by the river."

He didn't reply.

"I've told you just about everything about me," she said quietly, "but you haven't told me much about your life."

He remained silent for a long moment.

"What do you want to know?"

Anything. Everything. She tried to think of a safe topic. "What did you like to do when you were a boy?"

"Hunt." He kept his gaze on his plate. "Spent a lot of time in the woods. Liked it there because it was . . ." He seemed to search for the right word. "Quiet. Peaceful. In a big Irish family, that was hard to come by."

Annie nodded, imagining Lucas as a boy. Even when he was young, he had been of a quiet, independent nature. It probably hadn't been easy having three little sisters underfoot. But she had no doubt he had been a very protective big brother to them, even though he liked to get away by himself now and then.

"Got to be a pretty good shot," he said with a shrug. "Had to put food on the table in some tough times."

"During the war?" Annie asked.

"And before that." He lifted his gaze to hers. "We didn't grow up with money, you know. St. Charles wasn't much of a town in those days. Our place was just a cabin in the woods—like the one where you grew up."

Annie regarded him in surprise. She had assumed the McKennas always had money. But then, she and James had never discussed their families.

"Things were never real easy," Lucas continued slowly, "but times got tougher during the war."

Another thing they had in common, Annie thought, remembering how her own life had changed so drastically in those terrible years, after her papa ran off to avoid being conscripted. "Did your father join the fighting?"

Lucas nodded. "Ma and Pa were northern sympathizers, so that made us unpopular with some folks around St. Charles. When Pa went off to fight . . ." He glanced away. "He left James and me in charge. Told us to protect the womenfolk."

He became quiet, his gaze distant. Annie guessed that he must've only been about twelve at the time. James would've been about sixteen.

She didn't press him for details, didn't want him to tell her if it wasn't what he wanted.

But after a while he continued. "James was always better at book-learning than I was, and I was a better marksman. So that's how we divided things up. He took different jobs in town, made good money. Had a knack for that. I looked after the hunting." His gaze shifted back to his plate. "But toward the end, there wasn't much money to be made anymore, or much wildlife left in the woods. Not with all the soldiers and deserters and regulators moving through."

He halted again, running his thumb along the clean, white edge of the table.

"One morning," he said in a low voice, "a pair of soldiers came to the door. Union. Said they had known Pa, said they had food. They were officers, looked real clean and nice. And I . . ." His jaw hardened. "I let them in. Should've known better. It was just me and Ma at home that day."

Annie felt her heart beating hard as she saw a dozen emotions cross Lucas's face.

"Lucas," Annie said gently, "what happened to your mother?"

"I barely shut the door before I heard her . . . scream." His breathing was unsteady. "Then one of them hit me with the butt of his rifle. And the next thing I knew, James was waking me up. And the girls were there and they were all crying." He looked away. "And our . . . mother was dead. The Union officers stole what little food we had and killed her. For no reason at all. Just killed her."

Annie felt tears well in her eyes at the pain she saw in his. "Lucas, I'm so sorry."

"I was supposed to *protect* her." He swallowed hard.

" 'Protect the womenfolk.' That was the last thing Pa said before he left. Last words he ever said to me." Lucas got up from the table and walked to the fireplace. "When he explained to us why he had to go off and fight, that was what he told us—his favorite words from Psalm eighty-two."

Lucas looked down into the flames, his voice becoming rough. " 'Defend the weak and the fatherless, do justice to the afflicted and needy, deliver them from the hand of the wicked.' "

Annie felt a tear slip from her lashes, watching him, understanding only now why Lucas had become a lawman, why he felt so driven to defend and protect people—as he hadn't been able to protect his mother. "Your father died in the war," she said gently.

He nodded. "Shiloh."

Her heart ached for Lucas, and for James and their three sisters she'd never met. They'd lost their father and their mother, been left orphaned and alone to fend for themselves at a time when Missouri had been torn apart by marauders in both blue and gray. "What did you do?" she asked softly. "How did you all manage after that?"

"James managed," Lucas said simply. "He took the girls into town, where they'd be safe. I left. That same day."

She gasped. "Why?"

"To hunt them down—the men who killed our mother," he said, a razor-sharp edge in his voice even after all these years. "Took my rifle and tracked them like the animals they were." He turned his head toward her, the firelight casting his face in stark shadows. "But I never found them."

"Oh, Lucas." She closed her eyes, unable to bear it.

Everything was becoming so painfully clear to her now—why law and justice meant so much to him.

Because he had never been able to get the justice he sought for his own family, his own loss.

And that was also why he had been so determined to track down and bring to justice the person who had killed another member of his family. The woman who had taken his brother's life.

Her.

She looked down at her hands in her lap, wringing her napkin. "How old were you when you left them?" she whispered.

"Fifteen. Didn't go home for a long time. Couple of years. By the time I went back, James was already a success in the railroad business, living in a fancy house. I barely recognized the girls. Felt like I didn't even know them anymore."

So James had taken care of his family, while Lucas had chosen to become a lawman, and live apart from them. From everyone.

It struck Annie that they had that in common: they had both lived solitary lives. But while her isolation had been imposed by others, his was by choice.

Not because he was unfeeling, as she had once thought, but because he felt so deeply.

He was afraid to care, afraid to get close to anyone.

Afraid he would let them down.

She rose from the table and walked over to him. "And was that when you became a marshal?"

He nodded. "James helped with that, like he helped everyone with everything." He halted for a second. The two of them exchanged a glance.

They both knew James hadn't helped her when she needed it.

Lucas couldn't seem to look at her as she drew closer.

"He knew how much I liked it out West, and he knew some people. There was an opening for a deputy U.S. marshal. It went to me. I had some luck fairly early, got a bit of attention. Got promoted."

Annie knew he was being modest, just like when he described himself as a "pretty good shot" when the truth was he was lethally fast with a gun.

He called it "luck" and said he "got a bit of attention" when he had, in fact, methodically hunted down some of the worst, most notorious criminals ever to plague the territories; the earliest articles she had read from Travis's collection had been written when Lucas was only twenty.

"And ever since," she said, "you've been trying to protect people. To defend the good people of the world . . . like your father told you the day he left."

He turned toward her, his eyes dark with emotion.

She shook her head sadly. "And that's why you want to be able to tell the good people apart from the bad. So you won't make a mistake." She reached out to touch his arm. "That's all it was, Lucas, that day when you were fifteen and you opened that door. A mistake."

His muscles tensed beneath her fingers. "I failed them," he said hoarsely. "All of them. My mother was *killed* because of what I did. My sisters grew up without a mother because of what I did—"

"And you've been trying to make up for it ever since. Lucas, you've done so much good, for so many people. But you've never forgiven *yourself.*" She held his gaze. "And no matter how hard you try, you can't tell good people apart from the bad just by looking at them. People aren't like that. They're just . . . human. And even the good ones have flaws and weaknesses, and sometimes they make mistakes."

He shut his eyes. "Like James?" he asked gruffly.

Annie couldn't summon a reply. Her own heart was still full of hurt over the way James had treated her.

Lucas remained silent for a moment. Then he touched her face. "I've *tried* to understand what he did to you. But I can't. How could he toss you aside, you and your unborn child?"

He almost sounded angry at his brother for doing that to her.

"I—I don't know why he did it, Lucas." Annie had been struggling to understand the events of that night herself, for so long. "Maybe he . . . maybe he was tired and frustrated. Maybe he panicked." She took a deep breath. "Or maybe he just had one selfish, thoughtless moment. It doesn't mean he was like that his whole life."

Disbelief filled Lucas's eyes. "You're defending him?"

"I'm not defending him, I'm . . ." Annie searched for the right words, and felt like a weight had been lifted from her heart when she found them. "Understanding him, forgiving him," she whispered. "Lucas, he *was* a good man. You were right to believe that about him. He was good and kind and generous. But he wasn't a saint. He was just . . . human, like anyone else."

The disbelief in Lucas's eyes shifted to an emotion she couldn't name. His fingertips trailed through the wisps of hair that curled along her cheek.

She lowered her lashes. "He made mistakes. But so have I. It's . . . it's taken me a while to figure it out, but I know what I am—and what I'm not. I know I'm not perfect." She lifted her chin. "But I'm not what people in St. Charles always told me I was, either."

"No," he said softly. "No, you're not."

They stood in silence for a moment, surrounded by the silver moonlight shining through the windows and the golden glow from the fireplace.

When he spoke again, his voice had become hoarse. "There's something else I've been wondering, about that night. When James tried to take the gun from you . . ." He paused, searching her face. "Do you think it's possible he *knew* you meant to kill yourself?"

Annie inhaled a startled breath. "I—I don't know." The thought had never occurred to her.

"You had just told him you were carrying his child, and you were frightened, vulnerable. He had to see that. When he tried to grab that gun out of your hand, maybe he wasn't trying to save himself. Maybe he was trying to save you."

She closed her eyes, struggled to sort out the images in her memory, but they were blurred by the fear and shock and remorse that had gripped her that night. "All I remember is . . . I was so scared, and we were shouting at each other, and then . . ." Annie shook her head sadly, opening her eyes. "It all happened so fast. I don't know, Lucas." She hoped it was true, wished she could be certain, to ease his mind. "We'll never know. All we can do is—"

"Forgive him," Lucas said quietly. "Forgive him. And accept that he was only human."

Lucas suddenly looked as if he were exhausted, drained. He raked his fingers through his hair, walking over to the settee and sinking down onto it.

Annie felt another tug on her heart, remembering he wasn't fully recovered yet.

"Lucas, I—I almost forgot. I have a present for you." Annie walked over to the hotel desk on the other side of the room and took out the tissue-wrapped package she had hidden behind it, carrying it back to him. "It's just something small," she said. "Just something I wanted you to have."

He looked startled as he took the package and opened

it—to reveal the coverlet she'd been crocheting for weeks.

"You need something to brighten up your room," she explained. "It's sort of . . . empty in there."

He held up the bright red coverlet, a wry expression curving his mouth. "Just something small?"

"Well, all right, it's something kind of large. And there are some crooked stitches here and there. I was . . . still learning."

"I never would've known if you hadn't pointed them out. Looks perfect to me."

He wasn't looking at the gift as he said it; he was looking at her.

Their gazes held for a long, silent moment.

"I should've gotten something for you," he said apologetically.

"That's all right. You haven't exactly been in any condition to go shopping." She didn't need a gift; the way she felt tonight, the way he had opened up to her, was enough. "In fact, you look like you need some rest. I'll clean up." She moved back to the table and picked up a couple of empty dishes, heading for the kitchen.

"Annie."

It was the first time he had called her that in weeks. "Yes?"

"Thank you," he said quietly.

The sound of her pounding heart seemed to fill the whole room. From the emotion in his voice, she knew he wasn't thanking her for the gift she had just given him or the dinner she had made, but for listening.

"You're welcome, Lucas." She watched while he retreated to his room for the night.

Never had she guessed how good it might feel to be able to listen, to offer comfort. To ease someone's sorrow. It was something she'd never really had the chance to do.

All her life, she had imagined how wonderful it would be to have someone who truly cared about her.

She had never guessed it might be even better to truly care about someone.

18

After Lucas knocked for the third time, Holt yanked open his front door, his shirt and vest hanging unbuttoned, his eyes bloodshot. Though it was the middle of the day, the doctor looked like he'd just rolled out of bed after sleeping in his clothes—or hadn't slept at all. "What?" he snapped.

Lucas arched his brows in surprise and didn't say anything for a moment, standing on the front step, the collar of his black coat turned up against the snow blowing around him. "All right if I come in, Doc? Kind of cold out here, being January and all."

Without a word, Holt turned away into the house, leaving the door open.

Lucas took that as an invitation and stepped inside, closing the door behind him. "Tough week?" The parlor was dark; Holt had the curtains drawn, no lanterns lit. "You look as run-down as a two-dollar watch, Doc."

Only after Lucas's eyes adjusted to the dull glow that came from the fire on the hearth did he notice an open bottle of scotch on a marble-topped table in one corner.

Holt picked it up as he slouched onto a settee beside the fire. "Lost a patient last night," he said tersely, taking a drink straight from the bottle. "Don't feel much like seeing anyone today, McKenna."

"Sorry." Lucas moved toward the fire. "Someone you knew a long time?"

"Four-year-old boy." Holt let his head rest against the back of the couch. "Delivered him the night he was born. Poor kid was always sickly, but I thought he was going to make it. I thought I could . . ." He shut his eyes. "Why are you here, McKenna? Is this important?"

"Yeah." Lucas sat in a chair opposite him. "Yeah, it's important." He took off his hat, turning it in his gloved fingers.

His timing might not be the best, but Holt's reaction to losing a patient only reinforced for Lucas that he had made the right decision. And he couldn't keep postponing this discussion. He'd been thinking of little else for a week now.

Putting it off wasn't making it any easier.

"I need to know what your plan was for helping Annie escape."

Holt lifted his head and opened his bloodshot eyes. "What plan? We didn't have any—"

"I *know* you were planning something," Lucas said dryly. "I want you to tell me what it was."

The doctor regarded him in stony silence for a moment. "Why?"

Lucas dropped his hat on a low table to his left and took off his gloves. Then he just said it, calmly. "Because I'm not taking her back to Missouri."

"What?" Holt's eyes widened in shock.

"I'm not taking her back to Missouri," Lucas repeated. His fingers clenched around the soft leather of his gloves. "She'd be facing a judge and jury who'll never believe that what happened was an accident. Men who knew her mother, men who . . ." He paused, cursing under his breath. "Probably some who *slept* with her mother. They think of Annie as a whore, and it'll be a short damn trip to believing she's a thief and a murderer, especially with half the town lining up to offer evidence against her. Even if I talk to the judge, even if I can get the headmaster from that orphanage in Denver she donated the fifteen thousand to—"

"You've thought about this," Holt said in astonishment. "A lot."

Lucas nodded. He'd thought it through from every angle.

And come up with the same gut-wrenching answer every time.

"Even if they let me testify, they'll only claim she seduced me into lying for her," he said roughly. "And the donation to the orphanage isn't enough to prove her innocence. She gave it anonymously. Anyone could've sent them that money." He met Holt's steady gaze. "No jury will ever believe that my brother's death was an accident. They'll sentence her to life in prison. Or worse. She gets the wrong kind of judge . . ." The words almost choked him. "She could hang." He shook his head. "I'm not going to let that happen."

Holt's eyes narrowed. He set the bottle of scotch aside. "None of this seemed to bother you before, when you were so damned eager to haul her back to Missouri. What changed, McKenna?"

Lucas glanced away without replying. But something must have shown in his face.

"You care about her," Holt said quietly.

Lucas swallowed hard, still uneasy with that word, unwilling to put a name to the complicated feelings she stirred in him. All he knew was that Annie had become important to him, in a way no other woman had ever been. "I just think she's suffered enough."

"So what are you planning to do? Just set her free? You're going to break the law?"

"What I'm trying to do is get justice," Lucas said flatly, "and that means clearing her name. I have to go back to St. Charles and see what I can do to get the charges dismissed. And try to talk my sister-in-law into dropping the five-thousand-dollar bounty."

"And how likely is it you'll be able to do that?"

Lucas hesitated. "Not too damned likely," he admitted reluctantly. No matter how he argued Annie's case, he wasn't sure he could persuade the courts to believe him.

And he remembered vividly his last meeting with Olivia—how her blue eyes had practically burned with hunger for vengeance. She wanted Annie dead.

"But I have to try. However long it takes."

Understanding dawned in Holt's haggard face. "You're planning to send Annie out of here alone?"

"She can't stay in Eminence while I'm gone. The day I arrested her, I sent word to the constables back in St. Charles, telling them *exactly* where she is. Lawmen know she's here. Bounty hunters know she's here. As soon as those passes open, she has to leave—"

"But you're not going with her?"

"I can't." Lucas stood up, started pacing. "Try to imagine what would happen if I disappeared with her, if the famous U.S. Marshal Lucas T. McKenna of Indian Territory went on the run with an outlaw—it would stir up such a hornet's nest of publicity in the papers, posses from five states would be after us. My damned reputation would only *guarantee* she'd be hunted down." He shook his head. "The best thing for her is if I stay as far away from her as possible."

He turned to face the doctor. "But I can't just send her off alone. There are plenty more bounty hunters out there like the one that got to her before. She needs someone to protect her. You care about her—"

"McKenna, Annie and I have never been anything more than friends."

"I know that. But she *needs* a friend."

Holt still looked incredulous. "You haven't trusted me from the day you arrived in Eminence—and you're trusting me now, with this?"

"The irony hasn't escaped me," Lucas said dryly. "I considered all the possibilities; you're the best choice. I want someone who can look after her. You said you were a sharpshooter in the war. You're the best candidate to get her to safety." He sat down again. "So tell me what the hell your plan was."

The doctor didn't hesitate any further. "Canada. I have some old friends up in Montana Territory. Figured I'd take her there, and they'd escort her through the mountains on horseback, along some old Indian trails, get her safely over the border into the Canadian territories."

Lucas thought about it, then nodded. "Good. If I can buy her enough time, she'll make it." He ignored the burning, clenched-up sensation in his chest. "Help her disappear, Doc. Somewhere she'll be able to have what she's always wanted—a home, and friends." His throat tightened. "And a family."

The doctor slumped back into the couch, picking up the bottle of scotch again. "She deserves all that."

"Yeah." Lucas nodded. "She's suffered enough. I'm not going to let anyone else hurt her. At least I can give her that."

He had to give her her freedom, make sure she would be safe.

Protect her the best way he knew how.

Holt nodded. "You want me to tell her our plan?"

Lucas shook his head. "I'll tell her, Doc." He stood, picking up his hat and gloves. "Tonight."

"Rebecca?" Annie peered into the store's back room, putting on her coat. She saw Rebecca sitting on a crate, a lantern propped beside her. "It's almost five o'clock."

"Just about finished," Rebecca said, jotting figures in a ledger. "How many tins of Blanke's India Tea we got left?"

"Six." Annie picked her way toward her friend, around barrels of molasses and syrup, sacks of flour, coils of rope, and cheeses encased in wood.

Rebecca smiled. "Right soon, you'll know this place even better than me. Bet you can tell how many boxes of baking soda we got, too, right off the top of your head."

"Twelve," Annie said, pulling on her gloves. "Rebecca—"

"Looks like we made even more in the first week of January than in the last two of December put together." Rebecca held up the ledger, her face aglow with pride. "Never had a winter like this before. And it's all thanks to you."

Annie shook her head, blushing. "No, it's not."

"Sure it is. Folks like the way you've fixed up the store, they like how polite and helpful you always are. By the horn spoons, they just like being around you."

Annie blinked, feeling tears burn her eyes. She reached up and touched the gold locket she wore, a gift Rebecca had given her for Christmas.

It was a family heirloom, Rebecca had said as she pressed the velvet box into Annie's hand. But she didn't have a daughter of her own to pass it on to . . . so she wanted Annie to have it.

Annie knew she would wear it always. To remind her of this place, these people.

This brief, special time in her life.

"Come summer," Rebecca continued enthusiastically, "maybe we can talk to Cyrus Hazelgreen over at the bank, and see about us buying that empty millinery shop next door. If we knocked out the wall—".

"Rebecca, I won't be here come summer."

Her friend finally looked up from jotting in the ledger, her eyes large behind her spectacles. "But . . . well, I know we was *thinkin'* you'd have to go on your way this spring, but I thought . . . I mean, you and the marshal . . . I was thinkin' Lucas might not make you go back—"

"Lucas?" Annie looked at her curiously. "You called him Lucas. What happened to 'that ornery varmint'? I thought you didn't like him."

Rebecca set her pen and ledger aside. "He's sorta grown on me," she said grudgingly.

Me, too, Annie thought, lowering her lashes. Every time she even thought of him, her heart filled with emotions she had never felt before. For any man, or anyone.

"That lawman just has a certain way about him." Rebecca took Annie's hand. "And I been watching the two of you in the store for weeks now," she continued gently. "Annie, I seen the way you look at him. And the way he looks at you, when you don't even know he's looking. His eyes go all soft. Like a bee longing after a blossom. He cares about you."

Annie shook her head, blinking hard. Even if that were true, it didn't change the fact that he was a lawman, and she was a wanted criminal.

It didn't change what had to happen come springtime.

"Annie," Rebecca said insistently, "there once was a man looked at me thataway—and he proposed marriage and we spent near forty years together."

"That's not going to happen," Annie whispered.

"But I was thinkin' you two . . . might stay here, in Eminence. With all of us."

"No, I can't. I . . ." Annie dabbed at her eyes with her gloved fingers. How could she bear to tell Rebecca the decision she had made?

Since Christmas, she'd been thinking about it. But she hadn't even told Lucas yet, had been trying to work up her courage to say the words aloud all week.

"Rebecca, I really should go. It's almost sunset."

"Oh, lamb." Rebecca stood and enfolded her in a hug, sniffling. "I wish spring wouldn't never come."

"I know." Annie held on to her, this woman who'd been more of a mother to her than her own mama had ever been. "I'll miss you. I'll miss you so much."

As the sun began to sink behind the mountains, Annie climbed the hill to the cemetery, entering through the gate as she had so often. Even though Lucas had allowed her more freedom to go where she wished, she hadn't been up here in a long while.

But she wanted to spend a little time here today, before she went to talk to Lucas. Wanted to be close to her child.

Her heavy woolen coat wrapped close against the bitter wind, she trudged through the snow, toward the tree in the corner, its branches stark and bare against the winter sky.

But when she looked toward her baby's grave, she didn't see the little pine cross with the name *Baby Smith* on it. Her heart skipped a beat. Had somebody . . . why would anybody . . . ?

When she hurried over, she realized that it hadn't been taken away.

It had been replaced. With a new headstone of white

marble, that had a cherub carved into it, above different words.

Baby McKenna.

Annie gasped, sinking to her knees in the snow. She reached out to touch the letters of the name, and a Bible verse that had been added below it.

For the kingdom of God belongs to such as these.

She stared, astonished. Who could have . . . ?

Even before she completed the thought, she knew there was only one person who would do this, who would understand how much this gift would mean to her.

Who would care enough to claim the child she had lost. To give her baby a name.

Tears filled her eyes. *He cared about her.* Maybe he couldn't say the words, but he cared.

Annie remained there for a moment, very still, and felt as if her heart were healing and breaking at the same time.

Then she rose and went to find him.

19

"**L**ucas?" Annie was out of breath by the time she closed the jail's front door behind her; she had run most of the way. The setting sun cast long, slanting shadows across the furnishings and rugs in the main room.

He came out of her suite, still wearing his coat and hat. "There you are." He looked relieved, and a bit puzzled. "I went to find you at Rebecca's and she couldn't tell me where you'd gone, she was crying so hard. What's wrong?"

Annie shook her head, a tear running down her cheek.

"What is it?" He walked over to her, his expression concerned now. "What have you been running from?"

"Not from," she said breathlessly. "*To.*"

That was all she could get out before she started to cry.

"Annie?" He moved closer, reaching out to cup her face in his broad hands. "What's happened?"

"I—I found . . . your gift."

"Oh." He only sounded more confused, his voice becoming gruff as he brushed her tears away with his fingertips. "I wouldn't have done it if I'd known it would make you cry."

His caring words and concern for her only made her ache even more. She leaned forward and rested her cheek against the hard muscles of his chest, her tears dampening his shirt.

"Annie." He hesitated a moment before he wrapped his arms around her. "I'm sorry."

"No," she said painfully, trying to make him understand. "I . . . I'm . . ." She struggled to put her feelings into words. "Nobody's ever given me a gift that meant so much to me, Lucas." She closed her eyes. "*I've* never mattered to anyone that much."

His arms tightened around her, and even through the rough fabric of his shirt, she could feel his heart beating hard.

"Annie." He tilted her head up with one hand, his eyes dark as he looked down at her. "There's something I need to tell you."

She didn't prompt him when he hesitated, when she saw the emotions in his eyes; she knew he wasn't used to expressing his feelings in words.

Gently, he set her away from him, clearing his throat.

Then he finally spoke, "I'm not taking you to Missouri when the passes clear in the spring. I'm setting you free."

She stared up at him in astonishment. "Setting me . . . free?" she repeated blankly.

"It's the only way I can keep you safe."

He stated it calmly, as if it were a perfectly simple, clear, logical idea. Then he took off his hat and coat, turning to drop them over the back of the couch.

She was stunned. He was letting her go.

He was letting her go?

"But Lucas, I—I've decided I'm going back to Missouri with you in the spring."

"What?" He turned toward her. "What do you mean, you're going back to Missouri?"

"I'm going back to St. Charles to stand trial." She trembled as she said the words aloud for the first time. "I don't want to go on the run from the law again. I don't want to live the rest of my life always looking over my shoulder. I—I thought you would be happy."

He looked anything but happy. "I am not *taking* you back to St. Charles. You're going someplace safe."

"But where would I *ever* be safe?" She shook her head. "I would have to spend the rest of my life hiding and being afraid and lying to everyone I meet—I can't *do* that, Lucas. Not anymore. Not after the kind of life I've known here, the kind of caring I've known here."

"Annie, you can't stay here." He walked toward her. "You know that's impossible. I've talked to Holt. It's all planned. You're going to Canada."

"You and Daniel have it all . . ." She couldn't seem to catch her breath. "Lucas, if you try to help me, there might come a time when you would have to shoot it out with another lawman, to protect me. I can't ask you to do that." She clenched her fists. "I won't."

"So your solution is to go back and let them put you on trial? They'll never give you a chance!"

"It's the only way to clear my name. I have to go back and face a judge and jury, and just tell the truth—"

"And hope for the best? You could end up spending the rest of your life in prison. Or worse."

"It's either risk that or spend the rest of my life as an outlaw! I have to prove I'm innocent."

"There *isn't* any way to prove you're innocent. You *know* that." He grabbed her by the shoulders. "Annie, you have to let me handle this. I've thought it through. I'm sending you somewhere safe and then I'll appeal to the court, try to get the charges dropped—"

"You'll have a hard time doing that without me there.

How are you going to explain where I went? Tell them I escaped?"

"No," he said adamantly. "That would only make things worse for you. I don't want anyone sending out a posse to hunt you down. I'll tell them you're in protective custody—and it'll be the truth. Holt will be with you. He'll look after you—"

"Lucas, you can't do this." She pressed her fists against his chest, appalled at the sacrifice he was willing to make for her. "Have you thought of what it might cost you? If you let me go instead of taking me in—they could take your badge. It could cost you your career, your reputation—"

He cut her off with a curt shake of his head, a fierce look in his eyes. "That's a chance I'll have to take."

She stared up at him, stunned by the depth of his feelings.

His feelings for *her.*

"And what about your family?" Her voice wavered.

"I'll try to explain, make them understand."

She shut her eyes, unwilling to let him risk so much for her. "They'd never understand. Lucas, they'd never *forgive* you." She couldn't seem to catch her breath. "And you could be thrown in *jail* for letting a criminal walk away free—"

"You're not a criminal. You are *not guilty* of the charges against you."

"And I have to go back to Missouri and *prove* that."

He let her go, turning away with a frustrated curse. "I can't believe we're even having this conversation! *I* want you to escape and *you* insist on going back to Missouri—"

"Yes. Because it's the only way, Lucas." Tears blurred her vision. "I don't want to do it, but I have to. Because I want the kind of life I've had here, in Eminence. With the people I care about. Like Rebecca and Daniel and Katja and . . ." *You.*

He turned toward her, his gaze stormy.

"I'll lose all of that if I run." Her voice almost broke. "I'll lose everything. And I'm so *tired* of running, Lucas. My whole life, I've been running away from people who might hurt me. I have to stop running and stand up to them."

"But you could lose your *life* if you go back," he said hoarsely. "Those people you've been running from might do more than hurt you this time—they could hang you. Haven't you thought of that?"

She nodded solemnly.

"Annie . . ." He shut his eyes as if he couldn't bear to look at her anymore. "I admire the hell out of you for being brave enough to want to go back, *but you can't.*"

"I don't feel very brave," Annie admitted, her voice shaking. "I never wanted to set foot in St. Charles again. The idea of facing a courtroom full of people who look at me with contempt, who've despised me since I was a little girl . . . Lucas, it's terrifying."

He closed the distance between them and pulled her into his arms.

"But I *have* to go back." She rested her cheek against his chest. "I have to face them. It's the only way I'll ever really be *free.*"

"I can't let you do it, Annie." His words were stark, raw.

"Lucas, please, I'm so afraid. I can't do this unless you . . . unless you'll be there."

He drew her closer, surrounding her with the strength and warmth of his embrace. "I don't want *you* to be there. I am not going to let them anywhere near you. I won't let them get their hands on you."

"So you're sending me away," she choked out. "For how long?"

He didn't answer for a moment, his hand tangling in her long hair. "As long as it takes to get the charges dismissed and the bounty dropped."

"Months," she whispered. "Maybe years."

"I don't know," he admitted gruffly.

Annie knew. He might *never* be able to get the charges and the bounty dropped. She would be on the run . . . and he would be half a world away. Maybe in jail himself, his career as a lawman in ruins, his family lost to him forever.

"No." She lifted her gaze to his, blinking hard. "No, *I* have to make this choice, Lucas."

"You're going to Canada," he said stubbornly, "and that's final."

She smiled through her tears as she looked up at him—standing there so fierce and tough, so determined to wrestle the situation under his control. So much a hero.

But he couldn't rescue her. Not this time.

"I understand why you want to protect me." She reached up and touched his beard-roughened cheek. "I know how important it is to you—"

"No, you don't." His eyes burned into hers. "You don't know how I . . . damn it, *you* are important to me. *You.*" He tilted her chin up. "God help me, woman, I have tried so hard not to . . ." His voice became strained. "Not to . . ."

His mouth captured hers in a heated, breath-stealing kiss.

Annie melted against him, her heart racing, and surrendered to his passion, clinging to him. Her fingers gripped the heavy cloth of his shirt, her knees too weak to support her. The muscles of his arms went taut as he shifted his hold on her and buried one hand in her hair, deepening the kiss—branding her, claiming her.

His possessiveness set fire to her blood, sent need sweeping through her. Her arms tightened around him and she responded with a feeling that was wholly new to her. More than desire, deeper than caring, stronger than need.

He embraced her as if he would bind them together body and soul—until no force of law or man could tear them apart.

As if he would make her his, tonight and forever.

"Yes," she sobbed when he lifted his head, saying it again as he trailed hungering, urgent kisses down her cheek, her throat. "Lucas, *yes.*"

She wanted one moment with him, one memory to cherish when she was taken away from him. For now, for this night, they belonged to each other, and nothing could come between them.

Tonight, she wanted to dream of what could be, if only dreams could come true.

He swept her into his arms and carried her toward the suite they had once shared.

The bedroom was dark, the day's last light long vanished beyond the barred windows. He didn't take the time to light a fire in the hearth or even a lantern, letting go of her just long enough to lay her on the bed and pull the heavy velvet drapes shut. She held out her arms as he returned to her. He took off his gun belt, his boots, and then he was beside her on the bed. His weight pressing her down into the sheets was the only warmth she needed, the light in his eyes more than enough to chase the darkness.

Impatient hands tugged at clothing, hungry kisses dusted over bared skin. Her fingers glided along the smooth, corded sinews of his arms, his shoulders, the broad expanse of his back. Her dress drifted to the floor and his hands shaped her breasts, the tips beading beneath his fingers, teased, kissed. Her low moans blended with his as their mouths met again and again in hot, deep kisses.

He caressed her shoulders, her waist, her legs, until her whole body felt tingling and heated. Pleasure and need and a newer, deeper emotion twined and tangled within her as he opened her to his touch, finding her soft and wet and welcoming.

His fingertips whisked over her downy triangle, found the sensitive bud hidden within, stroked it. She arched beneath him as he urged it to fullness with his thumb, small, sharp cries tearing from her throat. Her hands kneaded his shoulders, his back, drawing him closer.

And as his body covered hers, there was no thought of past or future or the danger that awaited. There was only him, only now. Only this feeling of being safe and protected and cherished.

He fitted himself to her and a soft sound escaped her, a whisper of pleasure, of wanting, that came out as his name. And it was like one life ending, falling away from her like the golden sun that had set behind the mountains, and a new one beginning, a silver moon rising in the sky, defiant in its brightness against the night.

His gaze locked on hers as he penetrated her in one long, slow stroke, until that hard, male part of him was sheathed within her. Until he was deeply a part of her, a sweet pressure inside her. He moved his hips, alternating slow, silky caresses with sudden, deep thrusts that made pleasure coil tighter and tighter within her.

They rose and fell together, fire and steel, softness and strength, both offering and receiving, both taking and giving. The sensations in her body burned her like the fire in his eyes, those molten depths glittering with passion that startled her with its intensity. His mouth took hers in a kiss that was just as fierce and powerful.

Their sighs and whispers made the only sounds in the silence, and there was only him, inside her and around her, filling her body and her heart and her soul.

She arched her hips, taking him even deeper, their bodies moving together in a slow, endless rhythm that made the tension spin tight and low in her belly. Tremors began rivering through her and she felt him tremble in that same moment, felt his body go taut.

Together they reached for the light in the darkness, together they found it, shards of star-bright brilliance exploding around her, inside her, pleasure and joy cascading through her as he spilled his heat and life inside her.

He gathered her to him and she savored the sweet feeling, knowing she would never forget this moment as long as she lived, this feeling that overflowed her heart.

"I love you," she whispered in the darkness, in his arms. "I love you."

Lucas felt the touch of the sunlight seeping through the velvet curtains, but refused to open his eyes. All night, they had kept each other awake, making love again and again, fiercely, tenderly.

If he just kept his eyes closed, he could stay here, holding her close, and forget about the world outside this room.

Regret cut through him as he finally, reluctantly opened his eyes. She lay curled beside him, facing him, so beautiful in the light of dawn. He remained still and watched her sleep, memorizing every sweet curve of her face, every eyelash, every glossy tendril of her dark hair.

He had wanted her to be his, and his alone, if only for a brief time, a few stolen moments he would always remember, long after he had to set her free and watch her walk away.

She had to agree to leave him. Somehow, he had to persuade her to see reason.

But for now, just for now, he didn't want to wake her

from her dreams. Not when she fit beside him so perfectly, so soft and vulnerable, so fragile and small.

After a while, she must have felt the touch of the sun against her skin, because she stirred, her lashes lifting.

His heartbeat unsteady, Lucas reached out and brushed a stray curl back from her face.

She blinked drowsily, smiling. "Good morning."

He couldn't find any words. Why did they always seem to fail him at moments like this?

She touched his beard-stubbled cheek, and then ruffled the tangled hair on his forehead, almost playfully. "I don't regret last night," she said softly, "and I meant what I said. I love you."

"Annie . . ." He slipped his arm around her and drew her toward him.

"It's all right." She stroked his shoulder, soothingly, as if he were the one in need of care and comfort. "I know. You haven't changed your mind about me going back to Missouri."

"No." He hadn't changed his mind. There was no way in hell he was letting her put herself in the hands of people who would hurt her—who might kill her.

"But Lucas," she said in a tone that held a new, quiet strength. "I've made my decision."

"No," he corrected gently, "*I've* made your decision."

"Stubborn male," she teased.

"Maddening female." He kissed her shoulder. "Annie—"

"Lucas, I don't want to argue about it anymore." Her fingers threaded through the hair at the nape of his neck. "I don't want to think about what's going to happen when spring comes. Can we just . . . not fight about it anymore, for now?"

He nuzzled his cheek against hers, reluctant to deny her anything that would make her happy.

"There are only a few weeks of winter left." She

kissed his jaw. "And I don't want to spend them arguing with you."

With a sigh, he rolled onto his back, pulling her atop him. "How do you want to spend them?"

She snuggled closer, laying her head on his chest. "Like this."

"Annie." He closed his eyes. It had been unspeakably selfish to allow himself to make love to her for even one night, to accept her passion and her love when he had to send her away.

It was no way to treat a lady, especially not this sweet, brown-haired elf who had carved out such an important place in his life, in his heart.

He cleared his throat and forced himself to say it. "Annie, you should have everything you want—a home, a husband. And I want to give you that." His voice thickened. "By letting you go. You can have that life, somewhere safe—"

"But I don't *want* that life if it doesn't include you," she protested softly. "I want my home to be with you."

He reached up to thread his fingers through her long hair. "I don't even have a home," he reminded her. For years, the only home he'd had—the only one he'd wanted or needed—was what he could carry in his saddlebags. "And I don't know when . . . or if . . . I'll see you—"

She stopped his words with a fingertip against his lips. "Lucas, I know that we can't be sure what's going to happen. And when we get back to Missouri—"

"When *I* get back," he corrected.

She sighed in frustration but didn't try to argue for the moment. "Back in Missouri," she continued, "you'll see your family again and . . ." She paused. "That might change things between us."

"Seeing my family again will not change how I feel about you," he said gruffly. "Annie, you matter to me.

You're . . ." He tried to think of the right words. "Important to me in a way that I can't even . . ." He was making a mess of this. "I care about you, lady."

It came out as a half-growl, but his declaration still made her smile.

A dusky glow colored her cheeks. "I know, Lucas. You've shown me, in so many ways." She looked into his eyes. "But I don't want you to make any promises now that you might regret later." She shook her head, whispering, "Just give me today, and tomorrow, and however long we might have until spring."

Her plea wrung his heart. He brushed her tangled hair back from her face. "Just go on like we were before?"

She nodded. "Only without all the arguing."

He ran a fingertip along her cheekbone. "We'll be giving certain people in town plenty more to gossip about—"

"I didn't realize you cared so much what anyone thought about you," she teased.

"It wasn't me I was thinking of," he said dryly.

Her smile widened. "You're very sweet to be concerned about my reputation, gallant sir. But the people who matter to me already know how we feel about each other. In fact, I think Rebecca knew before I did."

He drew the blanket around her to keep her warm as she settled against him. "Holt knows, too."

She nodded. "As for everyone else . . . Some people will never accept me, no matter what. But for the first time in my life, I really don't care what people say or think." She sounded mildly surprised at her own words. "All I care about is how much I love you."

He shut his eyes, aching at the way those words made him feel.

"Lucas, just for these next few weeks, can't we pretend like . . . like there's nothing waiting beyond those mountain passes to hurt us. That for once, for a little while, we both have a place to call—"

"Home." He murmured his answer against her lips. "Yes."

20

Annie sighed and sank lower in the tub, watching steam curl upward from the water. The white tendrils that rose in the firelit darkness filled the room with the scent of meadow herbs from her favorite soap. She closed her eyes with a smile, the heat easing the soreness from her every aching muscle; it was Saturday, and she'd been at the store since six this morning, bustling and busy all day.

Lucas, bless him, had had the hot bath waiting for her when she got home, placed in front of the hearth in their room. He'd even lit candles on the mantel and the tables. The curtains were drawn, the whole hotel dark and silent.

"Better?" he asked softly from where he sat a few feet away.

"Yes." She rested against the edge of the tub, turning her head to smile at him. "Much better, thank you."

He returned her smile, reclining in the chaise longue wearing only his black trousers. There was a now-familiar gleam in his eyes as he watched her, a huskiness in his voice. "Happy to oblige."

Her cheeks warmed and she lowered her lashes. Even after weeks of sharing a home with him, she still blushed when he looked at her that way.

For the past month, they had spent their days as before, kept busy by their work. In the afternoons, she would sometimes visit her lady friends or they would visit her, filling the hotel's front room and kitchen with their chatting and laughter as they made tea and did needlework, or played cards, or baked some special surprise for their menfolk.

But the nights . . . the nights belonged only to her and Lucas. They spent every hour together, stealing every moment, giving themselves to each other as if each time might be the last.

And Annie had begun to realize that the hardest part of the choice she had made wasn't the idea of leaving Eminence and all her friends, or the fear of facing prison or worse.

It was the thought of being separated from the man she loved.

She bowed her head and rinsed her hair, letting the tangle of curls fall around her in a dark cascade. Once, it had seemed like she and Lucas were trapped by the winter snows that surrounded this isolated town; now it felt as if the blocked mountain passes offered their only protection.

And as the middle of February approached, bringing warmer temperatures, she knew that their sanctuary couldn't last much longer.

The water grew cool, but she took longer than necessary rinsing her hair, hoping Lucas couldn't see her expression. She had been trying so hard not to think about the future, not wanting to let sorrow or fear intrude on this special, magical time.

These few weeks of happiness that might have to last her the rest of her life.

"Ready to dry off?" he asked quietly. He came over and took a large towel from the chair beside the tub.

"Yes," she said, looking up at him, grateful to have her melancholy thoughts interrupted. As she stood, water sluicing down her body, he wrapped her in the towel, and in his embrace, his arms sliding around her. For a moment, he just held her.

Then he scooped her up and out of the tub, carrying her over to the chaise, setting her down at the end. After he picked up another towel he'd had waiting, he swung his leg over the long chair and sat down behind her.

She closed her eyes as he began to dry her hair. Of all the little customs and routines they had established, this Saturday night ritual was one of her favorites.

"Talked to Holt this evening," Lucas said after a moment.

"Oh?" Annie asked reluctantly. Her friend Daniel was not one of her favorite topics these days—because he agreed with Lucas that the best thing for her to do was go to Canada. The two men were working on a plan together, and they had Lily Breckenridge and some other experienced miners traveling out to the passes now and then, keeping an eye on the snows and reporting back.

While scouting, Daniel's friends had inadvertently solved the mystery of what had happened to the two prospectors suspected of poisoning Lucas at the Christmas dance: The pair had been found on one of the mountain trails, frozen to death. Apparently they had tried to get out of town rather than face Lucas's fury, and paid with their lives. The case, Travis had declared, was closed.

It also offered proof of just how dangerous the passes around Eminence were in the winter, Annie thought, a shiver going down her spine.

Lucas remained silent a long moment before finally sharing the news Daniel had given him. "Said it might be only another week," he told her quietly. "Maybe ten days."

Annie blinked hard, knowing that meant the two of them had even less time left together than they had thought. At the first opportunity, Lucas and Daniel intended to get her to safety.

And she was still equally determined to turn herself in and face the charges against her. "Lucas, I don't want to—"

"Shh." He stopped drying her hair, set the towel aside, and kissed her shoulder. "You know this is how it has to be, Annie. I want you safe."

He slid one arm around her waist and she covered his hand with hers. He threaded their fingers together.

She leaned back into his embrace, wanting so desperately to believe that his plan could work, that everything would be all right. But there were too many things that could go wrong.

And he would be risking too much, giving up too much. She couldn't let him do it.

"Annie, I'll come find you as soon as everything's taken care of back in Missouri," he assured her. "I know we said no promises—but I'm giving you one. However long it takes, I *will* come find you."

She closed her eyes, fighting the tears that threatened to spill down her cheeks.

"All you have to do is wait for me," he murmured encouragingly. "Just make sure you don't meet some nice Canadian man."

How did he keep managing to make her smile when she felt like crying? "I don't want to meet *any* nice man." She rubbed her cheek against his. "I want you."

He chuckled, low in his throat. "Thanks."

"I didn't mean it that way," she corrected quickly, nuzzling his beard-stubbled jaw. "You're very nice. And caring and gentle, and strong and brave. And I love you," she whispered against his mouth as he kissed her. When he lifted his head, she looked into his eyes. "I will never love *any* man but you, Lucas."

Their lips met again, and he held her closer, enveloping her in his strength and passion, and there were no more words between them. Tomorrow, or the next day there would be time enough to discuss what must be, Annie thought desperately. She didn't want the world to intrude on them. Not yet.

Please God, not yet.

She was late. Her woolen coat still unbuttoned, Annie juggled her gloves, a biscuit she had grabbed from the kitchen for breakfast, and a handful of hairpins as she closed the hotel's front door behind her, trying to do so quietly and avoid waking Lucas. Rebecca would never complain, but Annie felt terrible for being late. It was already a quarter to nine, and Monday was usually a busy day at the store.

With each new morning, she and Lucas had grown more and more reluctant to greet the dawn as it invaded the home they had made, reluctant to begin another day that carried them closer to the moment they had to part.

A week . . . maybe ten days.

Annie forced the painful thought from her mind, putting her gloves in her pocket and eating the biscuit in a few quick bites as she hurried down the board sidewalk toward the general store. She picked her way around icy spots and drifts sculpted by the wind during the night. Her gaze on the planks, she pinned her hair up, not even bothering to button her coat. The store was only a short distance from the hotel, and the air today had lost its bitter edge, seemed remarkably . . .

Warm.

She wasn't sure if it was that realization that slowed her steps, or the sound she heard.

The sound from the livery stable on the other side of the street.

Annie lifted her gaze and froze, her hands still raised to her hair, one hairpin still in her fingers. For a moment, she just stood there. Unable to think. Unable to move. Her heart was pounding so hard, it blotted out all sound.

The noise she had heard was the braying of mules and the jingling of harnesses.

A mule train. The first mule train of the season had arrived—a string of fifteen or twenty pack animals, loaded with provisions, accompanied by drovers with long whips. There was a laden wagon. And riders on horseback. Five of them.

A dozen thoughts all collided in her mind at once. The scouts had been mistaken. One of the passes was already open! She would have to leave Eminence. Now. Today. *Leave Lucas.*

Her fingers seemed to go numb. She let her arms drop to her sides, too stunned to take another step, to take a breath. It felt like she was being splintered in pieces, part of her numbly accepting that the inevitable had come too soon, part of her wanting to turn back, run to the hotel, to have just one more day, one more hour with him.

She took a step backward, shaking her head in denial, anguish.

And that was when she saw the woman.

For a second, some part of Annie's mind found it odd that a finely dressed lady should be among the rough muleskinners, odder still that she seemed to be in charge. The men who had been on horseback gathered around as she spoke with Mr. Ballard, the owner of the livery stable.

Then all at once, whether it was the woman's fine clothes or the way she held herself or the color of her hair, Annie realized that she looked familiar.

"Oh, my God." Annie flattened herself against the wall of the abandoned building behind her, feeling dizzy. Everything started spinning around her. *No. No, it couldn't be* . . . Annie had only seen her a handful of times, from a distance, from the window of her suite in St. Charles.

The men had started looking around at the few townsfolk who were out at this time of day—then one of them caught sight of Annie, said something to the lady.

She felt an icy chill go down her back as they all glanced her way. Her thoughts scattered. She obeyed the instinct to turn and start walking back toward the hotel. *Toward Lucas.*

"Antoinette Sutton?" one of the men called out, his voice sharp and challenging in the clear morning air.

"It's her!" another male voice shouted.

Not even thinking, Annie broke into a run. She heard them coming for her. Yelling at her to stop. Terror seized her heart. Their boots pounded the boardwalk. She kept running, blindly.

Hands fastened on her coat, her shoulder.

"No!" she screamed, her hair tumbling loosely around her as she was shoved back against the wall. There were five of them, their faces hard and angry as they looked at her. Two of them held her pinned, one on either side of her. All of them were wearing badges.

The lady had followed them across the street, her beautiful face a mask of fury as she approached, her voice shaking with outrage. "That's her."

Annie shook her head in mute disbelief.

It was James's wife.

"Antoinette Sutton," one of the lawmen said, taking out a pair of handcuffs, "you are under arrest on the charge of murder in the first degree."

They wrenched Annie's arms behind her. Her mind reeled. Mrs. McKenna came closer, until she stood only inches away. Her blue eyes ablaze, she glared at Annie as the cuffs were locked in place.

Then the elegant woman raised one gloved hand and slapped her hard across the face. Annie cried out and sagged in the arms of the men who held her.

"You murdering little *whore*," Mrs. McKenna snapped. "What in the name of God are you doing out of jail? What happened to my brother-in-law? Did you kill *him*, too?"

"Olivia!"

Annie glanced up the boardwalk at the same time Mrs. McKenna did—to see Lucas standing in the door of the hotel, wearing only his trousers and his unbuttoned shirt, his face stark with shock.

"Lucas!" Mrs. McKenna cried, looking relieved as she rushed toward him. "Thank God you're all right! We thought you were dead! Your sisters and I were worried *sick* when there was no word. I've been in Denver for a month waiting for . . . Lucas?"

He barely glanced at her, staring at Annie and the two lawmen who held her with an agonized expression. "Annie—"

"No." She shook her head, trying to tell him it was all right. For a moment, she had panicked, but this was what she wanted, what had to be. Tears blurred her vision and started to fall. "Lucas, no."

Mrs. McKenna looked at Annie, then at Lucas, her eyes narrowing.

Mr. Ballard had run over from the livery, and a few

other townsfolk came into the street. Suddenly the morning air was filled with noise, everyone asking questions and talking at once. One of the lawmen who had been standing apart from the others, a dark-haired young man with a beard, stepped forward as Lucas walked toward Annie. "Marshal McKenna, sir—"

"Weatherby!" Lucas looked surprised. "What are you doing here?"

"Knew something was wrong, sir, when you didn't write back after we let you know about Thompson and Reynolds," the young man said. "Sent a telegraph to St. Charles and they told us you'd disappeared. After we rounded up the last of the Risco gang, the boys picked me to go see if you needed any help—"

"I organized an expedition and set out as soon as I could." Mrs. McKenna's voice had shifted, become cool. "Lucas, would you mind telling me—"

"And who the hell are the rest of you?" Lucas challenged the other lawmen. "If you're from St. Charles, you're out of your jurisdiction—"

"Private detectives, Marshal," one of the men holding Annie explained. "Mrs. McKenna here hired us to find out what had happened to you and your prisoner."

Annie inhaled sharply as the two men holding her by the arms pulled her toward the street, their grips bruising.

"Hold on," Lucas snarled, stalking over to block their path.

"Lucas, don't, please, it's all right." With her hands cuffed behind her, Annie couldn't even brush her tangled hair out of her eyes, couldn't wipe away her tears. She knew he was trying to buy time until he could figure out what to do, but it was too late. "I'll go with them, willingly."

One of the other men took a sheaf of folded papers from inside his coat and handed it to Lucas. "We've been legally empowered to enforce the warrant for this woman's arrest, Marshal."

"Lucas." James's wife stalked toward him, her eyes full of suspicion. "What is going *on*? Why was this little tramp walking around free? And why do you *care* what happens to . . ." When he turned to look at her, whatever she saw in his eyes made her voice shift to a high pitch. "Oh, dear God."

"Olivia, there's a lot you don't understand—"

"It can't be." She stared at him in horror. "How *could* you? You let this whore *seduce* you, didn't you? You took her to bed! The tramp who murdered your brother—"

"She's not a whore. And it wasn't murder," he told her flatly. "It was an accident—"

"An *accident*?" Mrs. McKenna cried. "What are you *saying*? All this time we were all so *worried* about you, and *this* is what you've been doing"—she pointed at Annie—"sleeping with your brother's *whore*? Letting her trick you into taking leave of your senses?"

Annie shut her eyes, feeling sick, wishing she could sink into the wooden boardwalk beneath her feet.

"Olivia," Lucas said, biting off the word as if he were trying very hard to be patient. "I have to explain—"

"You don't have to explain a thing! I understand perfectly! She seduced you—just like she seduced James. She lured you into her bed with her harlot's tricks and played you for a fool!" She stepped away from him as if she couldn't even stand to breathe the same air. "Men are all such *swine*! It would be a miracle if just *once* a man could do his thinking with his brain instead of his . . . his . . ." She whirled on Annie. "You devious, low-born little piece of gutter trash! You've turned *everyone* against me."

"No," Annie sobbed. "No, that's not—"

"Don't you dare even *speak* to me!" Mrs. McKenna

gestured for her hired men to take her to the wagon. "Your lies and your tricks won't save you this time. "You're going back to St. Charles. And you're going to *pay* for what you've done."

21

Lucas found it hard to breathe, the courtroom was so packed. He'd attended dozens of trials before—but always as an arresting officer giving testimony.

Never as a loved one of the accused.

The trip home had taken twelve days, first on horseback as the mule train slowly made its way down the snowy mountain, then by stagecoach to Denver, then by train to St. Charles. He had stayed close every step of the way, refusing to leave Annie at the mercy of Olivia's hired muscle.

He had almost come to blows with one arrogant son of a bitch, but he had insisted on making sure she was well treated and unhurt. His deputy, Shane Weatherby, had come along to offer whatever help he could, and between the two of them, they'd managed to keep watch over her.

When he had been allowed to speak with her in the St. Charles jail, Annie had pleaded with him not to try anything rash to rescue her. Never had he seen her so brave, ready to stand up for herself and clear her name, assuring him that his presence alone would give her the strength she needed to face whatever might come.

Lucas felt his throat tightening. He intended to do more than lend her his strength.

To save Annie, he would move heaven and earth.

And now that his worst nightmares about the trial were coming true, that might just be necessary.

Lucas glanced behind him at the people filling every seat and standing in the aisles, some lounging against the mahogany paneling and marble pillars at the back: society ladies, shopkeepers, business associates of James's, constables, reporters, newspaper artists busily sketching on white pads of paper. All of them whispered and gossiped as they waited for the afternoon recess to end and testimony to resume.

For two days now, the population of St. Charles had hung on every word uttered by every witness as the prosecutor presented his case in lurid detail. The man had made it clear in his opening statement that he considered this crime so despicable, and Annie's guilt so clear beyond the shadow of a doubt, that the only possible justice lay in the most severe punishment: hanging.

Lucas clenched his jaw as he turned to face the front of the room, staring at the American flag behind the judge's bench.

Justice. For most of his life, he'd been pursuing justice, chasing it like it was something he could capture and hold on to. He had always believed there was a solid, unmistakable line between the saints of the world, and the sinners.

Lucas felt a hand on his arm and looked down into Rebecca Greer's face. Her eyes were filled with uncertainty and fear.

He covered her hand with his. If there was one thing he had learned in Eminence, it was that he couldn't draw boundaries around people and expect them to stay locked inside.

The bailiff entered the court from behind the judge's bench. "All rise for the Honorable Judge Knapp."

Lucas stood with everyone else. The gossiping on-
lookers scurried to reclaim their places; Olivia's friends
and supporters filled the entire left side of the room and
had overflowed onto the right, since supporters for the
accused were sparse.

In fact, they numbered four: the defense attorney ap-
pointed by the presiding judge, Lucas, Rebecca, and
Daniel. Annie's two best friends had followed them to St.
Charles as soon as they could.

This afternoon's witness was brought in: the defendant.

Lucas tensed as Annie was escorted into the court
wearing handcuffs. She looked pale, and her gown of
blue gingham seemed too big for her slender frame; he
had to fight the urge to walk over, pick her up in his
arms, and carry her out of here, take her someplace
safe. Somewhere he could protect her.

After the shackles were removed, two constables led
her toward the witness box. She walked with calm dignity, in spite of the looks everyone in the room gave
her—looks full of distaste, reproach, condemnation.

She didn't lower her gaze, didn't turn her face away
from these people who had hated her since she was a
child, who had always treated her as an object of scorn.

Lucas swallowed past a lump in his throat. For the
first time in her life, she faced them without flinching. As
if she finally realized that, in every way that mattered,
she was as good as any one of them. As worthy of respect and fairness.

And justice.

A hush fell over the room as everyone reclaimed their
seats—including the twelve men in the jury box on the
right side of the courtroom, some of them stonefaced and
impassive, others looking at Annie exactly as Lucas had
feared they would: with scathing expressions.

None of them looked inclined to be merciful.

As Lucas sat down, he saw his sisters file in from the back of the courtroom to take their places near Olivia and the prosecutor. Lucas had tried talking to Callie and Eden and Faith as soon as he arrived in town, but he'd been turned away; Olivia had gotten to them first, and they refused to see him. He wasn't welcome at James's house, wasn't allowed to see his nephew and niece, had been staying at a hotel with Daniel and Rebecca.

Every now and then one of his sisters would glance his way with a look of hurt and betrayal.

It felt like a fist in the gut every time.

Faith, the youngest, sat next to her longtime beau, the scion of a prominent banking family who had come all the way from St. Louis to be by her side. Callie was clearly trying to fulfill her duty as the oldest by being strong for all of them, holding her sisters' hands, trying to hold her own emotions in check.

And Eden . . . Eden, who had been his favorite when they were all young, who had always looked at him as if he could lasso the moon and stars and pull them down just for her, now refused to look at him at all.

It tore him up inside. And the worst part was that he knew what they were thinking: that they didn't matter to him at all. That they had depended on him and he had failed them. Again.

There was so much he wanted to tell them. That things weren't always as simple as they seemed at first glance. That he'd left here months ago determined to find a cold-blooded murderer and see her punished—and instead had found a woman none of them knew.

A woman who was nothing like what any of them expected, who was innocent of the charge against her.

A lady who had, day by day, earned his respect and his admiration . . . and claimed his heart.

The judge pounded his gavel to quiet the crowd, and Annie was sworn in and seated in the witness box.

Lucas kept his gaze on hers, seeing the courage in her eyes and trying to reflect it back, seeing the first spark of fear and trying to will it away. Legally, she didn't have to testify—and her defense attorney had advised against it—but Annie had insisted. If she didn't testify, she'd said, it would only convince everyone that she was guilty.

The prosecutor rose from his table. A tough, experienced attorney by the name of Drayton, he was an old friend and business associate of James—and it was obvious that he had taken a special interest in this case, that he personally wanted Annie punished.

Almost as badly as Lucas himself once had.

Drayton walked toward the witness box as he began his questioning.

"Miss Sutton, we have heard a great deal of testimony in the past days about your actions on the day in question. I wonder if you could clarify a few points for me?"

Lucas felt a muscle flex in his jaw. For two days, Drayton had called one witness after another to tell of Annie's relationship with James—from hotel and railroad employees who had seen them together on various occasions, to friends and colleagues who had known about her, all of them recounting how well James had treated her.

Of course, the prosecutor had made it all sound like Annie's doing, portraying her as a greedy, conniving tramp—neglecting to mention the fact that James had sought her out, that James had been purposely, willingly cheating on his wife.

Then the prosecutor had retraced her every step on that fateful day, calling to the stand the family servants, who'd told how they overheard her argument with

James, then the gunshot. Next had come the shopkeeper who had sold her the black dress she wore when she fled town, and later discovered her bloodstained clothes in an alley. The jury had even heard from the man at the stagecoach depot who had sold her a ticket west.

"My esteemed colleague Mr. Tanner informed us in his opening statement that this is all just a terrible misunderstanding," Drayton said now. "But if the shooting were really an 'accident' as you claim, you could have turned yourself in at any time and explained to the authorities. Why didn't you?"

"I didn't think anyone would believe me."

"There you are correct, Miss Sutton. We have nothing but your word to verify your version of events. Nothing . . . but . . . your . . . word. There are only two people who might tell us the truth about what happened that evening—and one was shot in the chest at close range with a .38 caliber revolver—"

"Your Honor, I object," the defense attorney called out.

"Mr. Drayton," the judge said to the prosecutor, "I sustain Mr. Tanner's objection. The coroner has already testified as to the nature of the wounds that caused Mr. McKenna's death. There is no need to keep restating the testimony of your own witness."

"Your Honor, I merely find it significant that the gentleman was shot through the *heart*," Drayton said. "And since there were only two people in the room at the time, either his mistress committed the crime, or he killed himself." He settled a steady gaze on Annie. "Is that your testimony, Miss Sutton, that Mr. McKenna committed suicide?"

"No—"

"You went there that evening to kill him, didn't you?"

"No!"

"You were angry because he had decided to end your relationship. You wanted revenge. You wanted money. So you went to Mr. McKenna's *home* where he lived with his *wife* and *children* and you shot him through the heart—"

"*No.*"

"Objection!"

The crowd buzzed with comments and exclamations. Lucas felt the anguish in Annie's eyes, so intensely that he had to grip the arms of his chair to keep himself from going to her.

"There will be order in this courtroom." The judge pounded his gavel on the bench. "Mr. Drayton," he said in a warning tone, "again, I sustain Mr. Tanner's objection."

"I will move on, Your Honor." Drayton turned away from Annie, folding his hands behind his back as he strolled toward the jury box. "Miss Sutton, your attorney, Mr. Tanner, has made a special point of stating that we do not have the murder weapon in our possession. And that is true. The gun was never found. Why do you think that is?"

"I don't know."

Lucas hoped that anyone who didn't know her as well as he did wouldn't notice the slight waver in her voice. Annie's attorney had instructed her to answer Drayton's questions as simply and succinctly as possible, offering no more detail or information than necessary. She would have the chance to explain her side of the story more fully when her attorney questioned her.

"You don't know?" Drayton gave the jury a dry look.

"I dropped it. It fell—"

"And no one ever found it? Come, come, surely you do not have so low an opinion of our local officers"—he gestured toward the constables sitting in the courtroom—"as to believe that they would fail to see a *gun* lying in plain sight at a *murder* scene?"

Every time Drayton said the word *murder* he made sure to give it special emphasis.

"I—I don't know what happened to it."

"Normally if a murder weapon isn't found, it's because someone has disposed of it," Drayton pointed out. "Such as the person who used it to commit the crime. The truth, Miss Sutton, is that you took that gun with you and threw it away as you fled, isn't it?"

"No."

"You disposed of that .38-caliber revolver the same way you disposed of your bloodstained clothes, didn't you?"

"No!"

"You shot James McKenna and took fifteen thousand dollars from his safe and left town. Are those the facts or are they not?"

"I . . . I—"

"*Fifteen thousand* dollars," Drayton repeated. "That's five thousand for each year you spent with him. Rather a nice salary for a woman who earned her living on her back—"

"Objection!" Tanner shouted, rising from his chair.

Lucas felt sick to his stomach. Only after the prosecution rested would Mr. Tanner have a chance to present his case for the defense. Annie would be able to tell the truth. Lucas would testify about how she had taken care of him when he'd been shot, when she could have left him to die. Rebecca would vouch for her good character, her tender heart. Daniel would tell everyone about the miscarriage Annie had suffered, and how she had mourned for her lost little one.

At Lucas's request, the headmaster from the orphanage that had received Annie's donation had even traveled from Colorado to make a plea for leniency.

Lucas felt his heart pounding as he looked at her, so small and alone. He could clearly see her trembling now—knew that everyone else in the room would interpret it completely the wrong way.

All their testimony might not be enough. Enough to erase the vivid picture Drayton was painting in the jurors' minds, the picture everyone in St. Charles was so eager to accept.

"Mr. Drayton," the judge was saying, "I must remind you to restrict your editorial commentary to the pages of the newspapers. The jurors are instructed to disregard the prosecutor's last remark."

"I withdraw the comment, Your Honor." Drayton walked slowly back toward Annie again. "Miss Sutton, after you took the fifteen thousand dollars from Mr. McKenna's safe, and after you disposed of your blood-stained clothing, and after you left town, you went West, is that true?"

Annie looked like she couldn't endure much more. "Yes."

"You fled to Colorado, you were hiding from the law, living under an assumed name, and you only returned here to stand trial after you were forced to do so. Isn't that the truth?"

"I . . . that wasn't what . . . I didn't mean to . . ."

"The truth is you fled because you knew that you had killed James McKenna. A respected member of this community. A business owner. A beloved husband. A father of two children. Isn't that the truth?"

"I—"

"*Yes* or *no*, Miss Sutton—*you* ended his life. *You* were responsible. *You and no one else.* Isn't that the truth?"

Lucas felt his gut clench, could see her eyes shimmering with tears, knew what she was going to say.

"Isn't it?" Drayton demanded.

"Yes." Annie lowered her head, one droplet sliding down her cheek. "Yes."

A hush fell over the courtroom.

Drayton turned to the jury, then walked back to his seat. "I have no further questions for this witness, Your Honor. The prosecution rests."

"Weatherby, I've got no right to ask you to do this," Lucas said in a low voice, as he and his deputy stood on the sidewalk at the bottom of the hill, looking up at the mansion, its windows gleaming in the late afternoon light. "If you want to walk away right now—"

"Sir, I know how highly you thought of your brother." Weatherby kept his voice quiet. "And I damn sure know you wouldn't be doing this for any outlaw. If you say Miss Sutton isn't a murderer and a thief, then she isn't." He regarded Lucas with a slow smile. "I've known you for four years, sir, and never once seen you knotted up like this over a woman. She must be something special."

"She is," Lucas said gruffly. "You go on around the front and create a diversion."

"Any particular requests?"

"Make it noisy, and make sure you keep the servants busy. Try to give me at least fifteen or twenty minutes."

"Consider it done, sir." Weatherby set off down the sidewalk, heading for the front gate.

Lucas circled around the back. Fifteen or twenty minutes should give him just enough time to do some investigating of his own. He moved through the hedges and into the gardens—retracing the steps Annie would have taken that day.

That fateful, tragic day that had changed so many lives forever.

Heavy clouds overhead made the afternoon unseasonably cool, damp with the promise of rain. He moved quietly through the gardens, glancing around, careful to avoid the groomsman who was tending mounds of daffodils and crocuses.

What he hoped—prayed—he would find was evidence. Not the kind of evidence he had once sought, to prove Annie's guilt, but evidence that would set her free.

There had to be *something*. Some detail that the constables had missed. That *he* had missed. Some clue that would help him prove that Drayton's portrait of a woman scorned bent on vengeance was all wrong.

When he reached the patio outside James's office, Lucas glanced in through the glass doors, tried the handle, and found it locked, as he had expected.

He slipped a small, steel tool from his coat pocket, and a moment later, he was inside, stepping into the room where it had all played out.

He felt his throat tighten, his eyes burn as he glanced around the spacious study with its gleaming teakwood paneling, expensive furnishings, framed works of art. There were no marks anywhere, not so much as one spot of crimson to mar the carpets; it looked like Olivia had had the place perfectly cleaned, tidied, restored to order.

Lucas choked back the emotions battling inside him and forced himself to focus, tried to picture the events of that day in his mind: Annie tearfully telling James about her pregnancy, James tossing his pocket change on the desk and ordering her to get out, Annie reaching for the money . . . and instead picking up the gun.

And James grabbing for the weapon.

Lucas clenched his jaw as he stared at the desk, hoping that James had been trying to protect her in that moment. That he had realized that the vulnerable young woman who was standing there, carrying his child, meant to shoot herself.

That he had died while trying to do the right thing.

Lucas shut his eyes. He would never know.

All he could do was forgive his brother for the events of that day, as Annie had forgiven him. And accept that he was only human.

Lucas moved behind the desk and bent down to start examining the wall, the floor. The office door on the other side of the room opened. Startled, he stood up.

"Uncle Lucas?"

It was his thirteen-year-old nephew, peering in, the door opened only a crack.

"Peter?" Lucas whispered, moving toward him quickly, afraid the boy would attract the attention of some servant or tutor. "You shouldn't be here—"

Before he could finish, the boy stepped inside and immediately shut the door, leaning back against it, wide-eyed and pale.

Lucas halted, feeling that look hit him like another blow to the gut. He wondered exactly what Olivia had told her children to explain why they were no longer allowed to see their uncle Lucas.

"Peter," he said quietly. "You don't have to be afraid of me."

"I'm not," Peter whispered, shaking his head emphatically. "I looked out my window and I thought I saw you in the garden and . . . Uncle Lucas, I want to . . . I have to—"

"Peter, you really shouldn't be here right now. And your mother doesn't want me to see you—"

"I know." The boy stepped away from the door, taking a deep breath. "Uncle Lucas, I'll be fourteen soon. Mother keeps telling me that I'm the man of the house now . . ." He squared his shoulders. "I *have* to talk to you."

"All right, Peter." Lucas noticed a grit and maturity in

the boy he had never seen before. "What is it you want to say?"

"I . . . I tried to talk to you before," Peter began haltingly. "That night when you left to go out west—but Mother stopped me. I came downstairs, remember, and started to tell you, but then Mother came over and she . . . she told me I shouldn't."

"Your mother told you *before* I left St. Charles that you shouldn't talk to me?" Lucas narrowed his eyes. "Why?"

"Because I wanted to tell you about Father," Peter blurted.

Lucas's heart started pounding hard against his ribs. "Tell me what?" He placed a hand on his nephew's shoulder. "Peter, what was it your mother didn't want you to tell?"

It was an hour later before they returned to the courtroom. Mr. Tanner was already questioning his first witness—Rebecca—as Lucas pushed open the doors, flanked by the two constables he had sent Weatherby to summon. His nephew was close by his side.

A hum of whispers and curious questions came from the crowd as Lucas strode down the center aisle with Peter, gesturing for the two constables to wait a moment. "Your Honor, I apologize for the interruption." He kept one reassuring hand on his nephew's shoulder. "But evidence has come to my attention that I think the court should hear. Mr. Tanner, I believe *this* should be your first witness."

Lucas slanted Olivia a hard stare, and saw that she was looking pale and panic-stricken all of a sudden.

Damn her, she did know. Olivia had known the truth all along. Had known before he left St. Charles.

Had been counting on his fearsome reputation to give her what she wanted: Annie, dead. He remembered how she had *encouraged* him to shoot without hesitation. *The West is an uncivilized place. No questions would be asked.*

And he had almost done it.

"Who is this boy?" the judge demanded. "Marshal McKenna, this proceeding is no place for a child—"

"My name is Peter McKenna." Though Lucas could feel his nephew trembling, the boy bravely spoke up for himself. "I'm James McKenna's son."

Another round of gasps and conversation rippled through the courtroom.

Mother and son exchanged a look across the crowded court, and Lucas saw a flash of betrayal in Olivia's eyes, felt Peter tense beneath his hand.

But even as he watched, all emotion in Olivia's expression was replaced by an icy dignity that descended over her like a protective cloak.

"Your Honor, I object!" Drayton called out amid the disruption. "This is entirely out of order."

"Your Honor," Lucas glanced over his shoulder and signaled the two constables, who came forward with a dirt-encrusted cigar box and placed it on the judge's bench. "I believe you'll also want to enter this into evidence."

"What the devil?" The judge opened the lid and his eyes widened, his gray eyebrows arching. "Mr. Drayton, perhaps you will wish to submit this new evidence to your experts for review . . ." He tilted the box up so everyone could see. "But I believe this may be the .38-caliber revolver you've been searching for."

Shouts and cries of disbelief filled the room. People were jumping to their feet for a better view.

"Young man," the judge said sternly, turning to Peter

again, "have you had this gun in your possession all this time?"

Peter nodded. "Yes, sir," he admitted. "I have."

"Very well, then." The judge motioned him forward. "Let us hear what you have to say. Mrs. Greer, you are excused for the present, but you may be recalled at a later time."

As Peter walked toward the witness box, Rebecca vacated it and joined Lucas to reclaim their seats behind the defense table. Lucas leaned forward and met Annie's confused, questioning gaze with one full of warmth and reassurance.

After Peter was sworn in, the judge questioned him directly. "What is it you would like to tell us, young Mr. McKenna?"

"I—I saw how it happened. I was there—"

There was such an uproar among the crowd, the judge had to pound his gavel almost a full minute before everyone quieted down enough for the proceedings to continue.

"What, specifically, did you see?" the judge asked.

"I was waiting in Father's study that night," Peter said, speaking quickly, as if he were eager to get it all out before he lost his nerve. "He was always busy all the time, always working, and I hardly got to see him much anymore. So I . . . I was on the couch in front of the fireplace, waiting for him to get home from his office, and I lay down and I must've fallen asleep. Because all of a sudden, I heard people arguing—Father and a lady. It woke me up, but I didn't know what to do. I thought Father might be mad if I let on I was there, so I just stayed quiet and stayed where I was. Then . . . then . . ."

For a moment, he couldn't continue. "Everything got quiet for a moment, and I thought it might be over, so I looked over the top of the couch." His voice wavered. "And that was when I saw it. I saw everything."

"What did you see?"

"She wasn't aiming the gun at my father, she was pointing it toward *herself*. I saw Father try to grab it from her and I heard him say, 'Annie, no, don't,' and that was when it went off. It just went off as he was trying to grab it from her. He was trying to stop her from shooting *herself*. It was an accident. It wasn't like everyone said later." Peter shook his head adamantly. "It was an *accident*."

A wave of noisy exclamations went through the courtroom.

Lucas glanced from Annie, who regarded him in shock, toward Olivia—who still sat in cool, tight-lipped silence, her spine rigid.

"Your Honor!" Mr. Drayton called out. "The testimony of a thirteen-year-old boy, who may have been coached by his uncle—"

"Let him finish, Mr. Drayton," the judge interrupted. "How did you come to be in possession of the gun, young man?"

"When Father fell, I . . . I couldn't even make a sound. I sunk down on the couch, and then the servants and Mother started pounding on the door, and when I looked again, the lady was gone. I ran over to Father, but he was . . . he was dead." Peter's voice broke. "The gun was on the floor and I—I picked it up and that was when Mother came running in from the garden. She thought *I* did something wrong. I tried to explain, but she made me run out and hide in the garden before she let everyone in."

He took a deep breath and continued. "That night, after I told her what I saw, she made me swear not to tell anyone. She said it had to be our secret—"

"And you agreed?" the judge asked.

Peter glanced toward Olivia, his voice becoming quiet. "She's my mother."

Lucas swallowed hard, picturing his nephew torn between loyalty to family and his sense of honor, wrestling with questions of right and wrong all these months.

Olivia still didn't say a word, kept herself utterly composed in front of her friends and neighbors.

"She said I was the man of the house now, and I had to put the *family* first," Peter continued. "She said the woman deserved to be punished, and I shouldn't say anything to the constables . . . or to Uncle Lucas. Then she asked what happened to the gun, and I told her I already threw it away. But I . . . I still had it," he admitted haltingly. "I buried it in the backyard, in that cigar box."

"Why, young man?" the judge asked gently. "Why did you do that?"

"Because I knew it was important, and I know it's wrong to lie." He shook his head, his voice becoming hoarse as he looked at Olivia. "I'm sorry, Mother. But Father always taught me that a man has to do what's *right*."

The judge turned to Olivia, an ominous expression on his face. "Is your son telling the truth, madam?"

"Your Honor," Drayton said, quickly coming to her defense, "Mrs. McKenna has not been sworn in as a witness."

Olivia remained as silent as ever.

"Mrs. McKenna," the judge said, glowering at her, "I can swear you in and call you up here, or you can tell us now."

She closed her eyes.

"Ma'am," the judge said sharply.

Her head came up and she rose from her seat, gracefully, all brittle dignity even as her plan fell to ruins around her. "My son is telling the truth."

"Are you admitting, madam," the judge demanded, "that you purposely withheld information material to this proceeding? That you knew your husband's death was accidental? That you knew an innocent person might be sent to the *gallows*?"

"Innocent?" The word seemed to shatter Olivia's composure like a rock thrown through glass. "She's *not* innocent! Why should it matter if it was an accident or not? That little *tramp* took my husband from me with her wiles and her tricks for three years. It's because of her that my children no longer have a father. I wanted her to pay." Her voice shook with bitter grief and fury. *"I wanted her to pay!"*

"Madam," the judge said slowly, as if he were struggling to be patient, "you should count yourself fortunate that I find reason to be lenient with you. Because you are a grieving widow, I will not bring charges against you for obstruction of justice—"

"But it *isn't* justice if she walks away free," Olivia cried. "We've lost everything and she hasn't suffered at all! It's not right—"

"Your Honor, there is still the charge of theft," Drayton said quickly, "the matter of the missing fifteen thousand dollars—"

"Your Honor!" Tanner stood up. "I have witnesses here who will testify as to the reason *why* Miss Sutton took that money. And to the fact that she gave it away after her arrival in Colorado, donating it to an orphanage in Denver." He glanced down at Annie. "And to the fact that this young woman has suffered a great deal."

"Gentlemen," the judge said, "the hour is late and I believe we have all heard enough. Mr. Drayton, in light of this young man's testimony and Mrs. McKenna's admission, the court will not pursue the lesser charge in this case."

Olivia sank back down, and for a moment Lucas almost pitied her, she looked so dispirited. But her son had done the right thing when it counted—and was well on his way to becoming a man his father would've been proud of.

The judge's voice rang out over the growing noise in the courtroom.

"It is my ruling that James McKenna's death was an accident. The charges against the defendant are dismissed." He banged his gavel, one quick, sharp strike. "Miss Sutton, you are free to go."

22

The rain that pattered down from the darkening sky couldn't wash away the smells of smoke and hot iron that filled the depot, as the engine a few yards away sent clouds of steam billowing upward. The train's bell started clanging.

Annie stood beside Rebecca on the platform, beneath the eaves, the two of them huddled close under an umbrella while Daniel took care of their bags. Her two friends and Lucas and Mr. Tanner had all escorted her out of the courtroom as soon as the judge pronounced her free, battling their way through the crowd, past newspaper reporters clamoring for interviews.

On the courthouse steps, her attorney had promised that he would take care of the press; he wanted them to report the full story, so that everyone might know the *truth* about who Annie Sutton really was—instead of the sordid version the prosecutor had been spewing in the papers.

Lucas's deputy Mr. Weatherby had been waiting with a carriage, and Lucas had told him and Daniel to get her and Rebecca to the railroad depot. He would follow directly, he'd promised.

"I'm sure he'll be along any minute," Rebecca said,

squinting as she peered through the rain in the direction of the road that led toward town.

"He will," Annie said, her heart pounding. She could still hardly believe that Lucas had saved her. That she was free.

But of course he had saved her. Lucas was always there when she needed him most.

He was a hero. Her hero.

When he had lifted her into the carriage and asked if she was ready to leave St. Charles once and for all, she had said yes, gladly; she didn't want to stay here one more night. A court of law had set her free, but there would always be people here who scorned and hated her.

Annie looked up into the clouds, the rain washing over her face. So much would never change.

But she had changed. She hadn't realized it until she returned to St. Charles, how different she felt. She wasn't her mother's daughter anymore. Would never be again.

And she wasn't frightened or alone anymore. She was leaving this place in the company of friends, and the man she loved. And she was free.

Really free.

The whistle sounded again. A few more passengers hurried out of the depot, juggling their umbrellas and baggage and tickets for the 6:15 to Jefferson City.

"Where *did* that man get to?" Rebecca grumbled worriedly. "Wait . . . is that . . . ?"

"Yes." Annie felt her heart soar as Lucas appeared out of the dusky shadows on horseback, galloping toward the train depot. She ran toward him, heedless of the rain, and Lucas pulled her into his arms as soon as he dismounted, the drops spattering down over them as he kissed her.

"Sorry I'm late," he said when he lifted his head. "Didn't mean to worry you."

"It's all right," Annie said. He had stayed behind to talk to his family. She had wanted to grant him time alone with his sisters, knowing how important they were to him. "Were they willing to speak with you?"

He nodded. "A little. Right now, they're in shock over what Olivia did, and they don't know what to think. I have to give them time. Things are still . . . tense."

Annie closed her eyes, knowing that his sisters might never be able to accept her as part of his life. She couldn't blame them for that.

And she couldn't force him to choose between her and his family. "Lucas, I can't take you away from them—"

"Annie." He tilted her head up, his eyes dark with emotion. "They're my sisters. You're the woman I love."

She hid her face against his coat *"Lucas,"* she whispered. She had thought she would never hear him say those words.

"I love you," he said gruffly. "And God help you, woman, you're going to be spending the rest of your life with me."

She smiled up at him through her tears, through the rain. "Have I ever mentioned that you can be a little stubborn?"

"Once or twice." He kissed her, threading his fingers into her damp hair. "Annie, your side of the story will be in the papers tomorrow, thanks to the interviews that Tanner and the headmaster from the orphanage are giving right now. I think that'll help everyone see you in a new light—including my sisters."

"But you could stay here, with them. They need you—"

"None of them are staying in St. Charles." He shook his head. "Faith and her beau are planning a summer wedding in St. Louis, and Callie and Eden are headed back to their studies at college." His voice softened. "I offered all of them train tickets to Colorado, told them they can take me up on it anytime. I said they'll always be welcome in our home."

Annie wrapped her arms around him and just held on to him, her heart too full of love for words, except for a silent prayer of gratitude to God for bringing this man into her life.

EPILOGUE

The warm March day had melted into hazy shades of violet and lavender as the sun drifted downward behind the mountains. A fresh excitement had arrived in Eminence with the first touch of spring, many of the town's former residents returning to work their claims, everyone filled with hope that a new silver strike might be found this year.

Mr. Hazelgreen had been talking to some investors about the narrow-gauge railroad he wanted. And Rebecca had bought the old millinery shop next to her store, and insisted on making Annie an equal partner.

But those weren't the reasons Annie's heart was beating so fast as she approached Reverend Gottfried's chapel.

When the door opened, the wind blew a strand of Annie's unruly hair into her eyes and she brushed it away, looking up with a sigh.

Because that was when she saw him. Watching her. He stood beside the reverend at the far end of the aisle, so tall and strong and handsome in his dark suit and white shirt, his town marshal's badge on his vest, Travis standing beside him as best man.

Lucas's grin widened until it brought out a dimple in

his cheek. The organist began to play and Katja and Valentina, Annie's matron and maid of honor, moved gracefully down the aisle. Everyone in the crowded pews turned to watch as Annie came into the church on Daniel's arm, wearing a gown her friends had made her of ivory satin, trimmed with pearls and silver embroidery.

Rebecca, who sat at the front, burst into tears as soon as she set eyes on Annie. The yellow and purple flowers on her new spring hat bobbed merrily as she dabbed at her eyes with a lacy handkerchief.

Lucas stepped forward when Annie reached the altar, and a hush fell over the gathering as the service began and the two of them made promises to love and cherish one another forever. Annie smiled up at her groom, letting all her love for him shine through in her eyes.

The rings they exchanged had been a gift from all their friends, made of silver that had been mined in Eminence.

And as they shared their first kiss as husband and wife, the dazzling evening light shone through the stained glass, painting the church with the vivid colors of sunset.